One night of passion changes
their lives forever…

New Arrivals

HIS EXPECTANT MISTRESS

REBECCA WINTERS
LINDSAY ARMSTRONG
CAROL MARINELLI

New Arrivals

COLLECTION

March 2015

April 2015

May 2015

June 2015

New
Arrivals

HIS EXPECTANT MISTRESS

REBECCA WINTERS
LINDSAY ARMSTRONG
CAROL MARINELLI

MILLS
BOON
&

Published in Great Britain 2015
by Mills & Boon, an imprint of Harlequin (UK) Limited,
Eton House, 18-24 Paradise Road, Richmond, Surrey, TW9 1SR

NEW ARRIVALS: HIS EXPECTANT MISTRESS
© 2015 Harlequin Books S.A.

Accidentally Pregnant! © 2010 Rebecca Winters
One-Night Pregnancy © 2010 Lindsay Armstrong
One Tiny Miracle… © 2009 Carol Marinelli

ISBN: 978-0-263-25377-1

010-0615

Harlequin (UK) Limited's policy is to use papers that are natural, renewable and recyclable products and made from wood grown in sustainable forests.The logging and manufacturing processes conform to the legalenvironmental regulations of the country of origin.

Printed and bound in Spain
by CPI, Barcelona

ACCIDENTALLY PREGNANT!

REBECCA WINTERS

Rebecca Winters lives in Salt Lake City, Utah. With canyons and high alpine meadows full of wildflowers, she never runs out of places to explore. They, plus her favourite vacation spots in Europe, often end up as backgrounds for her romance novels, because writing is her passion, along with her family and church.

Rebecca loves to hear from readers. If you wish to e-mail her, please visit her website at cleanromances.com.

CHAPTER ONE

Greek CEO of the Simonides Corporation, Andreas Simonides, thirty-three, astonished the corporate world by marrying unknown, twenty-six-year-old American, Gabriella Turner, in a private ceremony on Milos.

THE AUGUST HEADLINES in the *Corriere della Sera* caught Vincenzo Antonello by the throat. While in town he'd bought a newspaper before stopping off for lunch, never dreaming what he'd read when he opened it. In a gut reaction, his hands gripped the edges of his Italian newspaper so tightly, it started to tear down the middle.

"Papa? Are you mad?" His six-year-old son had stopped eating his pasta salad to stare at his father.

"No." Vincenzo caught himself in time. "It tore by accident."

"Oh. Can we go to the park now and play soccer?"

"In a minute, Dino. Let me finish my coffee first."

Sources close to the Simonides family have closed ranks on the press, but one rumor has floated that the elusive couple are honeymooning in the

Caribbean and won't be available for pictures or comments for some time to come.

The CEO's former Greek girlfriend, Irena Liapis, daughter of Athenian newspaper magnate Giorgios Liapis, was expected to become the bride of the brilliant Simonides tycoon. Since the surprise announcement, it has been learned that the twenty-seven-year-old Ms. Liapis, who heads the monthly lifestyle section of her father's newspaper, has resigned her position and dropped off the scene. Her location is unknown at this time.

An icy hand seemed to squeeze Vincenzo's lungs until he couldn't breathe. Since early July when Irena had returned to Greece, he'd honored her wishes by not going after her. Every day he'd expected to hear that she and the great Simonides were married.

When Vincenzo had first met her, he'd damned the man's very existence and had baited Irena constantly about her alleged feelings for the man she intended to marry. Those feelings had not stopped her spending one blissful night with him, though, Vincenzo thought angrily. He had hoped and believed that the night had been earthshaking for her, too, and that it had erased her desire for Vincenzo's nemesis.

But these headlines proved he'd only been deluding himself. Somehow he'd thought this was the one female on the planet who'd been different.

"Irena!"

"I know it surprises you to see me."

Deline hugged her. "Only because I thought you'd

already left for Italy. Why didn't you phone that you were still in Athens?"

"I—I didn't dare," she stammered.

"Not dare?" Her best friend's brown eyes looked at her with concern. "Come in and we'll talk." Irena moved inside. "I just finished feeding the twins. They're out in the garden room in their swings. Leon will be sorry he missed you. He left for work a few minutes ago."

"I know that, too. I came earlier and purposely waited until I saw his car disappear."

Deline had been guiding her through the Simonides villa, but after hearing that comment she spun around and put a hand on Irena's arm. "The minute I saw your face I could see something was terribly wrong. What is it that is troubling you, Irena?"

"My biggest fear right now is that your house staff will know I stopped by and mention it to Leon. *He just can't know I came here!*"

Unspoken words flowed between them. Deline was already reading between the lines and realized that whatever had brought Irena to the villa, it was deadly serious.

"The maids won't be in until this afternoon. The only person around at the moment is my housekeeper, Sofia. I'll find her right now and tell her that your visit is to remain private. She is a valued staff member and can be trusted, I'm sure. However, I will make it clear that if any of the staff or my husband hear about you having come over, she'll be in serious trouble."

No one ever had a better friend. "Thank you, Deline." They hugged again.

"I'll be right back."

As she darted away, Irena walked into the garden room. The five-month-old twins were in their swings facing each other. Each had a plastic toy and seemed perfectly content, but when they saw Irena, their little arms and legs started moving faster in excitement.

Irena knelt down next to Kris, who'd come through his heart surgery so well, you'd never know he was barely out of the hospital. She kissed his cheek, then turned to Nikos. Both beautiful black-haired boys had been made in Leon's image. Most people would assume Deline was their mother due to her black hair and olive skin.

But others who knew the Simonides clan well were aware of Leon's slip during a rough spot in their marriage. It had been a one-night mistake in a state of inebriation with Thea Turner, a Greek-American woman, now deceased, that had produced his beautiful children.

Incredibly, Deline, who was pregnant with Leon's child, had loved him enough to forgive him and take him back. They were now a family of four with another baby on the way.

"Problem taken care of," she announced as she hurried back in the room.

If only that were true…

"Tell me what's wrong," Deline begged after sitting on the sofa.

Irena eyed her dear friend who would have been her sister-in-law if fate hadn't stepped in to change lives.

Overnight, nothing was the same as it had been before. Leon's twin brother, Andreas, was the man Irena had thought she would be marrying. But two months ago she'd gone to Cinque Terre in Italy for her job and had met another man. So strong was the attraction and feelings between them, she hadn't wanted to leave him.

When she had returned to Greece to tell Andreas the truth, he had been unavailable because of some mysterious circumstance. Irena had soon learned that Thea's half sister, Gabi Turner, had appeared on the scene and Andreas had taken one look at her and had broken it off with Irena. The next thing she knew Andreas had married the blonde American woman and had just left on his honeymoon.

"Irena Liapis— Talk to me!"

Her body started to shake. "I don't know how to tell you this."

"What?"

"You're not going to believe it. *I* don't believe it."

"It's that bad?"

"Much worse."

"Are you dying?"

Irena knew it was a serious question. "No, but at least it would solve my problem."

Without warning Deline jumped to her feet. "That's *never* a solution!" she scolded. "I was about to say that unless an incurable disease is about to take your life, nothing else you could tell me would rival what I've lived through while I decided whether to stay with Leon or not."

"Try this. *I'm* pregnant."

Deline paled. "Andreas's baby…"

After a brief pause; "Probably," she answered in a shaky voice.

Her friend's eyes widened with incredulity. "What do you mean probably?"

"The doctor worked out the dates with me. He's ninety percent sure it's Andreas's, but it could be another's. Oh, Deline, what if it's Vincenzo's baby?"

"Who's Vincenzo?" Her friend's loss of color alarmed her so much, she guided her back to the couch where they could both sit.

"Vincenzo is a man I spent all my time with when I was in Italy doing my article for the paper. He is handsome and… Oh, what a mess!" Irena let her head drop into her hands, a sudden feeling of despair washing over her.

"How long have you known you were pregnant?"

"I've felt queasy for the last week and finally went to the E.R. yesterday. I thought maybe I'd come down with flu or something. The doctor there referred me to an ob-gyn who confirmed it this morning before I came here. I'm six weeks along."

She'd begged the doctor to go over the dates again… and again. When she'd left Greece for her newspaper assignment in Italy, she'd only slept with Andreas, the man she had assumed she would marry on her return to Greece.

But those ten days in Italy had changed the course of her life forever. There she'd met Vincenzo, had been hit hard and fast with feelings she had never experienced or felt before. So much so that she'd extended her stay to be with him and hadn't wanted to go back to Greece… or Andreas.

Her friend's eyes filled with tears. "Oh, Irena. No matter what, you're going to have a precious baby."

"I know." Moisture glazed Irena's cheeks. "I want it more than anything in the world." Wanted it to be Vincenzo's…she added silently.

"Of course you do." Deline squeezed her arm gently. "What are you going to do?"

Irena took a deep breath. "I know one thing I'm *not* going to do. Andreas will never learn the child I'm carrying is his, if it *is* his. I'm going to another OB this afternoon to get a second opinion. I *have* to be sure."

"I was just going to suggest that you see another doctor. This is too important."

"Oh, Deline…I want so much for Vincenzo to be the father."

"But if the next doctor tells you the same thing—"

"If he does, I still refuse to hurt Andreas and Gabi. You and Leon had to live through a nightmare when he came to you with the news that he'd fathered Thea's twins. I don't want to start another nightmare for them. They're in love. Andreas couldn't marry her fast enough. They're on their honeymoon making plans for their future. I won't do that to them."

Deline sat there shaking her head in disbelief.

"I want to be on *my* honeymoon with Vincenzo. I want to be able to tell him I'm carrying *his* baby. Sometimes I wonder how you got through it, Deline. I was so crushed for you." The twins were adorable, but they should have been Deline and Leon's.

"I'll never forget you were there for me." Her voice shook.

"I don't mean to bring up the past to hurt you. I just can't do that to them."

Deline got to her feet. "The truth has a way of coming

out, Irena. What if everything had remained a secret until years down the road? I'm not so sure our marriage could have withstood such a blow then. At least we're starting out with the truth now, before our own baby is born. And Leon has been so good to me—incredibly kind and understanding. Patient, you know?"

Irena understood. "Believe me, I'm thankful things are working out for you so well. But think, Deline— Maybe Gabi is pregnant already. I'm afraid of history repeating itself."

Her friend groaned.

"Wouldn't *my* news be a lovely belated wedding present for the two of them after they get back from the Caribbean… I can't do it to them."

"One day he'll find out, and when he does…" Deline actually trembled. "I know Andreas. Leon's brother is noble to a fault and he'll always care about you, but if you were to keep knowledge of that kind away from him and then he discovered it—especially after what he went through to make sure Leon was united with his own children—" She shook her head again. "I'd fear for you, Irena."

Put that way, so did Irena. She cleared her throat. "There's one way to handle it so he never finds out. That's what I came over to talk to you about."

"What? Move to another planet?"

"Not quite so far away. After I returned from Italy, I resigned my job at the newspaper. My plan had been to break it off with Andreas before I went back to Riomaggiore to be with Vincenzo. That's where I'm going now. What I'm hoping is that he meant what he said and still wants to marry me."

"Still? You mean in ten days you got to a point that he asked you?" Deline cried out aghast. "Not that you aren't the most beautiful and intelligent woman I've ever known. Any man would want you, but if he knew about Andreas—"

"It sounds complicated, I know. He didn't exactly ask. It more or less came out. But when I left, I couldn't give him an answer until I'd talked to Andreas first, and you know what happened next. He was totally involved with Gabi!

"When he told me about her, it struck me then that Andreas and I had never been in love, otherwise Gabi couldn't have stolen his heart any more than Vincenzo could have stolen mine. Vincenzo warned me that if I'd gone through with that marriage, it wouldn't have worked, that one day I would regret my mistake—he was right."

Deline stared at her before an odd expression broke out on her face. "What kind of a man could have caused you to fall for him so completely in a ten-day period, you want to marry him and wish it was his baby you're carrying?"

Irena averted her eyes.

"Come on. Out with it."

"His name is Vincenzo Antonello. He's an irreverent bachelor who's Italian down to the roots of his hair." Curly, untamed, overly long black hair. "He either walks or drives his used Fiat if he has to go any distance." Irena smiled at the memory, so different from her life where she had grown up in a world of luxury villas, elegant cars, limo service and helicopters.

"He was assigned to give me and my photographer

a tour of the liqueur manufacturing plant in La Spezia where he works. As he was putting me back in his car, he said he liked it that at five foot eight, I was closer to him in height. 'There's more to grab hold of.'"

His deep laughter had rumbled out of him along with the words spoken in heavily accented English. Insufferable, arrogant, but with those blue eyes piercing you through black lashes.

"Our whole meeting was absolutely crazy, Deline. The whole time I was there, he spent every waking hour with me. We laughed and ate and walked and talked. I've never talked with anyone else so much in my whole life. I don't think either of us got any sleep.

"We hiked, we played, we strolled. He bought me flowers and little gifts. I was showered with them. He... bewitched me."

Six feet of proud, hard-muscled male, handsome as the devil he mocked. The antithesis of political correctness.

Irena had grown up cautious.

He was a Catholic, albeit not a good one, he'd admitted with a rakish white smile. She didn't espouse one particular religion. Irena believed in the emancipated woman who could be powerful in the corporate world.

"He has an opinion on everything and isn't afraid to express it."

No worshipper of money, Vincenzo. As long as he made enough at his job, he was happy to let someone else handle the financial nightmare of being a CEO. Irena came from a monied background. Her parents' very existence was defined by wealth.

"Vincenzo went out of his way to show me his village. Our walks in the hills took all day because he kept pulling me down to kiss me. On my last night there I ended up at his apartment in Riomaggiore. It was very small and simply furnished. He fixed me an Italian meal to die for.

"We drank wine and danced on his veranda until it got dark. When he picked me up and carried me to his bedroom, it seemed entirely natural. I'd stopped thinking because these overwhelming feelings had taken over. Before I flew back to Greece, he said something totally ridiculous to me."

"What was that?" Deline had been watching and listening, spellbound.

"'We are opposites in every conceivable way, Signorina Liapis. I think we should get married.'"

"Irena—"

"He shocked me, too. He enjoyed doing it on a regular basis."

"What did you say to him?"

"From the beginning he knew how things stood with me, that I'd loved Andreas Simonides for a long time and expected to be his wife soon."

"How did he handle that?"

"He laughed at me. 'Love? If you two truly loved each other, you would be married by now and not here with me.'"

Irena bowed her head. "I have to tell you, Deline. Those words pierced me because I realized he was speaking the truth. Andreas and I had been drifting. If I'd felt for him what I felt for Vincenzo, I wouldn't have let my career take precedence over being with him whenever possible.

"Vincenzo kept firing truths at me. 'What is love, anyway? A word. It can mean anything you want it to mean at the moment. Then again it can mean nothing at all.'

"I asked him if he didn't believe in it. He shrugged his shoulders and did that Italian thing with his hands and arms. Then he said, '"I believe in forms of it. Who couldn't love a child, for instance?'"

"When I told him he was impossible to talk to, he said, 'Why? Because I don't conform to your misguided idea of perfection or feed you what you're used to consuming? Have you ever taken a good look at yourself?'"

Deline shook her head. "I can't believe he dared."

"He dared more than that. 'Ms. Liapis,' he said. 'You are like the geese that fly in chevron formation—cool and unflappable, you cruise above the world with your fine-feathered family unit as you were taught to do, careful not to be diverted by other species of birds or natural disasters.'

"'But I must tell you it would be fascinating to watch what would happen if just once you took a different course and had to wing it on your own.'"

"He *didn't* say that!" Deline cried.

"Oh, yes, he did, and his remark stung. When he started to make love to me, I didn't want him to stop. More than anything in the world I wanted to know his possession. He was a virtual stranger, yet nothing about him seemed strange. Everything we did felt right. It was like I'd met my soul mate."

In a rare moment of pique Irena had risen to the

bait and had done something foolish, if not dangerous, in order to prove he was wrong about her before she flew back to Athens. It had shocked her to the core, considering that from the moment he'd agreed to show her and the photographer around, she'd wanted to take him seriously, but was afraid.

Irena got to her feet. "After my new doctor's appointment this afternoon, I'm going to go back and tell Vincenzo he was right about everything. My being there will prove that I've taken a different course and want to be with him. We have this intense attraction and connection. It will be liberating to be able to admit it. If he meant what he said about getting married, I want it, too."

"What will you tell him about the baby?"

"The truth. As much as I've been told by the doctors. He has the right to know everything, including the fact that Andreas met someone else, too. If he can't forgive me for going back to break it off with Andreas, then he's not the man I thought he was." She bit her lip. "If he wasn't being serious about marriage, then I'll have to leave Europe."

"Where will you go?"

"I have no idea."

"Oh, Irena. I'm frightened for you."

"So am I. I'm terrified"

"Come on, Dino. You can do it."

"I'm scared, Papa."

Vincenzo could see the fright in his son's dark brown eyes. His medium-size six-year-old would only come as far as the edge of the hotel pool, but he wouldn't jump into his arms. No bribe would entice him. "Then what would you like to do before we leave?"

"I don't want to leave. I want to live here in Riomaggiore with you."

When Dino said it in that forlorn little tone, it gutted Vincenzo. "You know you can't, Dino. Come. We'll walk down to the beach and watch the boats."

"Okay," he demurred sadly.

"Would you like to go for a ride and catch some fish?"

"No. I just want to watch." Dino claimed he loved the water, but when it came right down to it, he couldn't bring himself to enjoy it. By now Vincenzo had hoped his son would have overcome some of his fears, but since his ex-wife, Mila, had remarried six months ago and moved to Milan from Florence, they seemed to have grown worse.

"Let's go!" He levered himself onto the tile. When both of them had slipped on their shirts and sandals, Vincenzo grasped Dino's hand and they descended the steps beyond the pool area that led down to the sea.

Tomorrow was the last day of his boy's one week summer vacation with him. Only a little more time left before he had to drive him back to Milan. Then the one weekend a month of visitation would begin again until his week in December. So much time apart from his son was killing him.

Before Mila had moved to Milan, Vincenzo had made that once a month sojourn to Florence where she'd lived with her family and Dino since the divorce. He'd found a small hotel located near the Boboli Gardens where you could look out over Michelangelo's city. The delightful spot had become a second home to him and Dino.

The hotel he'd picked out in Milan didn't feel like home to them. Neither did Milan itself, but rules were rules and had been set in concrete. Vincenzo was only given one week in summer and one week in December before the Christmas holiday to be with his son on his terms.

Nothing would change until Dino turned eighteen, unless of course Vincenzo married again. Such an eventuality would upset a small universe of people in more ways than one.

But after letting his father dictate an ill-fated marriage the first time around, he was through with the institution. His only choice was to bide his time until Dino was old enough to plead for a change in the visitation rules. Then Vincenzo would go before a higher court and appeal the decision. Hopefully that day would come years before Dino was considered an adult.

Later, as they walked along the cliffside path of Via Dell'Amore between Riomaggiore and Vernazza, his son cried, "Look, Papa. The sun fell into the sea."

"Do you think it scares all the fish to see a big light shining under the water?"

That brought the first laugh of the evening to Dino's lips. "No. You're funny."

Vincenzo looked down at his boy. He was the joy of his life. "Are you tired after all our walking? Do you want me to carry you on my shoulders up these steep steps?"

"I don't think they're steep." He trudged up ahead of him, then turned around. "What's steep?"

Laughter poured out of Vincenzo. "Almost straight up and down."

"Sometimes I think I'm going to fall over."

"You keep going up first then. If you start to tumble, I'll be here to catch you."

"I won't fall. Watch!"

His strong legs dashed up the steps to the winding road that led to Vincenzo's apartment. Dino had straight brown-black hair and brown eyes like his mother's. His body type, like Vincenzo's, had been inherited from their Valsecchi line.

Of course Vincenzo thought his boy brilliant like himself, and good-looking like Vincenzo's mother. The Antonellos had a proud nose and firm jaw. All in all his Dino was perfect.

"I'll beat you to our house," he cried before hurrying up the last part of the road to the apartment jutting out from the cliff. From their balcony giving out on the Mediterranean, they'd spent many an hour looking through the telescope at swimmers and boats. When the sky was clear enough, they could pick out the constellations among the stars.

Dino ran around to the front door with Vincenzo not far behind. To his surprise he heard his son say, *"Buonasera, signorina."* They had a visitor. Walking around the purple bougainvillea, his heart skipped a beat because he'd spotted the one woman he never expected to see again. His thoughts reeled.

In the fading light her glistening black hair fell like a curtain from a center part to her shoulders covered in a sleeveless lavender top. Standing there on those gorgeous long legs half-hidden in the folds of her white skirt, the impact of Irena Liapis on his senses had never been more potent.

"Buonasera," she answered with a discernible Greek accent.

"Who are you?" Dino asked, but by then her startled eyes, dark as poppy throats, had come into contact with Vincenzo's. Since he knew she couldn't understand Dino's Italian, he took over, but he had to be careful what he told him. Everything would get back to the boy's mother.

"This is Irena Spiros from Greece, Dino," he explained. "She doesn't speak our language. That means we have to speak English to her."

"But I don't know many words."

"That's all right. Do the best you can with what you've learned. We'll find out how good your tutor has been."

"Okay." Dino turned and shook her hand. "Hello, Ms. Spiros. I am Dino and this is my papa."

She looked startled to hear her mother's maiden name used and Vincenzo could tell that she was also shocked to discover he had a son. But she recovered enough from both surprises to smile at him. "Hello, Dino. How are you?"

"I'm fine, thank you."

"How old are you?"

"I'm six. How old are you?"

She laughed softly. "I'm twenty-seven."

"Dino," Vincenzo whispered in Italian. "You should never ask a woman her age."

He bit his lip.

"It's all right," she said to Dino, having understood

without translation. "You're a very smart, polite boy."
Her eyes lifted to Vincenzo, a question in them, and
he saw a glint of something undecipherable; anxiety
maybe. He decided to enlighten her.

"When you came to Riomaggiore two months ago,
my son was with his mother and stepfather in Milan.
I've been divorced five years."

"I see." She studied him intently. "Dare I tell you
he's adorable and that one day he'll grow up to be even
more handsome than his secretive father?"

Something about her was different. He had yet to discover what it was. "You mean as secretive as the *almost*
Signorina Simonides? According to the newspaper, she
hasn't been available since the CEO himself sailed away
with his new American bride."

He thought she might blush, or at least look away.
Instead she said, *"Touché."*

Her lack of outrage was as surprising as it was
intriguing.

Dino turned to him. "Papa? Can she come in?"

"Would you like that?"

"Yes. She's nice."

Agreed. "Then I'll ask her." He shot her a glance.
"He wants to know if you would like to come in."

She pondered the invitation for a moment. "Only if
it doesn't interfere with your plans."

"Signorina Spiros wants to come in," he whispered
to Dino, then moved forward to unlock the door.

Irena went inside but she feared her heart was pounding so loud, Vincenzo could hear it. After spending the
last night of her business trip here two months ago, she

knew his apartment fairly well. Comfortably furnished with a view of the sea to die for from the balcony, she found it incredibly charming. But something new had been added.

On the kitchen counter was an assembly of little boys' toys. The kitchen table had half a dozen board games sitting on top, one of matching cards still in progress. In the living room lay a soccer ball in one corner. A small golf club with plastic balls had been left in another corner. She saw a little bicycle propped against the outside railing near the telescope, all signs that a boy lived here.

Vincenzo had a son, but he'd never said a word about him. He came up behind her. His body was close enough she could feel his warmth. "Dino wants to show you his room."

She walked down the hallway to the door he'd opened for her. When she'd been here before, Vincenzo had indicated it was the guest bedroom, but he'd carried her past the closed door to his own room.

Inside she saw a lot more toys placed around, but what she noticed were framed pictures, some small ones on the bedside table and two large ones on the wall. They showed Dino and his father taken at different times and seasons.

Irena walked over to one of the photos where they were up on the turret of a castle in winter. Father and son were so attractive in their ski gear, she smiled. "I like this one."

"That is *Svizzera*."

"Switzerland?" she clarified. When he nodded she said, "Do you like castles?"

Vincenzo stood in the doorway. He translated for his son. "She wants to know if you like castles."

Dino looked up at her earnestly. "Yes."

"Do you have any soldiers? Or should I say knights?"

His son looked to him for help. After another translation Dino said, "I have um…forty."

"Forty?" she cried with a smile. "That's *molto!*"

When she spoke the Italian word, Dino laughed and rushed to a large case that he opened to show her all of his toy knights inside. She picked out one in full body armor and held it up to examine closely before putting it back. "This is an amazing army of warriors you have here." Vincenzo translated, causing Dino to beam. He was precious.

"Come in the living room," her host murmured. She moved past him and felt his gaze sweep over her. "Are you hungry? Thirsty?"

"Neither one, thank you. I ate at the Lido Hotel before I came here. It's where I'm staying whilst I'm here."

"Did you come to Riomaggiore by train?"

"No. I flew to Genoa, then rented a car."

She moved through the apartment to the kitchen table. One of the games of jumping monkeys needed no translation; Irena wanted a little more time to gather her thoughts so she opened the box. When she smiled at Dino, he scrambled around the other side of the table to help set things up. He seemed eager to play.

After she took a seat, Vincenzo found his place at the end of the table and they started the game. For half an hour they scrambled to make the monkeys cling to the spinning trees. Dino taught her to say *scimmia* for *monkey*.

Irena really got into the game, causing Vincenzo to step up the competition. Dino let out a shriek of laughter, followed by Irena's. Things came down to every man for himself with Vincenzo's continual chuckle adding to the fun. Pretty soon all the monkeys lay on the table or had fallen on the floor.

As she helped put the game away, she checked her watch. She'd been here long enough. It was time for his boy to be in bed. So far Vincenzo had said nothing of a personal nature in front of Dino, but naturally he wouldn't. Irena knew absolutely nothing about the dynamics between him and his ex-wife, he hadn't even mentioned his marriage the last time she had been here. Doubt filled her that maybe she didn't know Vincenzo as well as she had imagined. What if she had totally misjudged their relationship? She walked around the table and put a hand on Dino's shoulder. "Thank you for letting me play. Now I have to go. *Buonanotte,* Dino."

In the next instant he ran over to his father, letting go with a volley of Italian. A conversation ensued before Vincenzo eyed her in amusement. "My son doesn't want you to leave. I told him we'd drive you down to your hotel."

"That's very kind, but not necessary."

"I'm afraid it is," he came back in an authoritative voice. "Now that it's dark, a woman who looks like you out alone on a summer night is a target for every male from fourteen to a hundred years of age."

Irena tried to repress a smile. "Only a hundred?"

His black brows quirked. "You'd be surprised."

Actually she wasn't. Young or old, the male of the species was the same in Greece, but perhaps not as unique or fascinating as the Italian standing in front of her.

It warmed her heart when Dino took hold of her hand and led her outside past the mass of flowers growing in profusion everywhere. The pale blue Fiat was practically invisible. Vincenzo had parked it right up against the rear of his apartment to make room for other cars, which she'd observed were rare in the village when she'd come here the first time.

While she stood by with Dino, his father started it up and pulled out on the pathlike road so they could get in. Dino hopped in the back and strapped himself in his junior seat. Vincenzo reached across the front to open the passenger door for her and then they were off.

He drove at normal speed, but the dangerous curves and twists of the steep road made it seem like they were moving too fast past houses painted in oranges, pinks and yellows.

"You're as nervous as you were before," he said in his deep voice. "Don't worry. I could maneuver this cliff with a blindfold on."

She believed him, but had to admit she was relieved when they reached the parking area of the hotel. Before she could move, his hand left the gearshift to cover hers. It sent heat up her arm. "I'm taking Dino back to his mother tomorrow. Come with us, then we'll talk."

"All the way to Milan?"

"It's not that far."

Irena didn't look at him. "Do you think that would be a good idea? You know what I mean."

"Are you worried about my ex-wife? Don't be. If taking you with me were a problem, I wouldn't have suggested it. You *did* come to see me, did you not?"

She couldn't deny it.

"Dino enjoys your company." He kept talking as if she'd responded.

"Your son is like every child. They're happy with anyone who pays attention to them."

"True, but you turned him into a friend when you took the time to see the things in his room and remark on the castle. That's his favorite picture. With you along for the ride, the trip will turn into an exciting adventure for him."

He squeezed her fingers a little tighter before letting go. "Do I need to add how much I've longed to be with you again? Two months have felt like an eternity. Naturally I don't expect it has felt that way to you. Otherwise you wouldn't have gone back to Greece, leaving me without any hope of ever seeing you again."

Vincenzo had no idea of the depth of her feelings. But when she'd discussed her plan with Deline, she hadn't known he had a son. The very fact of Dino's existence altered the situation drastically.

Yet Vincenzo's words let her know nothing had changed for him personally. That tiny window of opportunity was still open for them to talk. If she didn't seize on his invitation, she might be sabotaging her only chance to salvage her life and that of the baby growing inside her.

The second doctor she'd gone to see hadn't been as convinced it was Andreas's baby. As he'd explained, pregnancy and conception were not hard and fast rules.

It was just as likely to be Andreas as it was Vincenzo's and no one could actually tell her this for certain, especially since she'd only slept with Andreas twice! No doctor could be one hundred percent certain based on a few fleeting encounters. The agony weighed heavily with Irena, more so every day, and she knew that she had to talk to Vincenzo about the situation. If only she could be sure that baby was his!

"How soon do you want to get away to Milan?"

"We'll pick you up at nine."

Irena nodded. "How do you say *tomorrow* in Italian?"

When he told her, she looked over her shoulder. "*Domani,* Dino." She got out of the car and hurried toward the hotel.

CHAPTER TWO

IRENA LAY AWAKE FOR a good part of the night. Her demons wouldn't leave her alone.

Though she'd been a career woman since college, in the back of her mind she'd always imagined that one day she'd get married and have children. Somewhere along the way Andreas had become part of that fantasy.

Over the years their families had been good friends and had often remarked that the two of them possessed the qualities for the kind of match that would last. Irena had thought so, too, but once they had begun seeing each other seriously, Andreas had waited a long time before making love to her. Their intimacy had been satisfying but not explosive. This had caused her to lose some confidence.

She recognized early that he was a cautious man. His reputation for not making mistakes put him, rather than his twin brother, Leon, at the head of the Simonides corporation once his father had to step down.

Though he'd assured her she was the only woman in his life, it hurt that he hadn't wanted to get engaged. He'd said he didn't believe in engagements. They'd know when the time was right to marry. She'd mistakenly assumed that the heavy responsibility placed on him as the CEO had dictated the amount of time they spent together.

If she were honest, she had to admit that between the hours he put in, combined with the travel she did for the newspaper, their relationship had suffered. When Vincenzo had pursued her so ardently, she'd been flattered and hungry for the attention.

But their ten days together and their one night of passion had turned into something more intense than a mere holiday fling. She knew then that her feelings for Vincenzo ran deep and now, seeing him again with his small son, those feelings were magnified. There was no question that Irena wanted this baby. She wanted it with all her heart and soul. And after witnessing Vincenzo's love for Dino, a part of Irena also longed for her baby to be Vincenzo's, too. But by the time she'd awakened at the hotel in Riomaggiore this morning, she'd changed her mind about following through with her agenda.

What she'd been planning since leaving the doctor's office was the act of a desperate woman. A *pregnant* one, she amended as she took the prenatal vitamins and antinausea pills he'd prescribed.

It was no use lying to herself. How could she think for one second that Vincenzo would feel the same way about her once she told him she was expecting a baby who might or might not be his child? He already had a darling six-year-old son of his own.

After brushing her teeth, she looked at herself in the mirror. Who did she think she was kidding?

What she needed to do was fly to someplace off the radar like Toronto, Canada. Her parents would understand she was trying to get over her heartache and wouldn't pressure her while she determined to make a new life for herself.

Toronto had a large Greek community. She could fit in using her mother's maiden name and have her baby. When it was a year old, she would go back to Athens, pretending to be a divorced woman. At that point she would be able to raise her child with no one the wiser and her secret forever safe.

Having made that decision, she dressed in white cotton pants and a silky, light blue blouse that tied at the side of her waist. The outfit would be comfortable to wear on the plane.

Before doing anything else, she wrote a note to Vincenzo explaining that it had been nice to see him and his little boy, but her plans had changed unexpectedly and she needed to make a flight.

Once she'd brushed her hair and slipped on her sandals, she was ready to check out of the hotel. It was only a short drive to the airport to return her rental car. If Vincenzo hadn't come to the hotel by then, she'd leave the note with the concierge.

At quarter to nine she arrived at the front desk and looked around. No sign of him. She paid the bill and left the note before walking out to the parking lot with her suitcase.

To her shock she discovered black-haired Vincenzo lounging against the driver's side of her car, causing a tumult of emotions inside her. How had he known which rental car was hers?

Tan cargo pants outlined powerful legs. In a claret-colored polo shirt with the kind of short sleeves that emphasized his hard-muscled arms, he could sell millions of magazines to any female who saw him on the cover.

He flashed her a stunning white smile. "Good morning, Irena."

"G-good morning," she stammered. "Where's Dino?"

"Buongiorno!" his son cried. When she turned, she saw him hanging out the window of the Fiat parked in the next row. She'd been concentrating so hard on getting away, she hadn't noticed his smiling face. He wore a cute white shirt with a big green dragon on the front. "How are you this morning, *signorina?*" He had that question down pat.

"I'm fine, Dino. How are you?"

"Wonderful!"

Vincenzo had probably taught him that word this morning. He said it with such an endearing accent. Her gaze swerved to blue eyes studying her beneath a sun growing hotter by the minute. He stood straight and moved toward her.

"Follow us to Genoa so you can return your car before we head for Milan."

She took a quick breath. "Vincenzo—something's come up and I can't go with you after all. I left a note for you at the desk when I checked out… I have to leave, Vincenzo."

His jaw hardened. "I have no intention of reading your note, and you can't leave…not yet. You made Dino a promise to come with us. He wants to show you Rapallo's castle in the sea, built to repel pirates. He hasn't stopped speaking of it—you can't disappoint him."

One more look at Dino's expectant expression and

Irena agreed. The only thing to do was drive to Milan with them. After Dino had been dropped off, she would ask Vincenzo to drive her to the Milan airport. She could leave for Canada from there.

"All right. A few more hours won't matter in the scheme of things." She reached for the key with the built-in remote and unlocked the door. He opened it and helped her inside, submitting her to another intimate appraisal before closing it. With an increased pulse rate, she started the car and waited to follow him.

During the short trip to Rapallo on the Italian Riviera, Dino turned in his junior seat and waved to her from time to time, making her smile. She waved back. When they reached the town, they parked in the historic center and ate gelato while they walked around the harbor.

She told Vincenzo to tell Dino that the tiny, picturesque castle out in the water looked like a toy castle. His son laughed and pulled her hand as they walked across the short causeway to explore it. Soon after, he begged her to ride the cable car up to Montallegro. Who could say no to him?

Along with other passengers they were treated to a panoramic view of the Golfo del Tigullio. After a lovely lunch at the restaurant on top, they took the funicular back down to their cars and drove on to Genoa where she returned hers to the rental company.

Vincenzo put her suitcase in the trunk of the Fiat where he'd stowed Dino's cases.

The sight of them and a bag of toys brought a pang to her heart. In a little while the two of them would have to part company.

Clearly Vincenzo adored his son. As for Dino, he was

crazy about his papa. How hard for them to have to be separated, yet Dino had a mother who must be missing him horribly.

More than ever Irena realized that in a few short months she, too, could be faced with a similar situation. If Andreas was the baby's father and he discovered the truth, then Irena would be forced to share visitation and the raising of her baby with him. But if Vincenzo turned out to be the father, then what would the future hold for them? Vincenzo already knew the pain of having to say goodbye to his child because of visitation; would he want to go through that again with this baby?

En route to Milan, Dino kept her entertained by teaching her a couple of simple children's songs in Italian. Vincenzo translated. She knew her accent was terrible, but she tried hard to memorize them and sing along. He corrected her here and there. By the time they reached the outskirts of the city, she could sing them without help.

"Bravo, *signorina*."

She shifted in her seat to smile at Dino. "*Grazie*. You're an excellent teacher."

He said something to his father in rapid Italian. Vincenzo answered back. Irena couldn't resist looking at him. "What did your son say?"

"He wishes you were his English tutor. Mr. Fallow was born in England, and moved here ten years ago. According to my son, he's strict and grumpy because of a sore hip. You're a much better teacher and you're very nice. He wants to know if you would you like him to teach you Italian."

Laughter escaped her lips. "I can't imagine loving anything more. How much does he charge?"

A smile lit up Vincenzo's blue eyes before he translated for his son. His boy giggled, then whispered something to his father.

Filled with curiosity she looked at him. "What was that all about?"

"He wouldn't say no to a chocolate bocci ball."

"Ah. A chocolate lover. I'll remember that, but what will his dentist say?"

This time Vincenzo chuckled hard. After he told Dino, all three of them were laughing, but it slowly faded as they were allowed through a security gate. Soon they pulled up in the courtyard of a luxury villa hidden from the road by foliage.

"I'll be right back." Vincenzo slid from the seat to get his son's bags.

Irena stayed in the car while Dino scrambled out of the back to come around to her door. She opened the window and shook his hand. "Thank you for a wonderful day, Dino."

"Thank you, too. You like Papa?" He looked worried. Of course he was wondering what was going on between her and his father. Did he want her to like his parent, or did he wish she'd go away and never come back? What would Dino make of a new baby brother or sister? A trickle of unease settled over Irena. Her baby could affect so many people's lives. She shook the feeling off and turned to Dino again.

"Yes, and I like you." She poked his stomach with her index finger.

He reacted with a grin. *"Ciao, signorina."*

"Ciao, Dino."

She watched the two of them carry all his stuff to the front door of the villa. A maid answered and let them inside. Assuming Vincenzo would be a while, she rested her head against the back of the seat and closed her eyes.

Though she knew what she was going to say to him when he came back out, she was full of trepidation. They hadn't been alone since she'd walked up to his apartment yesterday. Without Dino as a buffer, she didn't know what to expect from Vincenzo, and she had no idea how he was going to react to her news.

Vincenzo hunkered down in front of his son. "We had a good time, didn't we?"

"Yes. I loved it! Will Irena be with you the next time I see you?"

"I hope so."

"I do, too. She makes you happy, huh."

Vincenzo smiled at his son's insight. "Yes."

"Did you know she's afraid of the water, too? She told me while we were looking out of the castle window."

So…his son had an ally. "But she doesn't seem to mind heights because she liked the cable car ride."

"I know. So did I. She's fun!"

"I agree."

Lowering his voice to a whisper Dino said, "She's beautiful, too, but don't tell *you know who* I said so."

"Don't worry. I won't. Now before *you know who* comes downstairs, give me a hug." He felt Dino's arms wrap around him and squeeze him hard. "I'll see you at the end of the month."

"I wish we could do stuff more often."

"But this is working, right?"

As Dino nodded and wiped his eyes, Mila appeared in shorts and a top, looking immaculate as always. His son broke away and ran toward her, giving her a big hug. She kissed his head before flicking her glance to Vincenzo.

"You're later than I expected."

In a gush of excitement, Dino told her all about their outing to Rapallo with Signorina Spiros. Vincenzo was perfectly happy for his son to take over and explain.

Mila's expression hardened. "Take your things upstairs, Dino. I want to talk to your father alone."

"Okay." He turned to Vincenzo. "I love you, Papa."

"I love you, too."

He grabbed his sack of toys and started up the steps. When he'd disappeared from sight, Mila turned to him. "You've never introduced Dino to another woman before. How important is she to you?"

"Very." Last evening he'd come close to cardiac arrest when he'd seen Irena at his front door. If he wasn't mistaken, Mila lost color.

"And she's Greek?"

"Dino's already said as much. Now I have to go, Mila. Irena is waiting for me."

"She's here?"

"*Sì.* She is in the courtyard in my car."

"How dare you bring her here, Vincenzo! And how dare you sleep with a woman in the apartment while Dino's there on visitation!"

"Save your anger, Mila. She stayed at a hotel."

"I forbid it, Vincenzo."

Vincenzo felt his own anger toward his ex-wife bubbling to the surface. "Forbid what? I've obeyed every edict of the visitation stipulation to the letter. There's nothing in it that states I can't be with a woman in my car or my own apartment in Dino's presence. My life has nothing to do with you anymore, Mila."

"We'll see about that!"

"If you and your father want to throw more money away talking to your attorney, I can't stop you, but I promise you'll be wasting your time."

"You won't be so smug when I tell your father and he gets the judge to alter the stipulation."

"That's not going to happen. *Ciao, Mila.*" With Irena's arrival, Vincenzo now held the trump card and he would use it.

"Don't you walk out on me yet!" Her strident voice had risen higher. "I'm not finished!"

"If you aren't, you should be. Dino has missed you. Don't keep him waiting."

He left the villa, knowing he'd put the handcuffs on Mila for now. It was always a wrench to walk away from his son, but for once someone was waiting for him. He found himself somewhat breathless as he got back in the car and turned to Irena. Elation filled him that they were finally alone.

The richness of her black hair held his gaze, but it hid part of her features. He leaned closer to smooth it behind her ear, unable to resist touching her before starting the car. He studied her beautiful Grecian profile for a prolonged moment before pulling beyond the gate and out onto the main road.

"I took this week off from work to be with Dino and

don't have to report until tomorrow morning. Let's make the most of the time."

She stirred restlessly. "Vincenzo—I think we need to talk. You need to know the reason why I came...I didn't want to say anything in front of Dino."

"It's enough that you're here."

"I'm being serious."

"I never thought you weren't."

"Please listen to me. I won't be staying in Riomaggiore. I'm on my way to Toronto. If you'd be kind enough to drive me to the airport, I'll be grateful."

She was running away again. This time he wouldn't let her. "I thought you quit your job at the newspaper."

"I did."

"Then what's in Canada?"

"Another job away from Greece."

"If that's what you're looking for, I could offer you a public relations position at the plant in La Spezia."

He watched her hands clench together. "I don't speak Italian."

"I would teach you."

"Vincenzo—" she cried in frustration. "I stopped to visit you because I knew you would see the headlines about Andreas's marriage to Gabi. It was important to me that you didn't think I was a total liar.

"When I left Riomaggiore, I went back to break it off with Andreas. After I met you, I knew that my relationship with Andreas was doomed—you were right about that. Andreas figured it out for himself, too."

Vincenzo was silent for a moment before speaking. "Be thankful Simonides acted on his instincts."

"Whether he did or didn't, I acted on mine and slept

with you. That was the turning point for me." The attraction between them had been too powerful. They'd just gone with the moment.

He turned onto a road leading into a park. As soon as he could, he pulled to the side and shut off the engine before giving her his full attention. "Now tell me why you showed up at my door. The truth." Vincenzo was no one's fool.

"You're so sure I had an agenda?"

His penetrating blue eyes searched hers. "Let's just say you and I have a strong chemistry. Whatever the camouflage, I believe it brought you back."

He was right about the intensity of their physical longing for each other. "What if I told you the camouflage is hiding a compelling problem that has caused me to veer off course and fly alone?"

"I'm listening." He knew she was referring to the analogy about the geese.

Her heart thudded at the thought of her own daring. "Were you serious when you said you thought we should get married?"

"Perfectly."

She moaned. "That wasn't a fair question to ask you since the circumstances aren't the same as they were two months ago. I didn't know you already had a son and a troubled marital history."

"That's one way of putting it."

"I—I'm sorry your first marriage didn't work out—" her voice faltered "—but it's not just that. There is something else I need to tell you, something…"

"What is it, Irena? What is it that has changed since our last meeting?" Vincenzo was again silent for a

moment, clearly in deep thought, before his gaze shifted
to Irena once more. "Irena, are you pregnant...with my
baby?"

Shocked at his insight, Irena lowered her head, hating
what she had to tell him. "I'm pregnant, Vincenzo, but
I don't know if the baby is yours. I've been to two OBs
for opinions. Both worked out the timetable with me
and came to the conclusion that we can't be sure either
way who the father is."

"Simonides doesn't know?" Vincenzo was a proud
man. She'd been expecting that question and was prepared for it.

"I only came from the second doctor yesterday afternoon before I flew here."

"And he's on his honeymoon..." Vincenzo's eyes
narrowed on her face. "How soon do you plan to tell
him?"

"I don't."

"As in never?"

"If you think that makes me an evil woman, I'll
understand."

"Since I know you're not, why in heaven's name
wouldn't you tell him? He has the right to know."

"It's a long, complicated story."

"I doubt it rivals my own." There he went again al-
luding to a life that she knew next to nothing about. "Go
on."

"Look, Vincenzo. I've wasted enough of your time.
I shouldn't have come here. Please just drive me to the
airport."

"Not until you explain."

Irena threw her head back, causing her hair to resettle

around her shoulders, and closed her eyes. Then she took a deep, cleansing breath before she began to speak. "It all started over a year ago when Leon, Andreas's brother, and Deline, Leon's wife, had a very serious quarrel. He was working long hours as Andreas's assistant, was hardly ever at home and it hurt Deline a lot. She accused Leon of neglecting their marriage and her. She wanted to start a family, but hadn't been able to get pregnant and things were bad between them.

"They separated for a couple months. When Deline told him she was thinking of making the separation permanent, Leon was so hurt he got his friends together and took out the Simonides yacht. His friends invited some women on board and everyone got drunk. Then a terrible thing happened."

For the next little while Irena relived the nightmare that had come close to destroying so many families. "I still don't know how Deline is handling it. Besides being pregnant with Leon's baby, she's taking care of the twins he fathered on board the yacht with Thea Turner that night."

"She must love him very much."

"She does. I believe their marriage has a good chance of making it. But if I were to tell Andreas about our baby, it could destroy not only him, but his marriage, too. Gabi's an innocent in all this and went through hell when her half sister died in childbirth. Until Gabi contacted Andreas, she was the one who took care of the twins for the first four months of their lives. If this baby is Andreas's, how would this news affect her?"

Vincenzo moved his hand to play with the ends of her hair. "The more the plot unravels, the more it sounds like my own complicated family saga." This was the second time she'd heard him mention anything about them.

"All the families have been in crisis, including mine. My parents had been counting on my marriage to Andreas. They've been grief stricken since he married Gabi. They think I'm heartbroken over it! If they knew it was his baby, they'd insist he take responsibility.

"And Andreas would insist on taking control, because that's the way he's made. But then everyone would get in on the act to make things right with me. Nothing would ever be the same again."

Hot tears rolled down her cheeks. "It would ruin so many lives—that's the reason why I have to keep this a secret from Andreas."

Vincenzo cocked his dark head. "Does anyone else know you're pregnant?"

"Does it matter?"

"Yes."

"Why?"

"If we're going to get married, I insist that everyone believe the baby is mine."

Irena gasped. "Vincenzo, what I said earlier... You don't want to marry me! Especially not now."

"Irena, the baby you carry has as much chance of being mine as Andreas's. As you have explained, he already has a wife, therefore I insist on taking responsibility. You need a husband, the baby needs a father and I need a wife."

"Vincenzo..."

"I'll ask you the question again. Does anyone else know you're pregnant besides me and your doctors?"

"Yes."

"Who is it?"

She bit her lip. "It's Deline."

Vincenzo rubbed the side of his jaw. "Under the circumstances she's probably the only person you know who *could* be trusted. Do you think she'd be able to take our secret to the grave?"

Our secret. Irena couldn't fathom that he was really considering the idea of marriage to her, especially after what she had just told him.

"If I didn't believe that, I wouldn't have told her in the first place."

"Does she support you in keeping this from Andreas?"

"No. She's afraid that if I don't tell him, it'll come out one day anyway. But she would never betray me."

"Can you trust the doctors not to contact Simonides? He's too well-known for them not to make the connection."

"I did what you did when you told Dino my last name was Spiros. How did you know that by the way?"

"When you came before, I saw the name on your passport. Irena Spiros Liapis."

She blinked. "I'm surprised you would remember."

"I've forgotten nothing about you, Irena." His velvety words melted through to her insides.

"When I went to the E.R., I told them my name was Irena Spiros. I was referred to the OB under the same name. Including the doctor I saw yesterday, none of them has any idea I was the other woman mentioned in the headlines about Andreas."

"Then it's settled. We'll be married as soon as I can

arrange it. Since you don't subscribe to any religion, we'll say our vows in a civil ceremony."

"Stop, Vincenzo!" She shook her head. "You're going way too fast for me…and yourself."

"Don't presume to tell me my own feelings, Irena. If it had been possible, I would have married you when you were here before."

She took a shaky breath. "Without my having met your son first?"

"I would have introduced you. The three of us would have spent the day together before I asked him if he wanted to watch us get married."

Irena averted her eyes. "Whether he approved of me or not, he would have said yes because he loves you. He'll do anything to make you happy."

"But *I* wouldn't marry a woman unless she could make *him* happy, too."

"You hardly know me, Vincenzo. We hardly know each other."

"I know one of the most important things about you, Irena. You have an exceptionally kind nature that spoke to my son. After last night and today, Dino knows it, too. Shall I tell you what he whispered to me in the foyer before Mila appeared? He said he hoped you would be with me at the next visitation."

Her eyelids smarted. "He's very sweet."

"You took the time to play with him and make him feel like he was an important person."

"All children are important."

"Not everyone feels that way inside. I watched you with him last night. You put him at ease."

"I'm glad."

"Glad enough to marry me and help me raise my son while I father our baby?"

She avoided his gaze and stared out the side window. "It couldn't be that simple, Vincenzo."

"Of course not. I never suggested otherwise. We'll be one of those families of this generation that fits all the odd parts into one new whole. Hopefully it will work, but there are no guarantees."

Irena let out a sad laugh. "We're nothing alike."

His eyes grew hooded. "You and Andreas came from the same world, but you didn't make it to the altar. I wasn't as lucky as you, Irena, and didn't escape in time. My family thought I should marry someone like me, and you see what happened. I think being opposites with no expectations will be very good for us."

He'd said that before.

"I was in lust with you the second you walked in my office. That hasn't changed."

Her heart jumped. His honesty shocked her, but it was also that quality which had first attracted her. And his looks... She couldn't deny how physically appealing he was to her. Knowing he was already a father, having met his son, it surprised her that she found him more desirable than ever. But she couldn't allow that magnetism to blind her to the realities of the situation.

"I don't care what you say about Dino liking me. If we were to marry, he would feel another loss. You say you only get to see him one weekend a month and twice a year for a week. If we were to marry he would then have to share that precious time he has with you with me. The poor little darling would be so hurt."

In the next breath Vincenzo pulled her into his arms

and buried his face in her hair. "Once we're married, everything will change for the better for both of us."

"Vincenzo—we can't even think about it without Dino having a part in the decision."

"I'm way ahead of you, so this is what we'll do." He lifted his head, forcing her to look at him. "There's a hotel nearby where I always take Dino when I'm in Milan on visitation. I'll drive you there now and then I'll bring Dino back with me. We'll have an early dinner together and tell him our plans."

Everything was moving too fast. "That sounds good in theory, but you've only just dropped him back with his mother. What if she has arranged something special for him? He hasn't been home in a week."

A tiny nerve hammered at the edge of his mouth. She noticed it appeared when he was unusually tense. "If she has plans, it will be a first. As for my needs, this time they'll have to take precedence." After pressing a warm kiss to her lips, he let her go with reluctance and started the car.

CHAPTER THREE

BE THERE, ARTURO.

"Vincenzo! I saw your name on the caller ID and couldn't believe it. We haven't talked in ages. What can I do for you?"

"I need my attorney's help."

"Of course."

"I'm in Milan and am driving over to Mila's villa right now to pick up Dino. It's imperative I take him out for a few hours, then I'll return him. She's going to refuse because I only just brought him back from our holiday in Riomaggiore, but something's come up and it's vital I talk to him alone. Be the master counselor you are and call her attorney to let him know my special circumstances."

"I'll get on it right now."

"*Grazie,* Arturo." He clicked off.

Whether Arturo could reach Mila's attorney or not, Vincenzo had no intention of letting his ex-wife thwart him. She was already worked up because Dino had told her about Irena. He could just imagine the fireworks when he showed up at the door in a few minutes, but this was one time he didn't care, because hopefully it would be the last time he or Dino would ever be at her mercy in the same way.

"Signore?" The maid looked surprised to see him at the door.

"Would you tell Mila and Dino I'm here to see them."

"Sì."

He moved inside the foyer and shut the door. The noise resounded in the tomblike interior. Pretty soon he heard the patter of feet.

"Papa!" Dino came running into his arms.

Mila followed. "What are you doing back here?"

"Something important has come up. I need to talk to Dino for a little while. I hope you don't mind."

She had to think about it. "You can go in the salon."

"No, I meant I need to talk to him away from here, Mila."

"I don't want him leaving the house."

"Do you have plans for him?"

"We don't, do we, Mama?" Dino piped up.

"That's not the point, Dino."

"Then it won't matter if I take him for a few more hours. I'll have him back in time for bed."

"You've had your week with him, Vincenzo."

She didn't care that their son could hear this. Much as Vincenzo hated it, she'd left him no choice. "Legally I have the right to be with him until nine tonight. I bring him back early as a consideration to you, Mila. Go ahead and call your attorney. By the time you reach him, I'll have brought Dino back."

He glanced at his son. "We're going out to dinner."

"Can we get pizza?"

"If that's what you want."

"With *her?*" Mila demanded.

Vincenzo didn't answer. Dino walked out the door with him. It closed hard behind them.

"Mama's real mad."

"I'm sorry about that. She's missed you a lot."

They got in the car. "Are we going to eat with Signorina Spiros?"

"We are."

"Did she want me to come?"

"I'll say. In fact, she refused to eat with me unless you came."

A smile broke out on his face.

"Hey—our hotel!" he cried a few minutes later. "Is she waiting in our room?"

"Yes."

Irena thanked the clerk in the gift shop and took the two presents she'd bought back to the hotel room. Vincenzo had told her it was the one he and Dino always stayed in. They pretended it was their home away from home. The more she was getting to know him, the more she realized what an exceptional father he was.

If Vincenzo was the father of her unborn child, it would have no better parent. But she was getting ahead of herself. First they needed to broach the subject of marriage with Dino. These things took time.

Under the best of circumstances, his son might need months, even a year, to get used to the idea. Unfortunately Irena didn't have that long with a baby on the way. She still hadn't given up the idea of going to Canada.

Her ears picked up the rap on the door. Nervous over what was to come, she turned in time to see the two of them enter the room. It suddenly hit her they could be her future husband and stepson. As the thought penetrated, she was overcome by a myriad of emotions ranging from anxiety that it couldn't work, to excitement that it might.

"Hi, Dino!"

His brown eyes smiled. "Hi, *signorina!*"

Vincenzo's gaze traveled from one to the other. "I've just told him we're going to have dinner here. I'll call the kitchen. He wants pizza. What else would you like?"

"Salad? Coffee?"

He nodded and picked up the house phone to place their order.

"Come over here, Dino." She'd put one of her gifts on the table. When he joined her, she told him to open it. Out of the bag came a canister of fifty pickup sticks. "Have you ever played this before?"

When he shook his head, she looked at Vincenzo. "What about you?"

A gleam entered his eyes. "Once long ago. We called it Shanghai."

"Well, the game I know works like this." She opened the top and put all the sticks in her hand. Then she placed it on the table and let the sticks fall. Picking out the black stick she said, "The trick is to remove each stick one at a time so the others don't move. The person who can remove the most sticks is the winner."

She got busy and loosened ten sticks before disturbing

some. Dino couldn't wait to be next. The game entertained all of them until their meal was wheeled in on a tea cart.

While they ate, Vincenzo took over in the translation department. "Dino? We brought you here to discuss something very important. It's about me and Irena."

"What is it?" Above his lips he had a milk moustache.

Irena exchanged a private glance with Vincenzo and they both smiled. "Do you know how you always ask me how come I'm not married and I always tell you it's because I haven't found the right woman yet?"

He nodded. "But now you've found Irena, huh."

When Vincenzo explained what Dino had said, Irena expelled the breath she'd been holding.

"Yes. We want to get married right away. How do you feel about that?"

Once the question was posed Dino said, "Can I see you get married?" He'd asked it without hesitation. Vincenzo translated.

"We do everything together, don't we?"

Dino nodded. "Will Grandpa be there?" More translation.

"Not this time. Irena's family won't be there, either, because we're doing this too fast for everyone to get ready."

"It's not too fast for me!"

The look in Vincenzo's eyes as he translated said it all.

"Will Father Rinaldo marry you in the little church down the road?"

"I don't know. That's up to Irena." He explained what his son had asked.

Dino looked at her with entreaty. "It's a very pretty church," he said in English.

Irena didn't feel comfortable about that. Although she had strong feelings for Vincenzo, their marriage was going to be one of convenience first and foremost. Neither of them had expressed feelings of love for each other and they were really only marrying for the baby's sake. Vincenzo didn't even know if the baby was his or not!

"I tell you what, Dino. Your father and I will talk it over before we decide. Would that be okay with you?"

He let the subject go and asked another question before getting out of his chair to come and stand by Irena. He stared at her with an earnestness that melted her heart and asked her something in Italian. Again Vincenzo explained.

"He wants to know if you'll let him come to see us more often than once a month after we're married."

She didn't have to think about it. "Tell him I would love for him to come and live with us *all* the time, but I know he loves his mommy, too."

Vincenzo cleared his throat before enlightening his son. At that point Dino's spontaneous response was to reach out and hug her. Irena hugged him back, loving this precious boy already. Wiping the tears from her eyes, she told him to wait a minute. She got up from the chair and walked over to the phone table where she'd put his other gift.

"This is for you," she said in English, handing him the bag.

His face came alive in anticipation. "Two presents?" he said in the same language.

She understood what he meant. "Yes. Go ahead and open it."

He quickly pulled the little tied box out of the sack and undid it. Beneath the lid lay six chocolate bocci balls. *"Stupendo! Grazie, signorina."*

"Di niente, Dino." She'd heard that expression often enough. "Call me Irena."

Dino gave her another hug, then offered them both a chocolate. Irena declined hers, knowing how much he loved them, but his father had no reservations and popped one in his mouth. Dino followed suit.

"Delizioso," they both said at the same time. Just then she got an inkling of what Vincenzo would have been like when he was an irrepressible boy Dino's age. The image would always stay with her.

They settled down to a couple more rounds of pickup sticks, then Vincenzo made the announcement that they had to go. "Your mama is expecting you, and Irena and I have to drive back to Riomaggiore this evening." To her relief, Dino didn't act upset they had to go.

"The game is yours, Dino." She put it in the sack and handed it to him. In his other hand he had his bag of chocolate and they left the room.

In a minute they were on their way to the villa. Irena was content to listen while the two of them kept up a rapid conversation in Italian. Dino had a dozen questions, firing one after the other.

It was like déjà vu when they drove up in the courtyard and Vincenzo told her he'd be right back. Except that this time Irena got out of the car to give Dino another hug and say goodbye. "*Arrivederci,* Dino." She was determined to learn Italian as fast as she could.

He grinned in delight. "*Arrivederci,* Irena."

The die was cast. Irena had committed herself. There was no going back. Vincenzo was forced to suppress his euphoria as Mila herself answered the door, ready to castigate him. But for once Dino didn't seem to notice the tension coming from her.

"Guess what, Mama? Irena gave me presents. She and Papa are getting married and I get to watch!"

"Why don't you go up for your bath?" Vincenzo suggested. "I need to talk to your mama."

"Okay."

"I'll call you tomorrow night and let you know everything that's happening, okay?"

"Okay. *Ciao,* Papa." He raced up the stairs with a new spring in his step.

Vincenzo eyed his ex-wife. Beneath her anger she looked anxious, and with good reason. Since their divorce she'd had everything her way, but now that he was getting married, they could tear up the existing visitation agreement. "Thank you for letting me take him this evening. As you can see, it was important."

"I want to meet her."

"If you wish. Where's your husband?"

"Leo's in Rome."

"Shall I bring her in, or do you want to walk out to the car?"

Without answering him verbally, she moved past him and headed for the Fiat. Irena could see them coming and got out. She'd never looked more beautiful to him than right now standing there poised and elegant without being aware of it.

"Mila Ricci? May I present Irena Spiros from Athens," he said in English. "She doesn't speak Italian so we'll speak in English."

"How do you do," Irena said and shook Mila's hand. "You have a wonderful boy in Dino."

"Thank you," Mila answered in a brittle voice. She thrust Vincenzo an icy stare. In Italian she said, "How do you expect Dino to handle the situation when she can't even speak Italian?"

"She'll learn. Dino's anxious to teach her."

"I won't stand for it, Vincenzo."

He shrugged his shoulders. "You're going to have to."

"This won't change visitation."

She was in for a huge shock. Ignoring her warning he said, "You're being rude in front of my fiancée, Mila."

Her cheeks flared with color before she addressed Irena. "Do you have any experience with children?"

"No, but when Dino is with us, I'll try my hardest to make him happy."

Mila just found out Irena was a woman of high-class and breeding. It was impossible to fight good manners without looking like a shrew.

To Mila he said, "My attorney will be contacting yours. By Tuesday you'll know all my plans. *Ciao,* Mila."

Leaving her to digest that bit of news, he helped Irena back into the car. By the time he'd walked around to the driver's seat, Mila had gone back into the villa.

"I feel sorry for her." Irena spoke once they'd reached

the main road. "I don't think there's a mother alive who wouldn't feel threatened to know her child was going to be around the influence of another woman on a part-time basis."

He gripped the steering wheel tighter. "Perhaps now you have an inkling of how I felt when Mila re-married."

She nodded sadly. "Life shouldn't be this way."

"You mean everything should be perfect where every child gets to live with its own mother and father until he or she is happily married off and the whole wonderful process starts all over again?"

"Something like that," she whispered.

"You've already gotten a taste of what it's going to be like dealing with Mila. I'm glad she insisted on meeting you."

"So am I."

"In case her behavior has given you second thoughts, let me know now. I'll phone Dino to tell him there's been a change in plans. I don't want him to go to sleep tonight thinking that something's going to happen he's been wanting for such a long time."

"I don't understand. Why would your getting married make such a difference to him?"

"My story's as convoluted as yours. When I divorced Mila, I had to give up a lot to win my freedom from her. Dino was the main casualty, of course. He was so hurt by the tension in our impossible marriage, divorce was the only solution. But both our families disowned me over it."

"Are you joking?"

"I wish I were. If I wanted to see my child, I had to agree to abide by the severe stipulations she set up."

"Couldn't a judge have interceded?"

"Oh, he did, in favor of both our families. He and my grandfather were close friends, like your parents and the Simonides family. The order stated that Dino had been in jeopardy in a loveless home with a father who'd shown a flagrant disregard for his heritage and prominence, therefore was a poor role model."

"I don't believe it," she cried, aghast.

"There's more. Until the time came that I could show I'd come to my senses and had reconciled with my ex-wife, the visitation rules would stand."

"Oh, Vincenzo—that's horrible. None of those reasons make any sense."

"Of course not. Mila waited for me to go back to her, but she waited in vain. Finally she remarried six months ago, causing another change in Dino's life."

"Does he like his stepfather?"

"Not particularly. He's fifteen years older than Mila with a grown son and daughter at university. His wife died a year ago and it wasn't long after that he met Mila. He has nothing in common with a young boy like Dino."

"That must tear you apart."

"It does."

"So what will happen now?"

"Tomorrow morning I'll meet with my attorney to end the current visitation."

"What will you put in its place?"

"Joint physical custody. From now on Dino will have two homes."

"But the judge—"

Vincenzo shook his head. "Don't worry. After my attorney talks to Mila's attorney, everything's going to change in a big hurry."

"How can you be so sure?"

He sucked in his breath. "Because I'm prepared to do something I refused to do before. My father will be so overjoyed, he'll fall over backward to accommodate all my wishes, including that of influencing the judge to rescind his decision."

Irena had been listening between the lines. Whatever this something was Vincenzo had refused to do, it had to have been something big. So what was it the judge had meant about Vincenzo's heritage and prominence?

From the first moment she'd met him, she'd sensed he was a man of many parts. He knew too much, understood too much, had too much savvy to be an ordinary Italian male. There was an inherent authority and intelligence he emanated without conscious thought.

When they'd been introduced at the plant, she'd been aware of a certain deference the staff exhibited around him. Like he was someone elite.

She stared at his striking features as they sped along the strada toward Cinque Terre. Beneath his black brows, his aquiline profile gave him a fiercely handsome look. He had the most beautiful olive skin she'd ever seen. As for his eyes, they were so piercing a blue her body quickened just looking into them.

Irena felt like she was experiencing second sight. His sophistication couldn't be denied.

Who was this attractive man with unruly black hair

who drove around in a secondhand car and rented a tiny apartment on a cliff? He dressed in casual clothes you could buy in any local shop and wore flip-flops like his son.

Without clothes he'd looked like a statue of a god she'd seen in Rapallo that morning. The memory of them making love six weeks ago sent a wave of heat through her body. Did she even know him at all?

"You're very quiet all of a sudden."

His low voice curled through her nervous system. "I've been putting the pieces of a puzzle together."

"How close are you to being finished?"

He knew she was on to him.

"Several are still missing. Just how prominent are you?"

"Let's save all that until tomorrow."

What was she getting herself into?

"Don't be alarmed. Once I've seen my attorney, I'll explain everything. Go to sleep. I can see your eyelids flickering. We still have an hour's drive ahead of us. After such an emotional day, you're tired and need to take care of yourself, especially now that you're carrying our baby."

Our baby.

The baby *had* to be theirs. It had to be! But still that dark cloud of doubt lingered.

Irena *was* tired. In fact, she was exhausted from too much thinking and feeling. "When should we tell Dino about the baby?" she asked after closing her eyes.

"Most likely he'll decide the moment. He's an incredibly insightful little boy."

She chuckled. "How long do you think it will take me to learn Italian?"

"Two months for the basics if you work on it every day. The rest will come over a lifetime."

"A lifetime. That's a beautiful thought."

It was the last thought she remembered until the next morning when she awoke in Dino's bed feeling slightly nauseous. She was still clothed except for her sandals. She'd completely passed out last night, forcing Vincenzo to carry her into the apartment after they'd arrived.

The shutters were still closed, but she could see the sun trying to get in. She threw off the light cover and staggered to the window to open them. A glorious view of the Mediterranean greeted her vision. She checked her watch. Ten forty-five. Irena couldn't believe it.

Vincenzo had placed her suitcase in the bedroom. She got out her cosmetic bag and padded to the bathroom.

She called out to him, but there was no response. He'd said he was going to see his attorney this morning.

She could tell he'd been in the bathroom recently. It smelled of the soap and shampoo he'd used in the shower. A wonderful male smell she associated only with him.

Once she'd swallowed her pills, she undressed and got in the shower. After she washed her hair with apricot shampoo, she dried it the best she could with a towel, then hurried back to the bedroom.

With a change of fresh underwear followed by a cotton top and pants, she felt a little better, but she needed something to eat. In the kitchen she discovered a note on the table from him, written with a flourish.

I should be back by noon and I'll take you to lunch.

Feel free to nibble on anything that appeals. Crackers, toast might help with the morning sickness. There's tea or coffee in the cupboard, juice in the fridge. V.

She found a roll and grape juice. Perfect.

The food helped the emptiness in her stomach. She went back to the bedroom for her brush and worked on her hair until it fell in a swath. Since it was already warmer in the apartment than the other day, she arranged it in a loose knot on top of her head in the interest of staying cool.

Her pregnancy was causing her to notice everything. She'd thought her fatigue had been brought on by anxiety, but the doctor had assured her that it was normal to feel so tired, especially in the first few months.

Vincenzo already seemed to know and understand a lot more about her condition than she did. But then he had lived with his wife when she'd been expecting Dino. Irena had no doubts he'd taken amazing care of her.

She blinked back tears, not knowing the exact reason for being in such an emotional mood. Naturally it was a combination of everything, but she had to admit that part of it was the way Vincenzo had handled the situation. He was her rock.

Another part was her guilt. She needed to talk to someone about how she was feeling and reached for the phone to call Deline. Disappointed when she got her voice mail, she left the message for Deline to call her back. Then she phoned her mother, who answered on the second ring.

"Irena, my darling daughter. How are you? Where are you? Your father and I have been worried sick."

More guilt. She sank down on the side of Dino's bed. "I'm sorry. I meant to call you from the hotel in Riomaggiore, but the sightseeing trip with Signore Antonello took longer than I'd anticipated."

"You are with him again, in Italy?"

"Yes. You remember my writing about Cinque Terre in my article. It has those narrow, crooked streets lined with colorful old houses stacked haphazardly on top of each other. I think it's one of the most beautiful spots on the Mediterranean."

"You said that before. Is he a travel guide?"

"No, no. He works at Antonello Liquers in La Spezia. It's one of the places I highlighted in my article for tourists to tour. He was the man who took me around the village. Yesterday we went to a castle in Rapallo with his son."

"I'm glad if you're enjoying yourself a little bit. When I think what Andrea—"

"Don't go there, Mother. That part of my life is over. I don't want to talk about it again."

"I didn't mean to hurt you."

"I know. The fact is, Andreas and I weren't right for each other. I think we both knew it and tried to force something that wasn't there. Gabi's coming along proved it."

"What do you mean?"

"It's difficult to explain."

"But you *loved* him!"

It was hard to have a conversation like this long distance. "Yes, I loved Andreas. I always will." Frustrated, she got to her feet and began pacing right into Vincenzo who caught her by the upper arms to prevent her from falling.

By the enigmatic look in his eye, she couldn't tell what he was thinking, but there could be no question he'd heard that last admission. She eased away from him. "I have to go, but I promise I'll call you again tomorrow."

Irena hung up. "I—I was talking to my mother," she stammered.

"Have you told her about us?"

"Only in the sense that I knew you when I was doing the magazine article and since my arrival you've been showing me around. I don't plan to tell her anything else until our plans are formalized." She brushed her hands nervously against her hips, a gesture he followed with his eyes. "How did it go with your attorney?"

A heavy silence ensued. "Let's talk about it over a meal."

"Wait, Vincenzo—" He looked over his shoulder. "You came in before I finished making my point with Mother."

His face had become a mask of indifference. "You don't owe me an explanation of a private conversation with her. I walked in on *you*." On that note, he headed for the living room.

She followed him. "But I want to tell you."

He turned toward her with his hands on hips in a totally male stance. "Tell me what?"

"Mother's still living in denial about me and Andreas. If I'd finished that sentence I would have said, 'I always will love him as a friend, but I realize now that I was never *in* love with Andreas or he with me.'"

At the enigmatic expression on his arresting face, she added, "Otherwise I could never have gone to bed with you. No woman could do that if she were truly and deeply in love with another man."

"I agree," his voice rasped.

"Contrary to what you might think about me, in my twenty-seven years of life I've only been intimate with two men, and you're one of them."

His jaw tautened. "I never suggested you were promiscuous."

"No, but you'd have every right to think it after I fell like the proverbial ripe plum into your hands. I look back on it now and can't believe what I did. It still shocks me."

Miraculously, his compelling mouth broke into a half smile. "I confess I thought I'd died and gone to some heavenly place for a short while."

She'd thought the same thing, but couldn't bring herself to tell him that yet. "Vincenzo?" Irena eyed him frankly. "Can we put the past to rest? My relationship with Andreas? It's over."

He gave a slow nod. "Amen. Shall we go?"

Thankful they'd weathered that small storm she said, "I'm coming. Let me get my purse."

"How hungry are you?"

"I think a pasta salad would hit the spot."

"There's a trattoria across from the church Dino was talking about."

"I—I've been thinking about that," she stammered. "Maybe—"

"Irena—Dino assumed it would be a church wedding because that is what's real to him," he broke in quietly.

"We don't have to do it there, and I understand your concerns about such an arrangement, but it will convince other people that our marriage is real. Wouldn't that be best for all of us, especially the baby?"

She knew Vincenzo was right and sensed he wanted a church wedding, too. Could she go through with such a public display for the sake of the baby growing inside her? She looked at the handsome man in front of her who was doing so much to help her. Smiling, she touched his arm tenderly before speaking.

"You're right. After we have a visit with the priest, we'll walk over to eat."

CHAPTER FOUR

VINCENZO GRASPED HER HAND. They walked down the road and around the curve, breathing in the fragrance from the masses of flowers blooming in pockets of explosive array. In ways she felt like she was moving through some fantastic dream.

Before long she spied a centuries-old yellow church on the right. He tightened his hand around hers. "Dino likes to go to church."

"He's so sweet. If our getting married here will help keep his world intact, then it's important to me. I'm thinking ahead to the baby's baptism, too."

A gleam of satisfaction entered Vincenzo's eyes before he opened the door and they stepped inside the somewhat musty vestibule. Beyond the inner doors she gazed around the semiornate interior. The lovely stained-glass windows gave the small church a jewel-like feel.

"Vincenzo?" A tall middle-aged priest had entered through a side door. The two men carried on a conversation in Italian.

Finally, Vincenzo said in English, "Father Rinaldo, this is my fiancée, Irena Spiros. We would like you to marry us."

"That is a great honor for me."

"The honor's mine, Father. I've brought the signed document giving you permission to waive the banns so we can be married in a private ceremony on Thursday."

His eyes smiled. "You are in a great hurry, then."

"You could say that," Vincenzo responded in his deep voice.

Heat rose from Irena's neck to her cheeks.

"It's about time, my son."

"I had to wait for the right one, Father."

"And how does Dino feel about it?"

"When we left him a short time ago, he said he couldn't wait. Do you think you'll be able to fit us into your busy schedule?"

The priest's expression grew more serious. "For you, nothing is impossible."

Again Irena received the strong impression Vincenzo was someone of importance.

"Thank you, Father."

"Have you been baptized, Signorina Spiros?"

Irena nodded. "In Athens."

"*Bene.* Would one o'clock suit the two of you?"

Vincenzo glanced at Irena for her input. She nodded. "That will be the perfect time."

"Come ten minutes early to sign the documents."

"We'll be here, Father." The way Vincenzo was looking at her just then caused her legs to go weak. He cupped her elbow and ushered her out of the church. After the darker interior, the sunlight almost blinded her.

They walked across the street to the crowded

trattoria. Tourists were lined up to get inside. But she was with Vincenzo. When he appeared, suddenly they were welcomed on through and shown to a table on the terrace where the waiter hovered to grant them their every wish.

"You've made a conquest of him," Vincenzo murmured as the younger man hurried off with their order.

"You think?" she teased.

"I know. Have you forgotten I looked at you the same way when you swept into my office that day?"

Irena had to admit it had been an electrifying moment. At the time she'd tried to ignore what she was feeling, but apparently not hard enough as witnessed by the fact that she was seated next to Vincenzo and had just spoken to the priest who would be marrying them.

"Much as I like flattery as well as the next woman, I'm afraid the waiter's attention has everything to do with *you*. Who are you, Vincenzo? I'd like to know the man who's about to become my husband."

One of his brows quirked. "You know who I am better than anyone. If you recall, I told you my family disowned me. But so it won't surprise you when we sign the marriage certificate, you should know my legal last name is Valsecchi."

She thought she'd heard it somewhere, but she couldn't quite place the name.

"Thank you for telling me."

He smiled the smile that had seduced her on her first trip here. "*Di niente*. I can't have my pregnant bride suffer from an attack of the vapors on our wedding day."

"I'm not the type."

"Grazie a dio." He drank the last of his coffee. "I think you've toyed with your salad long enough. Your cheeks look a little flushed from the heat. Let's get you back to the apartment. While you nap, I need to run over to the plant for a brief meeting with the staff."

A nap sounded good. He escorted her through the restaurant to the street. Once again they walked the short distance hand in hand, this time uphill. Vincenzo was a demonstrative, physical man who touched her often.

Irena discovered that with each contact, she felt more and more alive. When he saw her inside the apartment and told her he'd be back later, she suddenly didn't want him to leave.

After he'd gone she decided to lie down for a few minutes. It surprised her that when she heard her phone ring and reached for it, an hour had gone by. The pills the doctor had given her seemed to have kicked in. They'd taken her nausea away, but she found she was sleepier.

"Deline?"

"I just put the twins down for their afternoon nap so we could talk. Tell me what's happening."

Getting up from the bed, Irena walked through the apartment to the terrace laden with potted flowers of every color. She leaned against the railing, feasting her eyes on the breathtaking view. "There's so much to tell you I hardly know where to begin, but in a word, Vincenzo and I are being married on Thursday."

The palpable silence coming from the other end wasn't surprising. "You're really planning to go through with this?"

"Yes. I just came from meeting the local priest who'll be officiating."

"You're having a *church* wedding?"

"It's what Dino wants."

"Who's Dino?"

She bit so hard on her lower lip, it drew blood. "Vincenzo's adorable six-year-old son."

"What?"

"I know this is a lot to absorb. For me, too. Let me start from the beginning." For the next little while Irena told her everything.

"Oh, Irena…I don't envy you for having to deal with an ex-wife."

"I'm not thrilled about it myself."

"Yet you still want to go through this. Obviously you're crazy in love with this man, right?"

"Love? I don't know about that yet, Deline. I thought I loved Andreas. I know one thing—he's bigger than life to me, Deline. Every minute we're together I find him more amazing."

"Maybe too amazing?"

She frowned. "What do you mean?"

"Have you asked yourself why he's willing to rush into marriage with you?"

"Deline—" she cried in exasperation. "I was the one who approached him, remember?"

"I know. I guess I don't know what I mean."

"He wants this baby and believes it's his."

"But it might not be his, Irena. If only you could find out before you go through with this marriage."

Irena sank down in one of the wrought-iron chairs. Her eyes closed tightly. "The last doctor I talked to said that only a DNA test could give me definitive proof of paternity."

"Then for all your sakes, I'd go get it done."

"I've been considering it."

"To tell you the truth, I'm surprised Vincenzo hasn't demanded it, especially as he is making such willing huge sacrifice as quickly as possible to keep you. He must be nuts about you!"

Irena jumped up from the chair. "I know exactly why he's marrying me, Deline. I figured it out the second I saw him with his son. That was no idle proposal he made two months ago. The fact is, he's bound to a strict visitation order. He wants his boy to be able to live with him and be with him as much as possible. For that to happen he needs a wife, but she has to be someone Dino can accept."

"Which means you've already won him over. There isn't a child in the world who wouldn't love you, Irena."

Tears pricked her eyelids. "You're a better friend than I deserve."

"Who helped *me* through the blackest period of my life?" she said almost angrily. "I'm glad if I can do anything for you."

"You already have by listening to me. In talking to you, I've come to a decision. No matter how painful it's going to be on everyone concerned, I'll never have a good night's sleep again until I know the truth about this baby's father."

Deline groaned. "Now you've got me worried."

"In truth it's all I have done since I found out about this baby, but for the first time my mind is clear. I know what I have to do. When I look back, I realize Gabi went to Andreas armed with the DNA results on the twins. Before he ever approached your husband, he immediately had them checked against Leon's DNA for a match. If I tell Andreas I'm having his baby, he'll want DNA proof, so that's the first thing that needs to be done."

All of sudden Irena heard Vincenzo calling to her. "Deline?" she whispered. "I have to go."

"Understood. Stay in touch."

This was the second time Vincenzo had walked in on Irena and found her on the phone acting furtive. She broke out in a smile. It didn't deceive him. "How did things go at your office?"

"Everything's been taken care of for the time we'll be away on our honeymoon."

Her smile cracked. "Vincenzo—"

"I was hoping some rest would have done you good, but you seem agitated. What's wrong?"

"There's something you need to know. We can't get married yet."

He was used to his gut taking hits, but this one penetrated. "If you're worried about a dress…"

She tossed her head back so hard, her hair came unfurled and the heavy weight swished against her shoulders. Much as he liked her gleaming black mane swept up, he preferred it undone. "You know I'm not."

Irena didn't have a vain bone in her fabulous body. "You said *yet*. What does that mean exactly?"

He could see her body trembling. "Once we're married I want to be a good stepmother to Dino, but first I need to consult another doctor and get a DNA test done.

It's for all our sakes—" she cried as if he'd already protested. "I know I told you I wanted to keep it a secret from Andreas, but that was hysterical talk on my part. Of course he has to know the truth if the baby is his. I want answers as soon as possible."

Vincenzo thought he wanted to know right away, too, but already he'd been living in a fantasy where the baby was his. The pulse throbbed at his temples. "When did you decide this?"

Her eyes, those mirrors of the soul, glistened with unshed tears. "While I was talking to Deline. If I get a test done, it will remove all uncertainty. I'm afraid at this point I can't live without positive proof. Once I know the truth, we'll go from there."

As long as she wasn't refusing to marry him, Vincenzo could live with it, although he dreaded seeing the evidence that Simonides was the father. "Then we'll take care of it now."

She looked at him with pleading. "You don't hate me for this?"

"*Irena*—your pregnancy could be in jeopardy if you don't have peace of mind. Are you ready to go?"

"Yes."

They passed through the kitchen. She picked up her purse and followed him out the door to his car. For once her thoughts were so heavy, she stared blindly out the window as they made their way down the dizzying cliff to the Via Colombo.

"We'll take the *litoranea* road to La Spezia. If you recall from the last time you were here, it's only a twenty-minute drive."

"The way *you* drive," she teased unexpectedly.

His lips twitched, relieved for the moment she didn't seem as tense. As she rested her head against the window, he turned on the AC and took advantage of the quiet to phone ahead to the hospital's E.R. Hopefully an OB would be available to cut down the wait.

Soon the traffic grew heavier. When they reached the sprawling city proper, he wound around to the hospital and parked. The lots were so crowded, Vincenzo was glad he'd called ahead to arrange for a consultation. After guiding her inside the E.R., they only had a ten-minute wait before an attendant called for Signorina Spiros.

They walked down a hall to a small office. The forty-ish female OB greeted them in good English. "I'm Dr. Santi. What can I do for you?"

This was Irena's arena. Vincenzo remained silent while she launched in with her request. While she gave the background that prompted her to come in, the doctor sat back in her chair, eyeing the two of them with compassion.

"I understand how anxious you must be to solve your dilemma. However, that kind of procedure called Chorionic Villi Sampling can only be performed between ten and thirteen weeks."

"But that's another month away!"

"Yes. And there is some minimal risk."

Vincenzo reached for Irena's hand. "Explain, please."

"The test is invasive because cells have to be collected and this can cause certain risks for the fetus. Besides that, about one in two hundred women suffer a miscarriage because of this test. You need to weigh that against your need-to-know information. For example, you should consider whether not knowing the results will cause anxiety and whether knowing will be reassuring."

"We've already determined we *have* to know," Irena insisted.

Vincenzo had his own thoughts on the subject. Whether the baby was his or not he wasn't happy about her having the test. He couldn't wait to be a father again and didn't like the idea that this could hurt the baby in any way. Worse, Irena could lose it, putting her own life in jeopardy in the process. To lose her was anathema to him.

He stared at Dr. Santi. "Do you perform this test?"

"I'll oversee it. We have a perinatologist who does the actual procedure."

He glanced at Irena. "I think we need to talk about this more."

"Why, Vincenzo? Please understand."

Her agony was so palpable, he couldn't refuse her. "How soon does she need to come in?"

"Don't wait any longer than two weeks."

"I won't," Irena answered.

"If you'll check with the desk in Outpatient and set up an appointment, the next time you come in I'll examine you and get the blood work done."

"Thank you, Dr. Santi."

"My pleasure."

Vincenzo shook her hand and ushered Irena through the doors to the outpatient department. Near her ear he said, "Make it for two weeks. We won't be home from our honeymoon until then."

She stared at him in surprise. "Where are we going?"

"I'll tell you later."

He waited while she made her appointment, then walked her out to the car, knowing better than to try to talk to her until she'd had time for the doctor's explanation to sink in.

"Are you upset with me?"

Exasperated, Vincenzo pulled her into his arms. "I'm worried for you, for our baby, but I could never be upset with you. I can see you need this test so you can relax. Whoever the father is, it's you and the baby I care about."

"Thank you, Vincenzo." She hugged him back with surprising strength before getting into the car. On the way to Riomaggiore he stopped for petrol. He didn't need much, but used it as an excuse to buy them both a soda. She thanked him and nursed her drink all the way back to the apartment, clearly in an emotional state. Evening had fallen.

"Feel better?" he asked once they'd walked inside.

"No." Her voice wobbled. He caught her in his arms before she broke down sobbing. The need to comfort her was paramount in his mind. In a swift move he picked her up and carried her to the couch where he could sit and hold her.

"I don't want to lose my baby."

Cradling her in his arms, he kissed her cheek and hair. "No procedure's been done yet. Let's agree that for the next two weeks, we simply enjoy our honeymoon."

She'd buried her face in his neck, soaking the collar of his shirt. "What do you have planned?" Her lack of enthusiasm would have been daunting if he didn't know the reason for it.

"We'll fly to Los Angeles with Dino and do it all. A Hollywood film studio tour, Disneyland, LEGO Land, Sea World."

He felt her stir before she lifted her tear-ravaged face. "You're serious?"

Vincenzo nodded. "He's never been there. Have you?"

"I've been to New York many times, but not California. Since I started working for the newspaper I've focused my travel articles in Europe. What about you?"

"I promised Dino I'd never go to those places until we could see them together. Part of the visitation stipulation forbids me taking him out of Northern Italy. There was one time I broke the rules to go skiing with him in Switzerland. Dino paid for it by not being able to see me for two months."

Irena threw her arms around his neck and hugged him. "How cruel."

She had no idea how cruel the powers working against him had been. He rubbed the back of her neck beneath her hair, needing this closeness like he needed water or light from a Mediterranean sun.

"If you haven't been able to spend more than a week with him at any given time, how can we be gone two weeks?"

"Being divorced tied my hands. On Thursday I'll be a married man and everything will change."

He heard a few sniffs before she sat up. "For both your sakes I'm glad things will be different. Looking back on my life, I loved my father so much that to imagine

I couldn't have all the access to him I wanted while I growing up is incomprehensible to me." To Vincenzo's chagrin, she slid off his lap before he was ready to let her go. "I want to make this trip with Dino so enjoyable, he'll remember it all his life."

"The wedding day, too," Vincenzo murmured. "He needs a suit. Since I'll be tied up most of Wednesday with more legal matters, let's go shopping tomorrow. I rather like the idea of my fiancée picking out my wedding attire."

She flashed him a smile that came off mysterious whether she'd intended it or not. "You trust a Greek woman with a responsibility like that? Italian men are the best dressers in the world."

"I didn't know that."

"You can fool some of the people." When she laughed gently, it gave him a whole new reason to be alive.

"I need to eat something. Come with me and I'll make you my own version of bruschetta. Dino can't get enough of it."

"I'm afraid I'm hungry again, too. The antinausea medication is working. Now all I do is eat and sleep." She followed him to the kitchen. "Unfortunately, every meal I've had in Italy has been divine."

Vincenzo chuckled. Her honesty was refreshing. When she liked something, she did it with her whole heart. While he got out the ingredients, she watched him. He liked that very much.

It didn't take long until he had their appetizers ready. "I'd offer you some of that local sweet dessert wine you tried the last time you were here, but it will have to wait until you've had the baby."

Their eyes fused for a moment. "The deprivation will be worth it."

He brushed her mouth with his own before he let her reach for a sample. The satisfaction of watching the food disappear pleased him no end. She stood at the counter next to him, munching away. Every so often she made a sound of pleasure.

Vincenzo loved that she didn't talk about how much weight she was going to gain. He liked every damn thing about her and needed another taste of her. This time when he claimed her lips, they were covered in extra virgin olive oil mixed with the tangy flavor of the herbs he'd added.

Divine didn't cover it, or the feel of her body as he pulled her against him. "I've been craving this all day. You could have no idea how much I want you." He kissed her long and hard. "The last two months were a desert after you left. Dino was the only reason I functioned. When are you going to admit you've missed me?"

"Isn't that what I'm doing?" Her muffled answer thrilled him.

"Irena—" Consumed with desire, he cradled her face, the better to kiss her features and eyelids, the passionate flare of her giving mouth. Back and forth they gave kiss for kiss, each one deeper and more prolonged.

They both heard the peremptory knock on the front door at the same time, effectively interrupting something private and marvelous. Irena's reaction was to pull away from him, but Vincenzo knew what the intrusion meant and clutched her to him possessively. The knocking grew louder.

She put her hands against his chest. "Someone isn't going away."

"News of our impending marriage has already leaked out through Mila's attorney." He kissed her palms one at a time. "One of my cousins has come to find out if it's really true. Probably Gino. Do you feel courageous enough to meet him if I let him in?"

"Should I be frightened?"

"He poses no threat, but *you* do by virtue of becoming my wife."

"Why?"

"Because I've been out of his hair for years, but after we get back from California he and my cousins are going to be seeing a lot more of me. I'll answer it before he breaks the whole place down. We'll offer him what's left of the bruschetta," he added, smiling.

But when he walked through the apartment and opened the door, it was his stepbrother Fabbio himself standing there. Apparently he hadn't trusted Gino or Luca to do his dirty work for him. Well, well… The whole nasty history between them flashed through his mind. Vincenzo could count on one hand the times he'd seen his flashy, dark blond stepbrother in the last seven years. *"Entrate, prego."*

"I prefer to stay where I am. Is it true?"

Some things never changed. Vincenzo looked over his shoulder. *"Innamorata?* Come and meet my stepbrother," he spoke in English.

Irena moved toward him. He knew he could count on her to remain calm in the face of surprise or an emotional storm, except when it came to the baby's paternity.

Vincenzo didn't miss the flash of stunned male interest in Fabbio's narrowed gray eyes when she joined them. After being thoroughly kissed in the kitchen, she'd never looked more desirable.

He put his arm around her shoulders, drawing her close. "Irena Spiros, meet Fabbio. Among his many talents, he's an *avvocato*."

"That means an attorney, doesn't it?" With the ease and unconscious dignity of a real lady she shook his hand. "How do you do, Fabbio."

Totally thrown, his stepbrother had trouble articulating. It had to be a rare moment when Fabbio, an inch taller than Vincenzo, was at a loss for words. "I've seen you before."

"People often say that to me. I must have the kind of looks shared by many women." Vincenzo had never met anyone who could think on her feet as fast as Irena.

"No." Fabbio wouldn't let it go.

She said something else to brush it off. "Won't you come in? Vincenzo just made us the most sensational food. If you don't finish the bruschetta, *I* will, and I've already eaten too much." With that voluptuous smile of hers, his married stepbrother's seduction was complete.

"Since I dropped in without invitation, another time perhaps." His eyes traveled from her glorious black hair down the curves of her body to her nylon-clad feet, presenting a picture of two lovers enjoying an intimate evening. He finally tore his gaze away to stare bullets at Vincenzo. Fabbio had wished him dead years ago. "If I could have a word with you."

Irena pressed his arm. "I'm sure you two have a lot to talk about so I'll disappear."

Before she could pull away, Vincenzo pressed a kiss to her red, slightly swollen lips. "I won't be long," he whispered.

She nodded. "It was nice meeting you, Fabbio."

Once she'd gone, Vincenzo lounged against the door-jamb, his hands in his pockets. "What's this about? As you can see, I have other matters pressing."

His cheeks went a ruddy color. "Mila just found out you're taking Dino out of the country for another two weeks on Thursday."

"That's right."

"The stipulation doesn't provide for changes."

"You know full well my marriage will have effectively done away with the rules of the divorce decree. The only reason you came here tonight was to see the evidence for yourself. Now that you've taken your full measure of my fiancée, I'd like you to leave."

His anger was near the surface. "You're not getting away with this without a fight."

"Surely that's for Papa to decide."

"He's ill."

"Only when it's convenient for him."

"Accidenti a te!"

"Curse me all you want, it will do you no good."

Now he was breathing hard. "The entire family stands against you."

"It was ever thus."

"You won't succeed."

"Careful, Fabbio. Your fear is showing."

"So is yours, or you wouldn't be doing everything in secret."

"Can you blame me for wanting to keep her away from the wolves for as long as possible? You're all waiting to tear her apart, but I won't have it. Irena is the most important thing in my life right now." He straightened and pulled his hands out of his pockets. *"Buonanotte, Fabbio."*

Irena appeared the moment he shut the door on him. "Don't you think it's time you told me about your family?"

He lifted one eyebrow. "Except for my mother who died seven years ago, I've been at war with them from birth."

She came closer, searching his eyes for the truth. "You're not joking." The pain in hers revealed she was devastated for him.

"Once upon a time I told you we were opposites. You come from a loving family and almost married into what I've gathered is a loving, forgiving family. I, too, love my father because he *is* my father, but I don't like him or my autocratic grandfather who's now deceased, or my stepbrother, or my uncles, not even my cousins once they started to resemble their fathers."

"Oh, dear."

"I sound like a monster," he ground out.

"No." After a moment of reflection she asked, "Besides your mother, are there no girls in this fearsome group?"

With a sharp laugh, he let out the breath he'd been holding and grasped her shoulders. "Dozens."

"But they hold no sway in the male-dominated

hierarchy," she divined with her rare capacity to discern the true nature of things. "How often is Dino around them?"

"Mila spends most of her time with them, so that means my son does, too. My father dotes on him."

"Who wouldn't? I'm crazy about him even after being around him such a short time. Does Dino share your feelings?"

"I'm not sure."

"How could that be? He tells you everything."

He shook his head. "Certain things he keeps to himself. In my case, I'm afraid my noninvolvement with family speaks for me."

"If he sometimes keeps quiet it's probably because he feels guilty."

Vincenzo kissed the end of her nose. "Why do you say that?"

"Because he knows how you feel and doesn't want to do anything that could upset or hurt you. *Or* get you in trouble," she added quietly before easing away from him. "From the sound of it, your intention to marry me has put flame to a fuse."

"You let me worry about that. The family has nothing to do with you and me. Our lives with our children will be our own."

She darted him a second glance. "I love Dino like my own child. Our *own* children… I want that more than anything in world."

Was Irena admitting she loved him because she'd accepted Dino? She still hadn't *our* baby yet. Vincenzo knew the doubt surrounding the paternity of the child weighed heavily on her shoulders. "I have a solution for us down the road, but only if you're willing."

"What's that?"

"One day we'll have another baby."

Her eyes suddenly filled. "Why do I get the feeling you think that one woman in two hundred will be me?"

Vincenzo reached for her and held her close to his chest. "You're wrong, Irena. If you do go ahead with the test I'm sure everything will be fine and we will have a healthy baby. I just want you to know how eager I am to have a child with you. *Our child.* With no shadow of doubt hanging over us, and a child that will never have to leave this home. Our home. The truth is, I was never in love with Mila and she knew it. But both our fathers wanted the marriage and my ailing mother urged me to go ahead with it because she was convinced Mila would make me a good wife. She worried about my wild side."

A faint smile broke the corner of Irena's mouth. "So I didn't imagine you had one."

He bit her earlobe gently. "Mama feared I was enjoying my bachelorhood too much. Like all mothers and fathers, my parents felt marriage would have a stabilizing effect on me, so Mila and I married. It was the worst mistake of my life. To pay me back for not loving her, she didn't tell me she was pregnant until her sixth month when she couldn't hide it any longer."

Irena's expression revealed her horror.

"Dino came four weeks early. The two months before she delivered were the happiest I'd ever known because the idea of being a father had taken hold. But it turned into a nightmare after he was born. She refused to let me be around Dino and help with him. Her doctor called it postpartum depression.

"I recognized it for what it was. She couldn't hold on to me, but she wanted our baby to herself, nothing more. By the time Dino was three months old, I was completely shut out of his life. I told her we couldn't go on in our marriage that way. She told me there wasn't anything I could do about it. I told her I'd divorce her. She claimed I wouldn't dare."

Irena let out a groan.

"Hideous isn't it? When my father found out I was leaving her and realized he couldn't stop me, he disowned me, shouting that he never wanted to see me again. The only reason I was granted any visitation at all was due to my mother who prevailed on Papa before she died. To this day we haven't seen or talked to each other."

"So the wedding—"

"Will be a new beginning for my father and me," he broke in.

"How will our marriage change anything in his eyes?"

"I know my father. He never wanted to disown me, but he had to save face in front of Mila's father. Now that he's heard I'm getting married again, I'll go to him a new man and tell him I'd like us to start over. By reaching out to him, I'll have allowed him to retain his pride. He'll be overjoyed and speak to the judge who will give me back my full rights as a father."

A glint of suspicion entered her eyes. "A marriage to

any woman could have helped you accomplish the same thing."

His spirits plunged. "Following your logic, I could have married years ago, but there's a flaw in your thinking. Why don't you sleep on it? Hopefully one day soon you'll have figured it out."

He drew in a ragged breath. "Go to bed, Irena. You look exhausted. I'll clean up the kitchen and see you in the morning."

CHAPTER FIVE

IRENA'S WEDDING DAY dawned, but she'd had a fitful night. It was a good thing Vincenzo had left early for the drive to Milan to pick up Dino. When she looked in the mirror and saw her drawn face, she was glad she had time to repair the damage before they returned.

Part of her restlessness stemmed from the fact that she hadn't told her parents anything since her last call to them. She vacillated whether to phone them now or after the honeymoon.

But as the morning wore on, she realized she couldn't put off telling them her news. To hurt them like that when they'd been such wonderful parents to her all her life would be unconscionable. She would have to tell them the truth. Not everything, but enough to satisfy them.

After getting ready for the big day, she walked through to the kitchen to take her pills and make her phone call. As it turned out, her father had already left for work, so her mother phoned him there and they set up a three-way call.

"Irena? I've been anxious about you," her father began without preamble.

"I know. How are you?"

"Fine, but that's not the point." Her father sounded upset. "What's this about sightseeing with some Italian and his son? Who is he?"

She took a fortifying breath. "His name is Vincenzo Antonello. He's divorced and has a six-year-old boy named Dino. He manages the Antonello Liquers plant in La Spezia."

"The one you covered in the magazine section."

"Yes."

"Is he the reason you're still in Italy?" Her mother's question wasn't an idle one.

The blood hammered in her ears. "Yes."

"I'll never forgive Andreas for what he did to you," her father blurted emotionally.

"Please don't say that. I believe it was meant to be. He couldn't help how he felt when he met Gabi a-anymore than I could help my feelings for Vincenzo."

Her words were met with silence before her mother asked, "What feelings?"

Now was the moment. "When I met him two months ago, we spent all our time together. I didn't mean to, but it just happened. By the time I had to leave, he'd asked me to marry him."

"When you were already promised to Andreas?" Her father sounded stunned.

"I wasn't promised to him, Father. We weren't even engaged! It's true we both loved each other, but apparently not enough to make it to the altar. There were times he turned to Leon before he turned to me. I know now I was never in love with him. That's why I came back to Riomaggiore."

Her mother made a sound in her throat. "So what are you saying?"

She gripped the phone tighter. "Vincenzo and I are getting married in a few hours."

"A few hours—" both parents cried in unison.

"Yes. There's a church down the road from his apartment. A Father Rinaldo is going to marry us. I know this comes as a huge shock to you. To me, too, actually. You have no idea how much I love him. He's a wonderful man with a darling son." The realization that her feelings for Vincenzo had grown into love came as a shock to Irena, but the moment she said the words she knew them to be true.

Her father was the first to recover. "Does the boy live with him?"

Irena closed her eyes. "No. Dino lives with his mother. They've worked out visitation."

"So you're going to be a part-time mama before *you're* a mama!" Spoken like a mother.

Tears slid out from beneath Irena's eyelashes. "I'm very happy about it and hope you will be, too."

"When are we going to meet him?" her father wanted to know.

"We're taking a honeymoon to California for two weeks. I'll phone you when we get there. After we return and everything settles down, the three of us will fly to Athens. Vincenzo's heard all about how wonderful you are and is anxious to—"

"Irena?"

It was Dino.

"I'm sorry, but I have to go. I promise to call you soon. Love you." She clicked off. "Here I am!"

Dino came running into the apartment wearing shorts and a dinosaur shirt. When he saw her in the dining room, he came to a full stop. "You are *bellissima!*"

It struck her how much she'd missed him. *"Grazie,"* she said with a smile before hugging him.

His brown eyes took in the cream-colored two-piece suit she'd bought in one of the boutiques. Around her neck she'd looped the matching colored lace mantilla she would put on when she entered the church.

While they'd been shopping she'd asked Vincenzo what he thought would look good in her hair. He'd said it didn't matter as long as she left it down.

"Is it time?"

She glanced at her watch. "Almost. I was afraid you wouldn't make it."

Vincenzo came in from outside, also dressed in shorts and a T-shirt. His eyes appraised her so intimately, she trembled. "After we left Milan, there was a terrible accident on the *strada* that held us up. Come in my room, Dino, and we'll both get ready."

"Your new suits are on the bed!"

"Fantastico!"

She could hear water running from the shower. Before long Dino came running back to the kitchen in his new navy blue suit and white shirt. Vincenzo had chosen the same outfit for himself. Both wore a blue-and-silver striped tie.

Irena reached inside the fridge and pulled out a florist's box that held two creamy baby roses and her corsage. She lifted Dino's from the tissue and pinned it to his lapel. When it was done, she kissed him on the check. "Now you look *bello* like your papa."

"Flattery will get you everywhere." Vincenzo spoke in his deep voice. She whirled around and met a pair of hot blue eyes. "Do I get a rose, too?"

He was incredibly handsome. Her mouth went too dry to talk. Instead, she reached for the other rose and walked over to him. Her fingers were all thumbs as she had to try several times to pin it on right. All the time she was fussing, Vincenzo placed little kisses here and there on her face, causing Dino no end of delight.

"Now it's your turn, Signorina Spiros." Near the shoulder of her suit jacket he fastened her corsage made of a cluster of cream-colored roses. "You do realize you won't be called that name much longer."

How could she possibly forget? Her impulsive trip back to Riomaggiore had come about half in a daze of pain and confusion, half with the ridiculous notion that Vincenzo might have meant what he'd said about the two of them marrying. Now here she was, ready to make promises to love, cherish and honor this man she'd only known for a short time.

Odd that she'd known Andreas for years, yet even after they'd started seeing each other as a couple, she'd never learned to know all the little things about him that she already knew about Vincenzo.

Every day with him, sometimes hourly, brought a new surprise. Part of the time she was breathless. The other part she found herself reeling with new information he fed her.

Feeling flushed and nervous, she turned to Dino. "I think we're ready."

"First some pictures." Vincenzo put his camera on the veranda table.

She caught his arm. "I just phoned my parents and told them we were getting married."

His eyes held a question. "Should I expect the police to descend on me before I can get you to the church?" he teased.

"No. They're not like that, but they'll want to see pictures."

"So will my father."

After he set the camera to take some timed shots, the three of them stood together in front of the climbing roses providing the background. After a dozen photos in quick succession, he said, "Let's go get married."

Dino led the way out of the apartment. They joined hands with him in the middle and made the same walk they'd done the other day beneath a hot, sun-filled sky. Tourists stopped them every few steps to congratulate them and take pictures. Her breath caught every time she looked at Vincenzo because he was so gorgeous. So was his little lookalike who wore a continual smile.

Soon locals had lined the road, clapping and cheering for them. To walk to the church for your own wedding surrounded by people who threw flowers petals at you was something Irena would never have imagined. But like everything else to do with Vincenzo in this dreamy garden paradise, it just felt right.

By the time they came in sight of the church, the crowd had grown larger. At first she'd thought this was something that happened to every couple who said their vows here, but the deference paid to Vincenzo became too obvious to ignore.

She realized something else was going on. Irena would have asked him about it, but it was too late. He'd

opened the doors and she had to let go of Dino's hand
to arrange the mantilla over her head. Vincenzo helped
her. "Have I told you yet how *squisita* you are?" he said
in a husky voice.

He led her through the vestibule and down the aisle
to the front where they sat on a pew. Soon a man and
a woman entered from a side door. They nodded to
Vincenzo before taking their places on either side of
the aisle. In another minute Father Rinaldo appeared.

When he walked over, the three of them stood up.
"You're late."

In a spate of Italian words Dino explained their
delay.

The priest winked at him and patted him on the
head. "Accidents will happen. I understand." He
glanced at Vincenzo. "We'll do the paperwork after
the ceremony."

"Grazie."

"Dino? Stand by your papa. Signorina Spiros will
stand at his other side. Vincenzo? If you'll take Irena's
hand, we'll begin."

She felt it curl around hers in a familiar hold that
warmed her heart. The priest performed the ceremony
in English. It was probably the shortest church service
ever given. No doubt Vincenzo had everything to do
with the choice of language and the length.

They both made their responses at the appropriate
time and he eventually said, "I now pronounce you,
Vincenzo, and you, Irena, husband and wife. Amen."

He smiled at Dino and said something in Italian.
Irena saw her new stepson grin before he answered,
"Sì," in a spirited voice.

Vincenzo turned to her. "Father Rinaldo just asked Dino if he thought I should kiss my bride now." On that note he lowered his mouth to hers in a kiss sweeter than anything she'd ever known. Touched beyond words, she scarcely heard the priest say something else to Dino in Italian.

"Papa—" He tugged on his father's sleeve.

When she looked, he'd handed Vincenzo a gold ring. He turned back to her. "This was my mother's. She told me to keep it for the woman I would marry." So saying, he slid it on Irina's ring finger.

He really couldn't have loved Mila or he would have given it to her and it would have remained in her possession, but the whole circumstance of his first marriage was still a mystery to her. Vincenzo was his own man. She couldn't understand him marrying Mila because of pressure.

"Irena?" Her head jerked up. "Father Rinaldo has asked us to follow him to the vestibule so we can sign the marriage certificate."

"Of course."

Dino hurried ahead of them. The witnesses signed first, then it was Irena's turn. She had to fill in Liapis after Spiros.

Vincenzo came last. She waited while he attached his signature. It took so long, she looked down at the paper. Her eyes widened in surprise because his name went on and on with a flourish.

Guilio Fortunato Coletti Vincenzo Antonello Gaspare Valsecchi.

After he'd signed it, the female witness gave Irena a

slight curtsey. *"Congratulazioni, duchessa,"* she muttered.

Irena couldn't have heard the other woman right, but when she looked around to talk to her, she and the other man had slipped away.

"Vincenzo?" She caught at his arm. He lifted his dark head.

"Sì, Signora Valsecchi? I don't know about you, but I like the sound of it. Very much in fact." The smoldering look he gave her melted her bones.

"That woman just called me *Duchess.*"

He had to sign another form. "Pay no attention," he muttered. "It's a defunct title now and has been for years, but some will still insist on using it to feel important."

She refused to be put off. "You're a duke?"

"It's meaningless, *tesora.*"

Irena turned to Dino. "Do you know who your father is?"

"Sì. He is Papa!"

"No— I mean— Oh—" she moaned in frustration. Vincenzo's low chuckle only added to it.

He finally stood up and handed the papers to Dino. "Will you run these inside to Father Rinaldo? We'll wait for you."

Dino nodded and dashed off. After he'd disappeared, Vincenzo pulled her into his arms. "All right. I'll tell you this once, and then we don't ever have to discuss it again. My father is the most recent Duke of La Spezia."

She blinked. "So the Valsecchis were once an important family."

"Once!" he emphasized. "At the time of my marriage to Mila, Papa was going through a cancer scare and had the title transferred to me. I couldn't have cared less about it. Unfortunately, the news made the papers. But then he recovered. After I divorced Mila he disowned me and the title was rescinded. That's all there is."

Irena shook her head. "That couldn't be all. Who was your mother?"

He studied her for a moment. "The Antonellos were a former royal family from the Ligurian region."

"And Mila?"

"Her family came from Florence and were of lesser importance. It means absolutely nothing, Irena."

"Except that in divorcing her, you were royally ostracized."

He gave an elegant shrug of his shoulders. "That's one way of putting it I suppose, but it's history now."

"Except that I'm a nobody."

"That's the beauty of it." His eyes blazed hotter. "I've finally gotten my heart's desire."

Before she could ask him what he meant by that comment, Dino came running back. Vincenzo picked him up and gave him a hug. The two of them had a major conversation in Italian. Whatever his father told him, Dino ended up shouting for joy.

As they went out the doors of the church, Vincenzo translated for her. "I asked him if he was ready to go on our honeymoon. He said yes and wanted to know if it was a long, long way. I told him we needed to fly to get there."

"Has he been on a plane before?"

"No. When I told him we'd be taking the Valsecchi company jet in order to reach Disneyland, you heard his answer."

* * *

"Irena? Are you sad we have to go home today?" Dino looked so cute in his Indiana Jones hat. Vincenzo had gone down to the desk to take care of the bill, leaving the two of them alone for a minute.

"*Sì*, but I know your mama can't wait to see you. She'll love the presents you bought her."

Throughout their trip they'd made arrangements for him to call Mila every late afternoon when she'd be up and available. Their conversations weren't long, but hearing his mother's voice every day probably cut down on any homesickness he might be feeling.

Irena couldn't believe that in the last two weeks she could actually understand some of his Italian and say a few phrases back, with lots of mistakes and plenty of laughs, of course. Still, they'd made a pact to speak it as much as possible and it was working. Vincenzo had told her she would learn Italian faster around his son than anyone else. It was true.

"Look!" she said to him. "We've had to buy two suitcases to hold all your new clothes and souvenirs!"

Her comment made him giggle as he ran around in his Indiana Jones costume. They'd bought him Indiana Jones LEGO to take home and build. Adventureland had been the biggest hit for him and they had gone there eight times, but he still couldn't find the courage to go on the jungle cruise.

Irena let him know she was nervous on boats, too, but would go on it if he would. She thought she was making progress when he got as far as the entrance to it, but then he had backed away.

Vincenzo kissed the side of her neck. "Thanks for trying to help him."

"Maybe I need to start with something simpler, like helping him get in a swimming pool. What if I took lessons with him? Do you think that would work?"

"Possibly. You have a special way about you."

"It's because I love him."

"He can feel it. That's why you almost talked him into it." *Almost* being the operative word. In the short time they'd been together, she felt like the three of them had become a little family. "Did I tell you you're going to be the most perfect mother? That little life inside you doesn't know how lucky he or she is."

She kissed the back of his hand. "He or she will adore you, too, Vincenzo."

They'd made the Disneyland Hotel their base. Dino had slept in his father's room containing two queen beds. Irena stayed in the adjoining room on another queen. Both she and Vincenzo had made that decision on the flight over. After their speedy wedding they felt it was important for Dino that she be eased into his father's life in increments.

In a few minutes, Vincenzo came back with a luggage cart and they left the hotel for the airport. Later on during the flight back to Italy, Vincenzo insisted she sleep in the bedroom while he and Dino bedded down on the fold-out bed in the club section.

It was Thursday when they landed in Milan. Two weeks had been but a minute. Irena found it difficult to let Dino go. Ahead of time they'd decided she would stay on board the jet. As soon as Vincenzo delivered him to his mother, he'd come back and they'd fly on to Genoa.

Vincenzo stood at the door of the plane. Irena walked

Dino toward his father and hunkered down in front of him.

"We'll see you next Wednesday after school for your overnight with us." Vincenzo had worked out the new parenting arrangement: every Wednesday night, three weekends a month, eight weeks in summer, every holiday shared and nightly phone calls just before his son's bedtime.

Dino nodded. Tears filled those brown eyes, but he didn't let them fall. "I'll bring my new Indiana Jones game."

"Good. And this time I'm *not* going to fall in the snake pit."

He giggled, causing one tear to dribble down his cheek.

"I'll miss you, Dino," Irena said, "While we're apart I'll study my Italian and you can test me. Is that a deal?"

Vincenzo helped with that word because he didn't know it. "We have to go now, son."

"*Ciao,* Irena." He followed his father out the door and down the steps to the tarmac. The steward joined them with all his luggage.

Irena walked back to the club section. Before she could even sit down, she dissolved into tears for Vincenzo and Dino, for Mila, for herself.

Years down the road she might have to face partings like this with her own child. Vincenzo had to do it all the time, already. How would he feel if the baby she carried was Andreas's? Would he feel the pull as much? Irena didn't know how he coped so well with the separation.

He made a magnificent role model who was a superhero to his son. The baby just had to be Vincenzo's!

But whilst her heart hoped, another part of her tried to accept the possibility that it was Andreas's child she carried, because to think otherwise, the joy would be too much!

She wiped her eyes and pulled out her cell phone. It was time to stop dwelling on her own worries and ask Deline how she was doing. With both of them pregnant, they had a lot in common.

"At last!" her friend cried after picking up. "It's been a week since you called me. Are you still on your honeymoon?"

"We're at the tail end. I'm waiting in the plane for Vincenzo to take Dino back to his mother's house before we fly to Genoa." She could hear a lot of noise in the background. Children's voices laughing and screaming. "Where are you?"

"On Milos. Leon took the day off and we flew out here until tomorrow. All the families are in or around the pool."

"Then you can't really talk."

"Actually, this is the perfect time. Leon's causing most of the havoc."

"You've both needed a break. How are things between you?"

"Believe it or not, we're doing much better. Tell me about you and Vincenzo."

"We've had a wonderful time with Dino."

"Naturally, but I'm talking about the two of you, if you know what I mean."

Irena sucked in her breath. "We haven't had a real

wedding night yet. I guess we already had it two months ago, but didn't realize it. Right now it's important to make sure Dino's secure."

"You've taken on a stepson. That's a huge responsibility."

"True, but he's adorable. If I'd given birth to him, I don't think I could love him any more."

"I believe it." There was a silence. "And what about the baby you carry…have you thought any more about that? Andreas isn't back from his honeymoon. Leon thinks it will be another few days at least."

She lowered her head. "Tomorrow will be my first appointment with my new OB. She'll draw blood for some tests. The CVS test I'm having done won't take place for another two weeks.

"I've made up my mind that if it's Andreas's baby, I'll tell him the truth as soon as I have the DNA result in hand. I don't want to think about that scenario too much, but if it does happen I was hoping I could call on Leon to help. I thought he might know the best way to handle it. He and Andreas have such a bond. However if you think that's too much pressure…"

"Not at all. He's been where you are now. If anyone will have insight in how to break the news, it's my husband."

Irena almost broke the phone clutching it so tightly. "I'm so worried about Vincenzo, Deline. He doesn't talk about it a lot, but I have a feeling he is hoping this baby is his. I've never wanted anything so much in my life. But I'm trying to face reality now."

"I admire you for dealing with this situation as honestly and discreetly as you can. Now you're married to an exciting man who has taken you on, warts and all." Irena half laughed through the tears. "Is he still exciting?"

"You have no idea." However, there was so much Irena hadn't told her yet. Vincenzo had glossed over everything to do with his family background. Until she had a better understanding of why he'd dismissed his illustrious heritage and wouldn't talk about it, she couldn't discuss it with anyone, not even her best friend.

"Vincenzo's so good to me, I can't begin to tell you, but I'd better get off the phone now. He'll be back soon. I'll call you again before I have the test. Thank you for being the best friend on earth."

"The feeling's mutual."

CHAPTER SIX

VINCENZO BOARDED THE JET and told the captain they could take off now. He found Irena in the club section, sitting back in one of the seats with her eyes closed. Even after the long flight she still looked fresh in her two-piece yellow linen suit. She had marvelous dress sense and a glow about her from being in the Californian sun, but some of it could be attributed to the fact that she was pregnant.

He'd had two weeks to think about the possibility that the baby wasn't his. He still found it difficult to accept and knew he would find it hard to let the baby go to its biological parent, especially after Vincenzo had been forced to go through the same experience with Dino all these years. But at this point in time he was much more concerned for Irena's health and the baby's.

Sometimes when he allowed himself to believe the baby was his, the joy that filled him was almost too intense. He let out a ragged breath. Two weeks from now they'd know the truth and they would deal with it. Though she'd pretended everything was fine in front of Dino, Vincenzo sensed Irena's anxiety was growing more acute.

Unable to help himself, he walked over and kissed her exposed throat, one of her many delicious parts.

"Vincenzo—" Her eyes flew open in surprise.

"We're about to take off. Let me help you." He fastened the seat belt for her, then took the seat opposite her and strapped himself in.

"How did it go? Was Dino happy to be home?"

"I'm sure he was glad to see his mother, but Leo was there and it made things less natural for him."

"After these weeks of being together, I know it will be hard on both of you to be apart. Thank goodness you only have to wait until Wednesday."

He gave her another prolonged kiss, loving Irena for loving his son, for understanding.

They'd already taxied out to the runway and were airborne. He waited until they'd attained cruising speed before undoing his seat belt. "Can I get you anything from the galley?"

"No, thank you. I had a soda while I was waiting for you."

He went in search of a cup of coffee. When he returned, she looked worried and gave him a searching glance. "How did Mila treat you?"

"Now that the tables have turned, she was unusually quiet."

Irena shook her head. "Surely she knows I could never replace her in Dino's eyes. She's his mother! If I can be his friend, that's all I'll ever be."

"There's more to it than that, Irena."

"What do you mean?"

"As long as Dino was our only child, Mila never

worried that he wouldn't inherit the title from my father one day."

"You said it was defunct," she reminded him.

"It is, but it's still of symbolic importance to her and her family. I could see it in her eyes tonight. She's almost apoplectic that there's the possibility you and I will have a baby in the future. That will mean Dino won't be the only one in line for the title and the money."

Irena left out a hysterical sound between a laugh and cry before eyeing him steadily. "Is it an extensive fortune?"

His lips tightened. "Yes."

"What does the Valsecchi family do?"

"Many things—investment banking, shipping, exports and manufacturing throughout eastern and western Europe. Now that my grandfather is deceased, my father, Guilio, is the CEO and oldest living member of the family."

"Is it a big family?"

"Average. The board consists of his two brothers, my uncle Carlo and my uncle Tullio. Reporting to them are their five sons, my ex-wife's brother and my stepbrother whom you've already met. Each one of them holds the position of vice president for the various departments within the business."

"Where do *you* fit in?" she asked quietly.

"That's a long story. I was twenty-six when my mother died. You already know her feelings about wanting me married to Mila, so I became engaged, but I didn't set a date for our wedding because I needed more time. Except for a war separating you, I don't understand putting off marriage if you sense it's right in your gut."

He put his empty coffee mug on the side table. "Within six months my father remarried a widowed aristocrat from Genoa. She had a son, Fabbio, who was twenty-seven and a bachelor. He fell for Mila. If her ambition hadn't been so great, she would probably have been happy with him.

"Father saw what was happening. About that time he announced he'd been diagnosed with cancer. I believed he might have been making it up to manipulate me. I'm sorry to say it worked. I acceded to pressure and married Mila. After she became pregnant, father ended up in the hospital with prostate cancer. At that point I felt guilty that I had doubted him.

"He thought he was going to die and appointed me acting CEO. Up until then I'd been his assistant. At that point he transferred the title to me. Naturally these moves infuriated the rest of the family and the lawsuits started flying. It was brother against brother, cousin against cousin.

"To defuse the maelstrom, I refused the title. That not only upset my father, it infuriated Mila and her family. They treated me like a pariah. In time my father recovered, but wasn't speaking to me."

Irena made another sound in her throat. "How ghastly for you."

"With our baby on the way, I won't pretend it wasn't a hellish period. I was away on business for a lot of the time. By the time Dino was born, we were at war. As I told you earlier, she wouldn't let me have anything to do with him, so I divorced her. You know the rest. The cruel part began with the visitation order that pretty well stripped me of my rights."

She stared at him in a daze. "Where were you living until then?"

"In one of the smaller family palazzos overlooking the water in La Spezia. After the divorce, Mila continued to live there."

"And your father?"

"In the former ducal palazzo with his second wife where I was raised. It's higher up the hillside."

"I thought Mila went back to Florence?"

"She spent time in both places, but when it was my visitation, she managed to be in Florence. Anything to make it more difficult for me. These days she splits her time between Florence, La Spezia and Milan. Again, when it's my time to be with my son, I have to travel, but naturally I don't mind."

"How did you come to live in Riomaggiore?"

"The Valsecchi company owns several hundred houses and apartments in Cinque Terre that are rented out. I decided to take the one I'm in because I favor it, and it's near the plant in La Spezia where I work. Antonello's was part of my mother's dowry when she married my father."

The fasten seat belt light flashed on. They were coming into Genoa.

"You're right," Irena murmured, fastening hers. "Your family life has been much more complicated than anything that has happened to me." She smoothed the hair away from her face. "Vincenzo? Why has marrying me allowed you to gain joint physical custody?"

He'd known that question was coming and had hoped he could put off answering it for a while longer. "I'll tell you when we're in the car. From the looks of it, jet lag is already catching up to you. Your beautiful eyes are doing that little flutter thing." His comment caused color to seep into her cheeks.

But Vincenzo knew that his wife, who still had yet to sleep in his bed, deserved to know what was happening. Their marriage might have been for convenience's sake, but he longed to make their marriage real. The truth was, he didn't dare make love to her until he'd cleared it with her doctor tomorrow. If being intimate could put the baby's life in any danger with the test looming, he would wait as long as it took. After all, he had the prize he wanted.

It was 10:30 p.m. by the time he'd ordered a limo to drive them to his car. Once he'd stowed the luggage and they'd headed for Riomaggiore, Irena had fallen asleep against the door. When he reached the apartment, instead of it being Dino he put to bed, it was his exhausted wife he carried to his son's room.

He removed her shoes and put a light quilt over her, relieved their talk would have to be postponed until tomorrow. Satisfied she wouldn't wake up, he went back to the car for their luggage and put as much away as he could.

After turning out the lights and locking up, he walked back to his bedroom and shut the door. Unfortunately he couldn't put off a certain phone call he'd promised to make as soon as he'd returned from his honeymoon. It was part of the bargain he'd struck with his father. With a sense of inevitability, he reached in his pocket for his cell and called him.

"So Vincenzo—you're home?"

"*Sì*, Papa."

"How's my little Dino?"

"After all his new adventures, he's thriving." He and Dino should have had a lot more like them over the years. Vincenzo struggled to tamp down his anger.

"Bring your wife to the palazzo tomorrow. Silviana and I have everything ready here for you to move in."

Bands constricted around Vincenzo's chest, making it difficult to breathe. "Tomorrow I'll bring her to the office. I'd rather your first meeting with her took place where I'll be working. I want to show her around, introduce her to everyone. Give us two weeks here at the apartment, then we'll make the move. Since we were married, I haven't had any time alone with her, Papa."

"You're that besotted?"

His father could have no idea. "I knew she was my soul mate the moment she was shown into my office and smiled." It got better from there. So much better that by the end of her business trip to Italy, they'd made love with a passion that still robbed him of breath. For those magical hours he knew in his gut she hadn't been thinking about Simonides.

"I guess I'm not surprised. I overheard Fabbio telling Tullio she was the most breathtaking woman he'd ever seen. That described your mother the first time I met her. How does Dino like her?"

Vincenzo cleared his throat. "I think very much, but you'll have to ask him if you want specifics."

"I intend to. Does your new bride want children?"

If a heart rate could quadruple, Vincenzo's did. With his next response, he would probably be struck by lightning. "To be honest, we've been so busy with Dino, there are many things we still need to explore. That's why we'd appreciate two more weeks without anyone else around."

"Then enjoy them while you can because you're going to be busy after that. I don't have to tell you how relieved I am you're going to be taking over, Vincenzo. As you found out when you looked over the books, we've had a downturn in profits over the last few years and we both know why."

"I agree the figures didn't look good."

"Your cousins simply don't have the grasp for business that you've always had. It's providential you came to your senses when you did. I'm tired of keeping it all together."

Vincenzo had come to his senses for the sake of his son and no other reason. His father wouldn't like all the changes he planned to make, but having been given two more weeks with Irena, he wasn't about to get into a detailed discussion tonight.

He thought ahead to tomorrow. Irena's doctor appointment had been made for midmorning. After they finished there, he'd take her to lunch at Spoleto's, one of his favorite spots. "We'll be at your office around one. *Ciao,* Papa."

"Ciao, figlio mio."

His father hadn't called him *my son* in seven years. All that time he'd held Vincenzo hostage over a title! Rage welled in his heart. He swore an oath that he would never allow anything like this to happen to Dino.

Frustrated once more that she'd fallen asleep on him, Irena had awakened soon after Vincenzo had carried her in the apartment. She'd thought he would have taken her to his bedroom tonight. They hadn't been intimate for over two months. Now that they were married and alone, she didn't understand it.

Anxious to ask him what was wrong, she'd padded down the hall, but his door was closed. She'd heard him talking to someone, but had no idea who it was or what they were saying.

Feeling shut out emotionally as well as physically, she took a shower and got ready for bed. Her heart thudded as she left the bathroom, hoping he was there waiting for her. But the apartment was dark and quiet. Dino's bed remained empty.

A pain pierced her heart. When she'd first met Vincenzo, everything had happened so naturally, she hadn't had to think about which foot to put in front of the other. Now here she was his wife and she didn't dare tiptoe down to his room and climb into bed with him.

No one could have been more loving and attentive than he'd been in California. There'd been great tenderness, but they were home now. She needed reassurance that he still wanted her the way he had before.

After she climbed under the covers, she remembered something Deline had said several weeks earlier. *Have you asked yourself why he's willing to rush into marriage with you?*

Irena's response had been immediate. He'd needed a wife to change the rules of visitation. Deep down she'd believed the attraction they had for each other portended something more significant. He'd said he'd gotten his heart's desire.

But if she was wrong and his desire for her was already fading, it was too late to do anything about it now because they were married. Dino was her stepson and trusted her. She had a baby coming. Although the paternity of the baby was still in question, Vincenzo had said he wanted to help her raise it.

Her parents knew they were married. While they were in California, Vincenzo had talked to them on the phone and he'd managed to charm them in his own inimitable way. Tomorrow she had her first medical examination with Dr. Santi. She'd gone past the proverbial point of no return. This was her life, the one she had made for herself. There was no going back.

This morning she took her time getting ready. Irena wanted to make herself look as beautiful as possible for her husband. She left her hair down the way he had said he liked it. After some deliberation she chose to wear a pale pink skirt with a shocking pink knit top. It had capped sleeves and a scooped neck. Combined with her tan and a new lipstick, she hoped she rated a second, even a third glance from Vincenzo.

He didn't disappoint her. She'd just finished her juice when he came in the kitchen and slid his arms around her. "You look good enough to eat." Irena turned around, anticipating a deep kiss, but it only lasted a moment. "You taste out of this world. If I nibble any more, we won't make it out the door to the doctor."

Another expectation dashed, but she hid her disappointment and reached for her purse. Following him out to the car, she could feast her eyes on his well-honed physique. Today he'd dressed in light tan chinos and a sport shirt in a brilliant blue that matched his eyes. Italian down to his hand-sown leather shoes, his dashing smile brought her senses alive.

As he escorted her into the outpatient department a half hour later, his potent male charisma drew the gaze of every female in the waiting room. It had been like that in California. He had admirers everywhere they went, yet he seemed oblivious to all the attention.

She had to concede he was more attractive than any film star or celebrity. It thrilled her that she was with him and could call this man her husband! Irena couldn't believe she was feeling and acting like a teenager when in reality she was a pregnant, twenty-seven-year-old woman.

"Spiros?"

Irena was so deep in thought, she didn't realize her name was being called until Vincenzo stood up. "That's you, *esposa mia.*"

She got to her feet and they walked back to a private examination room. After they sat down, Dr. Santi came in. She nodded to Irena. "You're looking well, *signorina.*"

"Actually, it's Signora Valsecchi now," Vincenzo corrected her. "We were married two weeks ago and just returned from our honeymoon."

"Ah…that explains the tan on both of you. Congratulations."

"Thank you," he answered for them.

"So, *signora,* have you decided you want to go through with the testing in two weeks? If so, we'll schedule it now."

"I made the decision the last time I was here. That hasn't changed."

The doctor switched her gaze to Vincenzo. "Are you in agreement, too? No second thoughts?"

"It's my wife's decision."

Vincenzo had said the words, but for some reason he didn't sound like he backed her. Perplexed, Irena turned her head to look at him. "I thought you were okay with it."

He covered her hand and squeezed it. "I am because it's what you want."

"But you still have reservations?"

The doctor stood up. "I'll leave you two alone for a minute to discuss it."

After she'd gone out, Vincenzo smoothed a lock of glistening hair behind her ear. "I told you before I'm not worried about you having a miscarriage, but I know that *you* are worried."

"Why do you say that?"

"Because you had nightmares on our trip—four of them, and another one last night. Something is bothering you."

Irena blinked in shock and covered her mouth with her hand, surprised and embarrassed by Vincenzo's insight. "How did you know that was what disturbed me?"

"You muttered the word *baby* each time. It shows how much you are thinking about this child you carry. I'm afraid you're the only one to determine if you can live with yourself if the test *does* cause you to miscarry. It appears you're going to have to weigh the possibility of suffering that guilt against your anxiety over waiting seven more months to know the outcome of the baby's paternity."

"They're all horrible choices."

He pulled her against him, molding his hand to the

back of her head. "Irena, no matter what," he murmured against her temple, giving her kisses, "I'm here for you."

"I know that. I'm the luckiest woman on earth." She embraced him once more, then pulled away from him before she drenched his beautiful shirt. "Will you find Dr. Santi and tell her I want to go ahead with the test?"

"I'll be right back."

Vincenzo had scarcely stepped out in the hall when he saw the doctor walking toward him. "My wife has decided she wants to schedule the test."

"I think it's a wise decision considering her emotional state. I've a feeling the waiting will be harder on her. We want her to have as normal a pregnancy as possible."

He nodded. "Before you go in to her, I would like to talk to you about something. Since our marriage two weeks ago, I've been afraid to make love to her. Knowing there's even a minimal risk to the baby because of the test, I've hesitated to do anything that could add to it."

She gave him a frank smile. "You've just saved me from telling you to hold off on the intimacy. Three more weeks with no problems and you can start to enjoy that side of your marriage.

"While I examine her, go to the outpatient center and have them direct you to the lab. I'll authorize them to do a swab of your cheek now. By the time the test is done and the results are in, you'll know if it's a match with your DNA. When your wife is through, she'll be waiting for you in the reception room."

"*Grazie.*"

He followed the doctor's directions and didn't have to wait long for his test. By the time Irena joined him in the lounge, he was still on the phone talking business with Bruno, his second-in-command at the plant. After hanging up, he walked her out to the car.

Before he helped her in he drew her close, looking down at the gauze taped to her arm. "Are you all right?"

"I'm fine."

"Are you hungry?"

"Starving." She said it a little too enthusiastically, but it meant she was making an effort even though she was nervous about the test. There was no one in the world like her.

"*Bene*. I'm taking us to a *ristorante* you're going to love." He kissed the lips he couldn't resist. Three more weeks… He didn't know how he was going to make it, but he had to for all their sakes.

Five minutes later they reached Spoleto's. The head waiter showed them through to the *terrazza* that gave out on a broader view of the Mediterranean. "Your usual table is waiting, Signore Valsecchi. Shall I bring the wine list?"

"Not today, Giovanni. We'd like iced tea and linguini for two."

When he nodded and walked off, Irena leaned forward. "What dish is that?"

"Linguini and their house sauce."

"That sounds delicious." She said the right words, but there was something else on her mind. "Before the waiter comes back, I'm waiting to hear the answer to the question I asked you last night. There's no royal line in my background, so how is it that your father has still been willing to get rid of the old visitation rules?"

"I've given him what he wants. Before we left on our honeymoon, I agreed to take back the title and be the cochairman of the company."

After a long period of quiet she said, "If you're not careful, you'll turn into my father. After he had to take over the newspaper business from his father, mother and I rarely saw him."

Irena's reaction was more than satisfying. It told him their time together was precious to her, too. He eyed her through veiled lashes. "But I won't let that happen to us, because I'm not like anyone else."

Her dark brows, perfectly shaped, knit together. "That's true, but a father and son running a conglomerate like yours will be consumed by business whether you mean for it to happen or not."

The waiter chose that moment to bring their food to the table. Once he went away again and they'd started to eat Vincenzo said, "Father won't be cochairing anything. His cancer has come back. No one knows how much longer he's going to live."

"I'm sorry," she whispered, putting down the iced tea she'd been drinking.

"I am, too. One good thing about the title is that it gives me absolute authority to choose the person who will cochair with me. What I need is a young outsider with business savvy and fresh vision. The company has been losing business over the last five or six years."

"Because you left," she stated baldly. Her confidence in him reassured him as nothing else could.

"It's more a case of mismanagement and a bad

economy. There are plenty of areas to attach blame. My way of doing things is to delegate once I've concluded the big contract negotiations. The detail work will be left to the others on the board who are capable of doing a good job if pointed in the right direction. Father didn't give them that much responsibility."

"That sounds good in theory."

"The changes I make will cut down on my workload. When I have to travel, you'll go with me and we'll turn those trips into vacations. Everything will be different."

"Are you thinking of asking Fabbio to help you? Being your stepbrother, he'd be a natural choice and is young like you."

Until Irena had come into his life, Vincenzo had felt like he was hurtling toward his old age at warp speed. Being with her was like finding the source of life all over again.

"There's no question Fabbio's an asset to the company. They all are in their own way, but after I chose to work at the plant, father did everything himself because he didn't trust anyone. No one has been taught to act or think outside the box. As a result, they're locked in a group mentality of business as usual. The company needs new blood for revitalization."

"It sounds like you've already made your pick."

"I have. It's a woman."

She looked down at her food. "In an all-male enclave?"

"Revolutionary, isn't it?"

"One of your dozens of female cousins?" Did he detect approval in her question?

"Not a cousin, but she *is* a relative."

At that revelation she lifted her head. Those dark, velvety-brown orbs had suddenly brightened. "Your father approves?"

"He doesn't know yet. When he does, it still won't matter. As I told you earlier, I hold the title now and can do as I please."

"I thought you hated it."

"This is the first time in my life I've had a change of heart about it. But I won't be keeping it for long."

She stopped eating. "Why?"

"When my father dies, I'll bypass Dino and bequeath it to my uncle Tullio while he's still alive. He's the next youngest Valsecchi brother. Knowing him, he'll think he died and went to heaven. His first item of business will be to throw me out and crown himself CEO."

"Be serious."

"You think I'm not? You have no idea how much my uncles have envied my father. Tullio particularly has coveted his position."

She kept staring at him. "Then what will *you* do?"

"Go back as head of the plant and work around the people I like."

Irena made a sound of exasperation. "Sometimes I don't know when you're being serious or not."

"I guess you're going to have to take this on trust."

Her eyes moistened. "I do."

"Bene." He put his napkin down. "How would you like to see Valsecchi headquarters?"

"Considering you're its head now, I guess I'd better. It would be embarrassing if someone asked me where my husband worked and I had no clue."

"It's only two miles from here in the marina district. Afterward I'm taking you sailing for the weekend."

A stillness enveloped her. He hoped it was because she liked the sound of it.

"I remember you telling me you had a sailboat when I was here the first time."

His eyes traveled over her features. "I wanted to take you out in it then, but it was in for repairs. It's a lucky thing."

"Why do you say that?"

"Because I might have sailed away with you and never come back. Once I met you, I couldn't keep things on a professional level with you."

"I'm afraid I couldn't, either, especially not that last night."

"Thank heaven for that. I was a thirty-four-year-old man you'd reduced to a besotted teenager who'd have done literally anything to get you to respond to me. I feared I didn't have what it took to entice the most beautiful woman I'd ever met in my life to stay with me another twenty-four hours."

Color seeped into her cheeks. "That last night with you was the result of a challenge you threw at me, one I couldn't *not* answer...." Her voice trailed.

One brow quirked. "For a woman as cautious as you, you showed a breathtaking response I suspected was in there somewhere, waiting to emerge."

"I had no idea I was that transparent."

"You weren't," he said in a serious tone. "It was wishful thinking on my part because I wanted you so badly and hated the thought of you ever leaving my bed."

"I didn't want to," she admitted, suddenly breathless at the memory of that night they had shared.

The chemistry between them was overpowering. Vincenzo reached over and held his wife's hand. "I'm longing to take you out on the water and show you some of my favorite places. There are isolated beaches where we'll relax and swim away from everyone else." He was counting the seconds until he could be alone with her.

CHAPTER SEVEN

IRENA'S HEART THUDDED to realize he didn't want their honeymoon to be over. Vincenzo intended to give her a true wedding night. Several of them in succession. She could scarcely breathe anticipating it.

Vincenzo fell silent as they neared La Spezia. Irena had found it perfectly charming before the way the city sprawled over the verdant mountains all the way down to the port. But this time as she looked up to take in churches and private estates clinging to the hillsides, she was aware that one of the more magnificent structures had to be Vincenzo's family palazzo.

The Valsecchi complex turned out to be a grouping of five buildings, each seven stories tall, surrounded by immaculately kept gardens. All of it was spread out over a large area. Vincenzo parked in the VIP lot and escorted her inside the first building with the family crest emblazoned on the main doors.

He nodded to the security people and ushered her inside a private elevator. "This will take us to my suite on the seventh floor."

When they arrived, he walked her to a door where they entered a spacious, elegantly furnished office with a superb view of the sea. Oriental rugs covered the inlaid wood flooring. It resembled a drawing room with paintings, a coffee table, matching love seats, occasional chairs and a library of books.

Vincenzo walked around the large oak desk and buzzed someone on his intercom. On the wall behind him hung an enormous oil painting dominating the room. Inside its ornate gold frame stood the full-length representation of the duke of La Spazia in his royal refinery. He was probably in his fifties when it was painted.

"What do you think?" Vincenzo had slipped his arms around her waist from behind. "See a resemblance?"

"Maybe in his body type," she ventured, slightly breathless because she'd been craving this closeness since they'd left the doctor's office. Whether it was unconscious or not, his hand slid to her stomach and caressed her, as if he wanted to feel proof of the baby growing inside her. The intimacy of the moment caught her off guard and made her tremble.

He smoothed the hair away and planted kisses along the side of her neck. "I'm glad you didn't say his arrogance or swagger. Otherwise I would have been crushed."

"Well, now that you mention it..."

He spun her around so fast, her head reeled. His blue eyes smoldered with desire before he lowered his mouth, kissing her with almost primitive hunger. This was what she'd been craving. It matched her needs that had been growing since their honeymoon.

To go to bed alone night after night in that hotel room suite knowing Vincenzo was only a wall away had been beyond hard. But she'd wanted Dino to enjoy that special time with his father and not feel threatened by her.

Voluptuous warmth filled her body. She didn't know where one kiss ended and another one began. Irena was so far gone she didn't realize that anyone had come in until she heard a discreet coughing sound from the other side of the room.

Vincenzo slowly relinquished her mouth. With his gaze still fastened on her he said, "Come all the way in, Papa, and meet my wife. Irena Liapis Valsecchi. This is my father, Guilio."

The timing couldn't have been worse. She eased away from him and turned toward the door leading to the private elevator. Her first glimpse of his father gave her some idea of what Vincenzo would look like when he reached his seventies.

Guilio Valsecchi was a handsome man with streaks of silver in his thinning black hair. Their builds were very much the same, but the ravages of illness had taken their toll. He no longer had his son's vitality.

Vincenzo's father drew closer. His biting brown eyes scrutinized her. Like his son he could almost make you believe he could see through you. He might be suffering physically, yet neither age nor cancer had robbed him of that aura of authority inherent in his son.

He reached for her hand and kissed the back of it. "I've been anxious to meet the woman who brought about this miracle," he said in English.

"Miracle?" she inquired softly.

"I never thought the day would come when Vincenzo would change his mind and follow in my footsteps." His gaze flicked to the painting. "My ancestor had a healthy fear of powerful women." He eyed her again. "After talking with Dino about you, I can understand why. He believes you love him as if he were *your* little boy."

Irena swallowed hard. "He's very easy to love."

Guilio pursed his lips. "My daughter-in-law is having a difficult time."

Irena already knew that, but was surprised this would be the first thing he had to say to her, except that knowing Vincenzo even for such a short time, she shouldn't have been caught off guard. Her husband had shocked her with his frank speaking every step of the way since their first meeting.

"I don't blame her. There's a fine line between a mother wanting everyone to love her child and accepting the fact that there's another woman, unrelated, whose love for that child goes deeper than the surface."

Judging by the strange flicker coming from the depths of his eyes, he didn't know if he liked her answer or not. "What do you know about being a mother?"

The question assaulted her body, a body that was already carrying a child. Would she come to know this baby? Would the test be a success, or would she lose this precious baby growing inside her? The fear at such a loss almost overwhelmed her, but she fought to stay composed. "Only what I learned from having a wonderful role model in my mother."

Vincenzo slid his arm around her shoulders and pulled her close. "Why don't you ask her about business, Papa? She grew up with an illustrious father who's one of the most revered businessmen in all Greece. Chief among his holdings is Athens's most prestigious newspaper. She grew up with it and worked in every department."

His father stared from one to the other without saying anything.

"Until two months ago she headed the coveted position of lifestyle editor, traveling all over eastern and western Europe. The photographer who came to Italy with her told me Irena has been her father's right hand for years."

Irena didn't know the two men had shared confidences about her.

"Rumor has it that when he's ready to step down, her father will name her to succeed him, but it's too late for that."

"How so?" his father finally spoke.

"Because I've made her my new cochair. She's going to help me run Valsecchi's. I've been single too long and do not want to be separated from my new wife now I have found her. Instead, we will work and travel together."

Irena almost dropped on the spot. She was surprised his father hadn't reached for a chair.

"I've brought Bruno over from the plant to be our assistant. This weekend he'll be setting up a desk and equipment for her in here."

Dr. Santi had cautioned Irena to take good care of herself and avoid any unnecessary upsets, but Vincenzo's bombshell had come close to blowing her away.

His father scowled at him. "You're not even going to throw Fabbio a crumb?"

"I have special plans that will challenge him and keep him busy. Since he seems to have a predilection for being enamored of the women in my life, I thought he would be better off in another building of the complex, separated from us."

The comment must have struck a chord with his father because Guilio didn't argue with him. "What about Dino?" he asked in Italian.

"When he's living with us, we'll be home with him or taking him on trips with us, of course."

"But this is absurd. Your wife can't do anything when she doesn't even know the language."

Her husband had put her on the spot in front of his father, but right now she didn't want to appear totally lacking in front of his parent. "Your son and grandson have been teaching me," she interjected in passable Italian. "Dino makes a great tutor."

While his father shot her another look of incredulity, Vincenzo went on talking.

"Bruno is giving out memos to make sure everyone is assembled for the first board meeting Monday morning at nine. It's imperative the family meets Irena so we can begin laying down new policies. I'd like things to start turning around by our next fiscal quarter."

Guilio's expression hardened. "The others won't stand for it."

Her very Italian husband did that thing with his hands again. "Then they will have to look for another job—the way I had to do when you disowned me. It *could* be the making of them, but I'm not holding my breath. Now if you'll excuse us, Irena and I are still enjoying our honeymoon and have other things to occupy our time. *Ciao, Papa.*"

Irena had no choice but to follow Vincenzo's lead.

"A presto, signore." She extended her hand, which he perforce had to shake. As her husband walked her out of the office to the private elevator, she felt his father's eyes boring into her retreating back.

On the way down, Vincenzo slipped his hand beneath her hair. He massaged her nape where the nerves were knotted from all the tension. "I can tell by your face you're not used to witnessing a relationship like I have with my father. Don't let it worry you. We understand each other."

"How ill is he?" she asked as he helped her into the car.

"That's difficult to say."

She bowed her head. "Your news set him back."

"Not as much as it astounded *you,* I'm afraid." Vincenzo flicked her an assessing glance after starting the engine. "But I know you and how much you love your work. Just because we're married doesn't mean you have to stop working. It will be fun running Valsecchi's together."

He was crazy, but it was a craziness that spoke to her soul. "What if the others revolt as your father said?"

"They won't. After what life has handed them, they don't have the kind of fire in the belly needed to break away and be self-starters."

Another fear grabbed hold of her. "You know the old adage about familiarity, Vincenzo."

"In our case it won't breed contempt. You need to understand something. I want you with me all the time."

In her heart of hearts she wanted it, too. When he'd first told her he was going to take over at Valsecchi's, she felt like she'd been tossed into a void. She could see years and years of separation ahead of them caused by their business priorities.

"Later, when the baby comes, we'll deal with any changes." Vincenzo reached out and laid a hand on her stomach. "If the baby's not mine, I'm hoping you'll be able to work out joint physical custody to coincide with our time when Dino's at the house. He needs a sibling, even if it's on a part-time basis. They're both going to be young enough to bond."

She nodded, saddened to think of the turmoil ahead of them if this baby was Andreas's. "I would have loved a larger family."

"By the time my father gave me a stepbrother, Fabbio and I were too old to relate."

And your marriage deprived you of being a full-time father to Dino. The pained nuance in his tone haunted her. Waiting to learn if he was the father of her baby had to be the hardest test he'd ever had to endure.

Twilight had descended over the Golfo dei Poeti. According to Vincenzo, this was the place where Byron and Shelley, the British poets, used to come and actually lived for a time. Irena could understand why.

The medieval fishing village of Portovenere they'd just left sat like a little jewel in this part of Liguria. She'd eaten mouthwatering fish and Vincenzo's favorite pear-and-chocolate cake with hot chocolate sauce. When she couldn't manage another mouthful, he reached for her hand in a possessive hold and they walked along the promenade banked by the fascinating multicolored tower houses.

At the end of it they climbed the steps to the San

Pietro church perched on a rocky outcropping. He pulled her back against his chest and wrapped his arms around her. With his chin buried in her hair, they had a superb view of Cinque Terre in one direction and the luxuriant green island of Palmaria in the other.

"That's our destination tonight," he whispered. "We'll anchor offshore until morning in a small sheltered bay away from people." Her body trembled with longing. She started back down to the port with him, eager to be away from the tourists milling about.

His gleaming white sailboat with thin black striping had a galley and one bedroom below deck. He handled the boat like it was a part of him. Having lived by the Mediterranean all his life, he'd grown up a water baby. When Dino had such a wonderful teacher in his father, it was strange he was still so frightened of it.

Irena wasn't that good at swimming herself. But Vincenzo loved everything to do with the water, so she was determined to learn, especially after he'd told his father he planned to vacation with her when they weren't at work.

"What does the *Spadino* mean?" The name had been painted on the side of his boat.

His white smile dazzled her. "Watch and learn." Once they'd moved past the buoys using the motor, the evening breeze picked up. He cut the engine and unfurled the white sail with a magnificent black sword imprinted on the canvas. It was so unexpected, she let out a cry. "Did you name it for a pirate, or because it cuts through the water like a sword?"

He sat at the rudder, guiding them toward Palmaria. "Neither reason, but I very well could have done and both would have made sense. The truth is, after Dino was born I bought the boat new and had the sail specially made to honor his name, which comes from Italian meaning 'little sword.' That's what a *spadino* is—a small or little sword."

"Oh, Vincenzo—how thrilling for him."

His smile faded. "You would have thought so, but he won't step on it. You saw how he was in Disneyland. He can't bring himself to go near the water."

"There has to be a reason." She walked over to him and put a hand on his shoulder. "Something has made him afraid."

He reached for it and kept it there while he kissed her fingers. "I don't know what it is. I fear he may have had an experience he won't tell anyone about, and the thought of him being afraid of anything saddens me."

Vincent didn't often show his brooding side, but when it came to his son she knew he couldn't help it. She turned to lean against the side as they drew closer to Palmaria.

He'd told her it was the first of three islands, the other two being Tino and Tinetto, charming names. As he angled them around the island she saw something unusual running down the steep hillside.

"What is that?"

"A slide where they once lowered black marble with gold veining from the quarry to the boats waiting where we are now." No ripple disturbed the surface here. "We'll sleep like babies tonight. If you want to go down and get ready for bed, I'll be there after I take care of the boat and lower the anchor."

"Don't you want some help?"

"I feel like waiting on you. It never leaves my mind for a second that you're carrying a baby." Tonight he didn't say *our* baby. Did Vincenzo fear that the baby might be Andreas's, too? Twelve more days before the test…

Irena left him and went below. She'd been hoping he would want to *help* her get ready for bed. On the night they'd made love—which felt like a century ago now—he couldn't help her out of her clothes fast enough. The sensual tension building for those ten days had exploded into a frenzy of need. Breathless, neither of them had held back.

But everything seemed different now that she was pregnant. Last night he'd taken them down the coast a little ways, telling her he'd join her shortly, but she'd waited so long for him, she'd fallen asleep. When she'd awakened, he was already up and dressed. He had breakfast laid out on deck for them.

He treated her like porcelain and at times with an aching tenderness that could make her cry. But the elemental fire burning between them before didn't seem to be there on his part anymore. If he hoped she would be asleep when he came down in a little while, he was in for a surprise.

The surprise ended up being on her. She waited an hour for him, but he never came down. Hurt beyond words, she put on her robe over her nightgown and went up on deck in her bare feet. She found him hunched forward on one of the banquettes, talking on the phone in Italian.

His conversation went on a long time. She couldn't imagine who it was on the other end at this time of night, unless there was bad news about Dino or his father. Nothing else could darken his handsome face with lines that made him appear older. She sat down on the same banquette to wait for him.

The second he felt her presence, he cut short his conversation and hung up. Because of the darkness, she couldn't read the emotion in his eyes, but she sensed he wasn't happy she hadn't fallen asleep by now.

"Who was that, or shouldn't I be asking?"

"You can ask me anything, but it was Bruno, my eyes and ears, nothing important. Everything's fine."

Without preamble she said, "Vincenzo, after telling your father that you'd chosen me to be cochair of the company with you, I made the assumption that we would now share everything—our work, our thoughts, our dreams, our hopes, our fears, your son, the baby to come and…our bed. Please don't insult my intelligence and tell me everything's fine because I know it isn't."

Vincenzo stood up and rubbed the back of his neck, a sure sign he was contemplating his response and would have to choose his words carefully. That small gesture incensed her, prompting her to jump up. She placed herself directly in front of him without touching him.

Her head flew back, causing her hair to swish against her shoulders. "Why don't you come out and say it—" she cried.

She heard his sharp intake of breath before he clamped his hands on her shoulders. "What in the hell are you talking about, Irena?"

"You—me—us! I thought you'd brought me sailing so we could have our own private honeymoon."

"How could you have any doubt of it?" he asked in

that silky voice guaranteed to render her witless with desire.

Fire turned her cheeks hot. "You're good at answering one question with another, Vincenzo. It's one of your best techniques when you want to evade an issue, but not this time!"

His hands flew up, palms facing her. "I swear I don't know what demon has gotten hold of you."

"I'm not a fool, Vincenzo." It thrilled her that for once her voice didn't tremble. "If you're suffering buyer's remorse for an impulsive moment you wish hadn't happened, just tell me! It can be fixed."

Lines bracketed his compelling mouth. "You're not making sense."

"Your marriage to me accomplished what you really wanted. Now that you have the title, you're home free, Vincenzo. If you think your father won't celebrate to see the back of me, then *you* don't have the sense you were born with."

This time he gripped her upper arms and gave her a little shake. "Get to the point," he ground out. She'd never heard him sound so upset.

"Dino's not my biological son, so it won't impact his life if we get a quickie divorce. Contrary to what you believe, a career as cochair of your company is not compensation for the husband I thought I was marrying."

He crushed her against him and kissed her so long and hard, she had no air left to breathe. "You know very well why I haven't touched you yet."

Through the layers of pain, the words resonated in her brain, leaving her reeling. She lifted her head, having to cling to him for support. "I have no idea what you're talking about…"

"Because of your pregnancy and the fact that the test is coming up! Dr. Santi told me that intimacy might hurt you or the baby at this early stage, especially with the test carrying so many risks for you both. She told me it would be better if we waited three weeks, until after the test, that way you'd be out of any danger."

Irena was silent for a moment, her features pale in the soft moonlight. She'd had no idea that her husband had been so thoughtful and suddenly Irena felt sick that she had reacted in such a selfish way. "I had no idea, Vincenzo…"

He groaned, pressing his forehead against hers. "I thought she would have talked about it with you, too. Obviously she didn't tell you the same thing."

"No," Irena murmured. "I wish she had— I've been so devastated, I haven't known what to do. It thought it was me.…"

"Irena—" he said emotionally, "since we took Dino back to Milan, it's taken every bit of willpower I possess to stay away from you. If I had my way, we'd never leave the bedroom."

The relief of hearing the truth left her physically weak. "Then let's go down below and we'll just hold each other."

In the next breath he wrapped his arms around her, pulling her right up against him until there was no air between them. She felt his hands rove over her back with growing urgency. "I'm holding you right now and it's not enough." His breathing sounded ragged. "The way I feel about you, I can't lie with you and douse the fire you whip up in me. It isn't possible."

The longer their bodies melted into each other, the more she believed his trembling equaled hers. It was a revelation. She suddenly realized how completely she'd misjudged his behavior.

"Will you forgive me for the things I said?" she whispered against his lips.

"I'm glad you lashed out at me— It helps me keep sane until I can love you the way I really want to. Go to bed, Irena, before I lose my resolve."

In this fierce mood she didn't care to disturb further. Her appearance had cut short his phone call with Bruno. Something was on his mind he had yet to divulge. But whatever else, Vincenzo still wanted her. For the time being she would hug that knowledge to herself.

"Where will you sleep?"

"Right here."

It was a beautiful night, warm and fragrant from the flowers growing in profusion on the island. She happened to glance down at the still water and saw something come up to the surface.

"Vincenzo? What's that? It must be almost two meters in diameter!"

His glance rested on the circular object. "It's the same moon fish that kept me company last night."

"Is it dead?"

"No. They sleep on the surface. I'll show you." He reached for an oar and dipped it in the water so it created a splash. The fish suddenly flashed its fin and descended below the surface.

"Oh, the poor thing."

He chuckled. "He'll find another spot in a few minutes and go to sleep again with nothing more to disturb his dreams than an irritating human. *Buonanotte, esposa mia.*"

On the way into the apartment the next evening, Irena heard her phone ring. It was the first call she'd had in two days. Not two hours ago Vincenzo had taken her to dinner at a delightful bistro in Vernazza, their last stop along the coast before coming home.

While he was bringing in their things from the car, she reached in her purse for the phone. "*Ciao,* Deline. *Come stai?*"

"It's scary how Italian you sound already."

She smiled. "That's because my husband is a wonderful teacher," she explained as he came in the living room. "It's Deline," she told him, knowing he was curious about her caller.

He pressed a kiss to her lips before carrying their bags on through.

"Call me when you can talk." Deline clicked off.

The abrupt cessation of conversation made her stomach clench in reaction.

Her friend had never done anything like that before. Vaguely alarmed, she tried to imagine what could be wrong. Of course, there could be a lot things. Deline could be having problems with Leon. Maybe she was having complications with her pregnancy. Yet Irena had the sinking feeling her phone call might have something to do with Andreas.

"That was quick." Vincenzo had come back in the room.

"She suddenly had to get off. I think a slight emergency with the twins. I'll call her back in a minute."

"In the meantime, do you want to talk to Dino with me? I'm going to phone him."

"I'd love it."

"Good. I'd like to pick him up in the helicopter, but he's never ridden in one before. I'll have to feel him out. If he's too frightened, then we'll take the plane to Milan and bring him back the same way."

She followed him over to the couch. After they both sat down, he punched in the digits. Before long Mila came on the line. In a brittle voice she said she'd put him on, but he couldn't talk long. A minute later they heard Dino's voice.

"Papa? Are you home?"

Vincenzo put him on speaker. "Yes. We just got back from a little trip on the sailboat."

"Is Irena with you?"

"Yes. She wants to say hello."

Irena had been practicing her Italian, hoping to surprise him. *"Ciao, amica. Come va? Mi sei mancato molto!"*

"Ehi—you have learned a lot!" he answered in Italian. "I miss you and Papa, too. Are you coming for me on Wednesday afternoon?"

"Sì," Vincenzo answered. "How would you like to fly in the company helicopter?"

"But there's no place to land!"

Vincenzo burst into rich laughter before translating

for her. Dino was adorable. "We'll land on the roof of my office."

"Is Irena scared?"

She thought she understood him. "No!" she called out.

On that note Vincenzo spoke to him a little longer, then ended the call. He pulled her onto his lap. "He said he'd do it because *you're* not afraid." His face sobered. "How have I lived this long without you?"

Her heart turned over. "Vincenzo—" She took the initiative and kissed the hard mouth she couldn't get enough of.

Irena hadn't meant to entice him. She wanted to keep her baby and had come to grips with the fact that they had to wait to make love until after the test. But she hadn't counted on the depth of her husband's passionate response or her susceptibility to his hunger that drove every kiss deeper and deeper.

Somehow they ended up on the floor with her half lying across him. This wasn't good. But it felt so good and so right, she couldn't stop what was happening.

"Irena," he said in a husky voice against her throat. "You're so beautiful it hurts. I want to kiss every part of you, but once I start, I won't be able to stop. We can't do this—"

He rolled her carefully to the floor, then got up to stand over her. His eyes burned with desire as he looked down at her. "I'm going out to cool off. I won't be long." In seconds he'd disappeared.

With her body still trembling from his touch, she got to her feet. Her hair was in total disarray. He couldn't seem to keep his hands out of it. As far as she was concerned, he could play with it forever.

When she saw her phone on the arm of the couch, she reached for it. Vincenzo's departure had given her the opportunity she needed to talk to Deline in private. She pressed the digits and walked out on the terrace where the heat of the day caused the air to hang heavy with the scent of jasmine and rose.

Irena was aware of an ache that brought warmth to the palms of her hands. Her pulse points throbbed in yearning to know his possession. That first time two months ago hadn't been enough. She knew it would never be enough.

A few weeks ago Vincenzo had admitted he was in lust for her. But what she felt for him was so much more than that.

She was a woman in love for the first time in her life. What she'd felt for Vincenzo paled in comparison to any other emotions of the past. She loved everything about the man she had married. If only she knew for certain that the baby she carried was his....

"Irena? Are you there? Can you hear me?"

Startled to hear Deline's voice, she cleared her throat. "Yes. I finally had a chance to call you back. You sounded so tense before you hung up."

"I take it you haven't seen a newspaper for a while."

She sank down on one of the chairs. "Go on."

"I think your father had an article printed to pay Andreas back."

"What do you mean?"

"I'll read it to you. The headline says, 'Only daughter

of prominent Athens newspaper magnate marries titled CEO in Riomaggiore, Italy. After a whirlwind courtship, Irena Spiros Liapis, once rumored to become the future wife of CEO Andreas Simonides, has wed Vincenzo Antonello Valsecchi, Duke of La Spezia, in a private church ceremony.'"

Irena smoothed the hair off her face. "When I talked with my parents, I didn't know Vincenzo was titled, so how have they found out?"

"Your father's not a newspaper man for nothing."

"No." He might just as well have shoved a boulder down the mountain. Once the momentum picked up, there was no preventing it from flattening everything in its path till it reached the bottom. "Has Leon seen it?"

"He's the one who showed it to me. I thought I'd better call you."

"Is he suspicious?"

"Incredulous is more like it. I told him I knew you'd met a man when you'd been there on business for the newspaper and that when you went back, everything had moved fast."

Irena stared into space. "When Andreas gets home from his honeymoon, that's probably the first thing Leon will tell him, but frankly, I'm much more worried about Vincenzo's feelings. I love him so terribly, Deline."

"I know. That's why I hate to have to tell you that Andreas and Gabi are already back. They flew in this evening. Leon went to the airport to drive them home. I would have gone, but Nikos has a cold. At some point your marriage will come up in the discussion."

"It will."

"I'm glad you're having that test done, Irena. If

Andreas puts two and two together and should call you, you'll be ready for him. Have you told your parents you're pregnant?"

"Not yet. Vincenzo and I have decided we'll fly to Athens with Dino and tell them in person after I've had the test. They always wanted to be grandparents. Deline? Thanks for this heads-up."

"Of course. We'll stay in close touch."

"Yes." Irena hung up and walked over to the railing.

That's where Vincenzo found her a few minutes later. She turned to him. "I'm glad you're back," she whispered emotionally.

He studied her with a questioning look in his eyes. "What did Deline say that has put that anguished look on your face?"

She told him everything. "I hadn't counted on my father being the one to inadvertently speed up the timetable."

Vincenzo stood there with his hands in his pockets, his expression solemn. "He loves his little girl and didn't like seeing her hurt. I can appreciate his reaction and the motivation behind his action. It was the most natural thing in the world for him to announce our marriage. He's a proud man."

"But he has no idea how the very existence of the title has caused you pain in your life. Now he has blurted it to everyone."

"You don't need to be concerned for me."

"But I am! I know how much you crave your privacy. I'm so sorry." Filled with pain, she hurried through the house to Dino's bedroom. She flung herself facedown on the bed, clutching the pillow like a life preserver.

In the next second, she felt the side of the bed give. Vincenzo leaned over her. "Forget everything, Irena. Relax." He rubbed her back "The only thing important now is you and the baby. We are going to have that test and then you are going to deliver a strong, healthy baby. I don't want you worrying about anything else."

CHAPTER EIGHT

IRENA HAD GOTTEN UP before Vincenzo. She'd prepared breakfast and had laid the table on the balcony. Along with a stunning linen suit in cream, the perfect foil for her dark hair and tan, she'd put on her serene countenance. You'd never know that within the hour she'd be walking into the conference room at headquarters to face a hostile environment.

During the drive into La Spezia, Vincenzo coached her on the opening remarks she planned to deliver in Italian. He felt an inordinate pride in her ability to be such a fast learner. Her accent wasn't bad, either.

Before long they arrived at the complex. Bruno, Vincenzo's auburn-haired confidant, stood at the entry to the conference room on the fourth floor. He'd met Irena when she'd come to Italy before. His smile grew broader as they exchanged greetings in Italian.

He flashed Vincenzo a silent message of approval. Vincenzo nodded before ushering Irena inside. The twelve, as Vincenzo thought of them, sat around the oval table in various attitudes of aggression, ready to pounce. Yet the moment they saw her, every jaw dropped. Fabbio's practically lay on the floor. Irena had the kind of looks that could stop weekend traffic on the autostrada.

He helped Irena to the seat next to his, but he remained standing. "Good morning, family. It's gratifying to know that during the years I've been away from the company, you've remained loyal to Papa. Before things go further, if any one of you, or all of you, wish to walk out now because you can't give me that same loyalty, I'll understand and we'll discuss your retirement privately."

As he'd predicted, none of them stirred.

"You've noticed several additions already. May I introduce my lovely wife, Irena Liapis, from Athens. I've asked her to be cochair of the company and she has accepted. We'll occupy the same office."

The pronouncement hit like a tidal wave, rocking them in their chairs. While they were digesting the news, he nodded to Bruno, who gave each of them a folder.

"Bruno Torelli worked with me at Antonello's. I've brought him here to be our personal assistant. He's an invaluable asset. If you'll take the time to read page one, you'll see the dossier on my wife's business credentials.

"She's a woman of many hidden talents. Her Italian is coming along beautifully, but it's not surprising. She speaks impeccable English. Because of her far-reaching family ties, she's also conversant in Serbo-Croatian and Slovenian. Those are areas where we do a great deal of business. I'm putting her in charge of them. She'll fit our needs like a hand in a glove."

While he heard coughs and quiet gasps, he glanced at his stepbrother, who so far hadn't been able to look him in the eye. "For years Papa has personally overseen the cottage industries, but now that he has stepped down, I'm giving Fabbio carte blanche."

Fabbio's gaze shot to his in astonishment. "You're eminently qualified for it and have been for a long time. Plan to set up your office in Building B with Gino and Luca."

He had two more assignments to make. "Uncle Tullio? With Papa gone, you will take over as company comptroller in Building C.

"Uncle Carlo? You'll take on Tullio's former area of responsibility along with your own and move to Building D." Tullio loved feeling important and Carlo disapproved of the way Tullio did business. These changes would satisfy both of them to some degree.

"All of you set up your new staffs and make the physical arrangements as you see fit." They needed their own space, something Vincenzo's father had never understood. "By Friday I'll expect reports on my desk. Irena will be taking the reports from Mario, Cesario and Valentino to get a grasp on the situation in the areas I mentioned. Now before this meeting is adjourned, she has a few words to say."

After his wife had delivered her small speech in perfectly adequate sounding Italian, he noticed a different feel steal over the room. She came across as a no-nonsense type, yet charming in her ultrafeminine way. They weren't happy with her, but they weren't feeling quite as mutinous as before.

Pleased that they all shook her hand before filing out, he liked the idea of working with his wife. As long as he kept her close to him, she would be forced to think about him. *Until the baby came.*

Last night he'd dreamed that the test results had shown Andreas to be the father. When she'd had to turn the baby over to Simonides for visitation, she'd fallen apart and Vincenzo hadn't been able to comfort her. He'd awakened in a cold sweat. He hoped with all his heart that the baby she carried was his child.

Irena eyed Dino across the kitchen table with her pocket dictionary in hand. Vincenzo had excused himself to take a phone call from Bruno. "Dino? Does your papa make you happy?" she asked in Italian.

"Sì."

"Do you want to make him happy?"

"He *is* happy."

She smiled. "I know. He likes his boat. He wants *you* to like it." She'd been working hard to get her pronouns right and put them in the right place.

He looked down. "I like it."

"Let's go with him."

Dino shook his head.

"Why not?"

"I can't swim."

"Why not?" she asked again.

He answered with a word she didn't understand. When she looked it up, it meant *fear.* "You have *pauro?*"

This time he nodded.

She hurriedly searched for another word. "You have fear of *pesce luna?*" The moon fish had startled her the other night, but she'd probably said it wrong.

"No." He bit his lip, then murmured, *"Squalo."*

Once again she dug into her dictionary and found the word. She lifted her head. He was afraid of sharks! She understood. *"Capisco."*

Irena knew a great white had been sighted in the Mediterranean some time ago. It was a rare occurrence, but clearly Dino had heard something about the animals that had instilled a deep fear within him.

Later when they'd put him to bed, she discussed it with Vincenzo who lay with his head in her lap on the couch. He'd put on some music he'd thought she would like.

"I think I can see why he doesn't want to swim, Vincenzo. If he learns how, then in his mind he'll think you expect him to ride on a boat. It's a short leap from there to falling in the sea and being attacked by a shark!"

He reached up and pulled her head down. "You've gotten something out of him I never could. My new cochair is brilliant." He kissed her mouth. "I've a feeling Papa told him something about the time he tangled with a shark when he was a teenager. It probably scared the daylights out of Dino."

Irena nodded. "I have an idea. When he comes on Friday for the weekend, why don't you ask him to swim with us in the Lido's pool because there aren't any sharks in there. Maybe it'll work and he'll slowly overcome his fear."

His eyes burned a flame blue. "I'll try it. Now I have another idea. Let's dance."

Yes!

The test was only nine more days away. If dancing was a way to get close to him for a little while, she'd take it. But the moment she stood up and melted into his arms, they clung to each other because he'd started devouring her with wild abandon.

Before she could say it, he told her it was time for her to go to bed in his bedroom. *Alone.* He would sleep on the couch as prearranged. What made any of it bearable was the fact that they went to the office together every day where she could feast her eyes on him and watch the genius at work.

On Friday Vincenzo's three cousins reported to her. She was still meeting with them when it was time to pick up Dino. She urged her husband to go without her. When the helicopter landed back at the complex, the three of them would drive home together.

Not long after he left, she was writing up her notes once the meeting had broken up when Bruno buzzed her from the reception room outside their office. "Are you free, Irena? There's a man here to see you."

She blinked because it meant it was someone not associated with the company. "Who is it?"

"He didn't say, but inferred it was urgent. Security has already searched him."

Irena had an idea who it was. Part of her had been expecting it. There was no one in the world more discreet than the man she'd thought she was going to marry. Andreas. That life and the woman she had been then seemed a century ago now. How much had changed!

"Please tell him to come in, Bruno."

"Bene."

She got to her feet and waited. "Leon—" she said

in surprise when Andreas's twin walked in the room wearing a tan business suit.

His gray eyes swept over her in alarm. "Sit down before you fall."

Irena didn't need to be prompted.

The man who would have been her brother-in-law rushed over to her chair with a glass of water he'd grabbed from a side table. "You've lost color. Here. Drink this. If you're not better in thirty seconds, I'm driving you to the nearest hospital."

"I'll be fine."

She drained the glass before looking at him. He was still hunkered down next to her. This close she could see the same expression he'd worn on his face for that month while Deline wouldn't have anything to do with him.

The time to speak gut to gut had come. "Does Andreas know about the baby?"

"No. He was sick when I picked them up at the airport. We called the doctor who thinks Andreas has picked up a bad bug on his honeymoon. He's in the hospital right now on an IV while he's being tested for everything under the sun."

"Andreas is ill?"

"I'm afraid so. His temperature's up and he can't keep food down." Irena heard the pain in his voice. Being Andreas's twin, she knew this had alarmed him.

"I can't believe it," she said in a quiet tone. "Poor Gabi. How is she?"

"Terrified for him, as you can imagine. She hasn't left his side."

"Of course not. Has he been ill long?"

"No. On the plane from Nassau he became so sick, his pilot and steward had to help him out to my car. When I eventually got home and told Deline, she broke down and it all came out about your pregnancy. She's panicked, we all are."

"In the beginning I was, too. But I'm not anymore, and she doesn't need to be." Irena put a hand on his arm. "Has he heard I'm married?"

"I don't know. He hasn't said anything." His breathing sounded labored. "Gabi's so terrified he isn't improving."

Irena could only imagine. If Vincenzo were lying in a hospital right now... "No matter what, you have to believe he's going to get better, Leon."

"One of the reasons I'm here is to make sure he doesn't get any worse. If he finds out about the baby..."

His words needed no translation.

"I can't stop people from talking, Leon, and I certainly can't prevent Andreas from jumping to conclusions."

"No. No one can do that."

"I have scheduled a test for a week from Friday. By the time Andreas is better, we will know who the baby's father is. If it turns out to be Andreas, then I'll deal with it when the time comes. But until then, Leon, I'm assuming and hoping that this baby is Vincenzo's."

"You're a strong woman, Irena."

While he gave her a hug, she heard a young voice. "Irena?"

She pulled away in time to see Dino at the door. Vincenzo stood behind him, his features unsmiling. His eyes were veiled so she couldn't see any blue.

"Come over here, Dino." When she motioned to him,

he ran to her so they could hug. "Dino, I'd like you to meet Leon. He's the husband of my best friend, Deline. I told you about her." The boy nodded.

Darting Leon a glance she said, "Leonides Simonides, this is my *stupendo* stepson, Dino." The way she'd worded it made him giggle.

Leon smiled. *"Ciao, Dino. Come stai?"*

She'd forgotten their family could converse in basic Italian. Her heart thudded as Vincenzo moved toward them. "Leon, this is my husband, Vincenzo Valsecchi."

The two men shook hands. "Congratulations on your marriage, Signore Valsecchi. Irena and her family have been friends of our family for many years. I've always said the person who won her heart would be the luckiest of men."

"Grazie, Signore Simonides." Her husband gave a polite response. "What brings you all this way?"

Her heart was jumping in her throat. "Andreas came home ill from his honeymoon and is in the hospital."

As Vincenzo's brows knit together, Dino tugged on her arm. She looked down. "What is it?"

"Who's in the hospital?"

"Leon's brother."

"Was he your friend, too?" he asked in all innocence. Both men stared at her till she could scarcely take another breath.

"Yes, he was."

"Oh."

"Dino?" Vincenzo put a hand on his son's shoulder. "We'll go out to the car and wait for Irena while she says goodbye to Signore Simonides." His civil demeanor didn't give away what he was feeling inside.

"I'll be right there," she assured him.

When he'd closed the door behind him, Leon let out a sigh. "I'm sorry, Irena. There's no easy way to handle any of this right."

"Don't worry about it. It's just that the wait for the test has made us both edgy."

"The man's desperately in love with you. Anyone can see that."

For Leon to say such a thing thrilled her; if only her husband had said those words to her. "He's the light of my life. I adore him, and would do anything to prevent him from being hurt."

He shook his head. "Now everything makes sense. For you to let Andreas go the way you did...no histrionics..."

"I'd already fallen for Vincenzo and was ready to break it off with your brother."

Leon's eyes were full of pain. "What a situation for you to be in now."

"Only you would understand how much I want this baby to be Vincenzo's. But if it isn't, I'm going to deal with it the way you did."

She walked over to her desk and got her purse out of the drawer. "Come on. I'll go out to the parking lot with you. There's a little boy and his papa waiting for me."

They rode the private elevator to the ground floor. Before they walked past security at the main door of the building she turned to him. "I can't believe Andreas isn't going to recover so I won't even consider it."

"That makes two of us." Leon gave her another hug. "Deline sends her love."

"Take mine back to her."

While Leon headed for his rental car in one direction, anxious to get back to Athens, she hurried toward the VIP parking in the other. Dino was leaning out the rear window of the Fiat, waiting for her. "Irena!" he called to her with a big smile on his face. It warmed her heart.

She gave him a kiss on the cheek before climbing in the front passenger seat. Vincenzo had leaned across to open the door for her. Without speaking to her, he started the car and they drove away.

"Where is your friend sick?" Dino wanted to know.

"He has a bug." She patted her tummy, a gesture Vincenzo noted. It reminded them both of the baby she was carrying. He translated for his son, who said, *"Che tristezza."*

Yes, it was sad. "*Sì,* Dino. But in time he will get better."

"The point is, will you?" Vincenzo threw out in a gravelly voice.

Leon's visit had brought the question of paternity to the forefront once more. Somehow she had to help get her husband's mind off it. When they pulled up at the back of the apartment, he announced they were going to the park as soon as they changed clothes.

Dino sounded delighted and scrambled out of the car. Irena followed him inside, deciding to put on white shorts and a matching knit top. Because the heat was particularly intense, she tied her hair back at the nape with a white scarf.

When she went back in the living room, she discovered Vincenzo had changed out of his suit into blue shorts and a lighter blue T-shirt, much like the outfit Dino was wearing. One day he would grow up to have the same hard-muscled physique as his father. No woman would be immune to him, either.

The park was just past the church on the same side. When they reached it, there were at least a dozen children playing. Vincenzo opened the duffel bag holding his son's equipment and pulled out a soccer ball.

"Watch me, Irena!"

Dino started kicking it around with his father. Vincenzo was a natural athlete and a natural with children. Pretty soon some other boys joined in. Irena sat in one of the swings, content to have a legitimate reason to look at her striking husband as long as she wanted. His powerful legs fascinated her. She remembered the way they felt entwined with hers.

A fierce ache passed through her body. Irena wished she could make her world perfect, but knowing she couldn't, she started swinging like she did when she was a child. Higher and higher.

"Careful," Vincenzo murmured, catching her midway, swing and all, bringing her to a stop from behind. "Remember the test. This close to the date you don't want to do anything that could cause a complication. If this broke…"

"You're right." She slid out of it and turned to him. "I wasn't thinking."

His gaze took her in, missing nothing from her sandals to the scarf holding her hair back. The little muscle at the corner of his mouth throbbed, revealing emotion held barely in check. "That doesn't surprise me. It isn't every day you hear Simonides is in the hospital."

"Vincenzo—" She lifted beseeching eyes to him. "I had no idea Leon had flown here. If I'd known, I would have told you."

"I believe you."

She moistened her lips nervously, aware of his scrutiny. Beyond his shoulder she could see Dino playing soccer with the other boys. For the moment the two of them were alone. "He's worried about his brother."

"I can only surmise he doesn't want you to say or do anything that could upset his twin."

For such a brilliant man, she couldn't understand how Vincenzo was so blind to the intensity of her feelings for *him*.

"I told him I wasn't going to worry about anything because I'm planning on *you* being the father. By the time he's recovered, I'll know the test results."

Vincenzo rubbed his lower lip with the pad of his thumb. "And then what?"

"If he's the father, I'll let Leon choose the moment to take the DNA results to him. But I don't want to think about it right now. I want to concentrate on us."

"So do I," he whispered against her lips. On that healing note, Vincenzo turned and called to Dino that they were leaving. He came running over to them, holding his ball. "What are we going to do now?"

She leaned down. "Shall we buy a gelato?"

"At the pool?"

Irena squinted at him. "No. At the *gelateria*."

"Don't you want to go to the pool?"

She didn't understand. "I thought you didn't like to go there."

He nodded his dark head. "Yes, I do."

Her pulse quickened to realize Vincenzo had managed some kind of breakthrough with his son. *"Veramente?"*

"Sì." Dino laughed. "There aren't any sharks in a pool! Everyone knows *that!*"

Overjoyed, she gave him a big hug. "I'm so glad you told me. Now I'll get in the pool with you."

"Fantastico! Let's get our bathing suits on!"

Irena was so happy with this much progress where his son was concerned, she wanted to hug her husband and never let him go, but the paternity of the baby still clouded their future. If the baby was Andreas's then their family would always be divided. Irena couldn't bear to think about it and so instead she showered all her attention on Dino, the child they had at the moment, pretending that Vincenzo's baby was growing inside of her.

By Sunday night they'd had such a wonderful time playing and swimming, there were tears from Dino at the helipad in Milan. Vincenzo stood outside the open door of the helicopter, but his son was all broken up and refused to get out.

"How come you can't come and get me next weekend, Papa?"

Irena had to clamp down hard on her emotions so they wouldn't show. Next weekend the test would be done and over, and a new chapter of their lives would begin.

"Because one weekend a month your mother wants you with her. It's all been planned, but we'll see you on Wednesday."

That cheered him up a little. "Okay."

"I'll study all the colors, *professore*," Irena promised. "You can test me to see if I make any mistakes."

A small smile broke the corners of his mouth.

"If she does them all correctly, what will you give her for a reward?" his father asked him.

"Do you like chocolate?"

"I can't live without it."

Dino laughed. It was good to see him leave in a happier mood. *"Ciao."*

"A presto, Dino. Ti amo." She'd wanted to tell him she loved him a long time ago, but until now it hadn't felt like the right moment.

"Ti amo, Irena." That was a first for him, too. He was the sweetest boy in the world. After a quick hug, he turned so his father could grab him.

Once they'd driven away in the limo, she phoned Deline. Since Leon's unexpected visit on Friday, Irena hadn't heard another word. To her disappointment it rang so long, she had to leave a message.

Five minutes later Deline phoned her back. "I'm so sorry I couldn't answer. We've been at the hospital with Andreas."

"How is he?"

"Yesterday they found out he has a rare parasite, but it's treatable. They started him on antibiotics and already his temperature has dropped. He kept down a roll and some juice tonight. If he continues to improve, he'll be able to go home in the next couple of days."

"That's good. Now I've got some wonderful news. Tonight Vincenzo's son told me he loved me."

"Oh, Irena…"

"Dino's going to make the most fabulous big brother for my baby. For the sake of all our sanity, that test can't come soon enough."

"It's only a few days away now. Hang on, Irena."

CHAPTER NINE

THE PERINATOLOGIST DOING the procedure came in the room. He nodded to Vincenzo before approaching Irena. "How are you feeling this morning, Signora Valsecchi?"

"Good. Anxious."

"I'm sure Dr. Santi told you what's going to happen. The ultrasound technician will be working with me. Once I've numbed your belly, I'll insert a long, thin needle. It will pass through the uterus to the placenta where I'll gather a sample of cells. You might feel a little cramping, but the procedure won't take more than twenty-five minutes. Do you have any questions?"

"No."

The doctor was ready to begin. Vincenzo was the one standing in the way of things getting started. He'd never liked the idea of her having this test and preferred to call the whole thing off, but Irena was determined.

He leaned over his wife, who'd drunk the necessary glass of water an hour ago and had been prepped for the ultrasound. "If you need me, I'll be as close as the reception room."

"I know." Her velvety-brown eyes pleaded with him to understand why she was doing this. But this kind of courage he didn't admire. It not only constituted a certain risk to the baby, but it also placed her in physical as well as emotional jeopardy. The thought of anything going wrong—or, God forbid, losing her—was incomprehensible to him.

She gripped his forearm as if sensing his inner turmoil. "It's going to be all right."

To the depths of his soul Vincenzo wanted, *had* to believe it. He kissed her lips before wheeling out of the room.

A month ago he'd had an inward struggle over the baby's paternity, but having just left his wife, he realized she was the only thing that mattered to him. So what if the baby wasn't his? He just wanted the baby and his wife to be safe and well.

Having met her, he was a changed man. Fulfilled on every level. As long as he had her, any other frustration or disappointment he could deal with.

Needing something to do, he headed over to the alcove to get himself coffee out of the machine. After draining the cup, he walked down the hallway to the lab and approached the fiftyish-looking female receptionist.

"Is there someone in charge I could speak to?"

One brown brow lifted. "I've worked here thirty years."

Her response would have amused him if he wasn't in such turmoil over Irena and the baby. "My wife's having a Chorionic Villi Sampling done as we speak to determine the paternity of her baby. When I came in to give a sample of my cheek tissue, the technician said the results for both of us would be ready in about ten days."

"But you want to know *now*."

Ehi. She'd been here thirty years all right. Vincenzo nodded.

"If you want to pay more money, you can know the results as soon as tomorrow."

His head reeled before he reached for his wallet.

She laughed. "Not to me. To the cashier down the hall. Everything's legal here."

He took a deep breath. He should have felt like a fool, but he didn't. "What's the protocol? Do I phone the lab?"

"You look like you're dying, so I'll call you by noon." She pushed a notepad through the window opening.

Vincenzo wrote down his and Irena's names and cell phone numbers and passed it back. "If you weren't sitting on the other side of the glass, I'd kiss you, signora."

"Signorina Loti. If there weren't any glass, I'd let you."

"Grazie," he said with heartfelt emotion before finding the cashier. After producing a credit card, he went back to the reception room.

He wouldn't tell Irena what he'd done. If anything, it could bring on more anxiety. Her health was all that mattered to him. Dr. Santi said to give her three days to recover. There could be some bleeding, which was normal. Plenty of bed rest, no strenuous exercise.

Once he'd heard from the lab, he'd tell her, of course. But until then, he'd wait out the next twenty-four hours without her knowing she'd be getting an answer much sooner than she'd expected.

"Signore Valsecchi?"

Infinitely relieved to hear his name called, Vincenzo

followed the nurse back to Irena's room. When he went inside, she was up and dressed, sitting in a wheelchair, looking too good for someone who'd just gone through such an uncomfortable experience.

He leaned down to press a brief kiss to the mouth he craved. "How are you feeling?"

"I'm really fine." *Grazie a dio.* "You've probably been going crazy waiting."

His pulse sped up knowing he needed to keep the truth from her a little longer. "I have, but everything's okay now that I can take you home."

"She's ready," the nurse said, putting a sheet of instructions in Irena's hands. "If you want to wheel her out, I'll accompany you to the entry and wait while you bring your car around."

Before long he'd helped her into the car and they drove out of the hospital parking lot. He looked over at her. "Are you hungry? Thirsty? I'll be happy to stop and get you anything you want."

"Thank you, but let's just go home."

He reached out to grasp the hand closest to him. "That's what I want, too."

She heaved an emotional sigh he felt go through him. "I'm glad it's over, Vincenzo."

"So am I. We will know soon and then we can start living our life. Are you feeling any discomfort yet?"

"No. There was a little stinging around the needle, but that soon left. I feel amazingly normal."

"You look it, but don't be deceived. You heard what Dr. Santi said."

"I know. I'll take it easy."

"We both will. I'll feed you grapes while you recite

your conjugations for me. By the time we go for Dino on Wednesday, he'll be so impressed with how much progress you've made, he'll ask me to buy you some chocolate bocci balls."

"One of those sounds good."

He rubbed her fingers before letting them go. "You're not pretending? You really do feel okay?"

"Yes. The only problem now is the ten-day wait. By then Andreas—"

"By then Simonides could have discovered about the baby, yes…" he cut in, trying not to sound harsh. "We'll deal with it when the time comes.…" His voice trailed.

"I'm sorry, Vincenzo. I don't mean to keep bringing him up."

"Don't apologize. If he is the father then he is going to be a fact of life like Mila." If it were true, somehow Vincenzo would have to learn to deal with it, but in his heart he still hoped…

When they reached Riomaggiore and he pulled up behind the apartment, she undid the seat belt and started to get out of the car, but he caught her arm. "You've just had surgery. Let me help you."

"I was only going to walk in the house. That's not strenuous."

Upset, he levered himself from the seat and went around to her side. "Whether it is or not, I'm carrying you inside."

She looped her arms around his neck. "You do too much for me. I feel like a fraud."

"Feel any way you like," he bit out. "I want to take care of you."

Irena kissed his cheek. "That's all you ever do. I'm the luckiest woman in the world." Tears filled her eyes at his gentleness.

He swept her through the front door, hoping she still felt that way after hearing the test results. "Do you feel like bed, or the couch?"

"The couch, but first I need to use the bathroom."

Vincenzo lowered her to the floor. "I'll make us something to eat."

"That sounds perfect." She gave him another kiss and started down the hall.

When she'd shut the door, he hurried out to the kitchen. His gaze caught sight of the homemade volcano sitting on the counter. She'd helped Dino make it on Wednesday. After several attempts, it finally blew and was such a huge success, his son wanted to do it again next week.

He pulled the food out of the fridge with more force than necessary. In his gut he wanted the baby she carried to be his; he wanted their family to be together always, without the fear of visitation always hanging over them. Once the results were in and Vincenzo had the truth staring him in the face, maybe then he could let everything go. But right now he felt like that volcano sitting there ready to go off.

Irena woke up the next morning with a start. It was almost ten. She'd been so nervous the night before, she'd stayed up late with Vincenzo watching a couple of old movies until fatigue took over.

To her surprise she'd slept soundly, but now that she

was awake, she remembered the procedure and hurried to the bathroom.

She could have cried out with relief because there was no leak of amniotic fluid and only a mere spot of blood.

After taking a quick shower, she brushed her hair and put on lipstick, wanting to look good for her husband. Next came a pair of jeans he hadn't seen her in before. She toned them with a sleeveless top in a café-au-lait color with white trim around the armholes and neck.

When she entered the kitchen, Vincenzo had already fixed their breakfast. His anxious gaze searched hers. "You're up!"

"Forgive me for sleeping in."

"Forgive you—" he cried out in exasperation. "You needed it. But for the last three hours I have to admit I've been checking on you every ten minutes, worrying you might not be breathing." Emotion had darkened his eyes to a deeper blue.

"I'm sorry." Since driving her home from the hospital, it was as if he was in a continual state of agitation, waiting to hear the worst.

"What's the verdict?"

"So far, perfect!" She smiled to reassure him, but he wasn't convinced. "Vincenzo—more than twelve hours have already passed. Dr. Santi said they were the most crucial, but everything's fine. Only the merest trace of blood, nothing else. If I were going to miscarry, there'd be more signs."

"No pain?"

"None!" She spread her hands the way he did, hoping

he'd see she was even learning Italian gestures, but by his expression they were wasted on him.

"You wouldn't lie to me—" His voice sounded unsteady.

"Why would I do that?" She took a step closer, not understanding this new side of him. His vulnerability was a complete revelation to her. No one seeing him like this would believe he was the confident, brilliant, in-charge Duke of La Spezia who was already making radically new changes at the Valsecchi corporation.

"You know everything there is to know about me. You *have* to know it! Believe me, if I were cramping and miserable, I would tell you, Vincenzo." She could see that something deeper was bothering him and that he wanted to talk to her about something so she tried to lighten the mood, hoping to get Vincenzo talking to her.

"Look, Vincenzo, if I was in any kind of pain do you think I would be wearing jeans like this for you? Do you remember how you once dared me to buy a pair like this when I came to Italy the first time?"

She modeled them in front of him, like she was on the runway of a fashion designer's shop. "Take a good look now because I won't be able to stuff myself into them much longer, not when the baby comes."

His jaw hardened, but his eyes watched every movement. That had to mean something. Now that the test was over and she hadn't miscarried, was Vincenzo worried about their future? Did he regret marrying her for the baby's sake? Irena continued, determined to find out what had caused her husband's sudden darkened mood.

"If you don't remember, *I* do. We were walking along the hiking path to Manarola behind a knockout Italian girl and her boyfriend. You challenged me to get a pair like she was wearing. As far as I was concerned, she might as well have not been wearing them for all the good they did her."

"That's a matter of opinion," he muttered, but she heard him. At least he was listening. It gave her the courage to go on.

"I told you a lady didn't pour herself into such an outfit. You said a man didn't always want the woman he loved to be dressed like a businesswoman. Maybe you don't remember, but you said a lot of things like that to me when we first met.

"When you told me you liked my height because there was more of me to grab hold of, I expected you to grab me. I *wanted* you to do it, and you *knew* it! But you teased me by not giving me what I wanted and drove me insane with wanting!"

That nerve at the corner of his mouth was throbbing again. "You were toying with me."

She put her hands on her hips, furious that she couldn't seem to get through to him. What was going on here? "I would never toy with you, Vincenzo."

"Then why did you come back to Italy? The truth now!"

"The truth?" she cried, baffled by his question. "You *know* why, Vincenzo." She went to him and placed her hand against his strong arm. He twitched, but did not pull away. Irena knew that she had to convince her husband of her true feelings for him. For so long she had been avoiding talking to him about how she felt, but with the test now behind them and their future ahead it suddenly felt liberating to say it.

"Vincenzo, the night I went to bed with you was the night I knew I'd fallen completely and irrevocably in love with a man for the first time in my life. That man was *you!* You were right about dreams, Vincenzo. You were right about everything! I did have a dream of being married to Andreas, but that's all it was, a silly dream, a fantasy.

"With hindsight I can see our relationship always lacked the fire, though we seemed like the perfect couple. Everyone thought so. But we were never true lovers and never felt it in our hearts. Andreas only ever made love to me twice."

"I don't believe you." His response sounded almost savage.

"Believe it. Both times were disappointing."

If anything, her husband seemed to pale with the revelation.

"Then I met you. Vincenzo Antonello. The most arrogant, gorgeous, impossible Italian male in existence with his beat-up car and his attitude that said to hell with the world. *Sì, signore*—" She nodded because he wasn't making any sound.

"You were that bad. Worse even. We were anything but the perfect couple. A mismatch in every way, shape and form. But by that first night, I felt like I'd met the lover I wanted to spend the rest of my life with. Every day after that I fell more and more in love even though you never said you were in love with me."

She took a fortifying breath. "I didn't want to leave you when it was time to go home, Vincenzo. I'd forgotten all about Andreas. I stayed in Italy three days longer than I should have because I couldn't bear to leave. I knew I had to tell Andreas about you, that I was in love with *you*. There was no way I could have gone back to him. My heart was with you, darling, and he had to be told.

"But he'd already fallen for Gabi so I never did get the chance to tell him about us. He was in a hurry when he came to my house and so full of his feelings for her, he did all the talking. It was a revelation to hear him pour out his heart. For once he was actually communicating to me, and everything he said I could relate to because love had happened to me, too."

Vincenzo still refused to speak, but Irena, filled with a courage she didn't know she had, continued. She knew that this was make-or-break for them—Vincenzo had to know her true feelings; she couldn't lose him now, after all they had been through!

"I gave up my job at the newspaper and made plans to fly back to you, Vincenzo, but I started feeling sick and the nausea was bad enough that I stayed in Athens to see a doctor. You know the rest of the story.

"So here we are, my love, together and married with a baby on the way. At first I feared that Andreas might be the father, but I can't worry about that any longer. He chose his path and I chose mine. It's in the past. My life is with you and Dino and the baby. We'll deal with whatever happens. All I know is, I couldn't live without you now."

A silence settled around them whilst Irena waited for Vincenzo to respond. He was staring at the floor and for a horrifying moment Irena believed that the marriage might be at an end. Perhaps this had been too much for Vincenzo to deal with? Then the silence was interrupted by the ringing of the telephone. Both of them seemed surprised by the intrusion, drawing them out of their solitude.

Vincenzo automatically picked it up from the counter, his eyes riveted on her mouth. *"Prego? Buongiorno. Sì. Momento."* Vincenzo handed the phone to her. "It's Dr. Santi calling to ask how you're doing."

"Oh—" She put it to her ear. *"Buongiorno,* Dr. Santi."

"How are you today?"

"Wonderful. Only a little blood. Nothing else. No cramps."

"Ah...that's what I was hoping to hear. Are you ready for some more good news?"

Her heart pounded harder. "Yes. Of course."

"While you were having the procedure done yesterday, your husband had a conversation with the head of the lab. He asked if they would rush the preliminary report. I have the results in my hand. Both your doctors were wise not to tell you anything definitive in the beginning. The baby is your husband's."

Irena thought she was going to collapse with joy. Her heart felt like it was flying on wings. "Oh, Dr. Santi—" Tears gushed from her eyes.

"What's wrong?" Vincenzo cried in agony.

"I'll see you in three weeks for your next appointment."

He rushed around the counter and caught her in his arms. "Tell me what's the matter, *innamorta.*"

She grabbed his face between her hands. "Not a

single, solitary thing. Vincenzo, *you're* the father of our baby! *You're* the one who made me pregnant. This is our baby, yours and mine."

"Irena—" He covered her face with kisses, unable to stop. "Our baby?"

"Yes, *mia amore. Ti amo.* If I didn't say that right, I don't care. I love you, Vincenzo. That night we made love, we created a family. *Our* family. Oh, darling—"

He started kissing her and couldn't stop. She didn't want him to stop. Before she knew it they were on the bed in his bedroom, entwined while they poured out their love. He hadn't brought her in here since the night their baby was conceived. From now on this was where she intended to sleep. In his arms.

"I know I have to slow down," he whispered on a ragged breath. "The doctor said three days. We've got two more to go before we know it's safe. How am I going to make it? You're going to have to help me." He kissed her long and deep. *"Agape mou."*

Her body quickened. "You just said you loved me in Greek."

"I've never told another woman I was in love with her, but I wanted to tell you that first night. I wanted you to hear me tell you in your own language first. Don't you think it's time I learned it? We want our son or daughter to be equally at home in both languages, don't we?"

"Oh, yes—" she cried softly, covering his face with kisses. "I'll teach you and Dino together. We're going to have the most wonderful life!" Her emotions burst their bonds and she broke down in joyful sobs. "I love you, Vincenzo. I love our baby. I love Dino. No woman in this world could be as happy as I am at this moment."

"Nor man," he said against her lips. "Today feels like the first day of life. Our lives." Vincenzo became serious for a moment as he looked deep into her eyes. "Irena, I'm sorry I was so distant before. The thought of anything happening to you or the baby filled me with fear. You have both become the most important things in my life and to lose you... I don't think I could have coped. I also feared that if the baby was Andreas's then the turmoil of visitation might destroy you. I felt helpless, for the first time in my life." He kissed her then and the kiss grew into something deep and intense, robbing them both of their breath.

"That's why we can't stay on this bed any longer. I don't trust myself not to make love to you."

"I don't want to do anything to hurt our baby, either, so I'll get up and we'll go in the other room to enjoy that fabulous breakfast you made in celebration of this incredible day."

"And while we do that—" He nibbled on her earlobe. "You phone the one person who needs to know our news. Then we're going to relax around here all day while I feed you chocolate bocci balls and we think up names."

"That sounds wonderful." She kissed his hard jaw. "And start planning a nursery."

"Did I tell you Papa has insisted that we live at the palazzo with him and Silviana? I agreed at the time to placate him, but have no intention of following through."

Irena shifted positions so she could look down at him. "Why not?"

He traced the line of her mouth with his finger. "You

know why, *bellisima*. We're both free spirits. I want our baby to be one, too, and I'm doing all I can to turn Dino into one."

"But what would it hurt for a little while? We'll keep the apartment and go back and forth. Your father might not have long left. Don't you think he made it a demand because deep down he was afraid you'd never come of your own free will?"

She kissed his mouth. "I think it's his way of trying to make up for the years you were estranged. Dino likes it there. Would it be so impossible for you? I know you love your father."

His hand tightened in her hair. Emotion had turned his eyes a deeper blue. "What did I ever do to deserve you?"

"I've asked that same question about you since the day you took me on that picnic. Beneath the tower you pelted me with flowers, like a knight might have done to his lady centuries before. I felt enchanted. You had enchanted me. Now that I'm carrying your baby, nothing could ever thrill me more. I don't care where we live as long as I'm with you."

"Irena—" He crushed her to him one more time. With reluctance he finally got to his feet and pulled her up with him. Arm in arm they left the bedroom and walked to the kitchen. Vincenzo handed her the phone.

Shaking with excitement, she called her friend. It was Saturday morning. She could be in Athens or on Milos. *Pick up, Deline.*

After six rings: "Irena?"

She put it on speaker for Vincenzo. "Yes! Where are you?"

"On the boat with Leon and the twins."

"Good. I have news you're both going to want to hear." Irena's gaze had fused with her husband's. His eyes were suspiciously bright. "Vincenzo is the father of my baby!"

Her friend's cry of happiness was so loud, it hurt their eardrums. She was already shouting the news to Leon.

Irena could hardly talk she was so full of emotion. "We're expecting a little Valescchi in about six and a half months. You'll have to come to La Spezia when we have it christened at the church. You'll stay at the palazzo with us, of course. Love you. *Ciao* for now."

She clicked off before clutching Vincenzo to her. "I love you. I love you so much you're going to get sick of hearing me say it."

"I'll get sick if you don't. Hand me the phone. I've got a phone call I'd like to make."

Irena was trembling so hard, she had to cling to her husband while he pressed the digits. He put the phone on speaker and all of a sudden she could hear her mother answer. Vincenzo asked her to put Irena's father on, too. He joined within seconds.

"We've been wondering when we'd hear from you two."

Vincenzo smiled down at her. "As you know, your brilliant daughter has been helping me get the company back on track, but we've taken three days off to celebrate and wanted you to do it with us since you're going to be grandparents in about six and half months."

"You're pregnant? Our little girl's pregnant!" her mother almost shrieked with joy.

"This is wonderful." Her father sounded all choked up.

"Irena will call you later and give you all the details. Right now we have to inform my father and his wife."

"Another little duke perhaps?"

"Or duchess," Irena teased, knowing full well how Vincenzo felt about that, but it never hurt to placate the parents while they were so delighted. "But don't you dare print anything yet!"

Her father roared with laughter before clicking off.

After Vincenzo hung up, she kissed him hungrily once more. "You're going to be the most wonderful father. Do you want a boy or a girl? Do you realize in all this time we haven't talked about that?"

He'd buried his face in her hair. "I don't care."

"Neither do I."

"Give me your mouth, Irena. It's life to me."

"I will after we call your father. Let me tell him. We've begun to be friends."

"I know. He's secretly crazy about you, but then, so am I. I'm hopelessly in love, *squisita.*"

Six and a half months later

"The head's crowning, Irena. Your baby's coming. One more push. You can do it."

"Come on, *cara,*" Vincenzo coached her.

Another push and she heard a gurgling sound

followed by an infant cry. She watched Dr. Santi hold the baby up before laying it across her stomach.

"You've got a sweet little girl here. She has a perfect set of lungs. Go ahead and cut the cord, Vincenzo."

Her husband, in gown and mask, appeared to have nerves of steel as he did the honors, but she knew deep inside he'd been terrified of anything going wrong.

In another minute the pediatrician took over and examined her. Once he'd cleaned her up, he put her in a blanket for Irena to hold. He glanced at Vincenzo. "She has her papa's eyes. They're already turning blue."

Irena sent her husband a secret smile. No one could know what those words meant to Vincenzo. He really was her papa.

"Everything looks terrific, Signora Valsecchi. She's eight pounds, and nineteen and a half inches long."

"Oh, darling—I can't believe she's here! Our baby at last!" Tears streamed down her face. When she looked up at him again, his were wet, too.

"She's perfect," he whispered in absolute wonder.

"She has the Valsecchi profile, just like Dino's."

"She's gorgeous, just like her mother."

"It doesn't seem possible we're holding our own baby." Irena couldn't believe how exquisite she was. She had tiny, feminine fingers and nails. But Irena saw other parts that belonged to her handsome daddy in the shape of her kissable mouth and head.

Vincenzo let out the joyous, uninhibited laughter of a happy, relieved father who no longer had to worry that the test done at ten weeks had harmed their baby in any way. The last shadow hanging over their marriage had just gone poof!

Guilio poked his head inside the door of her room, eyeing her with a smile. "Can people come in yet? Dino can't wait much longer."

"Of course," Irena told him, but Vincenzo asked his father to wait outside for a few more minutes. He was still examining their daughter with infinite care.

"You can't ask him to wait forever, darling."

"There's a whole crowd out there, Irena," he grumbled. "I don't think it's a good idea to let everyone in yet."

"But they want to see our baby."

"So do I," he said a little gruffly. "I'll let them in when I think you and Alessandra are ready and not before."

Whoa. She'd never seen him quite like this before. Another new aspect for her to love.

He pulled his mask off. "Are you all right? After what you've been through, I don't know how you could be so calm and look so beautiful." He brushed her lips with his own.

Irena adored this marvelous husband and kissed him back more thoroughly than he'd expected. "I'm not a fragile invalid," she whispered.

"Dr. Santi has put me in a bad mood. She said we have to wait six weeks."

"But I feel so wonderful I don't see why we'll have to wait that long. Do you?" The hungry kiss she gave him seemed to have done the trick. It was one of her wifely secrets that always worked because it had managed to put a gleam in his eye. For a little while she'd feared it had disappeared for a long time.

"We'll see," he teased. Then more forcefully said, "I

love you. You know that. If anything had happened to you…"

"But it didn't. Remember that I love you. And let Dino in. He's been waiting and waiting with your father. I don't ever want him to feel excluded."

"Neither do I." He walked over to the door. "One at a time, everyone. Dino first."

Taking hold of his father's hand, he walked gingerly toward the bed. She put out her arm. "I'm so glad you're here, Dino. I've missed you. Sit down in that chair and your father will let you hold your new little sister."

After Vincenzo took their precious bundle and placed it in his boy's lap, Dino studied the baby's face and hands for a long time.

"What do you think?" his father asked.

"She doesn't have any hair."

Irena laughed. "She will. My mother told me I was bald when I was born. Look at me now."

That brought a smile to his face. "Papa says he loves your hair."

"Is that true, *esposo mio?*"

For the first time since she'd known him, she believed he actually blushed.

"How soon will Alessandra be able to walk?"

Irena had to think. "Maybe a year."

"Nine months!" Vincenzo said in his authoritative voice.

She shot her husband a mischievous smile. "Do you know something that I don't?"

"She's a Valsecchi and therefore is already advanced for her age."

"Was I advanced, Papa?"

"Naturally," sounded another voice. Guilio and Silviana had come into the room. The old man's eyes were glazed with moisture as he bent over the newest arrival to the Valsecchi clan. He eventually lifted his head. Looking from one to the other he said, "You two do good work, both in and out of the office."

That was one compliment Irena would always hug to her heart. He patted Vincenzo on the shoulder. With a gorgeous nursery all decked out at the palazzo, the two of them had come a long way since the end of their estrangement.

"For a man who never jokes, that was pretty good, Papa."

"Do you want to hold her, Grandpa?"

"No, no. You're doing a fine job."

"Darling?" Irena whispered to her husband. "I can hear my mother's voice outside. I was afraid their flight would never get here. Tell them to come in."

The next few minutes were a blur as Irena's parents swept in the room with gifts and hugs. Both were beaming. They adored Vincenzo and Dino. Now they were ready to shower their love on their only grandchild.

Alessandra got passed around so much, it was worrying Vincenzo again, but she begged him to let his uncles and aunts have their turn first. Soon the whole place sounded like a party until the nurse came in and ushered everyone out.

Irena had to admit she was exhausted. She squeezed Dino's hand and asked him to come back later. The next time she awakened, the nurse came in with the baby to help her start nursing. Then she fell back to sleep again.

This time when she opened her eyes, she was surrounded by at least a dozen bouquets placed on countertops and carts. Just as she was wondering where her husband had gone, Vincenzo walked in the room with a vase of three dozen long-stemmed red roses. She let out a cry. "They're glorious!"

"Just like you." He set them on her side table.

"Vincenzo—"

"Quick, before our baby comes back." He kissed her long and passionately. When he finally lifted his head he said, "I've been needing that."

"So have I. Have you been with our daughter?"

"I spent part of the time in the nursery so I could bathe her. Dino watched through the glass. Afterward I took him for a meal in the cafeteria."

"Good. What does he think about all this?"

"He says he's going to tell his mother he has to come here more often because you're going to need help with the baby. He loves you, *tesoro*."

"The feeling's mutual."

"Dino's staying with my father and Silviana tonight so I can be here with you. Tomorrow if you're released, we'll all go home together."

"I'm too happy." She glanced around. "I can't believe all these flowers. Such an outpouring. Even from Fabbio."

"You've made a lot of friends and won him over too since you became my cochair. Later I'll give you the cards to look at, but there's a sealed note meant for you in one of the bouquets. Would you like to read it now?"

Obviously it was important to her husband that she did. As tired as she was she said yes.

He handed her the envelope. Inside was a florist card that read Congratulations from Andreas and Gabi. She broke the seal on the paper and opened it. Andreas had penned a message.

Dear Irena—

When Leon told me you'd married the man of your dreams and were expecting his child, I realized that the same thing that happened to me had happened to you. Fate had something wonderful in store for both of us that neither of us could have foreseen when we started down our path together. If you're feeling like I am, you've thrown off any residual guilt for unintentional hurt we might have caused each other.

Gabi and I are expecting a baby in three months. My joy is beyond words. What makes me so happy is that I know yours is, too. I'm anxious to meet Vincenzo. He has to be someone exceptional to have won you heart and soul. In the years to come, our paths will cross often, something I'll always look forward to.

Andreas.

Wordlessly, she handed it to her husband for him to read. She watched him pore over it several times. After a few minutes she heard him say, "He's not called the great Simonides for nothing, is he?"

She stared at the man she worshipped. "I love you, Vincenzo," she cried emotionally. "Come here."

* * * * *

ONE-NIGHT PREGNANCY
LINDSAY ARMSTRONG

Lindsay Armstrong was born in South Africa, but now lives in Australia with her New Zealand-born husband and their five children. They have lived in nearly every state of Australia and have tried their hand at some unusual—for them—occupations, such as farming and horse-training—all grist to the mill for a writer! Lindsay started writing romances when their youngest child began school and she was left feeling at a loose end. She is still doing it and loving it.

CHAPTER ONE

IT WAS a filthy night in the Gold Coast hinterland.

It hadn't started out as such, but severe summer storms were not unknown in the area and this series had sped across the escarpment, taking even the weather bureau by surprise. Rain was teeming down, and gusts of wind buffeted Bridget Tully-Smith's car. The ribbon of winding, narrow road between the dark peaks of the Numinbah Valley disappeared regularly as the windscreen wipers squelched back and forth, revealing and concealing.

She'd been staying with a married friend who had a hobby farm and was breeding, of all things, llamas. It had been an enjoyable weekend. Her friend had a young baby, a devoted husband, and their particular patch of the Numinbah Valley was wonderfully rural.

It should have been only an hour's drive back to the Gold Coast, but as the darkness drew in and the storms hit, somehow or other she got lost. Somehow or other she found herself on a secondary road, little more than a track, just as the rain became torrential—as if the heavens above had opened and were literally hell-bent on deluging the area.

Then she came round a bend to a concrete causeway-style bridge, or what had probably been one but was now a raging torrent, cutting the road in two. It came upon her so suddenly she had no choice but to brake sharply—and that very nearly proved to be her un-doing.

The back of her car fishtailed, and she felt the tug of the creek water on it, more powerful than the brakes or the handbrake. In perhaps the quickest-thinking moment of her life, she leapt out of the car as the back of it was slowly pushed to midstream, and scrabbled with all her might to attain higher ground.

She found a gravelly hillock supporting a young gum tree, and clung to it as she watched in horrified disbelief. Her car straightened, with its nose pointing upstream and its headlights illuminating the scene, then floated backwards downstream until it was obscured from view.

'I don't believe this,' she whispered shakily to her-self. She tensed as above the wind and the drumming rain she heard an engine, and realised a vehicle was coming from the opposite direction—and coming fast.

Did they know the road? Did they think speed would get them over the bridge? Did they have a four-wheel drive? All these questions flashed through her mind, but she knew she couldn't take a risk on any or all of those factors. She must warn them.

She abandoned her tree and ran out into the middle of the road, jumping up and down and waving her arms.

She was wearing a red-and-white fine gingham blouse, and she prayed it would stand out—though she knew her loose beige three-quarter-length pedal-pushers would not; they were plastered with mud.

Perhaps nothing, she thought later, would have averted the disaster that then took place. The vehicle was coming too fast. It didn't even brake. But as it hit the torrent raging over the bridge, just as had happened to her car, the back fishtailed, the stream got it, and it too was swept away at a dangerous angle.

Bridget winced and put a hand to her mouth, because she could see faces at the windows of the vehicle, some of them children, and there were childish cries as windows were wound down, one piercing scream. Then the car disappeared from sight.

She sobbed once and forced herself to examine her options, but they were pitifully few—actually she had none, she conceded, other than to try to reach the car on foot. Her mobile phone was sitting in her car…

But another vehicle suddenly appeared around the bend behind her, and this one managed to stop without skidding, well clear of the torrent.

'Oh, thank heavens,' she breathed as she started to run towards it, slipping and slithering up the muddy road.

A man jumped out before she got to it, tall, in jeans and boots and rain jacket.

He got the first words in. 'What the hell's going on? What are you doing out in this?'

Bridget tried to catch her breath, but it was a panting, emotional explanation she gave. She finished by saying passionately, 'There were children in the car! They'd have no hope against a torrent that can wash away cars. Have you got a phone? Mine's in the car. We need to alert—'

He shook his head.

'What kind of a person doesn't have a mobile phone these days?' Bridget demanded thinly. She was feeling thoroughly overwrought by now.

'I've got a phone. I've got no signal, though. The country's too rugged.'

'Then—' she wiped the rain out of her eyes '—should I drive your car back to get help while you see what you can do here?'

He shook his head.

She jumped up and down in exasperation. 'Don't keep knocking all my suggestions on the head—*why* not?'

The stranger took a very brief moment to examine her sodden, highly emotional presence. 'I'm not—' he began.

'Yes, you are!'

'You wouldn't get through,' he said precisely. 'There's a rock fall, and a washaway over the road a couple of kilometres back. It happened just after I passed.'

He stopped to open the back of the rather elderly Land Rover he was driving. 'So I'll go and see what I can do.' He pulled out a hank of rope, a knife in a leather holder that he clipped to his belt, a small axe and a waterproof torch.

'Oh, thank heavens— I'll come.'

'Nope. You stay here.'

'Mister!'

He turned to her impatiently. 'The last thing I need

is a hysterical slip of a girl to worry about. I only have one waterproof, that I happen to be wearing—'

'What does that matter?' she interrupted. 'I could hardly get wetter! And—' Bridget drew herself up to her full height: five feet two '—I'm not a hysterical slip of a girl! Let's go!'

Had it been doomed from the start, their rescue mission? She sometimes wondered. They certainly gave it their all. But climbing their way downstream beside the swollen creek, in pouring rain, with bushes and small trees whipping in the sudden gusts of wind, was not only heartbreakingly slow, it was exhausting.

It was also bruising and scraping, and before long, with still no sign of the car or any of its occupants, all her muscles ached.

That might have accounted for her slipping suddenly and getting herself caught up on an old piece of fence line at the edge of the creek. Somehow a piece of wire slipped into the belt loop of her pants, and she couldn't free herself however much she wriggled.

'Take them off!' the man yelled, and flashed his torch behind her. She looked backwards over her shoulder, and nearly died to see a dirty wall of water coming down towards her.

She didn't give it a second thought. She squirmed out of her pants, but the water caught her and she'd have been washed downstream if her companion hadn't leapt in beside her, managed to tie the rope around her waist and somehow drag and half-carry her to relative safety.

'Oh, thank you! You probably saved my life,' she panted.

He didn't reply to that. 'We've got to get higher. Keep going,' he ordered.

She kept going. They both kept going—until, when her lungs and her heart felt like bursting, he finally called a halt.

'Here—in here,' he said, and flashed the torch around. 'Looks like a cave.'

It *was* a cave, with rocky walls, a dirt floor and an overhang overgrown with dripping bushes and grass. Bridget collapsed on the floor.

When her panting had subsided a bit, she said with irony, 'Looks like the rescuers will have to be rescued.'

'It's often the way,' he replied, and set the torch on a ledge of rock.

Bridget sat up and looked around tentatively. She wasn't all that keen on small spaces, but the thought of what lay outside outweighed her tendency towards claustrophobia.

For the first time her partially unclothed state struck her. She looked down at her bare legs, then realised her blouse was torn and showing parts of her blameless pink lace and silk bra. It was also muddy and torn.

She looked up and discovered her rescuer on his knees, looking down at the dripping, twisted, half-clad length of her with a little glint of admiration in his amazing blue eyes—it was the first time she'd noticed them.

But just as she felt like squirming in embarrassment he looked away abruptly and started to undress himself.

She watched him in startled suspended animation as he ripped off his waterproof jacket, then his long-sleeved plaid shirt, revealing a tanned, muscular chest sprinkled with dark hairs and a pair of powerful shoulders. For a moment her eyes rounded in admiration of her own, then she swallowed with a strange little squawk of sound—a squawk of unwitting apprehension.

He said, matter-of-factly, 'I'm Adam, by the way. Why don't you take your blouse off and put my shirt on? It's relatively dry. I'll look the other way.' He tossed the shirt into her lap and did as he'd promised.

Bridget fingered the shirt. It *was* mostly dry, and it emitted a reassuringly masculine odour of sweat and cotton. It would be heaven—not only as a cover for the deficiencies of her attire, but also because she was starting to shiver with cold.

She pulled her blouse off, and her soaked bra, and slipped into his shirt as quickly as possible, buttoning it with shaky fingers. It was way too big for her, but although the sleeves hung over her hands, the length made her feel at least halfway decent. 'Thank you. Thank you! But will you be all right? I'm decent, incidentally.'

He turned back and pulled his rain jacket on again. 'I'll be fine.' He sat down. 'Not going to return the compliment namewise?'

'Oh, yes! I'm Bridget Smith.' She often used only the second half of her famous double-barrelled surname. 'Oh, no!' She put her hand to her mouth and her eyes darkened with concern as, for the first time since the car with the children had been washed away, she thought suddenly of her own plight. 'My car!'

'Your car will be found,' he said. 'I'm not sure in what condition, but once the waters recede—and they will—it will be somewhere.'

'Do you really think so? My windows were all closed but I didn't have time to lock it—my whole life is in my car!' she said, on a suddenly urgent little note.

He raised an eyebrow at her.

'My phone, my credit cards, my driver's licence, my keys, my Medicare card, not to mention the car itself.' She stopped helplessly.

'They can all be replaced or, in the case of credit cards, stopped.'

Bridget subsided, but her expression remained doomed.

'I take it it's Miss Smith?' he queried.

She shrugged. 'Not necessarily.' Her thoughts returned to her car.

'You're not wearing a wedding ring,' he pointed out.

Bridget hesitated, and stopped looking down the barrel of the chaos in her life if she didn't retrieve her car to look rather intently at the man she was trapped in a cave with.

Then she fished beneath his plaid shirt and pulled out the gold chain she wore around her neck. There was a plain gold wedding ring threaded onto it.

'I see—but why don't you wear it on your finger?' he queried.

Bridget blinked, and wondered how she could assess this man. Because, however good-looking, beautifully built and strong he was, the fact remained that she didn't know him—and one could never be too careful, could one? So it mightn't be a bad idea to have a husband in the wings…

'I've lost a bit of weight and it's just a little big.' The last part was true enough.

'So what's he like? Mr Smith?'

Was it just a casual query? Bridget wondered. To take her mind off the traumatic events surrounding them? Or had he doubted her?

'Actually, he's rather lovely, as Mr Smiths go,' she said lightly, and it was the invention flowing off her tongue so smoothly that caused her to smile apprecia-tively—not, she thought swiftly, that he would know it. 'He's tall, probably even a bit taller than you,' she con-tinued. 'And he strips to great advantage.' She stopped and asked herself where the hell that particular phrase had sprung to her mind from? A Regency novel? 'Uh…' She soldiered on. 'And of course he's devoted to me.'

'Of course.' A smile appeared fleetingly in those smoky blue eyes—a smile of genuine amusement that, all the same, made her uneasy for some reason. 'Does that mean to say,' he went on, 'he's waiting for you? At home, perhaps?'

'Oh, definitely,' Bridget lied with abandon.

'That's comforting to know. So when you don't show up, and you don't ring, he's liable to call the police, who in turn are liable to get onto the Emergency Services when they realise *you're* liable to be caught up in this situation?'

'Ah.' A tinge of pink coloured Bridget's dirty cheeks. 'Well, no. Not exactly. I was speaking more generally. He's—he's out of town at the moment. But only on a business trip—and—and—he'll be home tomorrow. Definitely. Or maybe the next day.'

Adam studied her. Her short cap of hair was a coppery bronze, and not even an extremely arduous hike through rocky, sodden terrain had been able to dim her sparkling green eyes, he reflected, and smiled inwardly. They were also very revealing eyes, and from the turmoil they'd revealed as a variety of emotions had chased through them he was fairly sure she was lying. But if she'd chosen to invent a husband, *why* had she?

He narrowed his eyes on the obvious answer. Never trust strange men. Of course. So Bridget Smith was a cautious girl, even on a night like tonight. Well, he'd go along with it if it made her feel safer…

'But hang on!' Bridget stopped looking guilty. 'The friends I was staying with—they'll probably worry and try to ring me. They wanted me to stay overnight, but I've got an early start tomorrow so…' She looked rueful. 'They might alert someone when they can't get me.'

'OK.' He shrugged and got to his knees. 'I'm going out to reconnoitre. If the water's still rising we may have to move again.'

The water *was* still rising, but not quite as fast.

'I think we can relax for a bit,' he said as he crawled back into the cave. 'The fact that it's not rising so fast may mean it's going to start falling soon.'

Bridget heaved a relieved sigh, but her relief was to be short-lived because there was an almighty crack of sound and something—a tree, they realised moments later—fell down the hillside from above, blocking the entrance to the cave.

She turned convulsively to Adam, her eyes wide and dark with fear. 'We're trapped,' she whispered.

'Trapped? Me?' he replied with a ghost of a smile. 'Don't you believe it, Mrs Smith.'

'But all you have is a small axe and a knife!' she objected.

'You'd be amazed at what I can do with 'em.'

'Are you—are you an axeman?' Bridget asked. 'Like those wood-chopping men you see at country shows?'

For some reason this question seemed to take him by surprise. Then his wide-eyed look was replaced by one of ironic amusement, and he responded with a question of his own. 'Do I look like one?'

'Not really. You look like—well, you could be anything.' She smiled anxiously. 'I didn't mean to be offensive—I think I'll just shut up.'

'Might be a good idea to save our breath,' he murmured, 'for what lies ahead. But, really, you have no need to worry about me. Nor would Mr Smith.'

'Thank you,' she said, but there was a question mark in those green eyes. As if she suspected she was being teased.

He waited for her to retaliate, but she dropped her lashes suddenly and folded her hands primly in her lap.

He was tempted to laugh, but reminded himself in time that, despite his assurance to the contrary, they *were* actually trapped in a cave by a tree at the moment.

* * *

An hour later they were free.

An hour during which Adam had used a combination of pure strength, some chopping, some manipulation with his rope, some propping with rocks and the sturdy axe to move the tree.

'I don't know how you did it!' Bridget gasped as the tree rolled away. 'You're actually amazing!'

'Leverage,' he replied, 'is what's amazing. One should always have a good understanding of levers and leverage.'

'I'll certainly put that on my list of things to learn—oh!' He'd swung the torch over the view from the mouth of the cave, and it wasn't a reassuring sight.

'Yes,' he agreed grimly. 'The water's still rising. OK, Bridget, we need to get out and up as fast as we can. Put the rope around your waist. That way we'll stay together. I'll go first. Ready?'

She nodded.

The next interlude, and Bridget had no idea how long it took, was sheer torture. The land above the cave rose steeply and was strewn with rocks. It was also slippery, but she followed Adam up the hillside doggedly, although at times it was a one step forward, two steps back kind of progress.

At one point she had to stop because of a burning stitch in her side, and she fell over once. Only the rope stopped her from cartwheeling down the incline.

Fortunately they were level with each other, and she caught sight out of the corner of her eye, during the regular sweep of his torch, of a rock he didn't see. A rock that looked to be teetering dangerously, directly above them. With a high-pitched yell, she cannoned into him, catching him off-balance and pushing him with all her might. They rolled away only inches from where the rock passed on its deadly way down the hillside.

Just as she felt she could go no further, they reached some flat ground, a grassy little plateau, and another sweep of the torch revealed a shed below the hillside, at the far end of it.

'Oh, thank heavens,' she breathed, but sank to her knees in utter exhaustion. 'I just need—a—little break, though. Not long,' she assured her companion, her voice coming in great gasps.

He came to stand over her and shone the torch down on her. She couldn't read his expression. She couldn't actually think straight, she just did as she was told.

'You hold this,' he said, and gave her the torch. She took it, and was completely unprepared to be hoisted to her feet and then up into his arms.

'But—but—what are you doing?' she stammered as he started to walk. 'I really—'

'Shut up, Mrs Smith,' he recommended. 'You've actually been rather amazing yourself, and you probably saved *my* life. It's the least I can do. Would you mind directing the torchlight forward?'

Bridget hastily repositioned the torch so he could see where he was going, and unwittingly began to relax. More than that, she had to admit to herself that it was heaven. His arms felt amazingly strong; she felt amazingly safe. And she had seriously to doubt she could have covered the remaining ground on her own two feet, because she felt as weak as a kitten.

They reached the shed.

'It's locked,' he said as he put her down. 'But on a night like tonight, and since we're not here to rob anyone, I don't suppose they'd mind if we do this.' And with a single stroke of the axe, pulled from his belt, he broke the padlock.

'Yes, well.' Bridget blinked a little dazedly. 'You're probably right. And we can always replace things.'

He looked down at her with a faint smile. 'We can, indeed. After you, ma'am.'

Bridget shuffled into the shed and made a sound of heartfelt approval at what she saw. In fact she discovered herself to be feeling a lot less sandbagged as she looked around.

It was an old shed, and didn't look particularly solid, but there were bales of straw stacked high against one wall, a double bed against another. There were some paraffin lamps, hanging on hooks, a kettle and a primus stove, some chipped mugs and a tea caddy standing on an upturned tea chest. There were racks of neatly sorted horse gear: headstalls, bridles, saddles and brushes. Three old thin towels hung on a railing, along with two light horse rugs.

There was also a wood-burning stove, with a chimney going through the roof. It was packed with paper and billets of wood.

'Glory be,' Adam remarked. He raised his voice against

the drumming of rain on the tin roof. 'In these conditions you could call this place the Numinbah Hilton.'

Bridget chuckled. Then she sobered. 'Those children—' she began.

'Bridget.' He turned to look down at her. 'We did our best. It's a small miracle we weren't drowned in the process. They will be fine, riding it out somehow. Just hold onto that thought.'

'But I was wondering—there must be a road to here, and maybe we could go for help.'

'I had the same thought,' he said. 'Do you have any idea where we are?'

'Well, no, but—'

'Neither do I,' he broke in. 'In fact I'm thoroughly disorientated after all the twists and turns that creek took. We could get even more hopelessly lost, whereas in the daylight this could be a good point of reference. We may even be able to flag a passing helicopter. There's bound to be some State Emergency Services scouting the area after a storm like this. But, listen, just in case there's a house attached to this paddock and shed, I am going to scout around a bit. As for you—' he scanned the dirty, sopping length of her '—first of all, do you have any sprains, strains, fractures or the like?'

Her eyes widened. 'No, I don't think so. Just a few bruises and scrapes.'

'OK—now, you may not approve of this suggestion, but it's an order, actually, and you can hold it against me as much as you like.' For a moment there was a rather mercilessly teasing glint in his eyes.

She stiffened her spine against that glint. 'What order?' she asked with hauteur.

He studied her tilted chin and smiled briefly. 'I don't know if you noticed a tank at the corner of the shed, collecting rainwater from the roof?'

She shook her head.

'Well, it's there, and it's overflowing. After I've gone, go out, take your clothes off, and stand under the overflow pipe. Wash all the mud, blood and whatever off yourself, then stand under the water for a couple of minutes. Do your bruises a world of good. But I'll get the fire going first.' He turned away.

'I—' she started to say mutinously.

'Bridget,' he returned dangerously over his shoulder, 'don't argue.'

'But I've got nothing to wear!'

'Yes, you have.' He pointed to one of the railings. 'You can wrap yourself in one of those horse rugs.'

He did get the fire *and* three paraffin lamps going before he left.

'Take care,' she said. 'I—I'm not too keen about being left on my own here. Naturally I wouldn't want anything to happen to you, either.' She grimaced. 'That sounds like an afterthought if ever I heard one! But I do mean it.'

He inclined his head and hid the smile in his eyes. 'Thank you. I won't be going too far. Not only because I don't want to get lost, but also because I don't want the torch to run out on me.' He touched her casually on the cheek with his fingertips. 'You take care too.'

She watched him walk out of the shed into the rain-swept night and swallowed back the cry that rose in her throat—the urge to tell him she'd go with him. Swallowed it because she knew that her brief resurgence of energy, such as it was, would not survive.

So she forced herself to examine his suggestion—or order. She looked down at herself. She was a mess of mud, his shirt was caked with it, and below her legs were liberally streaked with it.

It made sense, in other words, to get clean. If only she had something else to wear afterwards other than a horse rug...

It was like the answer to a prayer. Some instinct prompted her to look under the pillows on the bed, and she discovered a clean pair of yellow flannelette pyjamas patterned with blue teddy bears.

Under the second pillow was a pair of men's track-suit pants and a white T-shirt.

'You beauty!' she breathed. 'Not only can I be comfortable overnight, but I won't have to be rescued wearing a horse rug. And not only *that*, my fellow traveller can be decent and dry too—which is important, I'm sure. OK. Onward to the shower, Mrs Smith!' And she marched out of the shed.

It was a weird experience, showering beneath an overflow pipe in the middle of the night, in the middle of a deluge, in the altogether, even though there was a brief lull in the rain.

She took a lamp with her, and found a hook on the

shed wall for it. It illuminated the scene, and she could see a huge gum tree on the hill behind the shed, plus the ruins of some old stone structure.

Definitely weird, she decided as the water streamed down her body, and freezing as well. But at least the tank stood on a concrete pad, and there was a concrete path to it from the shed door. She'd also discovered a bucket tucked behind the tank, with a piece of soap and a nailbrush in it.

Did someone make a habit of showering from the rainwater tank? she wondered. Not that it would always be overflowing, but it had a tap. Maybe they filled the bucket from the tap and poured it over themselves?

She didn't stay around much longer to ponder the mysteries of the rainwater tank, but skipped inside and dried herself off in front of the fire. Then she examined herself, and, satisfied she would find no serious cuts, donned the teddy bear pyjamas.

'Sorry,' she murmured to the owner of the pyjamas. 'I'll get you a new pair!'

And then she turned her attention to the primus stove and the possibility—the heavenly possibility—of making a cup of tea.

Adam came back just as she was sipping strong black tea from one of the chipped mugs.

'I've just made some tea. I'll get you some. Any luck?'

He peeled off his waterproof. 'No—where did you get those?' He eyed the yellow pyjamas patterned with blue teddy bears.

She explained, and pointed out the track pants and

T-shirt. 'You know, I can't help wondering if someone lives here at times.' She poured bubbling water onto a teabag in the second mug and handed it to him.

'I think you could be right—thanks. There's no house nearby, but there's evidence of some foundations. They're probably using the shed while they build the house. The driveway leads to a dirt road—it's now deep mud—with a locked gate.'

'There may be horses out there—maybe fenced in.'

'I hope there are, so long as they're safe. The owners may come to check them out.' He put his cup down. 'You obviously took up my suggestion?' He inspected her clean, shiny face.

'I thought it was an order.'

His lips twisted. 'What was it like?'

'Weird,' she said with feeling. 'But if I could do it, so could you.'

'Just going, Mrs Smith,' he murmured.

Bridget watched the shed door close behind him and found herself standing in the same spot, still staring at the door a good minute later, as she visualised the man called Adam showering as she had done beneath the rainwater tank overflow. It was not hard to visualise his powerful body naked, that fine physique sleek with water...

She blushed suddenly, and moved precipitately— only to trip. She righted herself and castigated herself mentally. Anyone would think she was a silly, star-struck schoolgirl! All right, yes, she might have come out in sudden goosebumps, but at twenty-three surely she had the maturity to recognise it as a purely physical reaction to a dangerously attractive man? Besides which, she was allergic to dangerously attractive men who turned out to be less than likeable—wasn't she?

All the same, when Adam came back from showering wrapped in a towel, and she turned away while he dried himself in front of the fire and donned the track pants and T-shirt, she was aware of him again in her mind's eye. In a way that again raised goosebumps on her skin and caused her to feel a little hot.

Stop it, Bridget, she commanded herself.

An hour or so later another heavy storm broke overhead.

It was close to midnight.

Adam and Bridget were dozing side by side on the double bed when lightning illuminated the shed and a boom of thunder reverberated directly overhead, or so it seemed. Bridget woke and rolled towards Adam with a little cry of fear. He put his arms around her, but she started to shake with barely suppressed sobs.

'It's only another storm,' he said, and stroked her hair.

'I know,' she wept, 'but haven't we been through enough? And I can't stop thinking about those kids out there in this!'

'Hush… Listen, I'm going to put some more wood on the fire. Then I'll be right back.'

He was as good as his word, and when he came back, as if it was the most natural thing in the world, he piled the pillows up behind them and pulled her loosely into his arms. 'Tell me about yourself, Bridget. What do you do? Where were you born? What do your parents do?'

'I work in a television newsroom. At the moment I'm everyone's gofer, but I'm hoping for better things.'

She shuddered as another crack of thunder tore the night but soldiered on.

'I was born in Brisbane. My father died in an accident a few years ago, and my mother has remarried. She lives overseas at the moment. I did a BA at Queensland University, majoring in journalism. My father was a journalist, so I guess that's where I get it from.' She paused to consider for a moment.

She did enjoy her job, but *had* she inherited her father's passion for journalism? She sometimes stopped to wonder whether it had been her admiration for her father that had moved her to pursue the same career rather than a deep, abiding feel for it. She often found herself feeling restless, and as if she'd prefer to be doing something else—but what?

Adam broke the silence and the train of her thoughts.

'Now for the question of Mr Smith.' He looked at her with suspicious gravity.

Bridget bit her lip. 'There is no Mr Smith. The ring…' She fingered the chain around her neck. 'It's my mother's, but since I didn't know you, it seemed a good idea to invent a husband.'

'I wondered about that.'

'Why? I mean how could you tell I was lying?'

He considered. 'You have very revealing eyes. It also sounded like pure invention.'

Bridget blushed faintly.

He traced the outline of her chin lightly. 'So, no romantic involvement at the moment?'

Perhaps it was the storm raging overhead, perhaps it was the reassuring warmth of his proximity, but for whatever reason Bridget found herself telling Adam things she'd not told another soul. Things to do with how she had fallen madly in love at twenty-one, how it had led to an affair—a first for her—and how it had been a disaster.

'He changed,' she said sadly. 'He became possessive, and yet...' she paused '...oddly critical of me. But that was probably because I didn't—well—I didn't seem to be very good at sex. I think a lot of that was to do with the fact that I would really rather have waited—until we'd got engaged at least.'

She heaved a heartfelt sigh and continued. 'I—it didn't take that long for me to discover I'd gone to bed with a man I didn't seem to like much. Oh, he was good-looking, and fun to be with, but...' She trailed off. 'He became rather scary when I broke it off.' She shrugged. 'All of which amounts to the fact that I haven't tried again—I don't know why I'm telling you all this.' She looked into Adam's blue eyes, now thoroughly red-faced.

'Maybe it needed to be told?' he suggested, and stroked her hair. Creep, he thought at the same time, but didn't say it. He did say, 'Things could be quite different with the right man.'

Bridget looked unconvinced, but didn't pursue it. 'Why did I talk about it now, though?'

He stretched out his legs and pulled the one blanket

around them. 'It's been quite a night. Fear, stress, physical exertion, highs and lows, and now an almighty electrical storm.'

It's more than that, Bridget thought. There's something about this man that really appeals to me. He not only makes me feel safe, he makes me feel interested in him, as if I really want to get to know him and—

She stopped her thoughts there. And what? She was very conscious of him physically, she answered herself, and she just couldn't seem to help herself. Alive to all sorts of little things—like his hands. I love his hands, she decided suddenly. And the way his eyes can laugh, the way his hair falls in his eyes sometimes.

'Not only that,' he went on, and took his hand from her hair to rub his jaw ruefully, 'what it makes you, Mrs Smith, is simply very human. We all make mistakes and some dodgy judgements.'

Bridget thought for a moment, then said, 'I guess so.'

He grimaced at the lack of conviction in her voice. 'But there must be more to Bridget Smith.' He raised his voice as the thunder growled overhead. 'Tell me about your likes and dislikes. What makes you tick?'

'I'm very ordinary.' She paused and cast him a suddenly mischievous little look. 'Well, I do a lot of things fairly competently, but to date nothing outstandingly—although I'm living in hope that my true forte is still to make itself known.'

He laughed. 'What about all the things you do fairly well?'

'Let's see. I paint—at one stage I thought I might be

the next Margaret Olley, as I love painting flowers, but not so. I also like doing landscapes. I play the piano, but any hopes I would be the next Eileen Joyce were dashed early on. Mind you, I still enjoy doing both. I once thought I'd like to be a landscape gardener. My parents had a few acres and I loved pottering around the garden.'

She paused and thought. 'And I ride—I love horses. I don't have any of my own, although I did have a couple of ponies as a kid, and I help out at a riding school for disabled children. I seem to have a rapport with kids. Uh...I read all the time, I enjoy cooking, I enjoy being at home and pottering—oh, and I sing.'

'Professionally?' he queried.

She shook her head, her eyes dancing. 'No. I did believe I might be the next Sarah Brightman, but again not so. That doesn't stop me from singing in the shower and anywhere else I can manage it.'

'Sing for me.'

'Now?'

'Why not?'

So she sang a couple of bars of 'Memory', from *Cats*, in her light, sweet soprano. When she'd finished she confessed she was mad about musicals.

'You sound like a pretty well-rounded girl to me,' he said, with a ghost of a smile still lurking on his lips. 'In days gone by you would have had all the qualifications to be a genteel wife and mother.'

'That sounds really—unexciting,' she said with a gurgle of laughter. 'But it's probably in line with what one of my teachers told me. She said to me, *"You're not going to set the world on fire academically, Bridget, but you are a thoroughly nice girl.'"* She looked comically heavenwards. 'Unexciting, or what?'

'Oh, I don't know.' He grinned, and dropped a kiss on her forehead. 'It's nice to be nice, and I think you *are* nice.'

Bridget smiled back at him, unexpectedly warmed. Then a twinkle of humour lit her eyes. 'I showed her I wasn't such a disaster academically when I got to uni, and I got honours in a couple of subjects, but enough about me—tell me about you?'

His chiselled lips twisted. 'I wouldn't know where to begin.'

'Well, how old are you and where were you born? What do you do? That kind of thing.'

'I'm thirty-one—whereas you would be…twenty-two?'

'Twenty-three.'

'Twenty-three,' he repeated. 'I was born in Sydney. I've done many things. I'm also pretty keen on horses, but—' he raised his eyebrows '—since you ask, I'm something of a rolling stone.'

'You mean—no ties?' she hazarded.

'No ties,' he agreed.

'Did you get your fingers burnt by a woman once?'

For some reason that quiet question, uttered with a mix of wisdom and compassion, caught his attention fairly and squarely, and his remarkable blue gaze rested on Bridget thoughtfully for a long moment. 'You could say so.'

'Would you like to tell me?'

A little jolt of laughter shook him. 'No.'

Bridget faced him expressionlessly. Her hair had dried to a silky cap of copper-gold, brought to life by the firelight. Her eyes were greener in that same firelight. And, while the teddy bear pyjamas made her look about sixteen, there was, as the man called Adam knew, a perfect little figure beneath them, with high breasts, hips like perfect fruit and a slender waist.

She was also, he reflected, brave.

And no fool, he discovered, when she said, repeating what he'd said to her, 'But maybe it needs to be told?'

He pushed the blanket away and sat up beside her. The thunder was still growling, but it seemed to be moving away. The rain was still falling, but it was much lighter now. How did I get myself into this? he found himself wondering, and looked around somewhat ruefully, then down at the borrowed track pants and T-shirt he was wearing.

'I don't shock easily,' Bridget murmured. 'Did she run away with another man?'

He stared at her, and a muscle flickered in his jaw. Then he smiled, a wry little smile that didn't touch his eyes. 'How did you guess?'

'Well, with a woman involved, that's often how it goes. However…' Bridget paused, and wrinkled her brow. 'He must have had a lot more than you to offer *materially*, otherwise she must have been crazy!'

'Why?'

Bridget blinked and blushed. Then she grimaced inwardly and acknowledged that she'd allowed her tongue to run away with her. So, how to retrieve the situation with minimum embarrassment? Maybe just the truth…?

'You're pretty good-looking, you know. Not only that, you're amazingly resourceful, you're strong, and I couldn't think of anyone I would feel safer with.'

'Thank you,' Adam said gravely. 'None of that was enough to hold her, however. Although I have to admit the competition was quite stiff.'

Bridget frowned. 'But that makes her somewhat suspect, I would say, and maybe not worthy of too much regret?'

He waited impassively, and she tilted her head to one side enquiringly at him. Then he said, 'Have you quite finished, Mrs Smith?'

Bridget immediately looked immensely contrite. 'I'm so sorry,' she said softly. 'It still hurts a lot, I guess? Shall we change the subject?'

Adam swore as he rolled off the bed and went to put the kettle on the stove.

Bridget watched from the bed as he rinsed the mugs in a bucket. The paraffin lamplight softened the outlines of the piled-high bales of straw, but didn't pierce all the shadows in the shed. At least the worst of the storm had definitely moved away.

He spooned instant coffee into the cups and poured the boiling water in. 'Sugar?'

'One, thank you.' She hesitated. 'Look, I *am* sorry. I must have sounded unforgivably nosy.'

He shrugged and handed her a mug, then sat down on the floor beside the bed so he could lean back against it. 'At least it took your mind off the storm.'

'Yes. And I did tell you my life story, so I suppose I

was expecting something in return. We also saved each other's lives.'

There was silence, apart from the crackle of the stove and the now faraway thunder.

'She threw me over for my older brother,' he said. 'You're right. She's not worth it. But she—' He broke off. 'My brother is another matter, and one day he'll get his come-uppance.' He took a sip of coffee. 'Just a matter of finding the right lever.'

Bridget stared at his profile, her eyes wide and horrified—it looked as if it was carved in stone. She swallowed and said the only thing she could think of. 'You're hot on levers, aren't you?' Then, 'I don't think that's a very good idea. Much better for you to move on and—'

'Leave it, Bridget,' he warned, and flicked her a moody blue glance. 'Finish your coffee.'

'OK, I'm sorry,' she said contritely, and drank her coffee in silence.

He took the cup from her and placed it along with his on a ledge beside the bed. Then he climbed back in and took her in his arms again. 'Go to sleep,' he said, not unkindly.

Bridget relaxed and thought how good it felt. How reassuring, how warm and comfortable and natural, and she started to doze off.

Adam, on the other hand, found himself watching her in the firelight and wondering what it was about this girl that had prompted him to tell her things he'd never told anyone else.

Because she was entirely unthreatening? Because

she had no idea who he was? Yes, but there was more
to it than that. Rather, there was more to his feelings on
the subject of Bridget Smith, spinster, he thought wryly.

He felt protective of her, and he had to admire the
way she'd slogged through everything nature had
thrown at them, but, again, there was more.

As he watched her, he found himself wondering what
it would be like to make love to her. To part those pretty
pink lips that were twitching a little as she dozed—
what was she dreaming of?—and kiss her. What expressions would chase through her green eyes if he, very
slowly and gently, initiated her into the pleasures of sex
and wiped out the memories some oaf had left her with?

It would be no penance, he realised, and he felt his
body stir. It would be the opposite. She felt as if she'd
been made to fit into his arms, as if that tender little body
should be his property...

Then her eyelashes lifted, taking him by surprise, and
for a long frozen moment they stared into each other's
eyes. He held his breath as the expression in those green
eyes became an incredulous query, as if she'd divined
his thoughts.

But it was gone almost immediately, that expression,
dismissed with the faintest shake of her head, as if she'd
banished it to the realm of the impossible or as if it was
a dream, and she fell asleep again.

He released his breath slowly and smiled dryly.

No, it would not be impossible, Bridget Smith, he
thought, and nor was it a dream. But it was not going
to happen. For a whole host of reasons.

He lay for a while, listening to the rain on the roof, deliberately concentrating on it, and on the fact that it seemed to be getting lighter. But in fact the night hadn't finished with them…

CHAPTER TWO

AT ABOUT three o'clock Bridget woke, and this time Adam was asleep. She was still loosely cuddled in his arms, and there was a faint glow of firelight coming from the stove.

He looked younger, more approachable, but she paused and frowned as she drank his features in. A memory came to her. Could this man possibly have been watching her with desire in his eyes while he'd held her in his arms?

In this bed? In this shed, perhaps?

A little tremor ran through her. Had she imagined it or had she dreamt it? Even if she had, it filled her with a dizzying sense of delight to think of it.

But she put her hand to her mouth in a sudden gesture of concern. How could she feel this way so out of the blue, and about a man she barely knew?

Not only that, but a man who had made no bones about himself—he was a rolling stone, he was anti-commitment, and he had a score to settle over a woman.

Her eyes widened as she realized it didn't seem to

make the slightest difference. She still got goosebumps, she still felt those delicious tremors just to think that he might want her…

But would she be any good at it? she wondered. She'd certainly never felt like this before.

Half an hour later she knew she had to pay a visit to the outside toilet, much as she wished otherwise.

It was raining again, so she put on Adam's rain jacket, which covered her voluminously, and unhooked a lamp.

It was when her mission was accomplished and she was scurrying back to the shed that she came to grief— courtesy the mud and Adam's jacket. She tripped on the edge of the jacket at the same time as there was an ominous crack—the kind of crack she'd heard before, earlier in the night. She fell over in the mud and the source of the crack—a branch of the gum tree from the hill behind the shed—rolled down on top of her, bringing with it a smothering shroud of debris.

She got such a fright she blacked out for a couple of moments, and when she came to she couldn't see anything. The tentacles of hysteria started to claim her, and claustrophobia kicked in.

'Bridget, are you all right?' Adam called urgently. 'Bridget, answer me!'

She wriggled a bit. Nothing seemed to hurt desperately but… 'I seem to be pinned around my waist. I can move my legs, but I can't get out—oh, no,' she cried, as there was another crack and more rubble cascaded down the hillside.

'Bridget—Bridget, listen to me,' he instructed. 'Protect your head with your arms, if you can, while I get you out. Try not to move. I *will* get you out, believe me.'

But she didn't believe him, even as she heard chopping and sawing noises, even though she knew there would be more tools in the shed he could use, even though she'd seen what he'd done to another tree. That one had been much smaller...

There was something about being trapped that seemed to convince her she was going to die under the weight of all the rubble the hillside could rain down on her—including, she suddenly remembered, the ruins of the old building she'd seen while showering under the rainwater tank.

For a terrible moment even her legs wouldn't move, she couldn't feel them, and she all but convinced herself she must have broken her back. Later she was to realise it was hysterical paralysis, but at the time her life started to unfold itself in front of her. During the half-hour it took Adam to release her she became more and more convinced this dreadful night was finally going to claim her.

Her ridiculously short life, with no goals achieved, rolled before her eyes. Nothing much of importance to report at all, she thought groggily, and tears flowed down her cheeks.

She didn't immediately believe she was free, until Adam scooped her up in his arms and carried her into the shed.

'Am I dreaming? Is this heaven? Or the other place?' she asked dazedly.

He didn't answer, but put her gently down on the bed. Then he said, 'I'm going to undress you and assess any damage there may be. Try not to make a fuss.'

Bridget heard herself laugh huskily. 'I don't think I'm capable of making a fuss. I got such a fright—I thought I was going to die.'

Adam turned away and put the kettle on the stove. Then he turned back and pulled off the rain jacket and the sodden, torn pyjamas with as much clinical precision as he was capable of. He tested her limbs and her ribs. And when he was assured nothing was broken or twisted he told her she extremely lucky.

Bridget bore it all in silence, even when he filled a bucket with warm water and washed her. She was still grappling with the horrible feeling that she'd been about to die.

She hadn't noticed that he'd warmed one of the towels in front of the stove until he wrapped her in it and put her under the blanket.

She slipped her hand under her cheek and stared unseeingly into the shadows.

Adam gazed down at her for a long moment, then turned away to load the last of the wood into the stove. She had been extremely lucky, he thought to himself.

The strong PVC material of the rain jacket, even while it had actually become impaled on a sharp piece of wood and trapped her as much as the branch had, had also protected her from the debris. And the branch that had come down on her had had a slight bow in it, which had landed above her waist—thereby pinning her, but not crushing her. All the rocks that had come with it had miraculously missed her, although the other debris—leaves, twigs, grass and earth—had almost smothered her.

He looked down at himself. Once again he was a torn muddy mess, so he stripped, washed himself economically, then wound a towel round his waist. He doused the lamps, as the fire in the stove still roared and provided some light, and climbed into the bed beside her.

She didn't resist when he pulled her gently into his arms. If anything she sighed with relief, and he felt her relax slowly.

Finally she said, as their bodies touched, 'Thank you so much.'

'It was my pleasure,' he answered, with a wry twist to his lips. 'Go to sleep if you can.'

She did drift into an uneasy slumber for a while, but then she woke, shaking and obviously distressed, and suffering a reaction.

'Bridget—Bridget,' he said softly. 'You're safe.'

But she moved jerkily in his arms.

'Hey,' he added, 'it's me—Adam. Your axeman and wood-chopper. Remember?'

Her green eyes focused slowly and she started to relax. 'Oh, thank heavens,' she breathed. 'I thought I was out there again, with things falling down on me and suffocating me.'

'No. I have you in my arms. We're in bed in the shed— remember the shed?—and although the elements are playing havoc outside—' he paused to grimace as another storm cell erupted overhead '—we're warm and dry.'

But she grew anxious again. 'Is that more thunder and lightning? When is it going to stop?' she asked tearfully.

Adam studied her face in the dim light and felt that protective urge run through him again. She'd been through so much, and had borne most of it with a mixture of composure and humour, he thought. But how to comfort her now? More talk?

It came to him that there was only one way he wanted to comfort her—and the thought translated itself instinctively. He pulled her closer and ran his hands over her body.

She stilled, and her lips parted as her eyes grew uncertain, mirroring all her doubts. Was she dreaming again? And, if she wasn't, was she going to be any good at this?

And Adam discovered he couldn't help himself. He lowered his head to kiss her, with the express intention of not only comforting her but at the same time chasing away that look of uncertainty, proving to her she was infinitely desirable.

Bridget remained quite still in his arms for a long moment, then she seemed to melt against him and her lips parted softly beneath his.

Not only did she accept his kiss, but her senses flowered and brought her to a tingling awareness of his body against hers. And as that translated to a wave of desire for him, up and down the length of her, she felt soft and pliant. She felt as if none of her bruises or scrapes even existed, as if it would be the most natural, lovely thing in the world to open her legs and receive him.

And as all hell broke loose above them again, as thunder ricocheted around the ether and lightning flashed sparks of light through the old shed's dirty, high windows, they came together in the timeless act of love. Because, as both were to think later, they just didn't seem to have much say in the matter.

If anyone had told her how exquisite the act of love could be after her unhappy experience of it she would not have believed them. Not even when she'd felt herself come alive in that particular way in his arms had she expected such rapture.

The way he touched her breasts and teased her nipples was divinely thrilling. The way his fingers sought her warm, silken, most erotic spots almost took her breath away. And because he was extra-gentle, not only in deference to her scrapes and bruises, his final claiming of her and their subsequent climax was so different from what she'd known it was the most amazing, joy-filled revelation.

Most of all, the knowledge that she'd brought him equal pleasure was the cause of deep, deep satisfaction to her.

She was just about to tell him this when another huge crack tore the night air and the big old gum outside gave up its struggle to stay upright in the rain-sodden earth. With a crash, it cannoned down the hillside into the side of the shed.

They both moved convulsively, and Adam wrapped her securely in his arms. But although everything rattled, and a few things fell down, the shed withstood the impact.

'How do you feel?' he asked, after they'd waited with bated breath for more mayhem and none had come.

'Wonderful,' she said softly. 'I've never felt like that

before. I can't believe it.' Little lines of laughter creased beside her eyes. 'I mean…' She hesitated and changed tack. 'How about you?'

An expression she couldn't identify crossed his eyes. But it was with his lips quirking that he said, 'Wonderful.' He sobered. 'Bridget—'

'No.' She put a finger to his lips. 'I don't want to dissect it. I just want to go on feeling wonderful.'

'Then let's see if we can get a bit of sleep. Comfortable?'

'Mmm…' she murmured drowsily.

They fell asleep in each other's arms, until dawn filtered through the grimy shed windows and they heard a helicopter's rotors beating overhead.

'Bridget—' Adam said, and stopped.

Here it comes, Bridget thought, the parting of the ways, the thing that had been on her mind ever since she'd woken in his arms and been flooded by the memory of their lovemaking.

She wore—they both wore—State Emergency Services orange coveralls. Hers were way too big for her—but far better to be hoisted into a helicopter in something that nearly smothered her rather than an old towel.

And they did have to be hoisted into the helicopter, because the ground was too soft and waterlogged for it to land. By contrast, however, it was a bright sunny day, the sky was a clear blue, and the drenching rain, howling winds and pyrotechnics of the night before were like a dream—of the nightmare variety.

They were still sitting in the helicopter. It had landed on a tarmac driveway, and they were waiting for an ambulance to transport Bridget to the Gold Coast Hospital for a check-up.

She'd strenuously objected to this, saying she was quite fine, but Adam had sided with the paramedic on the helicopter and she'd been effectively outvoted. She had been uplifted by the news that the family in the car that had been washed away after hers had also been rescued.

'Bridget,' Adam said for the third time, and put his hand over hers. 'I'm not for you, and that's—'

'Not my fault but yours?' she murmured huskily, in a parody of the old 'it's not you, it's me' explanation.

He grimaced. 'Trite, but unfortunately true.' He paused. 'I'm lousy lover material, and I'd be terrible husband material.'

'Lousy lover material?' she whispered. 'I have to beg to differ.'

He lifted her hand and kissed her knuckles. 'You're sweet, but it was just one of those things.'

Bridget considered. It had seemed to her, from the moment they'd woken to the sound of the rotors and both leapt out of bed, covering themselves with whatever they could find and racing out to flag down the helicopter, that they'd been tied to each other by an invisible string.

She reconsidered. As if they belonged to each other! But she'd certainly felt that, and could she have been so wrong?

She recalled the way he'd taken her back inside the

shed and helped her into the voluminous coveralls, how they'd laughed a little together as she'd all but drowned in them. How he'd kissed her and told her it had to be an improvement on a horse rug.

Then they'd used a double harness to winch them up—he had seemed to know all about it, and also to know one of the crew—and she'd gone up in his arms.

He'd kissed her again when they were safely inside the helicopter, and she'd sat squashed up against him as it had risen and flown, squashed and in his arms, so her erratic heartbeats had normalised and she'd felt safe because they were *his* arms.

'Will you ever get over the woman who left you for your brother?'

He looked down at her, and there was something like compassion in his eyes that hurt her very much.

'I have got over her. It's my brother—but it's more than that. I'm far too old for you.' He stilled her sudden movement. 'In experience, in the kind of life I've lived, and in the far too many women I've loved. What you need is someone with no murky past, who can share an optimistic future with you.'

'And if I don't want—?'

'Bridget,' he cut in, and released her hand to wipe away the tears that sparkled on her lashes with his thumbs. 'If there's one thing you can take away with you, it's this: you were gorgeous in bed, and don't let any guy with an oversize ego tell you otherwise. You be selective, now, and make sure you give the men who are not good enough for *you* the flick.' He brushed away another tear and picked up her hand as his lips quirked. 'Incidentally, I'm one of those.'

'But I *loved* being in bed with you,' she whispered brokenly.

'There's a lot more to it than that.' He turned his head as an ambulance drove up and parked beside the helicopter. 'Your limo has arrived, Mrs Smith.' He raised her hand and kissed her knuckles again. 'So it's time to say goodbye. Take this with you.'

He rummaged in a seat pocket until he came up with a pencil and piece of paper, upon which he wrote a telephone number.

'If you need me, Bridget—' his eyes were completely serious now '—in case of any unplanned… *consequences*, this number will always get a message to me.'

Bridget took the piece of paper, but she couldn't see what was written on it. Her eyes were blurred with tears. Then it came to her that there were two ways she could do this. As a tearful wreck, or…

'And if you need me,' she said, dashing at her eyes as she raised her hand beneath his to kiss his knuckles, 'you know where to find me.'

They stared into each other's eyes until he said, very quietly, 'Go, Bridget.' His expression changed to harsh and controlled as a nerve flickered in his jaw, and he added, 'Before you live to regret it.'

Several hours later Adam Beaumont let himself into a hotel penthouse suite on the Gold Coast, and strode into the bathroom to divest himself of the orange SES cover-alls which had raised a few eyebrows in the hotel.

He took a brisk shower, dressed in jeans and a T-shirt, and padded through to the lounge.

But with his hand on the telephone he paused and thought about Bridget. Was she still undergoing examination for any unseen injuries? Or was she at home now?

It annoyed him momentarily to realise he couldn't picture her 'at home' because he had no idea where she lived. And it worried him obscurely to think of her at home, wherever that was, and alone. Not only after her amazing and dangerous adventure, but after their spontaneous lovemaking.

What had possessed him? he wondered rather grimly.

She couldn't have been less like the women he usually dated: soignée, sophisticated girls, well able to take care of themselves even when they discovered that he had no intention of marrying them. Not that he ever tried to hide it.

As to *why* he had no intention of marrying them, was it only a case of once bitten, twice shy? Once betrayed by a woman, in other words? Well, there was also the disillusionment of his parents' marriage at the back of his mind, but even that, painful as it had been as he grew up, did not equal his disbelief, the raw hurt, the anger and cynicism, the desire for revenge his now sister-in-law's defection had provoked in him.

Strangely, though, he hadn't thought about it in recent times—until a copper-headed girl with green eyes had winkled it out of him last night. And, yes, he thought harshly, it *did* still hurt, so it was better packed away—along with the whole thorny question of whether he would ever trust a woman again.

But to get back to Bridget Smith—why *had* he done it?

To comfort her? Yes. To prove to her that her one previous experience had been no more than a case of the wrong man? Yes.

Because he hadn't been able to help himself?

Well, yes, he conceded. And that had been due to a combination of those green eyes, that lovely, tender little body, her freshness, and the simplicity and naturalness of her reactions. Yes, all of that. Plus admiration—because she had been brave and humorous, and those little touches of hauteur had secretly amused him. Even her outrageous lies on the subject of the non-existent Mr Smith had amused him.

It came to him from nowhere. Perhaps, if he was ever to take a—how to put it?—convenient wife, Bridget Smith was the kind of girl he needed?

He stared out at the view from the penthouse as he pictured it. Mrs Bridget Beaumont. Then a frown came to his eyes and reality kicked in. He was better off steering clear of *any* commitment to a woman. Far better off.

He shrugged and lifted the receiver to organise the retrieval of his Land Rover and the possessions in it. He was about to put the phone down when he thought that there was one thing he *could* do for Mrs Smith. He could at least facilitate the retrieval of *her* possessions, if not her car...

* * *

Bridget had had to get a locksmith to let her into her flat, although not much later—after she too had showered and changed out of her coveralls—a knock on her door had revealed yet another SES officer, bearing her overnight bag and her purse, both retrieved from her car.

She was immensely grateful, even though the news about her car was not good. It was going to have to be taken out of its final resting place piece by piece.

She closed the door on the officer and bore her purse to the dining room table as if it were precious booty. Once she'd checked everything and found it all there she sat back and looked around, feeling suddenly sandbagged as all the events of the previous twenty-four hours kicked in.

It was small, but comfortable, her flat: two bedrooms, open-plan lounge, dining room, kitchen and a pleasant veranda, on the second floor of a modern two-storeyed building in a quiet suburb not far from the beach.

Although she could have owned it—her father had divided his quite substantial estate between her and her mother—she'd decided to keep her nest egg from her father intact in case she ever really needed it.

She'd put quite some effort into decorating her flat, though. She'd used a cool green for the walls, with a white trim, and cool blues for the furnishings and rugs.

Cool was the way to go on the sub-tropical Gold Coast. But there were splashes of yellow and pink. Some fluffy yellow chrysanthemums in a pewter flask vase on her dining table—the vase had been a present from her mother, who lived in Indonesia these days. And some pink cushions on her settee, a fuchsia lampshade atop a pretty porcelain lamp.

There were also some of her own paintings on the walls. Paintings of flowers that flourished in the tropics— orchids, frangipani and hibiscus. Oddly enough, despite her assertion to Adam that she wasn't much good, she'd entered some of her paintings in a local art show, and the owner of an interior design firm that specialised in decorating motels, rental apartments and offices had bought all six. He'd also told her that he'd take as many more as she could paint, and no matter if she repeated herself.

So far she hadn't done any more. She wasn't quite sure how she felt about her work gracing the walls of impersonal motel bedrooms, rental apartments and offices. Did that make her a real artist, or something much more commercial?

But now, as she looked around, art—commercial or otherwise—couldn't have been further from her mind. Why wouldn't it be when she'd just gone through a unique experience and then had it torn away from her?

But as she thought of the man called Adam she had to acknowledge that from the moment he'd so reluctantly revealed his past history she'd known he was bitter about women. He'd told her himself he was a rolling stone, so it shouldn't have come as such a shock that he would walk away from her like that.

But it had, she conceded, and wiped away a ridiculous tear. Because their intimacy, for her, had been so perfect and such a revelation.

Had she unwittingly translated that into the belief that it must have been the same for him?

She grimaced sadly. That was exactly what she had done. But perhaps the bigger question now was—What was she left with?

A memory, to be pressed between the pages of a book until it dried and lost colour like a forgotten rose? A memory that evoked a bittersweet feeling in her breast that faded with time? Or a raging torrent of disbelief and anger that he could have made love to her so beautifully she suspected she would *never* forget it and then simply walked away?

CHAPTER THREE

'WHO'S *this*?' Bridget Tully-Smith was holding a newspaper and staring at a picture of a man on the front page. Her expression was completely bemused. 'I don't believe it...'

Julia Nixon, her colleague and friend, put her red high heels on the dull commercial-grade carpet of the busy TV newsroom and wheeled herself in her office chair from her cubicle to Bridget's cubicle, next door. She scanned the picture and caption, scanned Bridget in turn, then said carefully, 'What part of Adam Beaumont don't you believe?'

'But that can't be Adam *Beaumont*!'

'Oh, it is,' Julia murmured. 'In all his glory.' She frowned. 'Why can't it?'

Bridget put the paper down and turned to her friend. 'Because I met him.' She paused, and thought how inadequately that covered her encounter with this man roughly three weeks ago.

'He was—' She stopped, then went on. 'He wasn't

part of the Beaumont empire! If anything he was very much a rolling-stone-that-gathers-no-moss type.'

'Well, he may be, but that doesn't stop him from being gorgeous or the real thing.' Julia stared at the picture with a pensive look in her grey eyes. 'Has he taken over from Henry Beaumont, his brother?'

Bridget perused the opening paragraph of the article accompanying the picture. 'There's a rumour, but that's all at this stage. How did you know?'

'High society is my department these days, darling,' Julia reminded her. 'You'd be amazed how many strange rumours I hear about the rich and famous when they party.' She smoothed her pale gilt hair and studied her long red nails with an expression Bridget couldn't identify.

Julia was in her thirties, an experienced journalist, with a penchant for red shoes, tailored grey suits and red nails to match her lips. She was extremely attractive, although she often exhibited a world-weary streak. She was unmarried but, talking of rumours, was said to have had—still had, for all Bridget knew—a series of high-profile lovers.

'For example,' Julia continued, 'Adam Beaumont is supposed to be estranged from the fabulous Beaumont mining family. He's certainly made his own fortune—out of construction rather than minerals.' Julia gestured. 'Further rumour has it that there's a blood feud between Adam and Henry Beaumont. And I wouldn't be surprised if Adam has finally found the lever to unseat Henry.'

Bridget's mouth fell open.

Julia raised a thinly arched eyebrow at her.

Bridget closed her mouth hastily. 'Nothing.'

'And I also wouldn't be surprised,' Julia went on, 'if he doesn't do as good if not a better job than his brother. I always had Adam Beaumont taped as a cool, tough customer who would be equally at home in a boardroom as a bedroom—he's as sexy as hell. Where did you meet him? It has to be him, I would say. You couldn't confuse that face easily.'

Bridget blinked at the picture in the paper and thought, No, you couldn't. 'Beside a swollen creek in a flash flood, trying to rescue a carload of people.'

Julia pursed her lips as she summed Bridget up from her short cap of coppery hair, her delicate features and her sparkling green eyes, her slender figure in a white-dotted voile blouse and khaki cargo pants to her amber suede pumps. 'You may have been lucky if you looked like a drowned rat.'

'Oh, I did.' Bridget paused with a grimace that turned to a frown. 'But—is he really a playboy?'

'He has escorted some of the loveliest, most exotic women in the land, but not one of them has been able to pin him down. Uh-oh.'

Julia wheeled herself back to her domain to answer her phone. And it occurred to Bridget as Julia did so that there was something in her colleague's demeanour that was a little puzzling. But she couldn't put her finger on it, so she turned her attention back to the picture in the paper.

Adam Beaumont was thirty-one, and good-looking. In the picture, he was wearing a suit and a tie, and he'd been captured on the move, with the front flap of his jacket flying open—not at all how she remembered him.

Despite his being soaked and unshaven that tempestuous night, and in jeans and boots, the two things she would always remember about him remained the same, however. It was the same tall, elegant physique beneath that beautiful suit, and the same haunting eyes—those often brooding or moody, sometimes mercilessly teasing, occasionally genuinely amused blue eyes.

It all came flooding back to her, as it had in the moments before she'd made the exclamation that had grabbed Julia's attention.

But for the time being she was to be denied the opportunity to think back to that memorable encounter with Adam Beaumont, whom she'd known only as Adam. It was an hour before the six o'clock news. The main bulletin of the day was to go to air, and the usual tension was rising in the newsroom.

She heard her name called from several directions, and she folded the newspaper with a sigh, then took a deep breath, grabbed her clipboard and leapt into the fray.

When she got home, she made herself a cup of tea and studied the newspaper again, at the same time asking herself what she knew about the Beaumonts.

What most people knew, she decided. That they were ultra-wealthy and ultra-exclusive. Adam and Henry's grandfather had started the dynasty as a mineral prospector, looking for copper but stumbling on nickel, and the rest, as they said, was history.

What she hadn't known was that the family was plagued by a feud, until Julia had mentioned it. The moment Julia had remarked on the possibility of Adam finding the lever to unseat his brother, Henry, it had taken her right back to the shed, the paraffin lamps and the storm, and that hard, closed expression on Adam's face. If she'd had any doubts that they were one and the same man, they'd been swept away.

Her next set of thoughts was that Adam Beaumont had probably gone out of his way not to reveal his identity—because, to put it bluntly, he was way out of her league.

Surely that was enough, on top of what he himself had said, to kill any lingering crazy longing stone-dead? she reflected—and wrapped her arms around herself in a protective little gesture.

Three weeks had seen her go through a maelstrom of emotional chaos. Her bruises and scrapes might have healed, but her mental turmoil had been considerable. And, as she'd postulated to herself the day she'd been both rescued and abandoned, she felt torn between a bittersweet *it was never meant to be* sensation and a tart resentment that left her feeling hot and cold. If he'd known he wasn't for her, why had he done it?

Of course she'd been more than happy to participate, but she hadn't had a cast-in-concrete conviction that she was a loner, had she? Moreover, shortly before it had happened, she had thought she was going to die. Had that accounted somewhat for her willingness in his arms?

But most of all, in these three weeks, she'd felt lonely

and sad. She couldn't believe she could miss someone so much when she'd only known him so briefly, but she did.

She sniffed a couple of times, then told herself not to be weak and weepy, and turned her attention to the newspaper again.

She reread the article, but there was not a lot to be gleaned from it. It was simply speculation, really, to the effect that there could be moves afoot on the Beaumont board, plus some of the company's impressive mining achievements.

It also detailed some of Adam Beaumont's achievements outside the field of mining, and in their own way they were impressive. He was obviously a billionaire in his own right.

So what was it really about, this article? she wondered. It did detail that Adam was not a major shareholder in Beaumonts, whereas Henry was. And how did that line up with what she knew? The fact that Adam had sworn revenge against his brother and was looking for a lever to unseat him?

She shook her head, a little mystified. She stared at the photo of Adam Beaumont and suffered an intensely physical moment. It was as if she were right back in his arms, with that chiselled mouth resting on hers, his hands on her body thrilling and delighting her.

What a pity there was never any future for us, she thought, and blinked away a solitary tear. It was no good telling herself again not to be weak and weepy, because the fact remained there seemed to have been awoken within her a chilly, lonely little feeling she couldn't dispel, and—she stopped and frowned—a strange little echo she couldn't place.

Of course there was also the fear that she might have fallen pregnant continually at the back of her mind. A state which came under the heading of *consequences*, no doubt, she thought dryly. Statistically, she had decided—the time of the month, it only happening once— it was unlikely. Although she was realistic enough to know it was a statistic not to be relied upon.

But now there was a new feeling added to all her woes, she realised as she laid her head back and stared unseeingly across the room. And it centred around the fact that he'd allowed her to think he was ordinary when in fact he was a billionaire.

What difference does it make? she wondered.

She sat up suddenly. It makes me feel like a gold-digger, or as if that would have been his automatic assumption as soon as I found out! she answered herself.

And that outraged her, she found. Although a little niggling thought came to her—perhaps that was the way a lot of women reacted when they discovered who he was? Perhaps that had added to his cynicism about women?

She heaved a huge sigh and deliberately folded up the paper so his picture was inside, not visible. She forced herself to concentrate on her upcoming weekend. She, several others and a party of disabled children were spending the weekend on a farm. It was going to be arduous, and she would give it her all. She would not allow Adam Beaumont to intrude. And her period would come in the natural course of events when it was due, on Sunday.

But her period didn't come in the natural course of events, and by the following Sunday it still hadn't.

It would be fair to say that Bridget had held out until the last moment in her belief that her cycle had gone a bit haywire, but when a home pregnancy test proved positive she had to face the cold, hard truth.

She was pregnant after a one-night stand with a man she barely knew—a man who had told her unequivocally that he wasn't for her…

It was a shattering thought.

Two days after she had made the discovery there was a crisis in the newsroom.

Megan Winslow, who was doing the news on her own because Peter Haliday, her co-presenter, had the flu, fainted half an hour before air time.

Out of the chaos, Bridget was chosen to replace her. In the normal course of events it would most likely have been Julia chosen to do it, but it was her day off. There were several reasons to choose Bridget. She spoke well, with good modulation—she'd belonged to her university dramatic society—and she was familiar with the autocue as she'd occasionally filled in for the weather presenter.

'You've also proofed a lot of the stuff, so you're familiar with it. We can find you something more formal to wear,' Megan's producer said to her. 'Make-up!' he yelled.

It was a miracle Bridget managed to speak at all, considering the emotion-charged atmosphere of the newsroom. Even more than that, her own inner turmoil was mind-boggling. She hadn't been able to come to grips in any way with the fact that she was carrying Adam Beaumont's baby. If anyone should be fainting, she should…

But she actually got through reading the news with only a few stumbles. And she had no idea who would be in the unseen audience for that particular broadcast…

Adam Beaumont unlocked the door to his suite in the luxury Gold Coast hotel and threw the keycard onto the hall table. He walked through to the lounge, shrugging off his jacket and tie, and switched on one table lamp.

The view through the filmy curtains was fabulous. The long finger known as Surfers Paradise stretched before and below him like a fairyland of lights, bordered by a faint line of white breakers on the beach and the midnight-blue of the Pacific Ocean, with a silver moon hanging in the sky.

He didn't give it more than a cursory glance as he got a beer from the bar and poured it into a frosted glass. He'd been overseas, and he was feeling jet-lagged and annoyed. One of his PAs had met him at the airport and given him a run-down of events that had occurred in his absence. One of them was a newspaper article described by his PA as a 'fishing expedition', to do with the board of directors at Beaumonts and a carefully worded suggestion that there was some unrest on the board.

Where the hell had that come from? he'd asked, but had not received a satisfactory answer.

The Beaumont board, he thought, standing in the

middle of the lounge, staring at nothing in particular. Ever since he could remember the family circumstances that had contributed to his distance from the board had galled him almost unbearably. And that had contributed, along with his faithless sister-in-law, to his determination to unseat his brother, Henry. But it so happened *he* hadn't done anything to create the rumours.

He put his beer on a side-table and looked around for the TV remote before he sank down into an armchair.

He was flicking through the channels when his finger was arrested, and he sat up with an unexpectedly indrawn breath as he stared at Bridget, reading the news.

She was wearing an elegant lime-green linen jacket, and her coppery hair was still short but obviously styled. Her eye make-up emphasised her green eyes, and her lips were painted a lustrous pink.

She looked, in two words, extremely attractive, he thought. But what the hell *was* this?

She paused, then launched into a piece she happened *not* to have proofed. Of all things, she stumbled on the Beaumont name. But she collected herself and went on to detail the fact that the rumours circulating were suggesting Henry Beaumont was about to be ousted from the Beaumont board by his brother, in a bitter power struggle.

It was the last item before a commercial break, and as had been agreed, to save viewers any confusion, Bridget said, 'I'm Bridget Tully-Smith, filling in for Megan Winslow tonight. Please stay with us for all the latest sporting news.'

Adam Beaumont stared at the television long after an

advertisement had replaced Bridget's image. *Tully*-Smith, he thought incredulously. You didn't tell me *that*, Mrs Smith. His mind ranged back. Although you did mention your father was a journalist and was killed in an accident. So it's more than likely that your father was Graham Tully-Smith, famous investigative journalist—or notorious, if you happened to be on the receiving end of it.

And it just so happens, his thoughts ran on, you're the *only* person I've ever told about finding the right lever to unseat Henry. Is there a connection between these rumours that have sprung up out of nowhere and you, Bridget?

Bridget was exhausted when she got home.

Although she'd been heartily congratulated on how she'd handled things, doing the news had been a huge drain. And on top of that the Beaumont piece had deeply perturbed her.

It had taken her back again to that night, to the events in the shed, back to Adam Beaumont again, and to what he'd revealed to her. But not only that. Adam Beaumont was where an awful lot of inner turmoil resided for her now…

She had come straight home, only to find she didn't feel like going to bed.

Then she got a phone call from the TV station, from a receptionist named Sally whom she happened to know, with the news that Adam Beaumont would like to get in touch with her. Could they pass on her number?

She took an incredulous breath. 'What for?'

Sally replied, 'I don't know, Bridge. He didn't say.

It wasn't actually him, anyway, it was his PA. Do you know him?'

'I—I've met him.'

'Well, maybe he wants to congratulate you on the news!'

'Uh…' Bridget thought swiftly. 'I really doubt it. I mean, I'd rather not.'

'That's OK. Although personally I would never say no to Adam Beaumont,' Sally remarked with a chuckle. 'I'll just say you're unavailable for personal calls. I've got it down to a fine art. Night, Bridget!'

Bridget put the phone down slowly, her eyes wide and a little stunned.

Why did he want to get in touch now? she wondered.

It must have something to do with the item about the Beaumont board she'd read on the news tonight. It couldn't be any other reason. But it had nothing to do with her. She hadn't even proofed the copy, let alone originated the item.

And there were several reasons why she didn't want to see him. Not yet, at least. Sheer panic was one of them. How was she to tell him she was pregnant? How would he react?

She wasn't at all sure of *her* reaction, other than stunned disbelief, so…

She hardly slept at all that night, but it didn't occur to her that Adam Beaumont wouldn't take no for an answer.

The next morning was Saturday, so she was off work. It was the day after she'd read the news for Megan Winslow and refused to talk to Adam Beaumont.

So what she was doing was strolling down the beach at Surfers, breathing the fresh salty air, hoping it would help her to clear her mind.

The tide was in, tracing silvery patterns on the sand, and the gulls were in full working mode as they swooped over the shallows, fishing for little bait fish. It was a clear, sunny day. There were swimmers and an army of walkers.

There were also families on the beach, with children of all sizes and ages, and for the first time she stopped and sat on a dune to study them closely. The crawlers, the toddlers, the paddlers, as well as a couple of pregnant mothers nearby. It occurred to her that in the company of her friends' children she thought loosely about having a family herself, but with one striking ingredient missing—a suitable father—it had never been more than that. She'd never imagined herself pregnant.

She was conscious again of that little echo she'd detected within herself but been unable to explain, and for the first time since disbelief and panic had gripped her it came to her that there was another life in her care and under her guardianship. In the normal course of events she would grow like the two pregnant women on the beach, and then that new life would be born and would carry her imprint.

But what about her life in the meantime? she wondered.

Would a reluctant father, even if he gave her and more particularly the baby material support, be better than no father at all? Or would she chafe at the fact that she'd never been good enough for her baby's father? If she did, how would a child react to that? Was she better off being a single mother or not, in other words?

How did you bear the burden of single-motherhood amongst your friends and in your workplace, though? It probably wasn't so unusual, but she couldn't think of anyone she knew who was pregnant and without a partner.

It was at this point in her musings that someone tapped her on the shoulder.

'Yes?' she said, with extreme surprise. She didn't recognize the man and couldn't imagine what a formally dressed middle-aged man in a suit and tie was a: doing on the beach, and b: wanting with her.

'It is Miss Smith, isn't it?' he said. 'Miss Bridget Tully-Smith?'

Bridget opened her mouth to say yes, but then said instead, with a faint narrowing of her eyes, 'Who wants to know?'

'Mr Beaumont, Mr Adam Beaumont, would like a word with you, Miss Tully-Smith. I'm Peter Clarke. I work for him, and I just missed you coming out of your building a little while ago. I was trying to park. I was forced to follow you on foot, and—'

'Please tell Mr Beaumont I have nothing to say to him at the moment,' Bridget interjected. 'And please tell him I don't appreciate being followed.'

She turned away and marched off, with her heart beating heavily.

She'd calmed down somewhat by the time she got home, and assured herself that if Adam Beaumont hadn't taken the hint before he would surely do so now.

Famous last thoughts...

She answered her doorbell late that afternoon to find him in person on her doorstep.

'You!' she gasped, and she tried to slam the door.

But he simply put his hands around her waist and picked her up, to deposit her inside the doorway.

'I'll scream!' she threatened, more out of frustration than fear.

'Scream away,' he invited. 'But I don't intend to close the door. I don't intend to deprive you of your liberty or harm you in any way, or stop you using your phone. I do intend to tell you this, though. The more you run away from me, Mrs Smith, the guiltier you look.'

This stopped Bridget dead.

She stared at him wide-eyed and with her mouth open. He was wearing the same suit he'd been photographed in, navy blue pinstripe, with a matching waistcoat, but today it was a pale blue shirt he wore, with a burgundy tie.

That dark hair was the same, though. So were the austere lines of his face and mouth. It was the same pair of broad shoulders beneath the faultless tailoring, the same narrow waist and long legs. The same blue eyes— but today they were accusing and insolent…

'G-guilty?' she stammered. 'I haven't done anything!'

'How about failing to give me your full name, Bridget?'

'Th-that wasn't—I often don't use my full name,' she stammered. 'People always ask me if—if I'm—' She stopped and pleated her fingers together.

'If you're Graham Tully-Smith's daughter?' he finished for her. 'Graham Tully-Smith, investigative journalist extraordinaire. But there's more, isn't there? You work in the news department of a television station. You've even climbed the ladder a bit to read the news. All of which places you perfectly to pass on a juicy titbit you picked up one wet, stormy night in the Numinbah, doesn't it?'

'What do you mean?'

'Bridget,' he said deliberately, 'you're the only person I've ever told about my ambition to unseat my brother. Yet now it appears to be common knowledge.'

Bridget breathed confusedly. 'I didn't tell a soul,' she protested. 'There's no way I could have used it, anyway. I'm just a very junior gofer. That's all.'

He raised a cynical eyebrow at her. 'Is that how you came to be reading the news last night? Look—' he turned back to the open door '—we can continue this in public if you prefer, or…?'

'Oh. Close it,' Bridget said, distraught, and when he did, she went on, 'We had a crisis in the newsroom last night. Megan fainted. That's how I came to do it. And reading the news doesn't mean I had anything to do with *compiling* it!'

'Is that so?' He came back to stand in front of her, and she could see the suspicion in his eyes. 'Are you *sure* you didn't mention it, even in passing, to someone who may have been able to use it?'

'No. I mean, yes, I'm sure!' she cried, her eyes wide and shocked. 'Anyway, it was common knowledge before I found out who you were.' And she told him about Julia's reaction to the first newspaper article, although she didn't mention her name. 'She, my colleague, even used the same word you did—a lever,' she went on. 'But up until that moment I had no idea who you were.' She closed her eyes and swayed suddenly.

'Bridget?' he said, on a different note as he scanned her now ashen face. 'Are you all right?'

'I—I'm, yes,' she murmured, but sank down on the settee. She rubbed her face and commanded herself to think clearly.

He hesitated, then sat down opposite her. 'Have you any idea how destabilising these kind of rumours can be? How shareholders can be affected—and share prices?' he added significantly.

'Of course.' She gestured. 'I mean, if I stop to think about it, of course. But I didn't. I haven't.' She grimaced as she thought that she'd had more than enough of an entirely different nature to think about recently. She lifted her lashes. 'Have *you* taken shareholders and share prices into consideration? You did tell me it was only a matter of time before you found the right lever to unseat your brother.'

He sat back. 'So I did. It so happens I haven't found it. It's a little complicated. But that's why I need to know exactly how these rumours started.'

He paused and studied her. She was wearing a white voile blouse and khaki cargo pants. Her feet were bare and her coppery hair was tousled. Her eyes were darker, and there was something about her that was different.

He removed his gaze from her as he pondered this, and looked around. It was pleasant, her flat, but very much exhibiting the simple pleasures of a home decorator. And rather reminiscent, for some curious reason, he thought suddenly, of the simple pleasure of making love to her.

In fact he had to confess that memories of that lovemaking had come back and taken him by surprise at some inappropriate moments...

Such as right now, he thought dryly. He could picture that slim, sleek little body moving in his arms, unfettered by any clothes. He could almost feel the lovely peachy curves of her hips beneath his hands, and he could feel his own body stirring in response. He suddenly realised she was staring at him with widening eyes, almost as if she could read his mind, and there was a tinge of colour mounting in her cheeks.

He looked away abruptly, but it crossed his mind to wonder about the power of the connection they'd made that night over four weeks ago. Of course circumstances had contributed to make it a unique occasion, but...

He deliberately stilled his thoughts there. It would never have worked then, and it certainly couldn't work now. If she had nothing to hide, why had she tried to evade him?

He sat forward. 'If I'm to get to the bottom of this, I need to know the absolute truth from you, Bridget,' he said. 'I'm prepared to wipe the slate clean if you had any involvement, *if* you agree to drop the matter.'

She took a deep breath. 'I had none,' she said simply.

He frowned. 'Why were you running away, then?'

Bridget stared at him. How could she tell this harsh stranger who believed the worst of her that she was

carrying his baby? It had been hard enough to con-
template telling the Adam she'd known and made
love to, but now…

She tilted her chin. 'I was told to stay away, if you
remember,' she said with quiet dignity.

He stared at her with several expressions chasing
through his eyes—one of them a certain scepticism.

It was that scepticism that made her blood boil and
her green eyes flash. 'But if you're imagining I spilt
your secrets out of pique on that account, you're dead
wrong, Adam Beaumont. Would you mind letting yourself out?' She came swiftly to her feet.

He stood up. And surprised her. 'Have you still got
my phone number?'

She could only nod.

'If you have any other thoughts on the matter, give
me a ring. In the meantime, I apologise if I misread you.'

'But you're not convinced?' she queried, barely audibly.

He shrugged and turned away, and she watched him
walk out of her flat and close the door behind him.

Bridget stared at the door, then dropped her head into
her hands. It was all so surreal, and she couldn't believe
it was happening to her. There seemed to be no link
between the events of that stormy night and the present
events. It was as if they'd happened to another person.

Come to that, it was as if there were two Adam
Beaumonts. The man she'd felt so safe with, the man
she'd loved making love to, and this formal stranger
who'd just walked out on her.

Yet for a moment there it had been as if the mask had

lifted a little. A moment when he'd concentrated on her figure and she would almost have sworn he'd been thinking about their time in each other's arms.

She rubbed her hands together as an extraordinarily clear mental picture came to her of his lean, strong hand on her breasts, her waist, her hips, of his mouth on hers and the way her curves had fitted into the hard planes of his body. It hadn't lasted, though, that moment when she'd thought he might have been thinking of them together that night. Perhaps she'd got it wrong?

As for his baby—she lifted her head and her eyes dilated—what was she going to do about that?

CHAPTER FOUR

ADAM BEAUMONT drove to his next appointment in a preoccupied frame of mind. There had been something about Bridget Tully-Smith he couldn't put his finger on—something that was puzzling him.

He'd been determined to see her because he'd been convinced she must be the source of the rumours sweeping the business world about the instability of the Beaumont board. And he'd been mentally kicking himself for allowing a slip of a girl to corner him into admitting what he had.

He hadn't thought he was going to die, he reflected with increasing irony, even if she *had*.

But if it hadn't been Bridget, who had it been?

He parked his BMW below a high-rise apartment building at Narrowneck and took the elevator to the penthouse, where his great-uncle Julius lived.

Now in his eighties, Julius Beaumont, his grandfather's younger brother, was confined to a wheelchair, but he still possessed a sharp brain and, at times, a cutting tongue.

The red velour drapes were pulled against the rainy dusk, and lamps gleamed on the polished surfaces of the heavy furniture. The building might be an ultra-modern tower, but Julius Beaumont was surrounded by antiques. Even his blue velvet smoking jacket belonged to another age.

And his chosen form of art—his passion in life, as it happened—adorned the walls: paintings of horses.

He inclined his white head as Adam came in, and by way of greeting said, 'Welcome, my boy, and what the hell is going on?'

Adam was under no illusions as to what he meant, and he replied accordingly, 'I don't know, Uncle Julius. How are you?'

'As well as can be expected,' Julius said testily. 'Help yourself, and pour me one at the same time.' He gestured towards the cocktail cabinet.

Adam poured two single malt Scotches into heavy crystal glasses and carried one over to his uncle. His own he took to an armchair.

'So you didn't decide to seize the bull by the horns and attempt to unseat Henry?'

'No.'

'Then who? And why?'

Adam sipped his Scotch. 'I'm somewhat at a loss. It could simply be shareholder uneasiness, but I've done nothing to promote that.'

'Hmm…' Julius swirled the amber liquid in his glass. 'You know, my boy, I've never meddled much in Beaumont affairs. It was Samuel's baby, not mine. But

I do have a fairly significant holding. And I suppose I was loath to meddle in the natural order of things. Your father taking over from Sam, Henry taking over from Kevin when he died from all his excesses. Now I'm not so sure—did it ever occur to you that you were lucky, by the way?'

Adam smiled faintly. 'Frequently, but what particular aspect do you have in mind?'

'Both Kevin and Henry suffered from "rich man's son" syndrome, that's what,' Julius barked. 'Everything fell into their laps, and that doesn't build strong characters. But because they contrived to hold you away from Beaumonts, other than what you inherited from your mother, you went out and proved yourself in another direction. Did you the world of good.' Julius broke off and sighed. 'I'm getting on, and thinking of getting out.'

'Only out of Beaumonts, I hope you mean?' Adam murmured.

Julius thumped the padded arm of his wheelchair. 'The rest of it's not much fun, and when your time comes it comes.' He grimaced. 'But there's still something I want to accomplish. I want to see you settle down, Adam, my boy!'

'Thank you, but I *am* settled and—'

'No, you're not,' Julius contradicted him querulously. 'For one thing, you're still single.'

Adam shrugged. 'In the normal course of events I do have a few years up my sleeve.'

'In the normal course of events you wouldn't still be

hankering for Marie-Claire, your brother's wife,' Julius shot at him.

Adam put his glass down. 'Uncle Julius,' he said coolly, 'don't.'

'You can't stop me!' Julius Beaumont had the family blue eyes, old and rheumy now, but for a moment they flashed fire. 'I may never have married, but I know all about these heartbreak girls: all eyes, all legs, take your breath away just to look at them. It's because of one of 'em I never did marry, if you must know.' He looked at Adam aggressively. 'Never told anyone that, and I don't expect you to repeat it.'

'I won't. She—broke your heart?' Adam hazarded.

'Damn near to it,' Julius agreed. 'And they may not make the best wives, necessarily. My nemesis married three times and never did get it right. Although in Marie-Claire's case she did marry Henry and give him two kids, whatever may—' He stopped rather abruptly.

Adam frowned, and waited as he wondered what Julius had been about to say. When his uncle didn't go on, he said briefly, 'That point has been made. And I'm getting a little tired of all this.' He picked up his glass to drain it.

'Then how about this?' Julius said sharply. 'If you show me you've consigned Marie-Claire and all that baggage to the past I'll hand over my proxies to you, so if there is uneasiness amongst the shareholders—and I wouldn't be surprised, because Henry's a fool—between us we would have the balance of power.'

Adam Beaumont found himself staring not at his

great-uncle but at a magnificent grandfather clock that had fascinated him for almost as long as he could remember. The long gold pendulum swung backwards and forwards behind its glass door.

He forced his gaze back to Julius. 'Why?'

'I want to see Beaumonts back to its former glory for my brother Samuel's sake. And I don't want to see you drift down the years like I did, a confirmed bachelor until you find yourself in a wheelchair, with no one but paid employees to care about your welfare.'

'Uncle Julius,' Adam said firmly, 'that is a gross exaggeration.'

'Well, maybe,' Julius conceded. 'You've been very good to me, my boy, I must say.' He looked fretful. 'I've also got no sons to leave my estate to. So? What do you think?'

'How am I supposed to prove anything to you?' Adam asked carefully.

'One surefire way.' The old man smiled almost demonically. 'Take a wife!'

'I can't just go out and *take a wife*.'

'I wouldn't be at all surprised if you could take your pick of dozens of potential wives. But I'll tell you something: what you need to look for is a thoroughly *nice* girl. They're the ones who won't break your heart.'

'Even if I were to find "a thoroughly nice girl",' Adam said, then paused and narrowed his eyes as the phrase struck a chord in his mind. He couldn't place it. 'It could take time—and I'm not saying I will,' he added, with a slight barb in his voice.

'It's six months to the next shareholders meeting—unless they force one earlier.'

Adam stood up. 'Look, I'm sorry, I have to go. But I'll come and have dinner with you on Thursday.'

'But you'll think about it?' Julius stared up at him.

Adam paused. 'It's not that I'm not grateful, but if I do ever get Beaumonts I'd rather do it on my own. I mean that, Uncle Julius. I don't want to inherit it, in other words.'

Julius Beaumont watched Adam leave and shook his head. 'A dead ringer for his grandfather,' he muttered. 'As stubborn as a mule, yet what potential.'

But Adam didn't leave until he'd spoken to Mervyn, in the kitchen. Mervyn fulfilled the role of housekeeper and valet for Julius, and was a devoted employee as well as having had some medical training.

'How is he at the moment?' Adam helped himself to a slice of prosciutto that was destined to be part of the salad entrée for his uncle's dinner.

Mervyn removed the plate from his reach. 'We're a little up and down, Adam.' He often used the royal 'we' when discussing his employer. 'I had the doctor over yesterday, but he didn't think it would do any good to send him to hospital. He was of the opinion it would upset him more than help him. But I'm keeping a close watch.'

'Thank you,' Adam said. 'Actually, I can't thank you enough for the wonderful care you take of him. Oh, and I'll come for dinner on Thursday.'

'I know he'll look forward to that!'

* * *

Adam drove away even more preoccupied than he'd been before, and pondered his great-uncle Julius's health. Was he nearing the end? Was this concern he was showing an indication that he could feel the sands of time running out for him?

Funnily enough, he conceded, a chilly little image had come to mind, of himself drifting down the years and ending up alone with no sons to leave his estate to. But for the rest of it…take a wife and get Beaumonts…?

Not so simple, he thought, and recalled with a dry smile his uncle's remark about how lucky he'd been. Yes, of course he had been lucky in lots of respects, but growing up with an older brother who'd been the apple of his father's eye had not been easy. And had been made no easier when his grandfather had taken it upon himself to favour his grandson Adam over his grandson Henry. For some reason that had infuriated his father. Or perhaps there was no mystery to it, really.

There'd always been deep tensions between his father and his grandfather. But, whatever the ebbs and flows of disapproval between Samuel Beaumont and his son Kevin, there'd been nothing unseen about Kevin's preference for Henry. Not only that, they'd even looked alike—whereas Adam had favoured Samuel, and they'd had the same interests.

Nor had it all ended there. Grace Beaumont, Kevin's wife and the boys' mother, had bitterly resented Kevin's indifference to his second son and it had affected their marriage. They'd ended up virtual strangers.

If I did ever have sons, if I did ever have children,

Adam Beaumont thought, I would never favour one above the other. Come to that, I'd *never* make them feel not wanted.

As for marriage—was it enough to marry even a thoroughly nice girl to ensure you didn't grow old and sad and lonely and ensure that you had heirs?

It was from that thought that he recalled where he'd heard the *thoroughly nice girl* phrase. The drenched Numinbah Valley via Bridget Tully-Smith, of course. The irony was that he'd even agreed with her at the time—but now…?

Bridget's mother rang her that night, and when she asked Bridget if anything was the matter it shot through Bridget's mind to tell her that she'd got herself pregnant by Adam Beaumont when she'd had no idea who he was. In the most amazing circumstances, granted, but that didn't absolve her from having acted incredibly foolishly. And, on top of all that, he now viewed her with extreme suspicion.

But common sense prevailed. The enormity of it all wouldn't fail to hit her mother and hit her hard. Probably enough to make her come racing home, which would be a pity. Her mother had been heartbroken at her father's death, and full of incredulity and anxiety when love had come to her again.

It had taken quite some power of persuasion on Bridget's part to get her mother to believe in this new love, and not to feel guilty about leaving her only child alone in Australia. Her mother's new husband, Richard

Baxter, was an academic, and he'd accepted a year's fellowship at a Jakarta University.

He had a grown-up family of his own: a son who'd followed in his footsteps and a married daughter who lived in Perth. Even more importantly, he was the perfect partner for her mostly delightfully, sometimes maddeningly vague and unworldly mother. He really looked after her and cared for her, and they had lots in common.

The last thing she, Bridget, wanted to do was spoil that.

That was why she reassured her mother again that she was quite fine before she put the phone down. But, sitting alone in her flat later that evening, after the call, she knew that she wasn't fine. There were all sorts of moral and ethical dilemmas in front of her, not to mention getting her mind around a baby...

This is probably where you finally grow up, she told herself. First of all, you can't go on *not* believing it. And you probably shouldn't go on berating yourself. It's done now, and what is more important is that you don't make any more dodgy decisions...

She paused in her reflections as the word *dodgy* raised an echo in her mind—and that raised the other Adam in her mind's eye. The unshaven one, the man who'd saved her life, whose hands on her body had been such a revelation to her and brought her so much joy. How could she not want this baby? it suddenly occurred to her. Not to want it would be like negating something perfect...

She swallowed suddenly. But that perfection *had*

been broken, she told herself. He didn't trust her, and there was no indication he could ever care for her...

She breathed in, distraught, and got up to get herself a glass of water.

If she decided to have this baby, she had to concede that she might have to do it on her own. Even if she did tell Adam Beaumont she was bearing his child, it would not necessarily lead to marriage—although she couldn't believe he would not offer some support. If she didn't tell him... Well, that had to be thought through thoroughly. It might, for example, suit her in some ways, but what about raising a fatherless child? What would that do to it?

She drifted over to the glass doors leading to the veranda and looked out at the night-time scene: the street lights, the garden inside the wall that protected it from the road, the cars, the wet slick on the road from an earlier shower. But she didn't see it at all as she grappled with what came to her suddenly as a crucial part of her problem. Whatever she did, she could not go on featuring as the villain of the piece.

She pulled a face at her turn of phrase, but it did clarify things for her. However she had this baby—whether there was a future or otherwise for her with Adam Beaumont—she had to clear herself of this stigma she'd acquired.

It was supremely important—because it affected her standing not only in his eyes but in her own.

How, though?

No answer came to her immediately, but in the middle of the night she sat up with a name on her lips—

Julia. Why not start with her? She did seem to know something about the Beaumonts. Maybe Julia could at least point her in the right direction…

'Going away?' Julia asked on Monday morning, during their coffee break in the TV station's bright, bustling, impersonal cafeteria.

'Away?' Bridget looked at her, mystified.

Julia frowned. 'Don't you have three weeks' leave coming up tomorrow?'

Bridget could have kicked herself. How could she have forgotten? But, come to think of it, how fortuitous?

'Yes. No,' she said, and bit her lip. 'I mean, yes, I do, and, no, I'm not going away. I was—that is, I'm planning to potter.'

'Are you all right?' Julia queried.

'Fine,' Bridget lied. 'Julia, tell me more about the Beaumont brothers.'

'Why?'

'Just interested. It seems to be a fairly topical subject these days.'

Julia cut her blueberry muffin in half and buttered it before she responded. 'They were probably destined to feud from day one. Henry was always the apple of his father Kevin's eye, but the fact is neither Henry nor his father had the approval of Samuel Beaumont, Henry's grandfather. He was the founder of it all. And, while he didn't approve of his son or his eldest grandson, he *did* increasingly approve of Adam and see him as a more suitable heir. But Samuel died unexpectedly, and Adam got pushed more and more into the background. He was only twenty when Samuel died.'

'I...see,' Bridget said slowly. 'That wouldn't make for a happy family, precisely.'

Julia shrugged. 'No. Mind you, Adam branched out on his own and turned a medium-sized construction company into a billion-dollar enterprise. So he did justify his grandfather's approval, you could say.'

Bridget's lips parted. 'So why does he still—?' She stopped.

'Hanker for Beaumonts?' Julia supplied with a world-weary little smile. 'That's probably men for you. Power is important. He *is* a Beaumont. And Henry is seen by some as not doing a great job with the company. But there's also more, a woman—'

Julia broke off rather abruptly, and Bridget had it on the tip of her tongue to say *His brother's wife?* But she stopped herself on the thought that she had not yet revealed one word of what he'd said that night, despite what Adam Beaumont might like to think, and she wasn't about to start.

'Are the brothers alike?' she asked instead.

'On the surface, in some ways.' Julia paused thoughtfully. 'Henry's very good-looking, and quite charismatic, but...' She put her cappuccino down and patted her lips with a serviette. 'Why do *you* want to know all this, Bridge?' she asked rather intently.

Bridget shrugged. 'Just interested,' she repeated.

Julia Nixon looked at Bridget closely and noted the faint blue shadows beneath her eyes, testament to several sleepless nights. And she recalled Bridget's earlier confusion on the subject of her upcoming leave.

'Uh-oh,' she said. 'You fell for him, didn't you? Look, I'm probably wasting my time, but don't go there, sweetie. It's a no-go zone. Both of them are—as I know to my cost.'

Bridget blinked at her. 'What do you mean? How do you know to your cost? And what?'

Julia shrugged. 'I was Henry Beaumont's mistress.'

That evening Bridget, still reeling with shock at Julia's incredible revelations, dialled the number Adam Beaumont had given her with a shaking finger.

A disembodied male voice she didn't recognise said, 'Adam Beaumont's line.'

'Could I speak to Mr Beaumont, please?'

'I'll just check, ma'am. Who may I say is calling?'

'It's—it's—Mrs Smith from Numinbah.'

'Please hold on for a moment, Mrs—uh—Smith.'

Bridget held on until the voice came back.

'Adam can't leave his guests at the moment, Mrs Smith, but he'd be able to see you tomorrow morning at nine o'clock at the Marriott. Just ask for him by name. Thank you for your call.' The line went dead.

Bridget took the phone from her ear and stared at it in frustration. She'd been about to say that she didn't need to see Adam, she'd only like to talk to him, but the knowledge sank in that she might only ever be able to get a message to him—it was what he himself had said in the helicopter, although she'd had no idea why he would go to those lengths to protect his privacy at the time.

Now she did, and it ignited a spark of rebellion in her. How could he treat her like this? Even if he didn't know she was to be the mother of his child, it irked her tremendously.

It also prompted her to review her situation and make some plans. And she looked up pregnancy on the internet, so she would have a clearer idea of what she was in for.

Yes, she would see Adam Beaumont tomorrow—but only to clear her name…

She dressed with special care the next morning, in a straight green linen dress that matched her eyes, teamed with a cream jersey jacket and high heels. It was one of her more sophisticated outfits, suitable not only for the Marriott but for the Beaumonts. Then she had second thoughts. She looked as if she was going to a lunch, the races, or a job interview.

She took it all off and donned pressed jeans, a loose knit top the colour of raspberries and flat shoes. She cleaned off all the make-up she'd put on, but then her face looked pale and there were shadows under her eyes, so she started again using the barest minimum.

She'd washed her hair, so it was bouncy and shining with gold highlights. She regretted she'd not thought to get her fringe cut, but it was too late for that—and anyway, what did it matter?

And anyway, again, she would be running late if she wasn't careful, after all this dressing and undressing.

She threw her keys into her purse and raced downstairs to her new second-hand car.

She walked across the Marriott foyer at two minutes past nine. Two minutes later she was being ushered into Adam Beaumont's suite.

He was standing at the windows in the lounge, looking down on the view of Surfers Paradise—not a sparkling view today, but cloudy and with showers scudding past. He turned as his assistant, a bright young man, the owner of the disembodied voice Bridget had heard the night before, announced her.

'Adam—Mrs Smith. Could I bring some coffee?'

Adam Beaumont raised an eyebrow at Bridget, who said, in a curiously heartfelt way, 'No. That is, no, thank you.'

The assistant withdrew, and they were left staring at each other. He wore a blue shirt with a white pinstripe, and navy trousers.

There were no blue shadows on his jaw, no other reminders of the way he'd been on that stormy night in the Numinbah. He was groomed and eminently businesslike, and he was alarmingly tall, but Bridget's heart did a somersault in her breast all the same.

How not to remember she'd been in his arms and loved it so much? she wondered forlornly. Then she took some deep breaths and spoke.

'I've found out who started those rumours.'

He blinked.

'It was my colleague. I mentioned her to you the other day. She—she's authorised me to tell you all this: she was your brother Henry's mistress until recently, when he dropped her.' Bridget hesitated, then went on, 'Dropped her rather brutally, I gather. So she looked around for a way to get even with him.'

'Are you—?' Adam Beaumont frowned. 'Is this for real, Bridget?' he asked with supreme skepticism, and added dryly, 'You're going to have to do better than that if—'

'No, please listen to me,' Bridget broke in. 'She said that during their affair she formed the impression that your brother, Henry, had always had the fear that you were going to try and oust him. It seemed...' Bridget paused. 'It seemed to her that if she planted this rumour judiciously it might open up the way for you to take advantage of it, thereby gaining her some revenge. And even if you didn't manage to take advantage of it, it would make your brother's life quite complicated and difficult.'

She did not add that Julia had also given it as her considered opinion that neither Beaumont brother would ever get over Henry's wife.

He looked incredulous. 'Who is she? And has she no fear of any repercussions?'

'Julia Nixon.' Bridget waited until she saw the recognition come to him. He narrowed his eyes and his mouth hardened. Then she went on. 'She has no fears because she's advised your brother that if there *are* any repercussions she'll reveal that she was his mistress. She wasn't the first and most likely won't be the last, and she'll reveal that to the whole world, so his wife, and eventually his children, will have to know.' Bridget swayed a little where she stood. 'I know it sounds awful, but I do believe it's true and I do believe he hurt her really badly.'

'So…' Adam continued to gaze at her with a myriad of expressions chasing through his eyes.

'So it had nothing to do with me.' She swallowed several times. 'Nothing at all. It was pure coincidence that it came out not long after we—after you told me—after we—' Bridget broke off desperately, and then added in a smothered sort of rush, 'Oh, please, is there a bathroom handy? I feel very—sick.'

She *was* very sick, in the powder room of the penthouse suite. What was worse, she had no hope of hiding it from Adam Beaumont, because he was waiting for her outside the door. He took one look at her and led her to the main bedroom, where he sat her on the double bed and fetched a couple of flannels and a towel from the *en-suite* bathroom.

He started to wipe her face until she protested.

'You don't have to! Thanks, but I'm quite able to—'

'Bridget,' he broke in sternly. 'I've done much more than this to you before, so will you desist?'

She desisted in a feeble way, as she was swept by a memory of the things this man had done for her, and how he'd made her feel so safe. All the same, she had to protest. 'But—' she began.

He folded the second flannel and put it to her forehead. It was blessedly cool and soothing. 'Don't say anything,' he ordered. Then, a couple of minutes later, when her breathing had returned to normal, he added. 'Something you ate?'

'Probably.' But, since I have a cast-iron stomach, much more likely to be morning sickness, she thought.

He took the flannel away and frowned at her. 'Are you sure?'

She moved her shoulders slightly. 'Maybe nerves as well. I wasn't sure whether you would believe me, but it is all true.'

'I do believe it's quite possible, although I'll certainly check,' he said dryly. 'I don't know her well, but I would imagine Julia Nixon is cool and clever, and women scorned…' He shrugged and got to his feet. 'Which means I owe you an apology, Bridget. I hope you can see that it was the only thing that seemed to make sense.'

Bridget looked up at him. 'You really don't trust women, do you?' she said quietly.

He shoved his hands into his pockets and looked down at her meditatively. 'I don't trust anyone on face value.'

The thought ran through Bridget's mind *Then you're just as likely to believe this is not your baby—and that would be the final insult.*

'Oh, well.' She stood up. 'I'm sorry this happened.' She gestured to the flannels and the towel. 'I'll go now.'

He made an abrupt movement. 'Stay until you're sure you're fine.'

'No, thank you. I am sure.' She ran her fingers through her hair and straightened her raspberry top.

'I hope I haven't made you late for work, but I'm flat out at the moment.'

'No. I'm on holiday for a few weeks, and—' But she didn't have time to finish what she'd been going to say because his PA knocked on the door and called through that he was so sorry but Adam's next appointment had arrived.

Adam Beaumont swore softly beneath his breath, but Bridget smiled at him briefly and said, *'Adios!'*

And she left, gathering her purse on the way.

Fortunately, because she'd forgotten about it, she was at home when her friend Sandra from Numinbah arrived, with her baby, to spend the afternoon with her.

The baby girl, Daisy, was three months old now, and she slept through most of the afternoon. It was just before Sandra was due to leave that Daisy, in her cot, opened her eyes, saw Bridget looking down at her and smiled a blinding toothless smile as she wriggled joyfully.

Bridget couldn't resist it. She asked permission to pick Daisy up, and as the tiny girl snuggled into her shoulder a primitive age-old instinct overcame Bridget. For the first time the baby growing within her became a precious reality rather than a burden, and her options narrowed.

She thought of herself and Adam. Not the new, hard Adam, but the man she'd trusted and loved to be with. Joined for ever in a little person who was the result of their rapture and passion. Be it a boy or girl, there would be some of its father, some of the features she'd loved linked with hers. And, even more than that, it was a part of *her*, and as such it could only be a joy to her.

* * *

After Sandra had left, Bridget took a long, hard look at her whole life. It occurred to her that all the things she did well enough, if not brilliantly, while they might not fit her out to be a cutting-edge journalist might be useful as a mother. And she suddenly discerned that she'd lacked a goal in life—could fate have provided her with one in the form of this baby?

It was a discovery that caused the path that stretched before her to look a lot less rocky.

CHAPTER FIVE

A LESS rocky path didn't have any effect on morning sickness, however, as she discovered the next morning.

To complicate matters, she'd just started to feel nauseous, but thought she was holding it at bay, when her doorbell rang.

She hesitated, then went to answer it. It was Adam.

They simply stared at each other for a long moment, then he said, 'May I come in? I want to apologise. I've spoken to Julia Nixon and she's confirmed everything you told me.'

Bridget put a hand to her mouth, then took it away. 'I'm sorry, it's not very convenient.' She took a step backwards, then whirled on her heel and raced for the bathroom.

When she came back, she was pale but composed—and he was standing in the middle of her lounge with his hands shoved into his jeans pockets and a frown in his eyes.

He took a long moment to scan her from head to toe. She wore a brown summery dress patterned with white dots, in a clinging crêpe material. It had a scooped neckline and came to just above her knees. With it she wore brown backless moccasins with white laces. Her face had obviously just been washed; it was free of any make-up and there were damp strands in her fringe. She looked younger than her years, though, and somehow vulnerable.

'Bridget,' he said abruptly, 'is this morning sickness?'

She looked away as she wondered how to deny it.

'Two mornings in a row?' he said, as he scanned her pale face.

Her shoulders slumped. 'Yes. But I wasn't sure how to tell you, or even if I would.'

'You weren't going to tell me?'

She winced at the way he said it, then soldiered on. 'There didn't seem to be much point, since there's no future for us. Besides which I wouldn't be at all surprised if you don't believe it's yours. But I absolutely refuse to go through any DNA testing.' Her eyes suddenly glinted green fire at him. 'I know whose baby this is, and that's enough for me.'

A long, fraught pause developed as he digested this. She couldn't read his expression, but she saw that nerve flickering in his jaw and knew what it boded—Adam Beaumont at his most controlled and harsh.

'You're not its only parent,' he said.

She shrugged. 'I may not be, but I'm its crucial parent at the moment, and to my mind that gives me the right to call the shots.'

As she said it tears ran down her cheeks, and she licked their saltiness from her lips and wondered why she should be crying when she felt so angry. It came to her that all her anger and hurt had boiled over at last—anger that he could have loved her and walked away from her; hurt that he could have believed she would spread rumours about him because it was in her blood, inherited from her father, or because she was silly and thoughtless.

He had also automatically assumed she would pursue him if she ever discovered he was who he was, so he'd let her go on thinking he was just a run-of-the-mill guy who was wary of any attachment...

She licked her lips and dashed at her eyes. 'You see, Adam Beaumont, not only am I its crucial parent, but I know you don't want me. You don't trust me, you couldn't have made it clearer. So I've made my own plans. You can stay and listen to them or you can walk away again, but this baby is *my* affair and will be quite safe with me.'

'Why?'

The one word seemed to echo around the room.

'What do you mean?' she asked at last.

'Why do you even want it if you hold such a list of grievances against me?'

Bridget put her hands on her belly. 'Because it's part of me,' she said, quietly but quite definitely. 'And because it's part of you—the part that made me feel as I'd never felt before. I know now that was not the whole you and never could be, but on that one night it was special to me,' she said with painful honesty.

'Sit down,' he said, and gestured to the settee.

'Look, this is my apartment,' she flashed back. 'I

can invite you to sit down *if* I want to, but you can't order me around!'

He grimaced. 'Would it be possible for both of us to sit down and discuss this rationally?'

She hesitated.

'Perhaps we could even have a cup of coffee—?'

'Don't mention coffee,' Bridget broke in with a shudder. 'It's what set me off yesterday morning.'

'Tea, then?'

'Black tea would be nice,' she said slowly, and moved towards the kitchen.

'I'd offer to make it, but I wouldn't want to upset you.'

'Sit down.' Bridget pointed to the dining table.

'And shut up?' he offered softly.

She had to smile—the most fleeting of smiles, gone almost before it was formed, but somehow the tension between them was reduced.

'So tell me about these plans,' he said when she'd made the tea.

'I thought I'd keep working for a while,' she said. 'But it's been dawning on me slowly that I may have taken up journalism as a tribute to my father's memory rather than because it was something I was passionate about. So to leave it is not going to be devastating.'

She nibbled a dry biscuit and went on. 'Naturally I would like to have a career, but until one recommends itself to me, and while I'm pregnant and then looking after a new baby, I intend to start painting again.'

She pointed to one of her pictures on the wall, a claret-red cluster of frangipani blooms on a heritage-green background, and told him about the offer that had been made to her. 'I think it would be a rather perfect occupation for the time being—and I'm actually looking forward to it. Financially I'm fairly secure in any event, until the baby is about two. Then I will need to earn somehow or other.'

Adam Beaumont sipped his tea. 'I take it you've thought all this out in the context of me not knowing about the baby?'

'Well, yes,' she conceded.

'And now?'

Their gazes clashed.

'I…' Bridget stopped and started again. 'I don't really know what to think now. I mean—do you *want* to have anything to do with it?' she asked in a strained voice.

He closed his eyes briefly, in obvious disbelief. 'Bridget, I may have let you down and not trusted you, but do you honestly believe I'd be content to let a child of mine go through life never knowing me?'

'But those are the things I *don't* know about you,' she said hoarsely. 'And I don't know how it would work—'

He interrupted her in a hard voice. 'Then I'll tell you about me. I grew up virtually without a father. He hated me because I reminded him of his own father, who was a cruel man. But Henry could do no wrong. From my earliest memories nothing I ever did was good enough for my father. He and my mother fought over it. They didn't speak to each other for years. I left home when I was sixteen because I didn't think I was wanted and I never went back. And the bottom line to it all is this,' he went on. 'No, I wasn't planning to have children, but now it's happened, and if you think I will allow any child of mine to suffer the lack of a proper father, you're wrong, Bridget.'

Bridget closed her mouth. It had fallen open not only at what he'd revealed but at the bitter intensity he'd shown.

And although his expression was wiped clean and un-readable as soon as he'd finished speaking, he got up and walked over to the window, and she could see the tension in the lines of his back as he stared out at the street.

She was not to know that Adam Beaumont had sur-prised himself with the depth of feeling this news had provoked in him. Nor was she to know that the more he thought about it, the more he was struck by the irony of the situation. His uncle causing him to look at his life and his future so recently was one of those ironies.

A certain rumour associated with his sister-in-law, although he didn't know if it was true, was another. But his mouth hardened at the thought of it, and the bitter-sweet revenge he could exact with this news...

There was also, though, the fact that even if he was suspicious of or impatient with this baby's mother, he still felt protective towards her.

In fact, he discovered, not only could he offer his own child a proper father, and that was paramount, but the more he thought about it he also had the belief that there was only one solution, and it was growing in him by the moment...

'I—I'm sorry,' she said, barely audibly. 'I had

heard… Julia did mention the divisions in your family, but I didn't realize—'

He turned back to her abruptly. 'It's over and done with now.'

'But what are we going to do?' she queried. 'Of course I wouldn't stop you from having access to it.'

Access… The word seemed to rebound on Adam, and he pictured it: a child with two homes, a child never quite sure where its allegiance should lie, a child possibly with a stepfather whose influence he, its real father, would have no control over.

'I don't want access when and where it suits you, Bridget,' he said harshly. 'There's only one thing to do. We need to get married.'

It took a moment or two for this to get through to Bridget, and when it did she stared at him incredulously. 'You can't be serious!'

'I am.'

'But we don't love each other. We hardly know each other! I don't even think we *like* each other now, and you certainly don't trust me—how can we?'

'Bridget.' He came back to the table and towered over her. 'You can't have it both ways.'

She looked up at him uncomprehendingly. 'I don't know what you mean.'

'You've laid a few serious charges at my door, but I'm offering to redress the let-downs and the hurt to the best of my ability. Don't you believe a child deserves both its parents?'

She moistened her lips. 'Yes, of course—although it

didn't seem to work very well for your parents, and that's what we would have to be afraid of—marrying then falling out badly,' she couldn't help but add. And then she thought of more objections. 'How come you're not accusing me of all sorts of crimes?' She waved a hand. 'Like trying to trap you or foist someone else's baby on you?'

'I was the one,' he said slowly, 'who initiated what happened that night. You were the one who got yourself clobbered by a falling branch. I really don't think you were in a fit state to set about trapping me.'

'I have to agree,' Bridget said dryly. 'But, to be scrupulously honest, I didn't do anything to stop you either.'

He grimaced. 'Also, I was wrong about you and those bloody rumours. That's why I'm here. And I can't mistake your determination to go it alone. None of it fits in with a girl on the make. The other thing is, you're a terrible liar.'

She moved convulsively but he took her hand. 'No, just listen. I mean that as a compliment—not that you lie really frequently or well. As in the case of Mr Smith.'

Bridget subsided somewhat.

'And—' he studied her narrowly '—you're deadly serious now, aren't you, Bridget?' He waited.

She nodded at last. 'But I'm not going to do anything I may later regret,' she murmured. 'And, forgive me— I do appreciate your feelings now I know them—but marrying you could fall into that category. We just—we just don't know each other.'

A fleeting look that was so grim touched his eyes as

their gazes locked. She shivered involuntarily, but she didn't look away.

His lips twisted. 'I should have known there was a touch of steel in you.'

Bridget raised her eyebrows.

'Yes,' he went on. 'A lot of girls would have been content to sit and wring their hands rather than put themselves at risk, struggling down a flooded creek in a God-almighty storm to save some children.' He shrugged. 'Think of this, though. *This* child is going to be with us for the rest of our lives. However it happened, we've forged that link and it can't be broken. But—and forgive me for saying this—' a wry little gleam lit his eyes '—the *way* it happened was quite amazing, I thought.'

Bridget's gaze fell before his at last, and a little pulse started to beat at the base of her throat. At the same time some pink coursed into her cheeks. If all that wasn't enough of a give-away of the power of her memories of that night in his arms, a little tremor ran through her.

He said nothing, but when she looked up she knew her disarray had been noted and filed away, probably for future reference.

She licked her lips. 'Are you not even a little surprised, let alone reeling from shock like I was?' she queried huskily.

He let her hand go, but pushed her hair out of her eyes with one long finger as a smile twisted his lips. 'Of course. But then nothing we do is simple and straightforward. It's always been one thing out of the blue after another.'

She had to concede this with a slight smile of her

own. It faded as a sudden thought came to her. 'Does this have anything to do with your brother's wife?'

He frowned. 'What do you mean?'

Bridget thought back to Julia's other revelation— her considered opinion that neither Adam nor Henry Beaumont would ever get Henry's wife out of their system.

She said slowly, 'If you can't have her you'll have to make do with second best, and *this* second best—' she patted her flat stomach '—has the advantage of coming as a package deal?'

'On the contrary,' he said, looking very directly at her. 'This has nothing whatsoever to do with my brother's wife. You never did, Bridget.'

'I wish I could believe you,' she murmured.

'Why don't you let me show you?'

She blinked at him and said a little warily, 'H-how?'

'Well, first things first. Come and see my place. It's about an hour's flight away.'

She lifted her eyebrows at him. 'Fly? Just like that?'

'I have my own helicopter.'

He not only had his own helicopter, he piloted it himself. And the speed with which he organised the day almost took Bridget's breath away.

He called his bright young assistant, Trent, and they went through all his appointments for the day and re-scheduled them.

'Uh, by the way,' Adam added, when his diary had been sorted out, 'I forgot to tell you, but I'm having din-ner with my great-uncle Julius—let me see—tomorrow night. Ring up his housekeeper and tell him I'm bringing a guest. Thanks, Trent.' He clicked off his phone and turned to her. 'Ready, Bridget?'

She was only able to nod dazedly.

He piloted her towards his property in the Rathdowney Beaudesert area, over the Great Dividing Range from the Gold Coast. They flew over rugged country and he actually circled the creek they'd followed that tempestuous night, and the grassy plateau that had been their saving.

The shed looked smaller than she remembered. The tree had been removed, but the scar where it had uprooted itself on the hillside was still a raw gash.

'I never did get around to replacing those pyjamas,' she said ruefully into her mike, above the noise of the rotors.

'Don't worry. I compensated the owners. They're a youngish couple, and they do use the shed on weekends while they build their house. See the foundations there?'

She nodded as she followed the line of his finger, then was struck by an unanswered question she had.

'What *were* you doing driving around the Numinbah Valley in that elderly Land Rover that night? Especially if you can fly in this?'

He patted the control panel. 'This bird had mechanical problems, but I needed to get back to the Coast so I took one of the property vehicles and took a back road. It's hard to imagine being worse off that night, but if I'd flown into those storms I might have been.'

Bridget shivered.

* * *

Half an hour later he landed the helicopter on a concrete pad and said, 'Welcome to Mount Grace, Mrs
Smith.'

Bridget stared around with parted lips. 'Oh,' she said.
'Thank you. It's—so beautiful.'

She was even more impressed after a guided tour.

Being over the Range was like being in a different
world from the sub-tropical coastal plain. Here there
were great golden, grassy paddocks, and there was little
humidity in the air. It was still hot, but it was a different kind of heat, and you could imagine cold, frosty
winters and roaring fires.

Nor did the vegetation resemble the tropical profusion of the Coast. There wasn't a palm tree in sight, but
the gardens were magnificent all the same—even if not
tropical—and the homestead, sheltered in the lee of a
wooded hill, was a delight.

White walls, steep thatched roofs, French doors
leading onto a paved terrace, and an unusual design of
circular rooms. And the whole length of the terrace was
dotted with terracotta tubs holding every coloured flow-
ering bougainvillaea you could imagine.

The occupants of the great grassy paddocks were
mostly horses, mares and foals, although deep rich red
cattle were to be seen too.

'So—you breed horses?' she turned to ask Adam.

'It's my hobby. My uncle Julius—he's my great-
uncle, actually—is my partner. He lives for horses. It's
his greatest ambition to breed a Melbourne Cup winner.
He used to go down for the race every year. He's not

well enough these days, but he's a mine of information on the Cup.'

Bridget smiled to herself, but didn't explain why. Instead she turned back to the house. 'It's—it's very unusual.'

'It's a South African design. Thatched roofs and ron-davels—round rooms—are traditional and common over there. My mother was South African. Her name was Grace.'

'So she's no longer alive?' Bridget queried.

'No. She and my father were killed in a car acci-dent.' He paused, then decided not to tell Bridget that his father had been drunk at the time. 'Come inside and have a look, then we'll have lunch. Do you feel up to lunch?'

'I feel…' Bridget drew some deep breaths of the clear air '…dangerously hungry, as it happens. I would kill for some lunch, in other words.'

He grinned.

Mount Grace homestead was vast and cool. There were no ceilings to hide the soaring thatch roof, the floors were polished wood, and there were stone fireplaces in all the rooms.

The main lounge-dining area was exquisitely fur-nished. Some of the furniture was in woods she didn't recognise, and looked very old. There was a zebra skin on one wall, and a Zulu shield that reminded her of the movie of the same name.

'All in all,' she said, breaking her rather awestruck

silence, 'there's one phrase that springs to my mind—out of Africa.'

'Yes—ah, there you are.' Adam turned at a sound behind them. 'Bridget, this is Fay Mortimer—housekeeper extraordinaire.'

'No such thing,' the middle-aged woman who stood before them replied. 'I'm sorry I wasn't here to meet you, but I had my hands full. How do you do, Bridget?'

They shook hands.

Fay Mortimer might be middle-aged, but she was slim and trendy-looking, with a shining bob of grey-streaked brown hair.

'Hands full?' Adam queried.

'I'm babysitting my granddaughter today. She's only three months,' she said to Bridget. 'But I have got lunch ready, and I thought it might be nice for you to eat on the terrace?' She raised an eyebrow at Adam.

'Sounds good to me. We're ready when you are. Bridget is actually starving.'

'Right-oh! You sit down. I'll bring it out.'

Lunch was delicious: a light consommé followed by a Caesar salad laden with smoked salmon, anchovies, and crispy bacon pieces. There were warm rolls to go with it, and it was followed by a cheese platter, biscuits and fruit.

As they ate, and Bridget sipped iced water while he had a beer, he told her about the stud and the stallions he had. He told her that Fay Mortimer's son-in-law was stud master, and lived there with her daughter—the mother of the three-month-old baby she'd been looking after. He also told her that they all lived in apparent harmony, although in separate cottages on the property.

It was utterly peaceful as they ate, with bees humming through the flowerbeds and dragonflies hovering, their transparent wings catching the sunlight. And the view was spread before them like a lovely sunlit tapestry under a blue, blue sky.

But when she'd finished Bridget laid down her linen napkin and said, 'I can't just walk into all this.'

Adam plucked a grape from the cheese platter and toyed with it in his long fingers. 'Why not?'

She hesitated, then swept her hair out of her eyes and took a sip of water. 'All this—it doesn't seem right.'

He ate the grape and plucked another, but it must have had an imperfection because after he'd studied it he tossed it into the shrubbery. 'I don't really understand what "all this" has to do with it. Are you trying to say if I'd been a wood-chopper at a country show you'd have married me?'

'That's ridiculous,' Bridget replied coldly.

'Why?' He stared at her derisively.

'Because—well, apart from anything else it is *obviously* not a good idea to marry anyone you don't really know!' she said through her teeth, and felt so frustrated she picked up the last few grapes on the stem and threw the lot into the shrubbery.

'Temper, temper,' he admonished softly.

'You started it!'

'Well, before we denude the table, may I point out

that we *do* know each other pretty well in one way—the way they euphemistically refer to as the *biblical* way.'

Bridget had gone from angry to feeling slightly embarrassed at her rather childish display, but this taunt brought a tide of bright scarlet to her cheeks. She said, with as much dignity as she could muster, 'It's not the only way you need to know someone.'

'No, but it helps greatly if all is well in that direction,' he said wryly.

It was Bridget's turn to stare at him, and then to draw a deep breath and say, 'I appreciate your offer, but I'm of a mind to do this on my own.'

He swore under his breath.

'As for all this,' she continued, with a sweep of her hand, 'it's a bit like a carrot being dangled in front of me.'

'I wouldn't put it like that.' He eyed her narrowly. 'But I would see it as an apt setting for a girl who's told me she loves horses, gardening, painting. It could be a landscape painter or a gardener's dream—and there's a grand piano in the music room we didn't get to see, as well as a harp, come to think of it.'

Bridget was silent.

'You don't think that would make life enjoyable for you?' he queried.

She looked around, and had to smile involuntarily as a mare and a frisky young foal wandered up to the fence on the other side of the garden. But she sighed as she said, 'You don't understand, do you? Or—and this could be another problem—you're so used to getting your own way you don't want to understand how I feel.'

'I have to admit I would have understood better if you'd jumped at the chance—not so much of marrying me but of getting my money.'

'Ah. Well, I'm glad I surprised you.' Her words were accompanied by a lethal little look.

It was his turn to stay silent. Then he pushed his chair back and changed the subject completely. 'Come and say hello.' He indicated the foal.

She got up and followed him to the fence. On the way she pulled up a dandelion, which she offered to the foal. The dark bay colt sniffed it, lipped it, then chomped it greedily.

She laughed and rubbed his nose.

Adam Beaumont smiled and turned to lean back against the fence. He said quietly, 'I've had cause to think I should rewrite my life recently.'

Bridget turned to him in some surprise. 'You have?'

He nodded and stretched his arms along the fence. And then he told her something of his last encounter with his great-uncle Julius.

'I don't want his proxies,' he said. 'If I do ever get to chair the board of Beaumonts I want to do it on my own. I don't want anyone ever to be able to say I rode there on my uncle's coattails. But for the rest—' he shrugged '—it is time to bury the past. Including Marie-Claire.'

Marie-Claire, Bridget thought. Just her name says it all...

'And I can't get this bleak little image of ending up on my own like Julius out of my mind,' he said with obvious frustration. He looked fleetingly wry. 'Perhaps that's why we need each other.'

Bridget opened her mouth, but he waved her to silence.

'I played God that night in the shed,' he said. 'I should have known better. I did. But it was a page we wrote together, Bridget. If it's brought more than you bargained for, the same goes for me. Even so, you obviously don't feel like tearing it up and throwing it away, and neither do I.' He paused. 'Despite everything, there's a *right* feeling to it.'

Bridget stared at him with her lips parted.

He had been looking into the blue yonder over her head, but now brought his gaze down to her. 'I know it's not a declaration of undying love, but that's the truth. And, contrary to what you said earlier this morning, I *do* like you.' His lips twisted. 'A lot.'

He reached out and brushed her hair out of her eyes. 'I don't like to think of you alone, and even if you have decided it's your brave new world—and I'm sure it will be that from time to time—it doesn't need to be.'

CHAPTER SIX

I⊤ was the sound of a car driving away that broke the spell for Bridget—that long, long moment when she was mesmerised by what he'd said, what he'd admitted, and the impact it had had on her.

'Who…?' she whispered.

He looked across at the departing plume of dust on the driveway behind the house. 'Fay. If we have no dinner guests she takes the afternoon off.'

'Oh.'

He looked at her wryly.

'I'm just a little speechless,' she confessed.

'You've offered me advice yourself,' he reminded her. 'To move on,' he elucidated.

'I know, but I didn't expect to—' She couldn't go on.

'To feature so prominently in it?' he suggested, humour glinting in his eyes.

'No.' She took a shaky little breath. 'But when you put it like that, it's terribly tempting. It sounds like a partnership. It sounds—sensible. But that's what it is, isn't it?'

He frowned. 'What do you mean?'

'It's…' She sought for the right words. 'It's a marriage of convenience, really.'

He didn't speak for a long time, then said, 'But that seems to recommend itself to you?'

She shrugged.

'Bridget,' he said slowly, 'I made some of the worst decisions of my life in a rush of—of passion, I suppose you could say. But respect, affection, and something to build on like a child, our child, recommends itself to *me*, yes.'

'I—I still need to think about it,' she murmured in some confusion—because his words, while so sane, seemed to strike a little chill through her. 'You must see that—well, it's the last thing I expected, and—'

'No, I don't think you need to think about it,' he contradicted. 'There can't be any reason why it isn't the best solution. You've told me your life—career-wise, anyway—is probably due for an overhaul. Is there *anyone* in your life it could make the slightest difference to?'

'No,' she denied. 'There's no one. Apart from my mother, and whatever I do is going to take her by surprise.'

'Then is there any reason to deny this baby both its parents in a secure home? Is there any reason not to put its welfare before everything else?'

Bridget turned away suddenly as his gaze bored into her. Was she thinking only of herself now? Was the fact that Adam had so much to offer—billionaire status, in other words—irrelevant really? She'd accused him of dangling a carrot before her, but perhaps that was immaterial. So what was behind her reluctance? Her own feelings?

Or a secret, inner suspicion that she was far better off without an Adam Beaumont who didn't really love her, even though he respected and felt some affection for her?

How selfish was that, though?

'Bridget?'

She turned back at last. 'I—maybe you're right.'

'Should we do it, then?'

Bridget discovered that she couldn't speak, because a fine trembling had started within her and had spread so that she was shaking from head to toe, shaking and feeling quite incapable of coherence.

She was unaware that she was also paper-pale and her eyes were as dark as emeralds.

Adam Beaumont cursed beneath his breath as he read accurately the enormous strain she'd been under, was still under, and did the only thing he could. He put his arms around her.

She didn't resist, but she didn't respond either—not for an age, at least. But gradually his warmth and the solid, secure feel of his arms got through to her, and she laid her cheek on his shoulder.

'I'm sorry,' he said, barely audibly. 'But you will be safe now.'

Bridget rested against him as all sorts of thoughts ran through her mind. One seemed to stand out. It was his child she was carrying and he did want it. Surely she owed that to the new life within her?

Her thoughts ran on. Did that not transcend any

doubts she had that he might never have her in his heart the way he did the mysterious Marie-Claire?

Here her thoughts performed a little jig, so much so that she suddenly found herself wishing she'd never heard that name—because it seemed to embody for her an allure and a magnetism no man could resist.

I'll have to get over that, she cautioned herself, if I do this.

'Bridget?' He slipped his fingers beneath her chin and tilted it so he could see into her eyes.

Her lips parted. 'All right. Yes, I will marry you. Thank you,' she whispered.

He hesitated, as if about to say something, then changed his mind and lowered his mouth to hers.

She stood quite still in his arms, waiting for the magic to start to race through her, but nothing happened.

He lifted his head. 'Still worried, Mrs Smith?' he queried.

'I think I must be.'

He looked pensive. 'You don't suppose I need to conjure up a wild storm and an old shed?'

Bridget's eyes widened.

He traced the outline of her mouth. 'You may not realise this, and I certainly have not given you cause to, but I've thought of us together, when it was the last thing I should have been thinking of.'

'You have?' She blinked at him.

'Yes. For instance, I happened to be in a business meeting and I found myself doodling something most—unusual for the kind of meeting it was—a blue teddy bear, of all things. And that led to all sorts of in-appropriate thoughts about you—and us. It wasn't my best meeting.'

Bridget smiled faintly and leant against him. 'That's nice, though. I don't mind being associated with blue teddy bears.'

His lips twisted and his hands moved on her hips. 'It was what was under them that caused me more embar-rassment.'

She looked into his eyes. 'Really?'

'Oh, yes.'

She studied the rueful look in his blue eyes, the darkness of his wind-ruffled hair, and a little inner tremor ran through her that was quite different from the panicky tremors she'd experienced before. Not, she found herself thinking, that he looked as he had that night in the shed. He was clean-shaven now, and although he'd discarded his tie, and his shirt was open at the throat, and he'd rolled up his sleeves, he was still Adam Beaumont—not just a man called Adam…

Or was he?

Had the way he'd recalled memories of that night brought the other Adam to mind? Something had. Some-thing about him was awakening her senses—senses that she had begun to think had been bludgeoned to death under the weight of all the trauma. Something was causing her fingertips to tingle with the longing to be able to touch him and her body to thrill at his closeness.

Perhaps it was something quite simple—he'd be-witched her almost from the first moment.

She took a breath that was a little sigh of relief. 'You're back,' she murmured.

'Back?' he queried, barely audibly, his breath stirring the fringe on her forehead, a question in his eyes.

'I—I've thought there were two of you. The man in the shed and Adam Beaumont. Sometimes,' she explained, 'I had these wonderful memories; at other times they were so sad because you were so different.'

'I'm sorry.' He kissed her forehead and then, after they'd stared deeply into each other's eyes, he sought her lips and they kissed deeply.

Bridget realised she was lost not much later. Just as lost as she'd been the night they'd first made love—only this time she was standing beside a paddock fence, with a couple of horses as spectators. But she didn't protest when he released her, only to take her hand and lead her back to the house.

Nor did she protest when she found herself in a round bedroom that might have been modelled on a traditional rondavel but was a symphony of sheer luxury. Beneath the soaring thatch roof, on the rich timber of a polished floor, stood a wooden four-poster bed with sheer white drapes. The coverlet was cream and the pillows lime-green. There were two beautiful sofas also in cream, with lime cushions, and wrought-iron candle sconces on the walls. The lamps were also fashioned of wrought-iron. The room felt exotic and slightly foreign, but it was breathtaking.

Even more breathtaking was the current that seemed to be flowing between her and Adam. She'd wondered at the back of her mind if the change of venue would stifle her urgent need of him—she was amazed at how urgent it had grown, when not that long ago she'd felt nothing but a sense of a partnership in the name of her baby.

Now, though, as he closed the door and took her in his arms again, the longing and thirst for him she'd escaped for a time in that strange little cocoon she'd inhabited became alive and vital. She breathed in the essence of him with a burgeoning feeling of joy.

She came alive beneath his wandering hands, and as he undressed her she returned the compliment. She undid his shirt buttons and slipped her arms around his waist.

'Mmm…' It was a sound of pure appreciation she made as she revelled in the long, lean, strong lines of him, and the feel of his shoulder beneath her cheek. But it wasn't only appreciation of the finer physical points of Adam Beaumont that prompted her appreciation. It wasn't only her growing desire and the waves of pleasure he was arousing in her. It was that warm, safe feeling he'd given her once before, coming back…

'Not a scratch or a bruise,' he said as he ran his fingers down between her breasts. They were lying on the bed, their clothes were lying on the floor, and he'd drawn the bed's curtains, so they were isolated from the rest of the room—the rest of the world almost, she felt.

'No, all healed,' she agreed with an effort as his fingers returned to her nipples. 'That's too nice.'

He grinned—a sudden, wicked little grin. Then he sobered and lifted his head to rest it on his arm so he could look down at her. 'Too soon?' he asked, although his wandering hand drifted lower.

'Oh, no,' Bridget gasped, and clung to him suddenly. 'I might die if you don't…don't…'

'So might I, Mrs Smith. Shall we do it together?' He rolled onto her, and the lovely rhythm of two bodies as one commenced and grew to fever-pitch, which he sustained for longer than she would ever have believed possible. Then the slow drift back to reality came, but the closeness remained.

'That was—so—so…' She tried to talk when she was able to speak again, but she couldn't put it into words.

He pulled the linen sheet up over them and took her back in his arms. 'It was.' He paused, then said with suspicious gravity, 'I can't think of the right word either.'

She laughed softly and ran her hand over his shoulder then through his tousled hair, and finally laid it on his cheek. 'One of my fears—one of my *many* fears,' she said, and looked askance, 'has been laid to rest.'

'Only one?' he queried.

'Well, probably a lot of them,' she amended. 'But this was a really awkward one. I don't know if that's the right word—but I'll tell you all the same.'

His lips twisted. 'Go ahead.'

'Why are you laughing at me?' She took her hand away and looked hurt.

'If I am,' he replied, 'it's because it seems that, far from striking you speechless, I've had the opposite effect on you.'

'Oh.' Bridget digested this. 'Is it not the right etiquette to be talkative after sex—glorious sex?' She lowered her lashes so that he wouldn't see the glint of humour in her eyes.

'Now, that puts it in a nutshell—why didn't I think of putting it like that?' he asked wryly. 'Anyway, you may talk to your heart's content. I'm listening.'

Bridget suddenly grew quite serious, 'I was afraid that I'd only be able to do it if I'd thought I was going to die—like before. I know it sounds ridiculous, but there you go.'

'You did happen to mention something about dying,' he reminded her.

She looked rueful. 'Not that kind of dying—that's a different kind of death. You know what I mean.'

He studied the serious green depths of her eyes, and the perfect skin of her neck and shoulders, then stirred. 'Precisely, as it happens since I was in the same boat. But I think you're right. Can we lay the other fears to rest now?'

Bridget opened her mouth and closed it.

'What?' He kissed her forehead. 'You might as well tell me all of them.'

She grimaced. 'I thought…' she began, and hesitated, then plunged on, 'I thought that you would insist on all kinds of tests before you accepted this baby—if you accepted it, if you even wanted it.'

He shrugged. 'You can go through life being cynical and skeptical, but there comes a day when…I don't know…to have faith seems more rewarding.' He looked at her penetratingly.

'You can trust me on this one,' she said steadily.

He kissed her and ran his fingers through her hair, then walked them down her arm to her waist.

Bridget took a breath, but he grinned and kissed her again. 'Unfortunately we need to go. Do you mind? Otherwise we'll be flying in the dark.'

'Is it that late? No, of course not.'

But he took his time to kiss her and hug her thoroughly, before he threw back the sheet and they got up to have a shower.

As he was driving her back to her flat, he said, 'Will you come and have dinner with my uncle Julius tomorrow night?'

Bridget, who'd been in her own private little world, and still spiritually seemed to be at Mount Grace, came back to the present with an effort. 'Yes. If you like. Will you tell him?'

'That we're getting married? Yes. About the baby? That's up to you.'

'I think,' she said slowly, 'I'd like to keep that private for a while. It's still very early.'

'Fair enough. Look—' he brought his BMW to a halt '—I'd love to spend the evening with you, but I'm going to be playing catch up this evening and tomorrow as it is. Will you be OK?'

'I'll be fine,' she assured him. 'It has—it did turn out to be a lovely day,' she added quietly.

'It did.' He closed his fingers around hers. 'I'll pick you up tomorrow, around six-thirty.'

* * *

Bridget spent that night feeling a bit like Alice in Wonderland.

One thing had caused her to sigh with relief: there was a message on her answering machine from her mother. She'd be incommunicado for a few days, as they were going up country for a break.

But it did cause Bridget to wonder whether, even in a few days, she'd be able to explain things coherently to her mother.

It had all—finally—made sense to her at the time, and in Adam's presence, but her mother could be a different matter.

She broke off her thoughts to bite her lip, and felt a little hot at the memory of being in Adam's presence. Then she realised that being alone in her apartment was another matter.

Alone in her apartment she was able to examine the events of the previous day in detail. Such as how she'd gone from anger, disbelief and hurt—from the conviction that she'd be far better off having her baby on her own—to allowing him to make love to her and loving every minute of it.

Would the Adam she remembered from the shed always have the power to seduce her?

And always be able to make her feel lonely and as if something precious was missing from her life when he wasn't there?

The other thing that perturbed her was the fact that she'd been able to take an impartial view of a woman Adam's brother had stolen from him—even offer advice

on the subject—but now she could only think of her
with a little bubble of dread.

She was ready when Adam pressed her doorbell.

She'd been to the hairdresser and had her hair
styled. She'd chosen a cropped jacket in a fine wool
plaid, black on blue-green, over a short fitted black
dress. With it she wore sheer black stockings and black
suede shoes.

When she stared at herself in the mirror and thought she
didn't look right—smart, yes, but too formal—she sternly
took herself to task and refused, simply refused, to indulge
in an orgy of redressing. Which was just as well, because
Adam arrived early, bearing a bottle of French champagne.

His reaction was satisfying and vindicated that
decision.

'How utterly elegant, Mrs Smith,' he murmured in the
moments before he kissed her. 'And how wise to have
waited to apply your lipstick,' he added, as he lifted his
head with points of laugher dancing in his eyes.

'It's not that I waited. I just hadn't got around to it,'
she denied. 'Truly! You're early.'

'I know,' he murmured, and pulled a long, slim box
from the pocket of his beautiful grey suit, worn with a
navy shirt. 'But I thought we might need a few minutes
to sort this out.' He put the box and the bottle on the
dining room table. 'Glasses?'

'Oh. I'll get them—but I shouldn't drink.'

He raised an eyebrow. 'Not even half a glass?'

Bridget moved into the kitchen and took two glasses out of a cupboard. She brought them back to the table as he expertly removed the foil and popped the cork. 'As a toast to us?' he added.

'Half a glass, then. Thank you.'

She accepted the champagne from him and they solemnly raised their glasses.

'To us,' he said.

'To us,' Bridget agreed, and took a sip.

'Open the box.'

Bridget hesitated. It couldn't be a ring box, it was too long, but it *was* obviously a jewellery box. Did she want jewellery from him? she found herself wondering.

She put her glass down and picked up the box. And she caught her breath as she flicked the catch. It wasn't a single ring box. There were four rings in it, all emeralds in different settings.

'I thought you might like to choose,' he said as she raised her stunned eyes to his. 'With those eyes I couldn't go past emeralds,' he murmured. 'But for the rest of it, it's up to you.'

Bridget dropped her gaze to the rings and licked her lips. 'They—they're all beautiful,' she said huskily. 'But I'm not sure I deserve an engagement ring like this— like these.'

'Why ever not?' he countered with a faint frown.

'I don't know,' she was forced to concede. 'I guess— perhaps I just wasn't expecting it.'

'Bridget.' He put his glass down on the table. 'We

have an agreement. We have more than an agreement, don't we?'

She looked up at him to find him studying her intently. 'What do you mean?'

'We not only went through all the pros and cons yesterday, we also sealed it, I would have thought, in a way that was essentially romantic.'

'Well, yes, it was…' She trailed off and blushed as his blue gaze seemed to strip away her smart outfit and expose the slender curves of her body.

'So what's wrong with the next step being an engagement ring, and shortly a wedding ring?' he asked quietly, but with a glint of sheer—sheer what? she wondered. Sheer determination?

Her shoulders sagged suddenly, because it felt as if she'd walked into a battering ram and didn't know how to deal with it at all. Why should she feel there was anything to deal with over this issue? It was only an engagement ring. The much more telling circumstance was going to be whether she allowed him to put a wedding ring on her finger. But hadn't she banished that dilemma yesterday?

'More fears, Bridget?' he said.

'No. No. Uh…' she scanned the rings, and her fingers hovered over them. For some reason—because it might have been the least expensive?—it was the smallest she was drawn to: a baguette-cut central emerald flanked by two smaller round diamonds on a gold band. She took it out and slipped it onto her ring finger. It fitted perfectly, and seemed to be just right for the size and shape of her hand.

She studied it, holding it up to the light, admiring the green depths of the central stone and the fire of the two diamonds. 'This one,' she said.

'Don't you want to try the others?'

'No, thank you. This is—very lovely.'

'And very discerning of you, Mrs Smith,' he murmured as he closed the box on the other rings. 'It's the best emerald, and the diamonds are flawless.'

Bridget took a frustrated breath. 'Well, maybe I will try the others.'

'Why?'

'They may not be as expensive.'

He looked at her wryly. 'Too late—but take the ring off for a moment.'

Bridget did so, and handed it to him.

He picked up her hand. 'Bridget Tully-Smith, will you marry me?' He held the ring, poised to slip it back on her finger. 'I know I haven't exorcised all your fears,' he added. 'But I do believe it's what we should do, and I have your welfare very much at heart.'

It was the last thing Bridget had expected to burst into her mind at this point, but it did, and it articulated her deepest fear: she didn't want to be married for her welfare, she wanted to be married because he was deeply, hopelessly in love with her—*as she was with him*.

Her lips parted and her eyes darkened as the knowledge slammed into her heart, almost taking her breath away. How had this happened to her? she wondered a little desperately. In such a short time? Was it the wonderful sex? The fact that he'd saved her life a couple of times? No, not only that, she acknowledged. Love was the simple factor that explained why she wanted to be with him, why she felt lonely without him even when she felt like fighting him—or throwing grapes around because he frustrated her at times—it made no difference.

It was why she'd been restless and edgy all day, why she'd missed Adam Beaumont as she would always miss him when he was gone from her—and why it might be more than she could bear if she ever lost him... She loved him with all her heart.

'Bridget?'

He was frowning down at her, and she was forced to hide her inner amazement at what had happened to her, the storm of incredible self-knowledge that was so much more powerful than anything she'd ever experienced.

'Yes...' she said. What else could she say? 'I mean—yes.'

He slid the ring onto her finger and kissed her lightly on the lips. 'Then why don't you put your lipstick on and we'll go and see my uncle Julius?'

She was quiet in the car, but he didn't seem to notice.

He did say, as he parked the car, 'Don't take any nonsense from my uncle.'

She looked at him, wide-eyed. 'What kind of nonsense?'

'He can be a pretty straight shooter. And this—' he switched off the engine and reached for her left hand to toy with the ring '—has come as a bit of a surprise to him.'

'Not only to him,' Bridget murmured.

'You mean your mother? Have you told her?'

'No.' Bridget explained about the message she'd received. 'But I was actually thinking of me. I feel a little shell-shocked. And I'm not sure if I feel like facing—anyone.'

'He's not well, Bridget. His doctors reckon he's living on borrowed time. But he's important to me, and I know this will mean a lot to him—the thought of me being settled.' He grimaced and released her hand, but took her chin in his fingers so he could look into her eyes.

'What if he doesn't like me?'

'What's not to like?' he queried, his lips twisting. 'Trust me, he'll like you. Just be yourself.'

Julius Beaumont stared at Bridget, then at Adam in turn, his bushy white eyebrows almost up to his hairline. 'Well, well, well,' he said. 'This is an unexpected pleasure, young lady. Sit down and tell me about yourself. All I got from Adam were the bare facts.'

Bridget relaxed a little, and she exchanged a little glance with Adam that Julius correctly interpreted as containing relief on her part and encouragement on his.

So, Julius found himself thinking, there *is* a bond of some kind between them. Not that I really believed he went out and chose the first girl he could find—or did I? Adam was a mixture of inspired long-term insight and the odd completely off-the-cuff, out-of-the-blue action...

'Thank you,' Bridget said, mercifully unaware of these thoughts, but warming to the old man. She sank onto a settee next to the wheelchair and accepted a glass of juice from Adam, who handed his great-uncle the one Scotch he was allowed.

'Tell me how you met?' Julius continued.

Bridget did so, leaving out the finer points. 'He saved my life—not once but twice,' she finished simply.

Julius Beaumont sipped his Scotch as his internal musing ran on… Not a bad beginning. In fact a whole lot better than he'd hoped for! 'Go on,' he encouraged. 'Tell me about yourself,' he repeated.

And then Bridget surprised him even further—but she also surprised herself, as his horse paintings caught her eye and dredged something up from the back of her mind, something she could share with this old man.

She said whimsically, 'I haven't done a whole lot with my life yet, although that could be about to change, but I believe we might have something in common. I can tell you the last twenty Melbourne Cup winners in chronological order.'

Not only Julius but Adam Beaumont stared at her in surprise.

'My father was fanatical about thoroughbreds,' Bridget went on. 'It was his hobby. Not that he was much of a gambler. Ten dollars each way was his maximum bet, but it was impossible to live in the same house with him and not imbibe some of that fanaticism.' She paused and her lips curved into a smile. 'And because my birthday is in the first week of November—Cup time—we used to study the Cup form together and he'd put an extra ten dollars on our choice for me, for my birthday present.'

'How often did you win?' Adam asked with a chuckle.

'Not always, of course, but over the years I totalled quite a nice, tidy sum.'

'Then you'd better come and study the form with me!' Julius remarked enthusiastically. 'My record has been abysmal lately.' He turned to Adam. 'Did you know this about this girl?' he barked.

'No,' Adam confessed. 'She keeps surprising me.'

Better and better! Julius thought, as Mervyn came to call them to dinner.

Before they sat down to eat, there was a surprise waiting for Bridget in the dining room. A wall of pictures that might have been gold-framed and artistically placed but weren't actually paintings. They were photos of Melbourne Cup winners.

And Julius Beaumont wasn't content to start his meal until she'd pinpointed all the ones she'd won on!

The meal flowed smoothly, and the conversation didn't flag.

But Bridget did look a little tired at the end of it, and Adam asked her in a quiet aside if she was all right.

She nodded, but he slipped her hand into his as they stood to say their farewells, and promised to come back soon.

Julius saw that little gesture, and it was on his mind after they'd left. Although there had been no other lover-like gestures, Adam did care about her welfare, he thought. And the absence of anything else lover-like might just have been a matter of good taste, he mused.

In fact there had been a lot of good taste about Bridget Tully-Smith, he reflected. No pretensions, no bravado, her own nails, no excessive make-up. In all probability a thoroughly nice girl.

So what could go wrong?

A face swam into his mind's eye: Marie-Claire Beaumont's. A flawlessly beautiful face, he had to admit, even although he didn't like the girl.

And it frustrated him unbearably for a moment to think that there was no way he could keep Adam and Marie-Claire apart if they chose otherwise.

But there is something I can do, he said to himself. If you think I'm going to tamely accept *all* your dictates, Adam Beaumont, think again. He rang the bell for Mervyn.

'You called?' Mervyn stuck his head around the lounge door. 'Ready for bed?'

'No, I am not, Merv.' Julius was the only one who had the temerity to shorten Mervyn's name. 'Get me my solicitor.'

Mervyn came fully into the room. 'You want to speak to him?'

'No, I want to dance the Irish Jig with him—of course I want to speak to him,' Julius said testily. 'Here. In person.'

Mervyn consulted the grandfather clock. 'It's ten o'clock. He may be in bed.'

'Then get him out of bed! And don't you go any-where. I may need you.'

'I do live here,' Mervyn pointed out. 'And I don't

think it's a good idea to get worked up over anything. We could regret it, you know.'

'Just do as you're told, Merv!' Julius ordered. 'And stop calling me *we*. It drives me insane. Pour me a Scotch while you're about it.'

'No,' Mervyn said. 'That I do refuse to do.'

CHAPTER SEVEN

BRIDGET stirred the next morning and discovered herself to be loosely wrapped in Adam's arms in her own bed.

'That's brilliant,' she murmured as she revelled in it.

He opened one eye. 'I haven't done anything.'

'You don't have to. You did enough last night. I'm enjoying things just as they are.'

He touched his forefinger to her mouth. 'You're easy to please.' He hugged her, then hitched the pillows up and sat back against them. They were both naked beneath the sheet and coverlet. She snuggled up against him and rested her cheek on his chest.

He stroked her hair. 'You were inspired last night with my uncle.'

'That was pure fluke. Seeing his horse paintings reminded me of what you'd told me about his passion for the Melbourne Cup.' She paused. 'I liked him.'

'He liked you.'

'You could tell?' she queried.

'Yes. What do you want to do today?'

Bridget sat up. 'You have a day off?' she asked, on a note of excitement.

He fluffed her fringe up with his fingers. 'Yes. Well, I'm taking one anyway. I thought we could—'

'Why did you ask me what I wanted to do if you've already got something in mind?' she broke in, and eyed him sternly.

'I…' He paused and rubbed the blue shadows on his jaw, then shrugged. 'You go ahead. I must tell you that you look like a disapproving governess, though.' His lips quirked.

'And I'll tell you about my parents. My father used to drive my mother mad doing something very similar.'

'He did?'

She nodded solemnly.

'What?' he asked, with an expression of mock fear.

'He used to say to her "We can do A or B. It's up to you." Then, when she chose B, say, he would agree, but add the rider that on the other hand A would be the more sensible choice, leaving her in no doubt that A was what he'd always wanted to do. "Why didn't you just come out and say so?" she would cry in frustration.'

'Ah. All right. What would *you* like to do today, Bridget?' he asked with elaborate courtesy.

Bridget pretended to mull over the possibilities. 'There is one thing,' she said at last. 'I'd just like to spend the day with you. That's all.'

'You're a tease, Mrs Smith,' he said ruefully. 'Well, I had this thought. Since I spend all my spare time up at Mount Grace, I don't actually have a house on the Coast.

I stay in hotels. So I thought we might look around for one—a house, not a hotel. Somewhere you'd be happy to call home while we're not up there. The question is, though, would you like a house or an apartment?'

'If by an apartment you mean a penthouse in the sky,' Bridget said thoughtfully, 'I think I'd rather have a house. Seems more appropriate for a child, and I'm not a fan of having to get into a lift every time you want to go out. It's also nice to have grass beneath your feet— I can't believe I'm saying this.' She looked conscience-struck.

'Why not? It makes sense.'

'Yes, but it's—well, I'm sure there's going to be an awful lot of money involved—your money—and it's going to be such a change of lifestyle for me.' Her eyes widened at the thought.

'Talking about a change of lifestyle…' He put his hand gently on her tummy beneath the sheet. 'When is this baby due?'

She told him a date in December. 'But that's by my reckoning. I haven't seen a doctor yet.'

'OK. That's something else we can do today.'

'Oh, but we might not get an appointment!'

'With my doctor, we will,' he said with a lurking grin.

'Life is so much simpler when you're a millionaire,' she responded with a faint frown. 'Nothing ever seems to stand in your way.'

'Things do, believe me.'

'Large things, maybe, but not small things?' she suggested.

He shrugged, but didn't comment on that. He said instead, 'We also have to set a wedding date.'

'Not today, we don't,' Bridget heard herself say. 'We have plenty of time for that.'

'But since we *are* getting married we may as well— in the next few days at least,' he replied.

She was silent as she grappled with a feeling she'd experienced before in relation to Adam Beaumont—the feeling that she was up against a battering ram. Yet since she *had* agreed to marry him, and since she *was* pregnant, what was the point in delaying it?

But it was a lot more than that, wasn't it? Last night she'd been struck by the knowledge that she'd fallen deeply in love with him. Last night she'd gone to bed with him willingly and loved every minute of it. Especially since she had been tired and a bit strung-up, so had really appreciated the gently warm experience he'd made it rather than the fireworks of the last time they'd slept together.

She articulated the thought that had been at the back of her mind ever since all this had come up. 'Let me tell my mother first.'

'Is she liable to change your mind?'

Bridget hesitated. 'She's liable to preach caution.'

He sat up abruptly and eased her up beside him. 'It's too late for that, Bridget.'

She said nothing, but pleated the sheet between her fingers.

'I know it's all a huge change for you…' He paused and studied the top of her head. 'But the sooner we get it under way, the sooner you'll get used to it and the easier it's going to be for you.'

She looked up at last, but he couldn't read her eyes.

'You don't rewrite your life without some upheavals,' he said quietly.

'I suppose not.' But she didn't sound entirely convinced. 'Is it not going to be a rather huge upheaval for you too?'

'Of course. But I'm looking forward to it more and more. And our own place—our very own, one you can fit out to your heart's content—will help.'

She looked around and thought of Mount Grace. She had to agree. Her mother's shadow seemed to hover over her in *this* flat; his mother's ghost—much as she'd fallen in love with Mount Grace—had to linger there.

She came to a sudden decision. 'All right. I'll look at houses with you, and I'll see your doctor today. But I'd still like to speak to my mother—no,' she said as he moved restlessly. 'I'm not going to let her change my mind, but I would like her to be here for the wedding, so any date needs to be one she can fit in with.'

'So long as it's not too far away.'

Bridget temporized, but he took her in his arms and lay back with her, fitting the curves of her body into the lean planes and angles of his. 'How right does that feel?' he queried, with a wicked little glint in his eyes as he cupped her breast.

'That feels like pure blackmail,' she replied, but a little breathlessly.

'It is,' he agreed. 'You seem to have brought out a

pirate-like streak in me, Mrs Smith. Is that the right word?' he mused.

'Pirate-like? Well, devious also springs to mind.'

He kissed the tip of her nose.

'I give up,' she said on a gurgle of laughter. 'You're a hard man to say no to, Mr Beaumont.'

A little later, far from feeling drowsy, Adam got energetically out of bed and announced that he was starving.

'Ah,' she said, curling up in his space. 'Yesterday I experimented with black tea and dry toast, and I didn't have any morning sickness, so I think I may stick to that. I don't think I should even *think* about cooking breakfast.'

'Don't worry, I'll take care of it all—including the black tea.' He headed for the shower.

'You cook?' Bridget asked with a tinge of surprise.

He turned back to her. 'In a limited sort of way. I spent a year after school jackerooing on a cattle station in the Northern Territory. Bacon and eggs is one of my strengths. Damper is another, but I'll make do with bread this morning. Do you have any plum jam?'

'Er—no. Do you like it?'

'I became addicted to it on damper. We used to get it in big tins and, apart from sugar, it was just about the only sweet thing we got.'

'How about strawberry jam?' she asked gravely.

He grinned. 'That'll do.'

'So that's where you got your expertise with ropes and axes and so on? Jackerooing?' she hazarded.

'Yes.' He grimaced. 'Such as it is.'

On his way to the shower he stopped and studied a painting on the wall—one of hers. A delicate study of some coral-pink ixora blooms on a velvety midnight background.

He turned back to her. 'I thought you said you weren't any good?'

'I'm average,' she answered.

'I disagree. In fact, I would be surprised if your new career *isn't* based on art. Have you started painting yet?'

She shook her head. 'I haven't had time.'

He squinted at the tiny initials in the corner— B T-S—then went to take his shower.

Bridget stayed cuddled up in bed and listened to him singing snatches of a sea shanty in a pleasant, husky voice.

It brought her a feeling of real contentment, although she smiled to herself to think of him as a closet shower singer. But *he* must be feeling contented, at least, she reasoned, even if she wasn't the love of his life…

She saw his doctor later in the day, and had her pregnancy officially confirmed. She also saw a number of houses, and fell in love with one of them.

It was on the Nerang River, behind Surfers Paradise, so it was peaceful but central. It had a lovely garden and a jetty, but it needed some TLC—mostly only cosmetic, so it wouldn't be a time-consuming exercise. She specifically asked not to be told how much it cost, although she knew that its position alone would guarantee a hefty price tag.

Inwardly, she discerned that she was a little uneasy about this house—to the extent that she did say to Adam that they had months up their sleeve and didn't need to rush into anything.

He simply shrugged—and told her the next day that it was signed and sealed.

The next evidence she got of his determination to get his own way was over her job. She still had nearly two weeks' leave in front of her, but happened casually to mention when she'd be going back to work.

Why not quit now and get it over with? had been his response. Why not start painting now?

She'd hesitated, and he'd reminded her that she'd been having second thoughts about it anyway. He'd also let drop that Julia had moved overseas.

'Did you have anything to do with that?'

They were dining out at a chic Italian café. The table-cloths were red, with green over-cloths, the glassware sparkled, the air was redolent with tantalising aromas, and the menu offered a delicious variety of pasta. It all faded into the background, though, as Bridget was unable to mask her surprise at this news.

He toyed with his wine glass. 'Yes.'

'How so?'

'I managed to get her a job in Singapore.'

'Why didn't you tell me? Did you coerce her?'

He rubbed his jaw. 'To a certain extent. I pointed out to her that spreading unsubstantiated rumours was not something to be viewed lightly.'

'They were true,' Bridget said.

'Not at the time, they weren't,' he said flatly.

'Your brother—' Bridget began, but he broke in.

'Look, Bridget, Henry is a married man with two children.' He gestured. 'I'm not making excuses for him, but Julia was always on shaky ground there. Don't you agree?' And he raised an eyebrow at her.

'I suppose so,' she said slowly. 'Is she all right? You must have threatened her with—something.'

'We did a deal. Materially, she drove a fairly hard bargain. But it's actually a much more challenging job there than doing the social rounds here.'

Bridget digested this for a long moment. They were both casually dressed, she in jeans and a blouse that matched her eyes, he in jeans and a sports jacket over a round-necked T-shirt. But it crossed her mind to think that whatever he wore these days, and even if his hair *was* wind-ruffled from their earlier stroll on the beach, there was no disguising that he was a powerful man. Capable of a lot more than railroading Julia Nixon out of town—and he had railroaded her, even if he had got her a better job.

And not only powerful, she thought, as something Julia had once said about him popped into her mind— he was as sexy as hell. She'd been so right. Apart from her own intimate knowledge of him, Bridget couldn't fail to by struck by the reaction of women who came in contact with him—or were simply sitting a few tables away from him, as one was now. She couldn't keep her eyes off him…

And it all caused her unease to surface again. What chance did she have of fighting him if he ever became minded to use his power against her?

'Did she mention me?'

'Yes.' He paused, looking completely unamused. 'She told me to get out of your life. It was advice I declined.'

'Do you still want to gain control of Beaumonts?' Bridget said slowly.

'Oh, yes.' He twirled some pasta round his fork. 'But not thanks to Julia Nixon.'

'So—so you've done nothing to take advantage of these rumours she spread?'

He smiled lethally. 'I've been sitting on my hands, you could say, other than persuading her to leave town. But the right moment will come.'

Bridget said no more on the subject, but it occurred to her that Beaumont Minerals was a factor she shouldn't discount in her relationship with Adam Beaumont, for the simple reason that it might mean more to him than anything.

The next day she sat down and wrote a long e-mail to her mother, who still had not returned from her 'few days' little break. She didn't send it, though.

She was aware that her mother had a rather vague concept of time. She remembered that both her mother and her new husband were keen amateur archaeologists, and she could imagine them on some dig, miles from anywhere, quite oblivious of the passage of time.

But, although she wanted particularly to speak to her mother, in some ways it was easier to lay the facts out in an e-mail, and she filed it in her 'drafts' folder, so as to have it on hand when she did speak to her. At the same time, seeing those facts laid out did make her stop and ponder her new life. And ponder, specifically, the speed with which it was all happening to her. Not only that, she was still unsure what to do about her job.

From a couple of remarks he'd let fall she knew Adam was getting more and more impatient about setting a wedding date. In fact, indirectly, they would have their first serious falling-out over it…

He rang her one morning and invited her to a dinner that night…

'What kind of dinner?'

'Formal, black tie,' he said down the line, and named a five-star restaurant she'd heard of but never been to, which happened to be in the hotel where he was staying. 'It's a business dinner, and most of the other guests will be Korean. I'm working with a Korean consortium at the moment on a construction project.'

'That doesn't give me a lot of time,' she said slowly.

'Doing anything else today?'

She bit her lip. 'No. When you say formal, do you mean long dress?'

'Yes. Is that a problem?'

Bridget came to the decision that she wouldn't be bested by a wardrobe deficiency. 'Not at all.'

'That's my girl. Look, if I don't get there myself, Trent will pick you up at seven and deliver you to me. See you!' And he rang off.

So, she thought, that's how high-flying businessmen do things. I wonder who he would have taken if it wasn't me? I wonder if it's some kind of test to see how I stack up against his high-flying business associates?

She stopped as this thought crossed her mind, and shortly took herself shopping.

It was Trent who was standing outside her door when the bell rang at seven, and he did the most gratifying double-take.

'Oh, do forgive me, Miss Tully-Smith,' he said ruefully, 'but you look absolutely stunning!'

Bridget looked down at herself. Rather than an evening dress, she wore fitted slim-line ivory taffeta pants, very high latest-fashion silver shoes and a silver spangled loose top over an ivory camisole. Her coppery hair was styled and bouffant, her nails were painted to match her glossy lips—she'd toyed with the idea of black nail varnish but decided against it—and the only jewellery she wore was her engagement ring. Her eyes were a clear, sparkling green.

'Thank you, Trent,' she said. 'But will it be appropriate, do you think? I wasn't quite sure.'

'Ma'am, you'll blow them away,' Trent assured her.

It was a view Adam seemed to share when she arrived at his suite. He was wearing black trousers, a white dress shirt and an undone black bow tie, and his dinner jacket was hanging over the back of a chair. His dark hair was tamed and tidy.

He put the phone down as she came in, and whistled softly.

'Oh, thank you!' She beamed at him. 'Every dress I tried on seemed to make me look—portly.'

His eyebrows shot up. 'Portly?'

She nodded gravely. 'I can't see any difference in my figure, but there must be some because that's how they made me feel.'

'I could give you my considered opinion,' he offered, 'but that would involve a minute inspection—and, of course, undressing you.'

A tide of pink rose into Bridget's cheeks as his blue gaze wandered up and down her. 'Er—thank you, but I don't think I'll…need that.'

He glanced at his watch. 'We have half an hour.'

Her colour deepened. 'You're not serious?'

'I couldn't think of anything I'd rather do at this moment in time.'

Their gazes clashed, and Bridget was assailed by a vivid image of his hands on her body as he undressed her item by item; by a breathtaking image of the tall, lean length of him also unclothed and intent on reducing her to a quivering state of desire. Not playfully, as he sometimes did it, but silently, and with all the erotic force he could bring to it.

'Adam…' She took a shaky little breath. 'If you mean what I think you mean, that—that—' she looked down at herself and gestured eloquently with both hands '—that would *wreck* me!'

There was a suspended moment when she felt she might almost cut the tide of suspense laced with longing that flowed between.

Then he grinned wickedly and held out his hand. 'Come here.'

She went reluctantly, unsure of what to expect.

'May I make a date to…if not wreck you, definitely undress you and make love to you after this dinner, Mrs Smith?'

She laughed in relief and leant against him. 'You may, Mr Beaumont.'

The dinner was a success.

Bridget held her own amongst the fifty or so guests, and was much complimented on her appearance—often in broken English, but the sentiments were obviously genuine. Any surprise that Adam Beaumont had ac- quired a fiancée was well hidden, but many of the guests were only business acquaintances and came from the other side of the world anyway. They might not even have understood the situation.

When they returned to his suite she was happy with the way things had gone, and a little surprised to realise how nervous she'd been about this event.

He poured himself a nightcap, and she had a cup of black tea and then yawned prodigiously. 'I should think about going home.'

He looked at her askance. 'What's wrong with staying here?'

She hesitated. 'I don't think I'd feel right about that.'

'Bridget.' He put his glass down and pulled off his bow tie. 'We are engaged.'

'I know, but—well, I didn't bring anything with me.'

'What does that matter? There are enough toiletries, shampoos, robes, and heaven knows what here for six people, let alone two.'

Bridget mulled over this. 'But you see,' she said at last, 'I would have to go home tomorrow wearing this.' She looked down at herself, at her spangled evening top, taffeta pants and high-heeled shoes. 'That would look— funny.'

'Nonsense. No one would give two hoots.'

She tilted her chin at him. 'I would.'

His lips twitched, then a tinge of impatience came to his eyes. 'You could get into the lift and go straight down to the car park.'

'Who knows who else could get into the lift?'

His nostrils flared as he took an irritated breath.

'Then I could send out for some clothes for you to-morrow morning.'

'Send who? Trent? No, thank you.'

He made a gruff little sound in his throat. 'Bridget, if you'd agree to move in with me—come to that, if you'd stop fluffing around and marry me—none of this would happen. Besides which, you promised.' He looked her up and down significantly.

She turned pink. 'You could come home with me,' she suggested.

'It is one o'clock in the morning. We're halfway across town.' He looked at her derisively.

Bridget rose and picked up her silver-beaded purse. 'Then I'll go alone. Incidentally, I'm not *fluffing* around, and I'm not even that sure that I *will* marry you, Adam!'

And she marched towards the door.

He caught her before she reached it, and detained her with his hands around her waist. 'I had no idea you were such a puritan,' he murmured. 'Although I should have known you had a temper.'

'Not only that,' she responded, her eyes flashing, 'but I've lost the mood—so please let me go.'

'I haven't. Lost the mood,' he elucidated. 'But here's a suggestion. What say that tomorrow morning I call down to the boutique in the foyer and get them to send up a selection of clothes for you? They don't even need to see you—you can leave here dressed as you see fit. I really don't understand what difference it makes, leaving in daytime clothes, but since it's so dear to your heart—'

He stopped and caught her wrist as she went to slap his face.

'Don't, Bridget,' he warned, on a cool, dangerous note.

'I'll tell you what difference it makes,' she said through her teeth. 'I wouldn't look so highly conspicuous. I wouldn't look like some good-time girl after a one-night stand. I'd look ordinary and un-noteworthy.'

He shrugged. 'Then we're agreed on this course of action?'

'Yes. No! I *really* don't like you for not understanding, and—'

But he pulled her into his arms and started to kiss her. She fought him briefly but it was a losing battle, especially when he lifted his head briefly to say, 'I'm sorry. I should have understood. I will try to be more understanding in the future.'

Despite the little glint of sheer devilry in his eyes, she felt herself melting…

'Was I silly?'

Bridget asked the question about an hour later, when she was lying beside him on the bed in a pool of golden lamplight, having been exquisitely made love to.

'Don't answer,' she went on, and smoothed her fingers through his hair. 'I'm talking to myself. I'm just trying to judge how legitimate my reaction was. In light of the fact that I will *still* be leaving here tomorrow morning—this morning—having spent the night with you.'

He kissed the bare curve of her shoulder. 'I wouldn't worry about it.'

'But I do. I mean, I like to have things clear in my own mind. It just…' She paused and thought for a moment. 'It just occurred to me that it could be really embarrassing—especially if I met anyone I know.'

'I can see that. Now,' he said gravely.

'Is it going to be any less embarrassing wearing jeans and a jumper, though?' she mused.

'Bridget.' He sat up, and couldn't go on for a moment because he was laughing. Then, 'If we make it a respectable time of the day, if you hold on to the thought that we *are* engaged, it should be a breeze. And I agree with you—you would have looked rather conspicuous in evening dress. Happy now?'

She snuggled up to him. 'Yes.'

'Now, I still have something to do—an inspection to

make,' he reminded her. 'Although you don't feel at all portly to me.'

She bore his 'inspection' with equanimity at first. But when he announced that there was only one change he could see, and his fingers stilled on her nipples, she had to draw several breaths to maintain her composure.

'These are different,' he said, stroking and plucking. 'Darker. But it's a very fine difference.'

'It's a very short time. Out of nine months, I mean,' she said with an effort.

'Still, time marches on,' he murmured, and she held her breath this time, quite sure he was going to make some remark about them getting married.

He didn't. He drew her close to him and kissed the top of her head, and started to make love to her again. She responded to the warmth and security of his arms and his body, to the pleasure he brought her, with a warmth and a bestowing of pleasure of her own. And she wondered, at the same time, why she didn't just marry him as soon as he wanted?

It is the one thing I can hold out about, she answered herself. It is the one thing—even although I've agreed to it—I can choose to do when I feel ready. And I know I don't want to keel over like a pack of cards over everything.

The next few days seemed to fly by.

They ate out a lot—once even going up to Mount Tamborine for lunch, in a fabulous garden restaurant. He also took her, wearing a hard hat and a fluorescent green overshirt, up one of his buildings in progress, via the outside construction lift. She gasped at the view from the top, and stopped to think about how highly success-ful he was.

She hadn't reversed her decision to not move into his hotel—another small holding-out against Adam Beaumont—so he'd moved some of his clothes and gear to her flat, although he still occasionally spent the night at his hotel.

When he did stay with her she discovered that he never went to bed before midnight, yet was always up by six. And he always went for a body surf or, if there was no surf, swam or jogged. And if she thought he was beautiful dressed in a tailored suit, he was even more so when he came back from those early-morning excur-sions, with his hair all ruffled, his jaw blue with stubble and his body cold and fresh.

'That's my axeman,' she said to him one morning, when he sat down on the side of the bed and pulled her into his arms hungrily.

'That's my essential Mrs Smith,' he replied. 'Not soaked to the skin, but with no make up, et cetera, and quite *au naturel.*'

One morning he came home with a dog.

'What's this?' she enquired, as the woolly, curly, cream and quite large dog followed him into the flat and sat down composedly.

'This is Rupert, according to his collar, although there's no other information. I found him on the beach, alone and possibly lost. I have not been able to detach him from my side since then.'

'But—well—' Bridget started to laugh. 'What are you going to do with him?'

'I was hoping you would offer to ring up the RSPCA and ask them to come and deal with him. He could be micro-chipped. Unfortunately—' he consulted his watch '—I'm running really late for a meeting now, so I won't be able to be of much assistance.'

Rupert had other ideas, however. He positioned himself outside the bathroom door while Adam showered, and Bridget tried to get hold of the RSPCA. But it was too early for them except in cases of dire emergency, as she told Adam.

He knotted his tie and scooped his keys into his pocket. 'This could be an emergency,' he said. 'Would you be a darling and look after him until they can take over?'

Bridget eyed the dog, now sitting at Adam's feet. 'Yes, if he agrees.'

'He's only a dog.'

'I know, but I just have a feeling he's attached himself to you.'

In the event, Rupert had. Because when Adam left he sat beside the front door and emitted ear-piercing yowls of complete devastation.

Adam came back in.

'What are we going to do?' Bridget asked helplessly. 'The neighbours... Anyway, I don't think you're allowed to have dogs in this building.'

Adam shrugged. 'I'll take him with me. Trent can look after him and sort things out.'

They left together, Adam and the dog, and Bridget was struck by a fit of giggles as she watched from the window as Adam loaded the dog into the passenger seat of his shiny BMW. Rupert accepted his status as number one passenger with aplomb and sat upright, staring ahead.

She was subject to similar fits of laughter on and off for the rest of the day. And never more so than when they returned, together, at about five o'clock.

'What's this?' she asked, as another gust of laughter shook her.

Adam glanced at the dog. 'Well may you ask—and it's no laughing matter. He tried to bite Trent, and he refused to have anything to do with the RSPCA. I drew the line at a containment net and a tranquilising dart.'

'So?'

Adam threw his car keys onto the dining table and shrugged out of his jacket. 'So I took him to my meeting. I took him to three meetings. He was perfectly well-behaved so long as he could sit at my feet and get taken for a walk now and then—I need a drink.'

'I'm not surprised,' she managed to say, having extreme difficulty in keeping a straight face.

'I know you're still laughing,' he accused, 'but have you any idea how traumatised my whole office is? I had the girls crying because they didn't want to see him hurt. I thought Trent was going to give notice on the spot. And I now own gifts pressed on me by those same girls: a dog basket, a set of bowls, a *huge* bag of dog biscuits.'

Bridget handed him a Scotch. 'There, there,' she said soothingly, and the front doorbell rang.

It was an RSPCA officer, together with a couple and a boy of about ten.

Rupert barked joyously and jumped up to lick the boy's face. The boy buried his face in the curly cream fur.

'So that's all sorted,' the officer said. 'They don't know how he came to get lost, but they're new to the area so that probably explains it.'

Before he left, Rupert came back to Adam and sat down in front of him.

Adam scratched the fur beneath his chin. 'I have to say it hasn't all been a breeze, mate, but you're a very fine dog.'

And, almost as if he understood every word, Rupert licked his hand then bounded over to his young master's side.

Bridget closed the door on them all, and Adam, with a sigh, sank down onto her settee. 'I must be a laughing-stock,' he said ruefully.

Bridget sat down beside him and snuggled up to him. 'On the contrary. There's obviously something very, very loveable about you.'

He put his arm round her shoulders and glanced at her with a wicked little glint. 'So you've noticed?'

'In the face of such canine devotion I could hardly fail to.'

'When are you going to marry me, then?'

Bridget sobered. 'I still haven't heard from my mother.'

'If we were to set the date for a fortnight from today, surely she'd be able to make it?'

'I—I guess so.'

'Well, why don't you start thinking about dresses and honeymoons and the like?'

Was that when it all started to tumble down like the house of cards it really was? Bridget was to wonder later.

She'd agreed to the fortnight time limit, and she'd asked what kind of wedding it would be. He'd told her with a lurking grin that it was up to her, but how did quiet, simple and very private sound?

'There you go again,' she'd accused. 'Giving me no choices!' But she'd almost immediately confessed that quiet, simple and private sounded fine to her.

She had, she saw later, still been caught up in the warmth and amusement of that day. She'd been convinced she loved Adam Beaumont—especially the very human side of him she'd witnessed that day.

She'd smothered the deep-seated reservations she had about marrying him, about rushing into things— or being rushed into things as if she were on a runaway train. She'd buried the instinct that had told her to hold back. It wasn't something she fully understood, anyway.

But the very next day it had become clearer.

Marie-Claire Beaumont announced her separation from her husband, Henry, citing irreconcilable differences. The couple's two children, four and two, had moved out of the family home with their mother, so it was reported in the paper.

It was noted in the same article that some

Beaumont shareholders were calling for an immediate meeting of the company's troubled board. And, although no parallel was drawn to deserting a sinking ship, if you read between the lines you could make the inference that the timing of this separation might have wider implications than two people who'd fallen out of love.

Since Adam had gone to Adelaide on a business trip, Bridget was unable to judge what kind of turmoil this announcement might have brought him. But she was in no doubt about the kind of turmoil it brought to her.

That hidden, mysterious little instinct buried in her psyche stood up well and truly now to be counted. What did this woman really mean to Adam? You couldn't love a man and not wonder about it, she saw. She might have been able to mostly ignore the question while Marie-Claire was safely married to his brother—or so she'd thought—but if she divorced Henry and was free…?

Had this been on the cards anyway? *Did* they have irreconcilable differences, Henry and Marie-Claire? Or was she deserting a sinking ship? Had Julia contributed, with all her bitterness?

And when Adam did come home, two days later, it was impossible to gauge his real state of mind on the issue. She might not have been able to anyway, she acknowledged. She was quite sure he was a master at hiding his feelings.

But what brought him home was traumatic anyway: the death of his great-uncle Julius, who had passed away peacefully in his sleep.

* * *

'I'm so sorry,' Bridget said down the line to Adam when he rang her with the news. 'I'm *so* sorry. I know he meant a lot to you.'

'Thank you,' he replied briefly. 'The funeral is the day after tomorrow. Will you come?'

'Yes, of course. If you want me to.'

'Why wouldn't I?' he countered, rather harshly.

Bridget took a breath. 'I wasn't sure whether anyone knew about us—apart from your uncle, of course. And some Korean businessmen. And Trent.'

'My uncle was the only one of the rest who mattered, but it's time everyone knew,' he said. 'Bridget, I'll be back tomorrow morning.' His voice softened. 'Take care of yourself in the meantime.'

'I will,' she promised, but she was disturbed when she put down the phone.

Did she want to go on show to the whole world at such a sad event? Who would be there? Surely there would be no wedding preparations now? No wedding, come to that, so soon after his uncle's passing? Not that she had done anything yet…

Marie-Claire Beaumont was at the funeral, surprisingly at her husband's side, and she was impossible to ignore—she was that kind of woman.

She was tall, with long fair hair and exquisite grey eyes. Black became her beautifully, and her designer suit with its short skirt set off her sleek figure and long legs.

No surprises there, Bridget thought. She'd already known this woman was something special, but had she anticipated that her looks, her elegance, her compo-sure—not to mention, of course, her history—would force her gaze to return to her again and again?

When she realised this was happening, Bridget took herself to task and thought instead of Melbourne Cup winners. She herself had chosen to wear the same outfit she'd worn to dinner with Julius Beaumont, and that helped to bring back the only time she'd met the old man.

But she couldn't help also studying Henry Beaumont. Julia had been right. He was as tall and good-looking as Adam, but there was a difference. It took some time for Bridget to put her finger on it, and then it came to her that, while Adam Beaumont had an inner stillness that translated to a harnessed kind of power, Henry looked discontented. He had a curious unfulfilled quality about him, and he looked older than the four years older than Adam she knew him to be.

The wake was held in Julius's apartment, with Mervyn in command of a discreet army of caterers. Champagne flowed, and the red velvet curtains were swept aside on the stunning view of the ocean from Narrowneck at its best, calm and blue and stretching for ever.

The wake started out quietly, but soon the hubbub of conversation rose and the temperature grew too, as many, many people came to celebrate Julius's life now they'd mourned his death. And there were plenty of raised eyebrows as Adam introduced Bridget as his fiancée.

But perhaps the sheer press of people would shield

her from too much attention—and anyway, there was Marie-Claire.

Had she always been such a scene-stealer? Bridget wondered. Or did it just come naturally? It might even be a form of bravado—it was to be noted that she and Henry were always on opposite sides of the room...

But when she was presented to Bridget there was more than bravado to Marie-Claire. She raised her eyebrows and smiled quite gently. Apart from a murmured 'How do you do?' she said nothing to Bridget at all, but the look she bestowed on Adam was a clear challenge, and what she said next was a clear invitation.

She said, in a fascinating, lilting voice, 'Despite today's solidarity for Julius's sake, you probably didn't think I'd do it, did you, Adam? But I have, darling—oh, I have—and now I'm on my own.'

And she moved away, but Bridget could literally feel the tension in the man standing at her side...

Those words might have meant anything, but to Bridget they contained a clear message. She must believe I don't know anything about her, she thought in a stunned kind of way as new arrivals presented themselves and she shook several hands and said she knew not what.

Not only that, her incredulous thoughts ran on, but she mustn't think I'm any threat, anything to take seriously, even although Adam and I are engaged...

Her thoughts ran along these lines for another twenty minutes or so, until she knew she couldn't go on any longer. She asked Adam if he'd mind if she went home.

He immediately looked concerned. 'What's wrong? Feeling sick?'

'No—not yet, anyway. But I'm *hot*, and I know—I know you can't leave, but I could get a taxi. Please?' she added.

He frowned. 'You could rest here in one of the bedrooms. There's the will to be read after—'

'No,' Bridget broke in urgently. 'I really want to go home, so I can get changed and comfortable,' she insisted, and tried to smile. 'I'll be fine.'

She must have convinced him, but even so he came downstairs and put her into a taxi himself, and promised to be with her as soon as he could, once the will had been read. Neither of them was to know that that would take longer than anticipated…

CHAPTER EIGHT

'How the *hell* did this happen?' Adam asked Julius Beaumont's solicitor, Mark Levy. 'I told him I didn't want it.'

They were alone in the library—apart from Mervyn, they were alone in the apartment.

All the guests had gone, as well as the caterers. Henry had departed mouthing threats and obscenities. Marie-Claire had just departed; Adam had been unable to decipher her expression.

As for Mervyn, he was sitting at the kitchen table in his shirtsleeves, not quite in command of himself as he drank champagne and contemplated, with amazement, the size of the bequest he'd received.

'Julius called me out in the middle of the night a week or so ago,' Mark Levy began. 'Well, not quite the middle of the night, but late. He wanted to change his will. I tried to talk him out of doing it there and then, but he was adamant.'

'So you gave in and let him do it?' Adam suggested, with some scorn in his voice.

'Adam.' Mark rubbed his brow. 'He was entitled to leave his estate as he saw fit. And, although I let him do it, I returned several days later and assured myself he was of sound mind. He was calm and alert. He was not on any mind-altering medication. Not only did I *judge* him of sound mind, he *was* of sound mind. He *insisted* he wanted the new will to stand.'

'So it's watertight?'

Mark Levy rubbed his hands. 'I deem it to be so.'

Bridget was wearing a navy tracksuit and socks when Adam came back to her flat.

It was getting dark, and she'd turned the lamps on. To take her mind off all her demons, she'd also concocted a snow pea, prawn and chilli fettuccine. She couldn't imagine that he would be starving, and had thought that a light meal would serve best. But even as she'd cooked she'd been mentally devastated, she realised. She couldn't get out of her mind that little scene played out at the wake between Adam and Marie-Claire.

She couldn't get over the conviction that had come to her that they were made for each other. In all their turmoil, in all their conflict, there was still a *matching* between them that seemed unmistakable. And she couldn't doubt the tension she'd sensed in Adam.

Some of her mental uncertainties showed in her face. She was a little pale, and her eyes looked huge. But that was nothing to the leaden feeling in her heart…

'Hi,' she said when he came in. 'All settled?'

He took his time about replying. He shrugged out of the jacket of his dark suit, undid his black tie and opened the top couple of buttons on his white shirt. He crossed over to the stove and lifted the lid on the casserole dish containing the fettuccine. He sniffed the aroma of garlic, cloves and chilli, then looked at her rather penetratingly.

'More or less,' he said at last, as he walked back into the lounge and threw himself down in an armchair.

Bridget hesitated, suddenly aware of how different he looked. He was also pale, and there were new lines scored beside his mouth—at least, lines she'd seen only once before. In a storm-battered shed in the Numinbah, when he'd told her some of his history…

She swallowed and poured herself a glass of water, then waved her fingers towards the fridge in unspoken query as to whether he'd like something to drink. She noticed at the same time that her engagement ring wasn't on her finger, and remembered that she'd taken it off and left it on the kitchen windowsill when she'd started to cook.

He shook his head at the drink offer, so she put her ring back on and took her water to the settee, where she sat down opposite him, with her feet tucked under her, and waited for him to go on.

'He left *you*,' he said, and dragged his fingers through his hair, 'his collection of Melbourne Cup photos.'

Bridget raised her eyebrows in genuine surprise. 'That was sweet of him.'

'Yes. He left *me* his entire holding in Beaumont Minerals.'

Bridget didn't look surprised. 'You would have expected that, wouldn't you?'

'No. I told him I didn't want it.'

'But it had to go somewhere, and if he disapproved of Henry it seems to make sense.' She shrugged, then frowned. 'Why didn't you want it? Because you didn't want anyone to think you'd been handed Beaumonts on a platter? Surely that's irrelevant now? Your uncle must have wanted you to have it.'

'It's not irrelevant,' he said irritably. 'I wanted to beat Henry fair and square. That's why.'

Bridget took a sudden breath as a kind of understanding came to her. 'Because of Marie-Claire?' she asked huskily. 'To prove to her you were better, smarter, cleverer, more powerful—whatever—than Henry?'

He raked a hand through his hair. 'Of course not.' But she could see that the tension she'd diagnosed in him in Marie-Claire's presence was still with him.

She swallowed several times, and took some deep breaths. 'Adam, I'll tell you the reason I came home this afternoon. Because your sister-in-law laid down a clear challenge to you, that's why. She's free and available. Or she will be.'

He stood up and towered over her. 'Do you think I *want* her?' he shot back. 'Do you think I *admire* her for leaving Henry when he's fighting for his business life?'

'She could be leaving him because he's chronically unfaithful to her, by the sound of it!' Bridget returned, with some fire of her own.

They stared at each other.

Until Bridget went on, 'Anyway, those are all side issues. I think the way you want someone is printed on your heart, maybe your soul, not on a table of pros and cons. But that—that's not the only problem.'

'Go on,' he said dryly, and with a touch of weariness in his eyes—as if the last thing he needed at the moment was more homespun wisdom from her. What he wasn't to know was how all her uncertainties and fears had crystallised.

'I think,' she persevered, 'that the real problem is—as I always suspected, funnily enough—the terrible cynicism she left you with, even if you can't get her out of your heart and soul.'

'Bridget—'

'No.' She raised her hand to stop him. 'That's why I haven't been sure about marrying you. Yes, it obviously seemed like a good idea for you to marry me *at the time*.' She put her hands on her stomach. 'When this happened. And you haven't stopped pushing me into it from the day you found out, but…' She gestured helplessly and wiped away an errant tear. 'Is it the right answer for you now?'

'If I'm *pushing* you into anything—' his tone was clipped and brusque '—it's because it is a good idea. It's the best idea available to us.'

Bridget put her hands together and prayed for some inner fortitude. She looked across at him, and something struck her that seemed to make terrible sense. 'Had you heard the rumours too, Adam? About your brother and his wife? Round about the time I came back into your life?'

'What—?' He broke off. Then, 'What difference does it make?'

'It could explain a lot,' she said, out of a suddenly dry throat. 'It could explain why you were so insistent about marrying me—so surprisingly insistent. Because if you hadn't forgiven her, hadn't stopped punishing her for leaving you—'

'Bridget.' His blue gaze was supremely mocking as he broke in. 'I know you find all that water under the bridge fascinating. I knew it that night when you started to offer me advice, although you didn't know me at all,' he said moodily. 'But you're wrong.'

She raised her chin, and hauteur replaced her tearfulness. 'I don't think I am—and don't patronise me, Adam Beaumont. I think we—this baby and I,' she said, 'appealed to you as a shield, just in case you were tempted to forgive Marie-Claire and love her again.'

He brought his fist down on the arm of the chair. 'That's all nonsense, Bridget,' he said shortly.

'You may see it as such, you may believe it as such, but I don't think it is.' She got up at last and went to the window. 'There's been something holding me back, something I didn't fully understand, but now it's all clear. It's what you feel for another woman and what she still means to you. And that has to affect us.'

'Nothing can affect us,' he said brusquely. 'Except this ridiculous shillyshallying. So let's get it over and done with, Bridget. Let's do it tomorrow—in fact I won't take no for an answer.'

She gasped. 'You can't make me!'

'You're right. But I can mention the child you're carrying, whose best interests you *should* be taking into consideration.' He ground his teeth.

Bridget took a shuddery little breath, but she said tartly, 'Maybe someone should take an overall view, Adam. Marie-Claire is going to be free. For whatever reason, she's admitting she made a mistake. So you won't have to end up on your own in a wheelchair,' she added, and couldn't hide the bitterness in her voice. She turned to stare out of the window and stiffened incredulously. 'Oh, no! I don't believe it!'

He frowned. 'What?'

'M-my mother,' she stammered. 'She's just walked into the building. With a suitcase. And a taxi is driving off.' She turned back from the window, with her eyes wide and horrified and her hand to her mouth.

CHAPTER NINE

'DARLING, you mustn't upset yourself any more,' Mary Baxter, formerly Tully-Smith, said soothingly. 'This is not the end of the world.'

Bridget raised her tear-streaked face to her mother. 'How can you say that? All I've ever done is be in the wrong place at the wrong time, and that's led me into getting caught up in an absolute maelstrom of— I can't tell you how much I wish I'd never heard of the Beaumont family!'

'If only I hadn't left you to go overseas!'

'Mum, this could have happened to me if you'd lived in—in the same street.' Bridget wiped her eyes with her fingers.

'What are you going to do?' Mary asked cautiously.

Bridget propped her chin on her hands and licked some salty tears off her lips. She'd probably never forget the awkward little scene that had ensued when she'd opened the door to her mother and received her embrace, plus her excited explanation that she had a whole week to spend with Bridget.

Then Mary had noticed Adam, and she'd started to apologise for barging in on anything, but Bridget had seen her mother's quick summing-up of Adam Beaumont as she'd introduced him, and how impressed Mary had been.

In fact she'd said as much—'What a pleasure to meet you, Adam! May I call you Adam?'

Then her eyes had fallen on Bridget's engagement ring, forgotten in all the trauma and still sitting on her daughter's left hand, and Mary had drawn a deep, deep breath.

Her next words had been, 'Is this what I think it is? But you've been so secretive, darling! Mind you, I have been away—oh, congratulations!'

Adam had been the one to find the right words.

He'd said quietly that they were engaged, but that things had got a little complicated between himself and her daughter and he knew Bridget wanted to speak to her alone. So he would leave them together but—and here he'd turned to Bridget with an unmistakable warning in his eyes—he'd be in touch tomorrow morning. And he'd left the flat, leaving her mother open-mouthed.

That was when Bridget had sunk down at the dining table in floods of tears, until she'd finally found some composure and told her mother the whole story.

'What am I going to do? I have no idea.' She sniffed and blew her nose, then reached out and pressed her mother's hand. 'Thank you for not reading me the riot act. I know you must be thinking I'm insane or something.'

'Oh, my dear.' Mary returned the pressure. 'Of course not. These things happen.'

Bridget closed her eyes. 'He doesn't love me. Adam.

Well, I knew that, but I didn't know what he felt for her—not really. She was a background figure, and as such I could ignore her—more or less. Now I can't.'

'No,' Mary agreed, and surprised her daughter as she added firmly, 'Therefore the last thing you want to do is marry him.'

Bridget opened her mouth but closed it again. 'I *am* pregnant,' she said at last, a little forlornly.

'Well,' her mother replied, 'that's going to take a bit of thinking about—but you have got me, darling! I'll be with you every step of the way.'

Uh-oh, Bridget heard herself say to herself.

She lay in bed that night and couldn't recall when she'd felt more lonely or miserable.

Yes, it was reassuring up to a point to know that her mother now knew it all, and was asleep in the spare bedroom. But how she was going to go forward, what she was going to say to Adam, were the kind of questions that resembled a secret form of torture.

Then there was the problem of her mother, even if it was reassuring to have her close by. Vague and unworldly Mary Baxter might be at times, but she could also be particularly stubborn once she set her mind on a course.

This could ruin her marriage, Bridget thought. It wouldn't be so bad if they lived here, but Jakarta was a long way away, and Richard had at least nine months of his fellowship to go. What was she going to do?

If these thoughts weren't bad enough, after she did fall into an uneasy sleep she woke and reached instinctively for Adam—and cried tears into the pillow as every time he'd made love to her came back to her. But he wasn't there. He wasn't there physically, and he wasn't there for her in any sense now. She couldn't allow him to be. Not now.

And nothing can change that, she thought. Nothing…

'Mum, I *need* to do this. Please believe me.'

It was early, about six o'clock, and cloudy, so it was grey outside and not a hopeful kind of day—which was in tune with Bridget's mood.

She'd got up to make a cup of tea, and her mother had appeared almost immediately in her favourite violet candlewick dressing gown.

'Well, I know I advised you not to marry him last night,' Mary said, 'and I stand by that. But to just disappear?' She stared at Bridget, anxiety written in her eyes.

'I need some time on my own, otherwise I might find myself getting married for entirely the wrong reasons,' Bridget said firmly—although she was feeling far from firm. She felt like a jelly inside, to be precise.

'So—what's he like? Apart from all this?' Mary queried.

Bridget stared out of the kitchen window. They were sitting with their tea at the kitchen table. 'That's the problem,' she said at last. 'He can be—' Her voice broke, but she took control. 'He can be lovely. But he can also be like a force that's impossible to resist.'

'Come with me, then,' Mary suggested. 'We'll go to Perth. That's where Richard is, with his daughter. We can both go to Perth. I know Richard will understand completely. And you can think things out there.'

'No. Thank you, Mum,' Bridget said warmly, 'but I just want to be alone for a bit. I'm not even going to tell you where I'm going, although I will be in touch, I promise. I don't really know where, but I need to go soon.'

'How soon?'

'In the next half-hour. I'm so sorry to leave you, but it's the best thing to do. Once he comes—if he comes—' She broke off.

Mary Baxter straightened. 'Let him come! I'll deal with him! No, Bridget, I simply cannot allow you to go off on your own. If you want to, we'll go now—we'll go wherever you want—but we'll go together!'

Bridget opened her mouth, but her mother simply said, 'You're not the only one with a mind of your own, you know.' She stood up and added, 'I haven't even unpacked, so it will only take me a moment to get ready.'

Bridget spent two weeks in Perth with her mother and Richard Baxter, at his daughter's house.

The only person she'd contacted was her boss, to ask for an extension to her leave, but she hadn't given him her whereabouts.

Every time a phone rang—although she'd left her mobile in her flat—and every time someone knocked on the door of the pleasant beachside home Richard's daughter and her husband lived in, she expected it to be Adam. But it never was.

At the same time as she cursed herself for living in

foolish hope, she couldn't believe it would have been that difficult to trace her movements—if he'd been so inclined.

But then she re-examined her assumption that he could have traced her easily. Maybe not. He didn't know her mother's surname, and even if he'd found that out, and found they'd flown to Perth, once they'd arrived there, it might be like looking for a needle in a haystack, without any idea of Richard's daughter's married name, mightn't it?

As the days slid by, her warring state of mind took its toll. If anything she lost weight, and she would have given anything for the peace and serenity the baby within her must surely need.

On one hand, she was sure she was doing the right thing; on the other, there were days when she felt so alone it was frightening. And times when she was filled with a raw, yearning ache for him there seemed to be no cure for.

There was also a looming decision to be made about where to go from Perth. And what to do about her mother?

Feeling traitor-like, now they'd been in Perth for two weeks, she prompted her mother and Richard to talk about their life in Jakarta, and they gave glowing reports of it. Yes, it was a big, teeming city, but they were growing accustomed to the local customs, and the whole thing was a splendid adventure, her mother said enthusiastically.

Bridget gathered herself to say that there was no reason for them not to return to Jakarta, that she was quite able to take care of herself.

But no sooner had she shown that enthusiasm than Mary took a deep breath. She reached for Richard's hand and said, 'Darling, I think—we think—you need to go back, and you need to see Adam Beaumont and talk this through with him. Or at least communicate with him somehow. I'll come with you if you decide to see him, and Richard will advise you if you decide to do it through a lawyer.'

Bridget could only blink several times. Then she found her voice. 'But you told me not to—'

'I know,' Mary interrupted. 'But I was extremely annoyed when I first said that. To put it mildly, I could have killed him for…' Mary paused and did not elaborate. 'I'm not suggesting you marry him. But it is his baby, so he bears some responsibility for it, and for you.'

Richard Baxter cleared his throat. 'I do feel it's the best way, Bridget. And we just want you to know that, wherever you decide to be while you have this baby, we'll be there too.'

Tears misted Bridget's eyes. 'Look, that's so—so wonderful of you, but what would make me happiest is for you both to go on being happy in your new life together. Anyway, there's the fellowship and so on.'

They looked at each other, Mary and her husband, and there was so much love and confidence in the mutual decision shining in their eyes as they shrugged almost identically, as if to say *that's a minor detail*, Bridget could hardly bear the pain that slammed into her heart.

If only she and Adam had that…

'Bridget,' her mother said quietly, 'you can't only think of yourself now, sweetheart. You need some kind of stability. It's important.'

Two days later she flew back to the Gold Coast. On her own. It was the one small victory she'd achieved, although she'd promised her life on the matter of staying in touch with her mother.

It was a bright day, lovely in the sun, but with a hint of winter in the air out of it.

She looked round her flat when she got in, and found she was happy to be home. Amongst her mail there was a letter from Levy, Levy & Cartwright, who proved to be Julius Beaumont's solicitors. They were holding her bequest for her, and required her to collect it and sign for it.

She picked up her mobile phone, lying exactly where she'd left it, but of course it needed charging. She hadn't left her landline answering machine on, so her mobile was the only way Adam might have tried to contact her. But as she carried it towards the charger it slipped out of her hand and crashed to the tiled floor.

She cursed herself for being unbelievably clumsy, and bent to pick up the pieces, but the phone was now history.

Since it was late afternoon, she decided she would spend the rest of the day laying her plans and working on what she would say, both to Levy, Levy & Cartwright, and to Adam Beaumont, should she be unable to avoid him.

She went into the bedroom to unpack, and her gaze fell on her painting of the coral ixora flowers that Adam had admired, and she stopped what she was doing as memories came crowding back.

There was something else about pregnancy she was

discovering, that often took her by surprise. She could and did sometimes fall asleep on the spot, and it had been a four-hour flight from Perth, with all the attendant travelling to and from airports on top of that.

Stopping only to pull her shoes off and wrap the doona around her, she slept through until early the next morning.

Anyone checking her flat for a presence, via some lights, for example, would have had no idea she was home…

'Miss Tully-Smith,' Mark Levy said the next morning in his office. 'I'm delighted to see you.'

'Thank you. Please call me Bridget. I've come to collect my pictures, and also to ask a favour of you.'

'I'm happy to help if I can, Bridget. Your pictures are boxed and ready for you. All I need is a signature.'

Bridget signed the form, then withdrew a package from her purse. 'Do you act for Adam?' she asked.

Mark Levy nodded. 'At times, but I'm not the only one. Is it—business?' he asked a shade cautiously.

'No. I just wanted this delivered to him, if you wouldn't mind.' She handed over the package. 'There's an explanatory note inside.'

Mark Levy studied her thoughtfully. He noted that although the only other time he'd met Bridget Tully-Smith she'd been wearing an engagement ring, this was no longer the case. It seemed, therefore, not unlikely that she and Adam had parted ways. In fact it wouldn't surprise him at all, he decided, if her engagement ring was in this package. Nor did she look well.

'I'll do my best, Bridget,' he said. 'But Adam is a little hard to pin down at the moment, so if it's urgent…?' He raised an eyebrow at her.

'No. Hard to pin down?' Bridget just couldn't help herself.

'I think he might be taking some time off,' Mark said. 'It will be common knowledge in the next day or two—he has ceded all his holdings in Beaumont Minerals to his brother, Henry, and since then he hasn't been around a lot.'

Bridget blinked, then stared at the solicitor, wide-eyed. 'Surely that's quite contrary to his uncle's wishes?'

Mark Levy shrugged. 'This is only my personal opinion, Bridget, but I think it's foolish to want to rule from the grave.'

'So do I, now I come to think of it,' Bridget murmured. 'But I don't understand,' she said helplessly. 'Has something happened in the family?'

Mark took his time. It *was* a known fact in the legal world that Adam had relinquished all his interests in Beaumont Minerals. What he did not know was why.

He stirred at last. 'I'm afraid I can't help you there. You haven't been in touch with Adam himself?'

Bridget cleared her throat. 'No. I was hoping…' She paused. Did it need to be a secret? 'I was hoping not to have to. Do you—would you know if Marie-Claire has gone back to Henry?'

Mark felt a pang of regret for this girl as he thought, So that's what's at the bottom of it all—for her, at least. But he could only tell her the truth. 'I believe not.'

* * *

Bridget didn't go home. She went to the beach.

She sat on a sand dune, her favourite spot, in the sun, and simply let the waves, the sunlight, the birds, and the clear blue sky soak into her psyche for a long time.

And gradually she realised why she was sitting so still, breathing it all in. It was in the hope that, just as the sea on the beach was scouring the sand clean, her dreadful confusion would be wiped away.

She put her hand on her stomach and let it lie there as she thought deeply about the baby she was carrying. Was it a boy or a girl? Would it have the Beaumont blue eyes, or green, like her own? Whatever, she reflected, the baby was her absolute priority now. And, whatever, nothing could change who this baby's father was. And, since they couldn't live together in harmony, some kind of arrangement had to be made. Not in anger, though.

But what had happened to make Adam relinquish his desire to take control of Beaumont Minerals? Yes, he hadn't wanted to get there on his uncle's coattails, so to speak, or on anyone's. But a legitimate bequest, his uncle's dying wish, had to be another matter, surely?

And as she thought about it, she realised she'd believed that he would see it that way eventually. She'd believed that over and above herself and the baby, even over and above Marie-Claire, that was what meant most to Adam Beaumont: control of Beaumont Minerals. It was the only thing that would redress not only Marie-Claire's defection and Henry's perfidy, but his father's treatment of him.

So what to make of this news?

She picked up a handful of sand and let it drift

through her fingers. It could have no bearing on her, though. And she thought of the note she'd written and put into the package with his engagement ring.

I'm happy to make some arrangement, not marriage, but an arrangement, whereby we live our separate lives but your child has your protection and love.

She'd penned a final line:

This is not negotiable.

Tears blurred her eyes and a song came into her heart. The Dolly Parton song Whitney Houston had made even more famous—'I Will Always Love You'…

Her tears had dried, and she was staring out to sea following a yacht sailing south when she decided it was time to go home.

She got up and brushed herself off, but she was still thinking of Adam Beaumont as she came to the road and stepped off the pavement—almost under the wheels of a car.

Someone saved her. Someone with a strong pair of arms pulled her away in the nick of time. And that someone was furiously angry.

Adam, who'd never looked taller, in jeans and a navy sweater, or more threatening.

'How can you just step onto a road without checking the traffic?' he ground out. 'How can you be so foolish?

Don't you know I've scoured the length and breadth of the country looking for you? And the moment I find you, you're about to wipe yourself out!'

His eyes blazed down at her and his mouth worked, then he pulled her into his arms and held her so tight she could barely breathe. Not only that, she could feel the heavy, slamming beat of his heart, and she couldn't doubt there was fear as well as anger driving him.

'Adam—Adam…' she whispered. 'I didn't think you cared—'

'Cared!' He held her a little away from him and stared at her.

'No.'

'Well, you're wrong,' he said shortly, then visibly took hold of himself. 'I'm sorry. You gave me a fright.'

Bridget swallowed. 'Who…how did you find me? Or is it just coincidence?'

'Yes and no.' He released her, but took her hand. 'Can we go back to the beach?'

She nodded after a moment.

He said no more until they'd reached the beach. 'I called in to see Mark Levy, so I knew you were back in town, and I got your note. You weren't home, so I— We used to come here together sometimes, remember?'

'Y-yes,' she stammered. 'Adam—' she couldn't help herself '—why did you let Beaumonts go? I thought it meant more to you than anything.'

'To prove to you I could live without anything, but not without you.'

Bridget stared at him with her lips parted and her eyes huge.

He rubbed his jaw. 'I know you may find it hard to believe after our last encounter, but when I discovered that I might never find you, that I didn't even know where to start looking, sanity kicked in—and I couldn't believe I'd been such a bloody fool. I couldn't believe I hadn't realised until then how much I loved you, and hadn't made you believe it.'

She tried to speak, but no words came.

'Where were you, incidentally?'

'Perth.' She explained about her mother.

He grimaced. 'You may not realise it, but there are two private detective agencies trying to track you down.' He sketched a smile, but it didn't reach his eyes. 'Because once that revelation hit me I knew I had to get you back.'

'So…' She had trouble making her voice work. 'But to walk away from Beaumonts…?'

He took her hand. 'Sit down.'

They sat down, side by side.

'I have no regrets,' he said, and paused, almost as if he was looking back down the path of his life. 'Beaumonts has been a torment, a real thorn in my flesh, ever since I can remember,' he said slowly, and stared out to sea. Then he turned back to her. 'Not only that, but it led me into making the worst mistake of my life.'

'Marie-Claire?' she hazarded, and held her breath.

'Yes. She epitomises all the blunders I've made in the name of believing I had some right to the company.'

He hesitated and seemed to gather his thoughts. 'It

wasn't only that she left me for Henry, it was the fact that she really left me for Beaumonts that made me so bitter and so hellbent on revenge. You were right about the cynicism she left me with—' He broke off and looked tortured. 'And you were right again. You and our baby *did* seem like a good way to keep her at bay, keep on punishing her. It was only looking back after you'd gone, when I remembered all my days in the sun with you.' He stopped. 'Anyway, it was only then that I saw what I'd been too blind to see—too wrapped up in my own ambitions, too wrapped up in all my old scars, going way back to my father. Marie-Claire meant nothing to me any more, and neither did Beaumonts. I *loved you.*'

Bridget moved her hands and discovered she had tears rolling down her cheeks.

'I didn't mean to make you sad.'

'I—I—I'm still amazed, though,' she confessed. 'You believed, and your uncle Julius believed, Henry wasn't doing a good job.'

Adam heaved a sigh. 'Henry,' he said, 'has his own demons. He's had me breathing down the back of his neck for years, watching every step he made. And he's had Marie-Claire manipulating him— I know he's been no saint in that direction but, well, things could change now. Anyway, it's no concern of mine. I've been a basket case since you left,' he went on. 'I can't seem to function without you. My staff are in despair because I'm never there, and I never know where I'm liable to be either.'

Bridget smiled a trembling little smile. 'Where have you been?'

'Chasing up leads on you, Mrs Smith. Hang on! I drove past your apartment last night but there wasn't a single, solitary light—when did you get home?'

She told him, and explained about the lack of lights too.

'Well, at least you got my demented messages on your mobile phone. Or—did you?'

Bridget shook her head. 'I didn't. I dropped my phone and smashed it before I could charge it.'

He swore under his breath, but there was a glint of humour in his eyes. He was silent for a long moment, then, 'Do you believe me, Bridget?' He stared deep into her eyes. 'You once said to me that if I needed you I knew where to find you—I need you with every fibre of my being.'

Bridget thought of what he'd given away, how he'd changed his life for her. She thought of his reaction to her all but stepping in the path of a car. 'Yes.'

'And—am I forgiven?'

She breathed in the very essence of him and felt her senses come alive. 'Oh, yes…'

He hesitated, as if he couldn't quite believe her soft avowal, then he swept her into his arms.

Some minutes later they became aware of a little boy of about six, standing nearby and watching them closely.

'What are you doing?' he asked.

Bridget released herself from Adam's arms and patted herself down self-consciously.

'I was kissing this lady,' Adam said gravely.

'Is she your mother?'

Bridget made a strangled sort of noise.

'No, but she's going to be my wife.'

'Oh. I only kiss my mother,' the boy asserted. 'My dad and I shake hands. Well, sometimes I kiss my grandmother, but she hugs me almost to death so I don't really like it.'

'I don't blame you. Uh—are you on your own, young man?' Adam enquired.

The boy swung round and pointed to a couple at the water's edge. 'I s'pose I better go back. They don't like me to wander away. Bye!' He ran off.

'Do I *look* like your mother?' Bridget enquired.

He smiled down into her eyes. 'No, you don't, Mrs Smith. And I also have to tell you that this beach is far too public for us.'

'And I have to tell you—' her lips curved '—I agree with you.'

'Your place or mine?' he asked quizzically.

'Mine is closer,' she said demurely.

'So be it. Race you?' he teased.

'No, you can drive me.'

But they were serious again as they lay in each other's arms in her bed.

'I can't quite believe I deserve this.' He ran his hand down her body, then rested it on her belly.

She looked into his eyes and saw they were sombre. 'I think I've always loved you,' she said quietly. 'One of the reasons I was so unsure about marrying you was because I didn't just want respect, care and affection from you. I wanted you to love me the way I love you.'

He closed his eyes. 'I can't believe I was such a fool.'

'Hush,' she recommended. 'We've got a whole new life in front of us. And I'm dying that special kind of death again. Are you?'

He groaned, and everything he did to her from then on showed unequivocally that he was…

They were married two weeks later.

It was small, simple and private, but the bride glowed in a strapless cream silk dress, and wore an emerald pendant to match her engagement ring.

The bride's mother, who had forgiven Adam Beaumont, was also radiant.

And in the fullness of time Adam and Bridget were blessed with a daughter they named Grace Mary. She had her mother's coppery hair and her father's blue eyes. This called for another celebration—a christening.

When the guests had departed, and Mount Grace was quiet and settled for the night, Bridget said to Adam, 'Your daughter requires your presence.'

He looked up. He was sitting on the chintzy settee in the lounge with his feet up, surrounded by the weekend papers. 'Since my daughter is only three months old and cannot talk, how did she indicate this to you?'

'I can tell.' Bridget had changed from her christening finery into slim cream pants and a green blouse, which she happened to be buttoning up.

'Here.' He got up. 'Let me—you've got them crooked.'

She accepted his ministrations, and her lips curved as he patted her down and murmured, 'All present and correct. For the moment.'

She looked into his blue eyes and deduced, correctly, that he would be undressing her in the not too distant future. And she was shaken inwardly by how much she loved Adam Beaumont; how, after all the trauma, the joy of being married to him never left her.

She was still, at times, amazed at the change in him—wrought by freeing himself from the yoke of his bitterness, and helped by their closeness. There were no longer two men in her life, just the one Adam Beaumont—the one she'd loved right from the start.

She slipped her arms around his neck. 'Do you ever think of that night in the Numinbah?'

'Yes. Do you?'

'I do,' she concurred gravely. 'I used to think that it was the most foolish act of my life, to sleep with a man I'd never met before because I thought I was going to die. But I don't think it's turned out to be such a bad thing after all.'

'Ah. One could even say you showed not only great judgement but great taste,' he offered, with a perfectly straight face.

Bridget looked at him in mock disapproval, then had to laugh. 'Don't get too swollen a head,' she warned, all the same.

'Why would I do that?'

'Since you have not one but two adoring females in

your life, it's quite possible. Now, Grace won't go to sleep until she sees you. Trust me. I know this.'

He laughed and kissed her lightly. 'I don't believe you for a moment, but I'll come—in a moment.'

She raised her eyebrows at him.

'It's simple,' he said. 'All I want to say is—I love you. The only problem is I keep on wanting to say it, over and over.' His blue eyes were quite serious.

Bridget melted against him. 'It's not a problem,' she assured him.

ONE TINY MIRACLE...
CAROL MARINELLI

Carol Marinelli recently filled in a form where she was asked for her job title and was thrilled, after all these years, to be able to put down her answer as 'writer'. Then it asked what Carol did for relaxation. After chewing her pen for a moment Carol put down the truth—'writing'. The third question asked: 'What are your hobbies?' Well, not wanting to look obsessed or, worse still, boring, she crossed the fingers on her free hand and answered 'swimming and tennis'. But, given that the chlorine in the pool does terrible things to her highlights, and the closest she's got to a tennis racket in the last couple of years is watching the Australian Open, I'm sure you can guess the real answer!

CHAPTER ONE

A NEW DAY.

A new start.

Another one.

Walking along the beach, Ben Richardson was head down and too deep in thought to really notice the glorious pink sky over the smooth waters of Port Phillip Bay. He had been accepted for a position as Emergency Registrar at Melbourne's Bay View Hospital and would be there in a couple of hours to start his first day, only there were no first-day jitters as he made his way along the beach—after all, he'd had plenty new starts before.

This would be his fourth job in the three years since Jennifer's death…no, it was nearly four years now. The anniversary was coming up soon and Ben was dreading it. Trying and failing not to think about it, trying and failing not to constantly think how life should be, had *they* lived. Had he stayed put at Melbourne Central, had life not changed so dramatically for him, he'd have been starting to apply for consultant positions now. But staying there hadn't been an option—there were just too many memories there for him. After six months of trying, Ben had realised that he couldn't keep working in the same place that he had once worked with his wife and had accepted, after some soul-searching, that things would never be the same again, could never be the same again. So he had moved on to Sydney—which had felt right for a while, but after eighteen months, well, that restless feeling had started again and he'd moved on to another Sydney hospital. Only it had been the same tune, just a different song. The place was great, the people too…

But it just didn't work without Jen.

So now he had returned to Melbourne, but on the outskirts this time, and it was good to be back closer to his family and amongst old friends again.

No, he wasn't nervous about this new start—the difference was that this time he was looking forward to it, ready for it, excited even by the prospect of finally moving on.

It was time.

He had decided to live by the beach and take brisk walks or jog each morning…except on day three after moving in he'd already pressed the snooze button on his alarm a few times!

Ben picked up speed, even broke into a jog, his large, muscular frame belying his deftness, and all too soon he reached his destination—the house that he had had his eye on for a couple of weeks now.

While working through his notice in Sydney, Ben had made the trip down to find a home close to the hospital. Looking online, speaking on the phone with real-estate agents, he had found several prospects to view over the weekend, determined to secure a home before he started his new job—deciding that maybe if he owned a property then he'd be more inclined to settle for longer.

The real-estate agent had been showing him a typical bachelor apartment, a new development along the beach, with gorgeous bay and City views. It was bright and airy and had all mod cons with the bonus of a huge balcony which would be nice when he had friends or family over. It had everything, really, and Ben had come close to purchasing it that day, but, standing on the balcony as the agent sorted out the documents, Ben had seen the house next door. An older house, it jutted out a touch further onto the beach than the apartment block. The garden, which had direct beach access, was an overgrown green oasis compared to the swish decking and clear-walled balcony that he'd stood on.

Instead of looking at the glorious beach, Ben had found himself gazing into his potential new neighbour's garden. A huge willow tree shaded most of it, there was a slide and swing and a trampoline, but what had really caught Ben's eye had been the boat parked along the side of the house—a man in his forties had been hosing it down and he had looked up and waved as they'd stepped out onto the balcony and Ben had given a quick nod back, only realising then that the man had actually been waving to the real-estate agent instead of himself.

'I'll be with you shortly, Doug,' the agent called, then took a seat at the well-positioned glass table, sorting out brochures and papers and finally locating the contract.

'Is it on the market, then?' Ben asked.

'Sorry?'

'The house next door—is it for sale?'

'Not yet,' the agent said with a noncommittal smile. 'Have a seat, Dr Richardson, and we'll go through the small print.'

'But is it coming onto the market?' Ben persisted.

'Perhaps. Though, really, it has none of the specifications you outlined. That house needs a lot of work, it still has the original kitchen and the garden's a jungle...' Only Ben wasn't listening and the real-estate agent suddenly had that horrible sinking feeling that he was losing his grip on his certain sale. 'The apartment complex is maintained, regularly serviced, there's the gym and lap pool for tenants,' he pointed out, pushing what he assumed were the benefits of living here for this tall, rugged-looking bear of a single guy, with the title of doctor. He had been so sure that low maintenance was the key to this sale.

He was wrong.

Ben was fast realising that high maintenance would be fantastic!

This was a garden and a house he could lose himself in, what with house repairs and oiling decking. And how about a boat...? How much better to fill up his limited spare time renovating a house or out on a boat on the bay than to be confined to modern, sleek lines of the apartment or burning off his endless energy in a lap pool? For the first time in a very long time, Ben found himself interested in something that wasn't work, and, staring at the house, he could almost glimpse a future, a real future... So, instead of closing the deal and moving into the plush apartment complex, to the agent's obvious annoyance, Ben took a gamble, put his furniture into storage and rented one of the cheap furnished units at the other end of the street, prepared to sit it out till the house came on the market.

It was win-win really, Ben thought this morning as he walked along the beach access path to the front of the house. In that short space of time, the bottom had fallen out of the housing market and the developers were having trouble selling the luxury apartments. Already the price had gone down a few thousand, so, if nothing happened with the house…

For Sale by Auction

He saw the board and gave a smile as he read that the auction wasn't far off, just a few weeks away, in fact. And there was an 'open for inspection' scheduled at the weekend. Walking back toward the beach, this time he noticed the glorious skies and the stillness of the morning, seagulls sitting like ducks on the calm water, a dog running in and chasing them away. And then he saw *her*, standing in the glassy ocean, the water to her knees, legs apart and stretching, her hands reaching for the sky. She stood still and held the position and then slowly lowered her arms.

And then did it all over again.

God! Ben rolled his eyes. He had a great physique and made a very half-hearted attempt to keep it, relying mainly on walking a thousand miles a day in Emergency then burning it off with a swim, but this new-age, welcome-the-day-type stuff, or whatever she was doing…

Please!

Still, Ben conceded there *was* something rather spec-tacular about her lack of inhibition, something about her that made Ben smile as he walked.

And then she turned and his smile vanished as she bent over...doubled over, actually. Ben saw her swollen stomach and realised she was pregnant *and* visibly in pain. Picking up speed, he walked a touch more quickly along the sandy pathway and onto the beach—not wanting to overreact as maybe it was part of her exercise routine. But, no, she was walking uncomfortably out of the shallows now, still bent at an awkward angle, and Ben broke into a light jog, meeting her at the foreshore. He stared down at a mop of dark curls on the top of her head as, still bent over double, she held onto her knees.

'Are you okay?' he asked in concern.

'Fine,' she moaned, and then looked up. She had amber eyes and big silver earrings and was gritting her very white teeth. 'Stupid yoga!'

'Are you having a contraction?' He was assessing her. Not wanting to just dive in and place his hand on her stomach, he thought he ought to introduce himself first. 'I'm Ben, I'm a doctor...'

'And I'm Celeste.' She blew out a breath and then slowly unfolded. 'And I'm not having a contraction, it's a stitch.'

'You're sure?'

'Quite sure!' She stretched and winced and then rubbed the last of her stitch away. 'Stupid new-age stuff!' He couldn't help but smile and then so did she. 'According to my obstetrician, it's supposed to relax both me and the baby. It will kill us both, more like!'

He tensed, standing on the beach on a glorious warm morning, and was slammed back there again—just as he was almost every day, every night. Not all the time now but surely, given it was nearly four years on, *too* many times.

'So long as you're okay,' he clipped, and went to go, but she was holding her swollen stomach now with both hands and blowing out a long, slow breath. 'That,' Ben said firmly, 'is *not* a stitch.'

'No.' Her eyes screwed up just a touch and this time he did place his hand on her stomach, felt the weak tightening flowing around her uterus, and held his hand there till it passed, satisfied that it was nothing more than a Braxton-Hicks' contraction.

'It's just the baby practising for its big day.' She smiled. 'Honestly, I'm fine.'

'You're positive?' he pressed.

'Absolutely.'

'If they get stronger, or start coming—'

'More regularly, I know, I know.' She gave him a very wide smile. The sun was up now and he could see her tan and her freckly face. She really did have an incredible smile… 'Well, thanks anyway,' she said.

'No problem.'

She turned to walk along the beach, in the direction he was going, and as he started to walk behind her, he half watched her to make sure she didn't stop again, but she seemed fine now. Dressed in white shorts and a white tight-fitting top, she was curves everywhere, and Ben felt a touch awkward when her head turned around.

'I'm not following you—I live up there,' he explained.

'Good!' She slowed her pace down. 'Where?'

'In the units at the end.'

'Since when?' she asked.

'Since the weekend.'

'We're neighbours, then.' She smiled. 'I'm Celeste Mitchell, I live in Unit 3.'

'Ben, Ben Richardson—I'm at number 22."

'You're at the quiet end, then.' Celeste rolled her eyes.

'Are you sure about that?' Ben said, raising an eyebrow. 'It certainly hasn't been quiet the last two nights. Fights, parties…'

'That's nothing compared to *my* neighbours,' she retorted.

They were there now, at the row of one-bedroom units that were a bit of an eyesore in such lovely setting. No doubt one day a developer would come in and swoop up the lot of them and build a luxury complex or a hotel, but for now they were just an old and rather rundown row of units that offered cheap rental and beach access—and were filled with backpackers looking to settle for a few weeks and the occasional regular tenant, which Celeste obviously was.

As they walked past her unit, it stood out from the rest—the little strip of grass at the front had been mowed and there were pots of sunflowers in the small porch.

Clearly this was her home.

'Thanks again for your concern.' She grinned. 'And if you need a cup of sugar…'

He laughed. 'I'll know where to come.'

'I was going to say you'll have to go next door. The doctor just put me on a diet.'

He laughed again and waved goodbye. Heading up to his unit, he let himself in, put on the kettle and peered around the gloomy interior before heading for the cranky shower, wondering if it would spurt hot or cold this morning.

He hoped her flat was nicer than his. It was an odd thought to pop into his head, but he just hoped it was, that was all. It was certainly as neat as a pin on the outside—maybe her husband had painted it. And hopefully she had nicer furniture than his landlord had provided. Still, that wouldn't make up for the noise...

Coming out of the shower, he could hear his neighbours fighting again and for Ben the auction couldn't come soon enough.

He made some coffee and smiled again as he spooned in sugar.

She didn't need to be on diet—she was curvy, yes, but she was pregnant. He thought of that lovely round bottom, wiggling up the beach in front of him, and just the image of her, so crystal clear in his memory, startled him, so that he immediately turned his mind to more practical thoughts.

Her blood glucose was probably high. She'd be around seven months or so...

He forced himself to push her out of his head, and wouldn't let himself give her another thought—till he drove out of his garage, feeling just a touch uncomfortable in his slick four-wheel drive, and saw her watering her sunflowers and waving at him.

He waved back—reluctantly. Ben didn't like waving to neighbours or, despite what he had said, dropping in for sugar, or popping over for a chat. Had she not appeared in pain, he'd have kept right on walking, have kept himself to himself—which was just how he liked things to be.

Whoosh!

As he drove past, Celeste could feel her cheeks redden even as she, oh, so casually waved.

He. Was. Gorgeous!

Gorgeous! Well over six feet and broad, his legs were as thick and as solid as an international rugby player's, and that longish brown hair flopping over his eyes as he'd stared down at her on the beach already had her wanting to run her fingers through it. As for those green eyes...why the hell didn't they have doctors like that where she worked?

Then she stopped being twenty-four and single and remembered she had sworn off men for the next decade at least. Also, she was, in a few weeks, going to be a mum.

Funny, but for a moment she'd forgotten. Talking to Ben, chatting as they'd walked, for a moment there she'd forgotten she was pregnant, had just felt like, well, a normal woman! Which she was, of course—there was nothing more womanly or normal than pregnancy. But this morning she'd been one who'd fancied and blushed and said all the wrong things in the face of a very sexy man. Celeste had assumed, though she'd neither read nor been told it, that the 'fancy' switch remained off during pregnancy—that you went into some sort of hormonal seclusion, where men were no longer attractive and you didn't flirt or even look twice. And for six months it *had* been that way...

Would stay that way, Celeste told herself firmly.

Not that she needed to worry. A deft kick from her baby reminded her that she had no choice in the matter—she was hardly a candidate for romance!

CHAPTER TWO

'CELESTE, what are you doing here?' Meg, the charge nurse, shook her head as Celeste handed her a return-to-work certificate as she joined the late-shift emergency nurses to receive handover.

'I'm fine to work. I saw my obstetrician again yesterday,' Celeste explained.

Meg scanned the certificate and, sure enough, she had been declared fit, only Meg wasn't so sure. 'You were exhausted when I sent you home last week, Celeste. I was seriously worried about you.'

'I'm okay now—with my days off and a week's sick leave…' When Meg didn't look convinced Celeste relented and told her everything. 'My glucose tolerance test came in high, that's what the problem was, but I've been on a diet for ten days now, and I've been resting, doing yoga and taking walks on the beach. I feel fantastic—some people work right up to forty weeks!'

'Not in Emergency,' Meg said, 'and you're certainly not going to make it that far. How many weeks are you now?'

'Thirty,' Celeste said, 'and, as the doctor said, I'm fine.'

Which didn't give Meg any room to argue and,

anyway, here wasn't the place to try. Instead she took them through the whiteboard, giving some history on each of the patients in the cubicles and areas. 'When the observation ward opens, Celeste can go round there…'

'I don't need to be in Obs,' Celeste said, guilty that they were giving her the lightest shift, but Meg fixed her with a look.

'I don't have the resources to work around your pregnancy, Celeste. If your obstetrician says that you're fine for full duties and you concur, I have to go along with that—I'm just allocating the board.'

Celeste nodded, but no matter how forcibly Meg said it, Celeste knew she was being looked out for as far as her colleagues could—and for the ten zillionth time since she'd found out she was pregnant she felt guilty.

Finding out she was pregnant had been bad enough, but the fallout had been spectacular.

Her family was no longer speaking to her, especially as she had steadfastly refused to name the father, but how could she? Having found out that not only was her *boyfriend* married but that his wife worked in Admin at the hospital she worked in, even though no one knew, would ever know, guilt and shame had left Celeste with no choice but to hand in her notice. Then, just as it had all looked hopeless, she had found out that she been accepted at the graduate emergency nursing programme at Bay View Hospital, which was on the other side of the city.

She hadn't been pregnant at the time of her application and the polite thing to do might have been to defer—perhaps that was what had been expected of her—but with such an uncertain future ahead, a monthly pay cheque was essential in the short term, and, as a clearly single mother, more qualifications wouldn't go amiss. Also, moving away from home and friends would halt the endless questions.

It was lonely, though.

And now her colleagues were having to make concessions—no matter how much they denied that they were.

'Cubicle seven is Matthew Dale, eighteen years old. A minor head injury, he tripped while jogging, no LOC. He should be discharged, Ben's seeing him now.'

'Ben?' Celeste checked.

'The new registrar. He started this morning. Here he is now…' Meg waved him over. 'What's happening with cubicle seven, Ben?'

'I'm going to keep him in. Sorry to open up the observation ward so early but…' His voice trailed off as he caught sight of Celeste, but for whatever reason he chose not to acknowledge her, just carried on giving his orders for the patient. Although she had to offer him *no* explanation as to her being here, and though there was absolutely no reason to, again, for the ten zillionth and first time, Celeste felt guilty.

Almost as if she'd been caught.

Doing what? Celeste scolded herself, as she walked round to the closed-off observation ward, flicked on the lights and then turned back a bed for Matthew.

She was earning a living—she *had* to earn a living.

She had ten weeks of pregnancy to go and the crèche wouldn't take the baby till it had had all its inoculations, so if she stopped now she wouldn't be working for almost six months.

The panic that was permanently just a moment away washed over her.

How was she going to cope?

Even working full time it was a struggle to meet the rent. With no help from her family, she was saving for the stroller and cot and had bought some teeny, tiny baby clothes and some nappies, but there was so much more she needed. Then there was her bomb of a car…

Celeste could actually *feel* her panic rising as she faced the impossibility of it all and she willed herself to be calm, willed herself to slow her racing mind down. But that was no help either, because the second she stopped panicking all Celeste felt was exhausted.

Holding the bed sheet in her hand, she actually wanted to climb in, to lie down and pull the sheet over her head and sleep—and get fatter—and read baby magazines and feel kicks and just *rest*.

'Feeling better?' Celeste jumped at the sound of Ben's voice. 'After this morning?'

'I had a stitch,' Celeste responded just a touch too sharply. 'And, before you ask, I am quite capable of working. I'm sick of people implying that I shouldn't be here. Pregnancy isn't a disease, you know!'

'I was just being polite.' Ben gave her a slightly wide-eyed look. 'Making conversation—you know, with my neighbour?'

She'd overreacted, she knew that, and an apology was in order. 'I'm sorry—I've had a bit of trouble convincing the doctor that I'm capable of coming back to work, and I've got Meg questioning me here. I just…'

'Don't need it.'

'Exactly,' Celeste said. 'I'm hardly going to put the baby at risk.'

'Good.'

She waited for the 'but,' for him to elaborate, for the little short, sharp lecture that she seemed to be getting a lot these days, but 'good' was all he said. Well, it was all he said about her condition, anyway.

'I've booked Matthew in for a scan. He had a small vomit, and I'd rather play safe. He's a bit pale, and I'm just not happy—they should call round for him soon. I've also found a hand injury to keep you occupied...' He gave her a nice smile and handed her the notes. 'Fleur Edwards, eighty-two years of age. She's got a nasty hand laceration, probable tendon, though the surgeons won't be able to fit her in till much later tonight. Given her age, it will be under local anaes-thetic, so if you can give her a light lunch and then fast her—elevation IV antis, the usual.'

'Sure.'

'Could you run a quick ECG on her, too? No rush.'

He was nice and laid-back, Celeste thought. He didn't talk down to her just because she was a grad, didn't ream off endless instructions as if she'd never looked after a head injury or hand laceration before. And, best of all, he hadn't lectured her on whether she should be here.

The observation ward was rather like a bus-stop—you were either standing or sitting around waiting, with nothing much happening for ages or everything arriving at once.

Matthew was brought around first, pale, as Ben had

described, but he managed a laugh as he climbed up onto the bed as Celeste had a joke with him.

'You do know exercise is bad for you?' His mother and girlfriend had both come around to see him into the observation ward, but now he was there and settled they would be heading home. Celeste did a careful set of neurological observations, warning Matthew this would be happening on the hour, every hour. 'Whether you're asleep or not…'

She told Matthew's family about visiting and discharge times and wrote down the hospital and extension numbers for them. Just as she was about to get started on the admission paperwork, the doors opened.

'Another admission for you…' Deb, a fellow grad, was wheeling round a rather delightful Fleur—with rouged cheeks and painted on eyebrows, she was dressed in a blue and white polka-dot skirt with a smart white blouse, which unfortunately had been splattered with blood. 'Fleur Edwards, 82, a hand injury—' Deb started.

'Ben's already told me about her,' Celeste said, sensing Deb was in a rush. 'Any family?'

'Her daughter's coming in this afternoon.' They flicked through the charts. 'No allergies, she suffers with arthritis, but apart from that she seems very well…'

'I'll sort things out, then,' Celeste said, smiling over at Fleur, who was patiently sitting in a wheelchair, her arm in a sling. 'Is it getting busy out there?' she asked Deb.

'It's starting to—we've got a multi-trauma coming in.'

Though she smiled as she went over to help Fleur, Celeste was hit with a pang as Deb left, just a pang of *something.* She should be out there, would have loved to really immerse herself in this emergency programme, and though she hoped to when she came back from maternity leave, Celeste was also realistic enough to know that her head would be full of other things by then, and that she'd be exhausted for other reasons, namely the baby who was kicking at her diaphragm right now. Still, it wasn't Fleur's problem.

'Hello, Mrs Edwards.'

'Fleur.' Fleur smiled.

'I'm Celeste—I'll be looking after you this shift.'

'You should be the one being looked after.' Fleur clucked. She really was gorgeous. Widowed for twenty years, she was an independent old lady, and she had cut her hand peeling an orange for her morning snack, Celeste found out as she took her history.

'Well, for now we'll get you into a gown and into bed, so that we can elevate your hand on an IV pole. You've had something for pain—has that helped?'

'I can hardly feel it, the bandage is so tight.' Fleur said. 'Would you mind taking me over to the ladies' before I get into bed?'

'Of course.' Only at that moment Matthew sat up, with that anxious, frantic look Celeste knew all too well, and with a quick 'Won't be a moment' to Fleur she raced over, locating a kidney dish just in time and pulling the curtain around him.

'It's okay, Matthew,' she soothed. 'I'll just fetch you a wet cloth...' And run another set of obs, Celeste thought. He really was terribly pale.

'I've got to get work,' Matthew muttered. He wasn't

a particularly large 18-year-old, but none the less he was trying to climb out of bed and he resisted as Celeste tried to guide him to lie back down. 'I have to get to work, I'm going to be late…'

'You're in hospital, Matthew,' Celeste said. 'You've had a bang on your head, remember?'

She was trying to reach for the call bell to summon help, worried that if he became agitated he might fall if he did get out of bed and hurt himself further, but as quickly as it had happened, Matthew seemed to remember where he was and stopped trying to climb out of bed and instead lay back down. 'Sorry.' He gave a wan smile and said it again. 'Sorry. I'm fine now.' And he seemed so, except, like Ben, Celeste was now worried.

'Matthew. Do you know where you are?'

'Hospital.'

She went through his obs—they were the same as before, his blood pressure a smudge higher, but his momentary confusion still troubled Celeste and she buzzed on the intercom. 'Can you send a doctor round to the observation ward?'

'Is it urgent?' Meg checked. 'They're just assessing a multi-trauma.' Celeste looked over at Matthew's pale but relaxed face and wavered for a moment. He seemed absolutely fine now and his obs were stable but, still, she just wasn't sure.

'I need the head injury assessed again,' she said, thinking it was likely Meg was rolling her eyes now. 'Let Ben know—he saw him.' She headed back to Matthew and Fleur gave a worried nod when Celeste said, 'I'll be with you soon.'

'Look after him!' the old lady said. 'Don't worry about me.'

Of course, by the time Ben arrived Matthew was sitting up and joking about his moment of confusion and refusing the oxygen that Celeste was trying to give him. 'Look, I'm sorry to pull you away,' she told Ben.

'No problem. The trauma team is with the patient and he's actually not that bad. So what's going on with Matthew?'

'Nothing!' Matthew said and it certainly looked that way.

'He was fine,' Celeste explained. 'In fact, he seems fine now, but he had a vomit a little earlier and was certainly confused and restless for a moment. He didn't look at all well—' She was trying to think up reasons to justify pulling a registrar out from an emergency, but Ben quickly interrupted.

'I agree.'

He didn't seem remotely annoyed that she had called him. Instead, he was checking Matthew's pupils and his blood pressure for himself as Celeste explained that he had tried to climb out of bed, insisting he had to get to work.

'How are you feeling, Matthew?'

'Fine. Well, a bit of a headache...'

'Okay,' Ben said, 'I'm just going to lay you flat and have a good look at you.' It was Ben who never got to finish this time as Matthew started to retch again, his face more grey than pale now, and he was moaning loudly about a pain in his head.

'How do you get urgent help around here?' Ben

asked, and it was only then that Celeste remembered that it was his first day here—he seemed so assured and competent. He was also a lot bigger than Matthew. He ignored the patient's protests to push off the oxygen mask and attempts to climb out of bed as Celeste pressed the switch on the wall. The light flashed above the door like a strobe as one of the team came to the intercom and Celeste explained what was happening.

The trauma team was still with the multi-trauma, so it was Belinda Hamilton, the rather snooty but exceptionally good-looking senior emergency registrar who came, along with Meg and a porter to get the patient to Resus if required. Had Matthew still been on a gurney it would have been easier to wheel him straight to Resus, but time was of the essence and the observation ward was set up, like any other ward, for such an emergency, so instead Celeste wheeled over the crash trolley. Matthew was like a tethered bull now, and it was Ben doing the tethering as he rapidly explained what had occurred to his senior. But he didn't await her verdict, just told her what was required. 'He needs to intubated and sent for a scan,' Ben said. 'Can you alert the neuro surgeons?'

Celeste was busy opening packs for the intubation, her heart hammering in her chest, stunned at how quickly Matthew had deteriorated.

Though Meg had also come to assist, she didn't take over, just guided and advised Celeste, who was setting up for the intubation. Raji, the anaesthetist, arrived just as Matthew started seizing, his body jerking violently. The whole thing was horrible. In a matter of moments

Matthew's condition had become critical—his family would have barely made it to the car park.

Raji was shooting drugs into the patient as Ben gave him the lowdown and thankfully the jerking stopped. Matthew was taking long, laboured breaths, but at least he wasn't seizing or fighting any more, though Celeste could feel her blood pounding, surely up near Matthew's as she wrestled to remove the bedhead to give Raji more access to the patient's airway.

'Here.' Ben must have seen her struggle and removed the bedhead easily for her. Raji was a pleasure to work with, a laid-back guy who really just got on with things, checking all the drugs she had prepared and pulling up for himself the others he required. Matthew was on a cardiac monitor, the seizing had stopped, but he was gravely ill and as Celeste watched Raji intubate the patient, Meg liaised with the porters and Imaging.

'Should we let his family know?' Celeste asked. 'They only just left.'

'Let's just worry about the patient for now,' Belinda snapped, and Celeste felt herself redden.

'I'll call them as soon as I can,' Ben said. 'He'll probably go straight up to Theatre from Imaging.'

It took ten, maybe fifteen minutes at the most before Matthew was paralysed and intubated and on a trolley, being wheeled up to Imaging and probably then on to Theatre. All that was left from his time in the obs ward was a mountain of paperwork and a lot of chaos. The suction equipment was still on and gurgling, and would need cleaning, the oxygen tubing and masks would need replacing; the bedhead was abandoned on the other side of the room, there were packs open everywhere. The crash cart was in chaos and there were syringes and vials on its surface. Everything would need to be tidied and checked and replaced and then checked again.

'So much for giving you a quiet afternoon!' Meg gave her a sympathetic smile, but her pager went off, and there really was no chance of her staying to help.

Letting out a long breath, forcing herself to just get on with it, Celeste turned around and saw Fleur's worried face.

'Will he be okay?' she asked worriedly.

'I think so,' Celeste said, and came over, her heart sinking as the proud, dignified lady burst into tears and said sorry over and over.

'I've wet my pants!'

'I'm so sorry!' It was Celeste saying it to Fleur now. 'It was my fault for not taking you.'

Ben was at the desk ringing the unfortunate family to tell them what had happened to Matthew, and Celeste and Fleur were in the bathroom. Fleur's wet clothes were off and her hand was wrapped in plastic and elevated on an IV pole, with the old lady sitting in a little shower chair.

'Let's both stop saying sorry, shall we?' A lot older and a lot wiser, Fleur caught Celeste's eyes and smiled. 'You could hardly leave the young man, could you?'

'I know.'

'I just don't want my daughter to know that I've had an accident—she'll be in soon, and she'll think I'm losing my faculties.'

'Of course you're not!' Celeste exclaimed. Still, she'd have been embarrassed too, so she came up with a plan. 'Why don't I rinse out your clothes?' Celeste suggested. 'They're covered in blood anyway. I'll tell your daughter that's why I washed them.'

'What about my knickers?'

'I'll wash them and hang them by the vent.' A little bit ditzy at times, Celeste could also be very practical. 'They'll be dry by the end of my shift—no one will ever know.'

'You're very kind.'

Not really, Celeste thought. Anyone should do it. She still winced when nurses stuffed filthy clothes into bags for relatives, wondering how they'd like it. Still, she couldn't change the world, only her own actions. So she filled a sink with water...

'Cold water for blood,' Fleur prompted, and Celeste did as she was told then set about showering her patient. Firm friends now, Celeste smiled when Fleur asked what was surely a rare favour. 'Would you mind giving my back an good wash?' she asked. 'I can never reach it.'

'Of course.' Fleur's back was indeed grubby from, most likely, years of neglect, as her arthritis simply wouldn't allow her arms to reach it.

'I bought a brush from the chemist,' Fleur said as Celeste gave it a good scrub. 'You know, on a long stick, but I still can't get there.' So Celeste took her time to wash it as thoroughly as she could, wondering how best to approach this proud lady.

'You'll be needing some help with your hand out of action...'

'I will not!' Fleur said, as Celeste wrapped her in towels. 'I'll manage fine with one hand.'

'You probably will,' Celeste said, 'but there are so many aids, like hand-held showers, and there are brushes for your back but with curved sticks. I'm not sure of all the things that could help, but maybe we could get you assessed.'

'I like my independence.'

'Well, this will help you keep your independence.' Celeste shrugged. 'You may as well while you're here… Have a think about it.'

Fleur was right, Ben thought. Sitting at the desk for a moment, having made a very difficult call to Matthew's mother and not ready to head back out there, he'd overheard the conversation between the two women. Celeste *was* kind, very kind indeed.

It was so easy to become hard working in Emergency— he'd seen it happen to so many colleagues. It was necessary almost if you wanted to survive in this area. He had become hardened too—switched off on certain occasions, because at times it was easier to deal with a patient than a person, kinder to yourself not to think about a family and friends and futures that were being obliterated, to just get on with the job in hand, rather than look at the bigger picture. But watching Celeste wheel out a smiling Fleur, all powdered and warm and well looked after, Ben was a mite conflicted.

Because pregnancy was his *thing*. One of his many *things* if he actually stopped and thought about it, which he tried very hard not to do.

Most people had one—Belinda had just told him on

the walk back from Imaging how her younger brother had almost died from a head injury. The staff hadn't noticed his deterioration and it had been Belinda herself who had recognised the signs when she had come to visit. Yes, they all had their *things*. And pregnancy was Ben's—the one thing where he just had to detach and deal with a foetus rather than a baby, look at a set of numbers instead of the person.

He didn't want to be hard, didn't want to be bitter—except he was.

Yet watching Celeste rub her back after helping Fleur into bed, reluctantly watching the shape of her pregnant belly, he resisted the urge to just walk away, to shrug his shoulders and let her get on with it. She wasn't a nurse, or a set of numbers, or a pregnant woman, she was Celeste, who was kind and tired and had had a difficult start to her shift and a lot of mess to clean up.

'I've spoken to Matthew's family...' As he chatted to her, he lifted the metal bedhead from the floor and replaced it, then easily dragged the portable oxygen cylinder back to its spot—just doing a couple of little things that he didn't need to, in the same way Celeste had done for Fleur, only she could never know the effort behind his easy gestures, because being around her was becoming unbearable for Ben. 'They're on their way back. I've told them to come to the front desk, but if they arrive here, just give me a buzz.'

'I will.' She pulled over a linen skip and stripped the bed. 'Do you think he'll be okay?'

'He'll be in Theatre by now,' Ben said, 'so, hopefully, yes. I'll let you know when I hear.'

Her quiet shift was anything but. By the time it came to a close the crash cart was checked and put away, the eight beds had been filled with patients, Fleur had agreed to a visit from Occupational Therapy and now that visiting time was over, the ward was actually neat and in order—at least the night nurse should have a quiet shift!

'Thank you, Celeste.' Fleur smiled as Celeste helped her into clean, dry undies before she headed off home. 'For all your care and for washing out my clothes—my daughter never suspected a thing.'

'That's good. Theatre just called and it shouldn't be too much longer till they're ready for you.'

'And I'll just stay in for one night?'

'If all goes smoothly, which I'm sure it will, I'll see you in the morning.' Celeste smiled. 'I'm back on at seven.'

'You work too hard,' Fleur fussed. 'I know it's what you girls do now. Still, I hope your young man's at home with dinner waiting so you can put your feet up.'

'I shall!' Celeste smiled and then blushed as she realised that Ben had come in. ''Night, Fleur.' She walked over to Ben. 'I don't want her worrying.'

'Sorry?'

Celeste hurried to explain. 'Well, it's just easier to sometimes let people think that there is a Mr Mitchell at home…' Her blush darkened as it was only then she realised Ben would have neither known nor cared that she had just been caught fibbing to Fleur. 'Have you heard anything about Matthew?'

'That's what I was coming to tell you about. I'm heading home, so I just rang ICU. I didn't get a chance till now. Apparently his pupil blew in Imaging. They got him straight up to theatre and evacuated a massive subdural haematoma—so I came to say well done. It was a good pick-up—a lot of people might have hesitated seeing as his symptoms were so fleeting.'

'How is he now?' Celeste asked, warming at his praise. Matthew's brain had been bleeding, the pressure building inside his skull, causing his symptoms. It was the scary thing about seemingly benign head injuries—and the reason patients were often admitted for observation afterwards. She had read about it, studied it, learnt about it, but now she had witnessed it for herself. The *chore* of regular neuro obs would never be considered a chore again.

'On ICU. It will be a good forty-eight hours before we know anything, but there is hope…'

Which was always nice.

She handed over her patients and headed for home in a car that was making more new and rather worrying noises. She slowed down at the gates and indicated left for the block of units. She climbed out of the car, leaving it idling, too worried to turn off the engine, because one day it surely wouldn't start again! Absolutely bone weary, she opened the gates and then realised someone had pulled up behind her.

'I'll close them,' Ben called out, which he did, and she drove another hundred yards and then pulled on her handbrake and climbed out of her idling car again to open the garage, because the landlord was too mean to put in automatic doors.

'I'll get that.' He walked over from the gates and made light work of the garage door, and even waited till she had driven inside and closed it for her as she walked out.

Which didn't sound like much, but every stretch was one less stretch that she had to do and she was so tired that all she was was grateful.

'Thanks for that.' Celeste was too weary to even summon a smile.

'No problem,' Ben called, heading back to his own car to repeat the ritual for his own garage. And still he didn't deliver a lecture. Still didn't check that she was okay, or ask if she was sure she should be working.

Had he asked, Celeste thought, as she let herself into her little unit, she might just have burst into tears.

She had to eat, but she was too tired to cook, so she had a bowl of cereal instead.

Then a very quick shower. Knowing she'd regret it if she didn't, she put out a fresh uniform for the morning, checked her alarm and slipped into bed, too tired to worry, too worn out for tears or even to think really.

She had to be back there tomorrow at ten to seven!

CHAPTER THREE

BEN didn't worry.

He was concerned for his patients at times, but he didn't do worrying.

The worst day of his life had happened a long time ago and he knew things could never be that bad again, so consequently he just got on with things, didn't fret or dwell—or, well, worry!

He hadn't in years.

Yet there was this niggle now and, no matter how he tried to ignore it, still it persisted.

His second day at Bay View Hospital and the flood-gates had opened.

One drowning had been brought in as well as victims of a multiple pile-up on the beach road. It was over forty degrees and people were collapsing everywhere. It was just one of those days where everyone ran to keep up and everyone worked up to and beyond their limits.

Including Celeste.

He could see her ankles swelling as the shift pro-gressed, see her blow out of her mouth and onto her red face as she stripped yet another trolley and prepared it for the endless list of recipients, could see the *effort* in her movements, and then finally the sheer relief on her face at 3:30 p.m. when her shift ended. As he watched her waddle out, like it or not, Ben *was* worried.

'What are you doing tonight?' Belinda was tapping away on the computer. In her late thirties, and absolutely stunning, she was also witty. With a tumble of black hair, she had almond-shaped brown eyes, full red lips, and dressed like she'd stepped out of a magazine. Thankfully, *very* thankfully, Ben didn't fancy her a jot, which meant there was no trouble sharing a tiny office and they could chat easily about things—which they did as Ben wound up his day and packed up his briefcase. It was only his second day and already paperwork was starting to pile up.

'I'm stopping in at the real-estate agent's, then the deli to buy salad and chicken instead of a burger and then…' Ben thought about it '…I will *make* myself go for a jog this evening. What about you?'

'I'll show you…' She gave a wicked smile. 'Come here.'

Curious, Ben walked over and looked at the screen and stared at the image of a rather ordinary-looking guy.

'A GP, late thirties, has children but doesn't want to involve them yet…'

'Sorry?' Ben had no idea what she was going on about.

"That's good,' Belinda said. 'The last one I saw brought his children along on the second date! We've chatted on the phone,' Belinda explained to a bemused Ben, 'and he seems great—we're meeting for coffee tonight.'

'You're going on a *date* with him?'

'Coffee.' Belinda laughed. 'You should try it—you'd be a hit!'

Ben shook his head. 'Internet dating isn't for me.'

'Don't knock it till you try it.'

'Be careful.' Ben frowned. 'Shouldn't you go with someone when you meet him? He could be anyone!'

'He's who he says is.' Belinda winked. 'I've checked his registration.'

'Well, good luck.'

The real-estate agent was being nice to him again—there had been a little bit of initial sulking when Ben hadn't bought the apartment, but he'd obviously got over it and he was Ben's new best friend again now that he had a genuine prospective client for the house.

'Can I have a look around?' Ben asked.

'Not till the "open for inspection" at the weekend,' the agent said. 'After that, I can arrange a private inspection for you.'

'I'm actually working this weekend,' Ben said, 'so don't worry about it.'

'You will come and have a look, though?' the agent said anxiously.

'Like I said…' Ben shrugged '…I'm working—but it's really no problem. I'm actually going to look at another house tonight.'

That soon got him on the phone! A private inspection was arranged within the hour and Ben wandered through the house he was seriously thinking of calling home. It did need a lot of work—the kitchen was a bomb and the downstairs bathroom would need to be ripped out, but the master bedroom had already been renovated, with floor-to-ceiling windows that took in the bay view and a fantastic en suite that did the same.

Yes, it was way too big for one, but it just felt right.

He could renovate it, Ben thought, take his time, pull out the kitchen, do up the back garden… Standing in the master bedroom, staring out at the bay, Ben felt the first breeze of contentment he had in years, the first, the very first glimmer of how finally coming home should feel.

Despite his nonchalance with the agent, despite the shake of his head when he found out the reserve price and that the vendor wanted a quick settlement, he was just playing the necessary game. For Ben, the auction couldn't come soon enough.

A wall of heat hit him as Ben opened the door to his unit. He opened the windows, turned on a fan and put his dinner in the fridge then peeled off his clothes and hoped that the shower ran cold this evening—which thankfully it did.

After showering, he pulled on some shorts and nothing else, then headed for the kitchen. Suddenly, out of the blue, there was this sort of long groan as everything ground to a halt.

It had been happening all over Melbourne—the power outages every evening as the lucky people who had air-conditioning selfishly cranked it up to full. Ben just had a fan—which now, of course, wasn't working.

He went outside to check the power box, just in case it was only him, and glancing down the row of units he saw Celeste checking her power box too.

She was in lilac shorts this time, and a black singlet. Her hair was wet and she looked thoroughly fed up.

'Again!' She rolled her eyes, gave him a brief wave and headed back into what would surely soon be a furnace—unlike his unit, Celeste's got the full questionable glory of the afternoon sun.

And that was when that niggle hit him again—an unfamiliar, long-forgotten feeling that gnawed at his stomach as he pulled open the dark fridge and pulled out the plastic containers he had got from the deli—a strange niggle of worry for someone else.

Ben didn't want neighbours who dropped in on him and he had certainly never thought he'd be a neighbour who did just that—but there he was on her doorstep. She had come to the door holding a bowl of cereal and was clearly irritated at the intrusion but trying to be polite.

'The electricity should come back on in a couple of hours—it's been happening a lot lately,' Celeste said, and went to close the door. She wasn't actually irritated with him and didn't mean to be rude, she was just trying not to notice he was wearing only shorts. Which was normal, of course, in the middle of a heat wave. Had he knocked just two minutes later, she'd have had to put her top back on herself before answering the door!

The sight of all his exposed skin made her own turn pink, though, and she didn't want him to notice!

'Have you had dinner?' he said to the closing door, and she paused, glancing guiltily down at the bowl of cereal—which was probably not the best dinner for a heavily pregnant woman and she was instantly on the defensive. 'I can hardly cook with no electricity.'

'No need to—I've got plenty.' He held up the dishes to tempt her. 'Let's go and eat on the beach—it will be cooler there.'

It was. There was a lovely southerly breeze sweeping in and Celeste walked in the shallows. Ben could practically hear the sizzle as her hot, swollen, red ankles hit the water.

'I should have come down earlier.' Celeste sighed in relief. 'I keep meaning to, I mean, I'm so glad I did when I get here…'

'I'm the same.' Ben smiled, and it was so nice after such a busy day to just walk and say not much, to watch the dogs and the boats and the couples—to just *be*.

And then to sit.

Chicken in tarragon and mayonnaise, with a crisp Greek salad, was certainly nicer than cereal, and washed down with fresh fruit salad, it was bordering on the healthiest dinner of her pregnancy. The baby gave an appreciative kick as she sank down onto her back.

'That was yum—thank you!'

'You're welcome.' Ben gave a small uncomfortable swallow. 'Look, I'm sorry if I dismissed you a bit at work.'

'You didn't.' Celeste frowned.

'I did,' Ben said, 'or rather I didn't let on that we'd already met.'

'That's okay.'

'I just like to keep work separate…'

'That's fine,' Celeste said. 'This evening never happened.' She turned and smiled at him where he still sat. 'How are you enjoying your new job?'

'It's good.' Ben nodded.

'You were in Sydney before?' Celeste checked because she'd heard Meg say so.

'Yes.' Ben didn't elaborate. 'How long have you worked there?'

She didn't reply for a moment as she was busy settling herself back on the sand, closing her eyes in sheer pleasure. 'Nearly three months.' One eye peeked open. 'I don't think they were particularly thrilled when I turned up for my first shift.'

Thankfully he wasn't so politically correct that he pretended to have no idea what she was talking about. Instead, he just grinned and Celeste closed that eye and finally, finally, finally she relaxed.

'God, this feels nice,' she sighed after five minutes of lovely comfortable silence.

And it also looked nice, Ben thought, it looked very nice indeed. Her lashes were fanning her cheeks, her knees were up, and her stomach was sort of wriggling of its own accord—like Jennifer's had, Ben thought, and then abruptly stopped that thought process.

'So there is no Mr Mitchell?' he asked.

'Nope.' Her eyes were still closed.

'Do you see him at all, the father of your baby?'

'Nope.'

'Does he know?' Ben asked, even though it was none of his business. 'I mean, is he helping you out?'

'He thought he was,' Celeste said. 'He gave me money to have an abortion.'

'Oh.' Ben stared down at her.

'I was on my maternity rotation at the time I found

out I was pregnant, babies everywhere—not that it made me want one, it terrified me actually, but…'

'You don't have to say anything else if you don't want to.'

But she did want to—lying there with her eyes closed, lost and lonely and really, really confused. Maybe, as everyone said it would, talking might help clear her head. It was worth a try, anyway, because yoga certainly hadn't worked!

'He's married.' She opened her eyes then and closed them—and even in that teeny space of time she saw *it* pass over his features. That moment where you were judged, where opinions were cast, where assumptions were made. 'I didn't know that he was, not that that changes anything.'

'Did you go out for long?' he wanted to know.

'Three months.' Celeste sniffed. 'He was my first real… I just believed him. I mean, I knew why we didn't go out much, and why we couldn't go to each other's homes…'

'Sorry?'

'It doesn't matter,' she muttered.

'So where did you go out?'

'For drives, for dinner, to a hotel sometimes…' She gazed up into his clear green eyes. 'He's a bit older than me, quite a bit older actually,' Celeste said, and then she was silent for a while.

Rightly or wrongly, he did judge—he tried not to, but he did.

Why didn't people think? Why were people so careless?

And now there was this baby…

He closed his eyes and thought of Jennifer—of the plans they had put in place, how much they had wanted a baby, and though he didn't say a word, she could feel his disapproval.

'So you've never made a mistake?' she said defensively.

'I've made plenty,' he admitted.

'But no affairs, nothing you regret.'

'Oh, there's a lot that I regret,' Ben said.

'You're single, divorced…?' It sounded like the questionnaire on Belinda's dating site, and he winced inwardly.

'Widowed,' he said, and it was her turn to judge, Ben knew—he had been through it many times before.

'Do you miss her a lot?' she asked gently.

'Yep,' Ben admitted, and that was enough. He ran some sand through his hands, concentrated on the little grains instead of himself then glanced at his watch. 'The power must be back on by now.'

'So what if it is?' Celeste smiled. 'I'm enjoying talking—you were saying how much you miss her?'

God, she was persistent. Really, he should stand up and leave, but she'd said so much about herself and, picking up another handful of sand, he let it run through his closed fist, and admitted some of his truth. 'I miss it for Jennifer too.' Her silence was patient. 'She loved living.' He looked out to the water and could almost see her, blonde ponytail flying as she jogged. 'She'd be out there running or swimming now—cramming some exercise in after work.'

'Was she fit?'

'Very.' Ben nodded, but there was this savage rip of

thought there because, despite doing everything right, despite her healthy lifestyle, it hadn't counted for anything in the end.

'What did she do?'

'She was a doctor as well—in Emergency.'

'What happened?' Celeste asked, but Ben shook his head, not willing to go there. 'Come on.' It really was time to go now, and not just because he didn't want to talk about it. He was doing her a favour. A woman in Celeste's condition really didn't need to hear about how Jen had died. So he held her hands and heaved her up and they walked back slowly, idly chatting about not very much at all, till Celeste wormed her way back in again.

'Have you dated again—I mean since…?'

'She died three, nearly four years ago,' Ben said, answering the unspoken question.

'Oh.'

'A bit.' He gave a shrug. 'Though it was probably too soon.'

'Are you still comparing them to her?' Celeste asked, boldly striding in where no one else really dared to go, but Ben just ignored her question and, glad of the diversion, opened the gates to the units, but Celeste stood patiently waiting.

'Are you?' she asked.

'Sorry?'

'Comparing them?'

She was a persistent little thing, like a little woodpecker, peck, peck pecking away—

'I used to,' Ben admitted. 'But not now—that's not fair on anyone.'

'Especially as she sounds like Superwoman,' Celeste grumbled, and her response was so refreshing Ben actually smiled. 'So,' she pushed, 'are you ready now?'

'Perhaps, though not anything serious.'

'Ooh, I'm sure there'll be plenty of takers.' Celeste grinned. After all, she'd heard the giggles and gossip in the staffroom—Ben could take his pick!

'What about you?' They were sitting on her steps now, the conversation, and the friendship, too new, too fragile to snap it by asking him in. And anyway the power was still off, so they sat on the steps and got to know each other just a little bit better.

'I'm hardly in a position to date.' Celeste rolled her eyes. 'Can you imagine me out clubbing?'

'I guess not!'

'And I'm still in that "all men are snakes" place.'

'It's probably a very wise place to be right now,' Ben agreed. 'I've been a bit of a snake myself lately.'

'Do tell!' She did make him laugh, she was so eager for gossip, and so easy to talk to, that somehow he did.

'I went out with someone for a while—she was great, but even though I told her from the start—'

'She didn't listen?' she finished for him.

'She did at first, said she wanted the same thing— then, well, it got a bit more serious. She started to hint at wanting different things.' He looked into her smiling amber eyes. 'Like moving in.'

'Not for you?' she said wisely.

'Maybe one day, but she also started talking about children. And one thing I do know is that I don't want kids.'

'Never?'

'Never,' he said emphatically.

She got the message and was actually rather grateful for it. Oh, they hardly knew each other, had barely scratched the surface, but there was certainly if not an immediate attraction then at the very least an acute awareness. Which was something she hadn't felt in the longest time—had been sure, after the way Dean had treated her, that she'd never feel it again. But sitting here, looking into Ben's green eyes, hearing his words, Celeste suddenly realised that he felt it too. That he was carefully reading out the rules of any potential relationship should they choose to pursue one.

'We couldn't be less suited really,' Celeste said after a moment's pause. 'I'm not looking at all, you're not looking for serious and…' she patted her large stomach '…this isn't a hernia!'

'I had worked that out!' Ben smiled. 'So how about we just be friends?'

She stared into his green eyes and this time she didn't blush. Oh, she had a teeny crush on him—what heterosexual woman wouldn't?—but her heart was way too bruised and her ego far too raw and her soul just too tender to even fathom going there again. It was simply nice to have an adult to talk to. Her world had changed so much, and with her family not talking to her and her struggle to fit in on her new course, it was just nice, very nice to have Ben in her life, to talk to a person instead of staring at the television. 'A friend would be lovely.'

And still he stayed. Celeste went in and brought out two glasses of water, and then picked at daisies as they chatted, shredding them with her fingers, joining them up, and when she wasn't looking at him, somehow it made it easier for Ben to talk.

'You see, I had it all with Jen...' He pushed his fingers through his hair, tried to sum up how he was feeling, because she was so easy to talk to. Maybe because she hadn't known Jen, maybe because her eyes didn't well up with tears as friends' and family's did when he spoke about her, or flinch in tiny reproach at his sometimes bungling efforts to try and move on with his life. 'I don't want to try to re-create it—I don't want to do it again with someone else. I've already been there and done it.'

'Lucky you, then.' Ben blinked at her response. Really, he felt anything but lucky, but he supposed that, yes, she was right, he had been lucky to have Jen in his life for a while.

'I'd give anything to be able to say to this little one that its dad and I were in love.'

'Were you?' Ben asked.

'I thought so.' She shrugged. 'But looking back it was just infatuation, I guess—it sounds like you had the real thing.'

He didn't answer, because at that moment her television started blaring through the window, a cheer coming from the unit opposite as the power kicked back in.

'I'm going to do some work...' Ben stood up.

'Well, thank you for dinner...' Celeste smiled '...and a thank-you from the baby too.'

'You're very welcome.'

'I'd offer to return the favour, only I'm having enough trouble rustling up dinner for one at the moment,' she said wryly.

'I don't expect you to.'

He didn't expect her to. Celeste knew that and so too did Ben.

But next night when he came home from work he could see pots of sunflowers on his doorstep, her way of saying thank you, he guessed.

'I have some good news for you,' Ben said as he knocked on her door.

'I could do with some. Come in,' she invited.

'Matthew was extubated this evening,' Ben explained as he followed her into her tiny kitchen. 'He's doing really well—they're hoping to move him from ICU in the morning.'

That *was* good news!

'It could have been a very different story. I've had Belinda patting me on the back and the neuro consultant even came down to Emergency to say well done. I have told them that the credit goes to you.' He watched her face pink up with his praise. 'I know it's tough deciding whether to wait and see or call for help.'

'It can be,' Celeste admitted, as she pulled a vast jug of iced tea from the fridge and poured them both a long glass. 'I mean, you don't want to look like an idiot or that you're overreacting to everything…'

'Overreact!' Ben said simply. 'For now at least—until you've got more experience and your hunch button's working properly.'

'Hunch button?' Celeste frowned at the unfamiliar term. 'What's that?'

'When you have a hunch about something, when you're almost sure but not quite.'

She'd already worked out what he meant even before he explained it, but as he did explain it, she felt that glow in her cheeks darken just a touch, aware that he wasn't quite meeting her eyes. Her hunch button was tapping away, but for different reasons now, and she flicked it off quickly.

She was so not going to develop a crush on *another* man from work!

Look where that had got her!

And it *was* nice to have a friend.

They sat in her little living room, watching the 'weigh-in' on her favourite show, Celeste grumbling that she should be a contestant. Ben was more than a touch uncomfortable and trying not to show it—he could see the little pile of baby clothes all neatly folded on the ironing board and even though it was weeks away, there was a slight baby smell to the house—which probably had something to do with the baby lotion Celeste was rubbing into her hands, but still... So he went to get the jug of iced tea and when he came back, he poured her one into the glass she was holding, and he wouldn't have been human if he hadn't noticed her cleavage—would have to be blind to miss it actually, only Ben wasn't usually a breast man. Except that they were so jiggly and voluptuous that he was suddenly kneed in the groin with an unfamiliar longing.

So he sat down. He realised he couldn't smell that baby smell any more, just the unsettling scent of Celeste. The room was too hot, so of course she kept lifting up her arms and coiling her hair onto the top of her head as she chatted away, and then it would tumble down again, and she'd lift her arms once more.

'I'd better go…'

'Already?' Celeste said, but then they got talking, oh, just about this and that, and suddenly it was after ten. As he stood at the door to really go this time, Celeste found herself thinking that she'd had the nicest night in a long time.

Too nice, even.

Because of all the stupid things to be thinking, she was wondering what it would be like to be kissed goodnight by him.

Wondering what she'd do if that lovely mouth came a little bit closer.

'Thanks for the flowers, by the way.' Ben broke into her thoughts. 'You shouldn't have done that.'

'It's no problem.'

'No, you really shouldn't have done that.' Ben grinned. 'They'll be dead in two days—I'll forget to water them.'

'I won't.' Celeste smiled. 'Just enjoy.'

It was a relief to close the door on him!

CHAPTER FOUR

THEY ignored each other at work, of course.

Well, they didn't mention their evenings by the television or walks on the beach and sometimes as she sat in the staffroom and listened as Deb rattled on about how sure she was that Ben was going to ask her out (when Ben had already told her that he was embarrassed by Deb's constant flirting), or when the gorgeous Belinda started talking rather too warmly about him, though Celeste sat like a contended Buddha, inside she was fuming and could have cheerfully strangled them quiet.

She liked him.

Which was okay and everything. After all, half the department liked him in that way too, she was hardly in a minority—no, there was a slightly bigger problem than that.

Sometimes, *sometimes* she got that nervous fluttering feeling, which could only be generated by two.

Sometimes, *sometimes* she got this fleeting glimpse that Ben liked her too.

She told herself she was imagining it—as surely as

Deb was. Because there was no way Ben could possibly be interested in her.

So why was he acting so strangely?

Coffee break over, she headed back to Cots—and tried to tell her stupid heart to stop beating so quickly at the sight of him, except it didn't listen. It picked up speed half an hour later, only for different reasons as a rather frantic mother handed Celeste a very floppy baby.

She pushed on the call bell even before she unwrapped him.

He was big and chubby and barely opened his eyes as Celeste swiftly undressed him and ran some obs.

'He keeps vomiting…' The mum was trying not to cry. 'He saw the GP yesterday, she said it was gastro and to push fluids into him…'

No help was coming, so Celeste pushed the call bell again. The baby's pulse was racing and his temperature was high, so she put him on some oxygen and pushed the call bell *again* as she pulled over the IV trolley, resorting in the end to sticking her head out of the cubicle.

'Could I have a hand?' she snapped, and shot a frantic look at Ben, who was showing a patient his ankle X-ray. 'Now!'

'Press it three times for an emergency!" Ben snapped back, when he saw the baby.

She was still learning which way was up—only yesterday she had been warned for overreacting and pressing three times for everything remotely urgent and now she was being scolded for doing too little.

Some days this job was just so hard!

'Depressed fontanel.' Ben swiftly examined the listless baby, as Celeste quickly lifted him off the scales and set up for an IV. She was terrified of putting an IV line in such a sick baby, but it was part of her course and something she had to learn to do. She'd started on big, strapping, muscle-bound men with veins like tram lines, and then on sick adults. She had even put IVs in a few children now and a couple of babies as well, only not one as unwell as this and not with Mum anxiously watching—and now Meg was here too! 'Poor skin turgor.' Ben continued with his assessment then shook his head as he saw the slight shake of her hands as Celeste held the floppy arm with one hand and poised the needle with the other. 'I'll do it.' He took over without further comment and she was glad that he had. As a fat little baby, his veins would be hard to find at the best of times, but collapsed from dehydration they were proving extremely difficult and even Ben, with very steady hands, took a couple of goes to establish IV access, eventually finding a vein in his foot.

'I'm in.' He took some bloods and held the IV in firm place as Celeste connected it to a drip and then taped and wrapped it, carefully splinting his foot as Mum hovered close. As Ben relayed the IV fluids he wanted the babe to receive, he glanced up at Celeste with a quick addition. 'Could you put on a mask, please?'

She didn't see *him* putting on a mask, and neither was he asking Meg to. She gritted her teeth, for now she did as she was told. It was becoming an all too familiar pattern—in the couple of weeks that they had been working together Ben had become rather—for want of a word—annoying! She was already being looked out for by her colleagues and was uncomfortable enough with that, but Ben seemed to be on a mission to ensure that she saw only the safest, calmest, least infectious patients and if he wasn't suggesting that she put on a mask he was reminding her to wash her hands!

As if she needed reminding!

Still, with Ben now speaking with the mother, it was hardly the time or place for discussion—she'd save it for later.

'He's nine months old,' Ben checked with the anxious mum as Celeste sweated behind her mask. 'Is that right?'

'Only just nine months,' his mum said. 'I know he looks older.'

'How long as he been sick?' Ben asked.

'He started vomiting yesterday, three, maybe four times.'

'And this morning?' He fired questions as he continued to examine the baby and ordered a bolus dose of fluids for him. Celeste had already put him on oxygen and the paediatricians were on their way down, but Ben was examining his abdomen carefully, concerned that it was the surgeons that they needed. 'What colour is the vomit?'

'Green.'

'Okay…' He checked the baby's nappy and, still not happy with the abdomen, asked Meg to page the surgeons. Having spoken briefly with the mother, he rang Imaging to order an urgent ultrasound.

'I think it's an ileus,' Ben said, standing on hold on

the phone at the nurses' station as Celeste pointedly washed her hands at the little sink there, yet annoyingly as she dried her hands he pushed the bottle of alcohol hand rub towards her.

'Does that diagnosis mean I can go in there without a mask now?' Celeste asked, and then she frowned. 'Or is that suddenly an airborne disease too?' She watched his jaw tighten.

'You just need to be careful,' Ben pointed out. 'At that age, he could have measles, chickenpox, slap cheek…'

'Here.' He pushed the bottle of hand scrub to her again as she climbed onto the stool to write her notes, but she ignored it.

'You should use this,' he insisted.

'Why?' Celeste challenged.

'Because we don't know what's wrong with the baby yet, because you should—'

'Ben.' She clicked off her pen and put it down. 'While I appreciate your concern, I really don't need you to look out for me.'

'I'm not looking out for you—I'm just—'

'Making me paranoid!' Celeste said. 'Ben, I can beat you on the paranoid stakes with this pregnancy any day!'

He doubted that, but bit his tongue.

'I'm just ensuring that you take sensible precautions,' he said instead.

'I've spoken with my obstetrician, with the infectious diseases nurse, with Meg, and I'm using universal precautions. I'm being as sensible and as careful as possible, but dealing with sick people is part and parcel of nursing,' she said calmly.

'I don't see that it can hurt to take a few more precautions,' he muttered.

'I can't walk around in a spacesuit,' Celeste said, 'and neither can the nurses on the children's or oncology wards, neither can the nurses or radiographers who don't even know that they're pregnant but might be...' She could see his frown descending as the grad nurse gave the registrar a stern talking to. 'And all we can be is sensible, *all* the time, not just when we're visibly pregnant, so thank you for your concern and, no, I won't be using this...' she pushed back the bottle of alcohol scrub '...because I happen to be allergic to it.'

'Fine!' Ben snapped, more annoyed with himself than her. If her doctor was happy to let her keep working, and the hospital was still employing her, if Celeste wanted to keep working—well, it wasn't his concern.

So why was he so worried about her?

It niggled at him all day and later into the evening when, confused, he stood at the supermarket, basket in hand, and chose organic steak, because it was better for the baby—which, again, wasn't his concern, but he just stuffed it in his basket and added a carton of orange juice with added iron. He knew he was overreacting and he had every reason to. It was the anniversary of Jen's death in a couple of days, so it was no wonder he was upset. But then he did what he always did—and chose not to think about it.

A very vague routine had developed—not every day, not even every other day but now and then. He'd wander down and ask if she fancied dinner, or he'd hear her watering the sunflowers at his front door and pop his head around and ask her if she wanted to watch a movie, or whatever.

It was company, that was all.

And she was so-o-o glad of it.

So glad not to have to be as bright and bubbly as she pretended to be when she was at work—so nice to chat and moan, or sit with her feet up on his coffee table and watch a movie.

And never, not once, did he lecture her, or question her decision to keep working.

Till at the end of thirty-three weeks, till *that* night, when, full from organic steak and salad washed down with orange juice with added iron, she heaved herself off the sofa, and Ben glanced at his watch.

'It's only eight-thirty.'

'I just fancy an early night.'

'You're on a day off tomorrow.' Ben frowned, reluctantly seeing her to the door. His own company was the last thing he wanted over these next few nights. 'Are you sure you're okay?'

'I've got a doctor's appointment tomorrow. I want to—'

'Make sure that you look well rested, so you can fool him,' Ben said, and then stopped, his jaw muscles clamping, because it was *none* of his damn business what she did.

'I need to work for a few more weeks,' Celeste said, and Ben said nothing. He just forced a smile, and opened the door, telling himself that she didn't need a lecture, just a friend, but it was getting harder and harder to hold his tongue.

Then she burst into tears.

Celeste, who always smiled, always laughed, always came back with a quick retort, crumpled and gave in.

'I can't do it any more!'

All he felt was relief, relief that she'd seen it, relief that she wouldn't be doing it any more, and he pulled her, sobbing, into his arms and let her weep.

'Then don't,' he said gently.

'I can't afford not to,' she argued, but with herself now. 'Only I just can't face going there again…'

'I know.'

'I'm so tired.'

'I know.'

'And I'm scared of the germs too.'

'Come on.' He led her back to his sofa, fetched some cold water from the fridge and then gently he spoke with her, just as he would a patient, and explored her options. She had everything in place, even had some savings, but it would only just cover the rent and not much else. There would be a bit more money once the baby came along, but undoubtedly things were impossibly tight for her financially.

'The car's about to give up,' Celeste sobbed. 'And I haven't got a baby seat for it. I was going to get that with next month's pay…'

'My sister has had hundreds of car seats—the garage is full of them. She had twins…so that's sorted, okay?'

It was just the tip of a very big iceberg, just another thing on her endless list, but it was a relief to tick it off, to share, to finally admit just how drained from it all she really was.

'I need to work, but I really think that if I carry on,

it will affect the baby.' She was so glad that he didn't jump in and confirm her fears. 'I've got all this fluid...'

'Look.' Ben was supremely gentle. 'You've done well to get this far.'

'Some women work right to the end.'

'And some women don't,' Ben said. 'Some women can't, and it looks as if you're one of them.'

'I'll speak to the doctor tomorrow.' She nodded. 'I'll be honest.'

'Good,' Ben said, then he paused. And dived in where he didn't want to, got just a little bit more involved. 'Have you thought of asking the father for help?'

'Never.' Celeste shook her head. 'And please don't give me a lecture saying that he's responsible too, and that I've every right—'

'No lecture,' Ben interrupted. 'What about your parents?'

'I've written to them.' He realised how hard that would have been for her—knew from their chats how outraged their response had been, how they had cut her off. The fact that she had written and asked them for help after they'd done that to her showed she was thinking about the baby.

'Well done.'

It was the nicest thing he could have said. 'I only posted it yesterday, so I haven't heard. I've asked if I can move back, just for a few weeks...'

He'd miss her, Ben realised, but it was the right thing for her now. She needed family, needed someone to take care of her during these last difficult weeks—and it certainly wasn't going to be him.

'I'm going to speak to the doctor tomorrow.' Her voice was firmer now. 'And then I'll tell Meg.'

'Good.'

'And now…' again he pulled her up from the sofa as she went to stand '…I'm really going home to bed.'

He smiled at her as they reached the door. 'You'll get there,' Ben said, 'you really will.'

'I know.'

She was so tired and so weary and lost, trying to be brave in the dark, that this time when he pulled her into his arms, it wasn't because she was crying, it wasn't because she was upset. He didn't actually know why he'd done it, it just felt very right to hold her.

And for Celeste it felt so wonderful to *be* held for a moment.

A lovely, lovely moment to just stand and lean on him, to feel his words in her hair, his assurances that she had made the right choices, that she would be okay, and that she was doing well.

'I'm scared.'

She had never, not once, admitted it to anyone.

Defiance had become her middle name, because if she stopped for just a second, if she questioned her wisdom to keep the baby, to go on working, to not publicly name the father, to admit, even to herself, that she was struggling, then surely, *surely*, all the balls she was juggling would come clattering down. It was easier to cope, to insist she *was* coping, to just get on and do, rather than stop and think.

Yet in his arms she stopped for a moment—admitted the truth and waited for the crash.

Waited for the balls to clatter to the floor, for everything to grind to a halt, for hopelessness to invade, yet as she stood there, held by him, all she did was pause, just this blink of a pause where she told her truth and, safe for a moment, regrouped.

'Scared of what?' After the longest time he asked her.

'The baby deserves better.'

Ben closed his eyes in regret. Shameful regret because he had, at one time, thought the same too.

Two affluent parents, conceiving a baby that was planned, loved, wanted…

It had been his blueprint, his rage at the universe, because if he and Jen, with all they had, with all their plans and dreams, couldn't get there, why should anyone else?

Only now he held Celeste and realised that, despite the circumstances, the woman in his arms met the last two on the list and, despite the odds, she'd make up for all the rest.

'It's got *you*.' He stayed there, still holding her, and thought about it—thought how lucky that little baby was to have her, unplanned or whatever. It had Celeste—and he thought how she'd made him smile so many times, thought of the warmth of her affection and how lucky the recipient of that would be, and his neat blueprint faded from his mind.

'Am I enough, though?' she asked anxiously.

'Oh, yes,' he replied definitely.

She was absolutely enough.

More than enough.

So much more than enough, only he wasn't talking

about the baby now, because holding her, for the first time holding her, he forgot what they were talking about, forgot that she was pregnant. She was simply Celeste, funny, kind and terribly, terribly sexy. The scent of her up close, the soft feel of her head against his chest, overcame him, and he was lost in her. As naturally as breathing, he told her how he felt with a kiss instead of words, just pulling up her chin and kissing her. He lowered his head onto dark red lips and confirmed how *enough* she was with his mouth, and as their lips met Ben experienced this heady rush, like sugar dissolving on his tongue, as he tasted temptation.

She was stunned, because this was nothing like she had ever felt before, because in Ben's arms she felt safe, and just herself. Good, bad, whatever, she was herself with Ben. She had admitted to him that she was scared and the world had carried right on moving, only now it was even better than before.

His hands were in her hair and his mouth was moving with hers and she felt sexy—for the first time in her life she felt sexy and cherished and safe. And Ben felt it too, this tenderness and want rushing in that was *finally* without comparison. There was no logical thought to it—it was just a kiss, but one that tasted like heaven, surrounded by the scent of her hair and with her tongue cool from water. It was instinct, just the haven of instinct.

She kissed him back.

Kissed Ben in a way she never had before.

Not a practised kiss, not the type you have to think about—it was all about tasting, sharing, which was just how it should be. Ben's privacy, the isolated place that was him was suddenly hers to explore, and it tasted divine. Celeste had stepped inside the exclusive inner sanctum of this guarded man and she gloried in it.

'Celeste.' He groaned her name into her mouth, so she knew that she was there, knew she *was* the woman he was kissing tonight. One of his hands was on the back of her head, bringing her face to his, the other was on her bottom, her big fat dimply bottom, she vaguely thought, except he cupped it and stroked it till all it felt was fabulous. She hadn't really known what sexy was, yet she was discovering it now, right now, when it should be the last thing on her mind. Yet she was only a woman and, as his hands gathered her closer to him, it was all she wanted to be.

He had never come closer to escape—to a place where it was just him.

It wasn't a selfish escape.

Because also in that place was Celeste, and for a blissful few moments Ben was himself—the real him, the one that had been lost for ages. So he kissed her, tasted her, wanted her, without past or future, just succumbed to the heady taste of the present. He was hard, and he could feel her lovely bottom in his hands; he was in the place where bliss was no longer enough and then you reached for more, so he pulled her into his hardness, wanted to feel her softness against him, to shed her clothes, to drown in her. But instead he felt the solid weight of the baby that had been there only on the periphery of his mind now pressed into him. He could feel the dense weight of it and, tonight of all nights, it felt like a punch to the stomach, and it was Ben who pulled back.

'I'm sorry.' He released her so quickly it felt as if she were falling. 'That shouldn't have happened.'

Maybe it shouldn't have, but it had. It wasn't the kiss that embarrassed her—she was saving that for later. Right now it was his reaction—he was acting as though he was completely appalled at what he had done.

'Forget it…' She attempted casual, with a heart rate topping a hundred, as if shot awake from a blissful dream. Only now she was facing stark reality and just wanted out of there, as soon as she could. 'Really, it's no big deal.'

'Celeste…' Hell, he didn't want to add to her problems—only he just had, Ben knew that. But he had forgotten in that moment that she was pregnant. As he'd held her, all she had been was Celeste. 'Like I said, I'm not looking for—'

'I get it, Ben,' she interrupted. 'And neither am I. It was just a kiss, just…' She shrugged helplessly, because it had been so much more than just a kiss. She could still taste him on her lips, still feel the delicious crush of him holding her, and now he had taken it all away. 'Just one of those things that should never have happened. It doesn't change anything.'

CHAPTER FIVE

ONLY everything changed.

He saw her come into work around lunchtime the next day and speak with Meg. Trying to pretend nothing had happened, she gave him a quick smile as she passed. It had been a kiss between friends, Ben told himself, that had maybe got just a little out of hand. He was certain they could move on from it, so when a little while later he met her in the corridor, he asked how she was.

'Not bad.' She gave him a breezy smile. 'I'm officially on maternity leave.'

'How are you, Celeste?' Belinda clipped past on high heels and stopped to ask.

'I was just telling Ben that I've been signed off.' He could see it was with great effort she was maintaining that smile. 'So I guess I'll see you both when I'm a mum.'

There was a message for him in there, Ben knew it, and, feeling guilty, he was almost relieved to hear it. He was having trouble believing how stupid he'd been last night. She had enough on her plate without him messing things up, and a waif with a baby was the very last thing he needed right now.

'I hope she's okay,' Belinda said as Celeste waddled off.

'She will be now she's not working,' Ben answered.

'No.' Belinda gave a little shake of her head. 'I meant that I hope she'll be okay on her own with a baby.'

'She's not a teenager…' They were walking back to the office, and Ben was getting more and more irritated with Belinda's gloom. 'She'll be fine.'

'But, still, it isn't going to be easy. I wonder who the father is? I mean, she's never said, and surely he should be responsible for something…'

'How's your new man?' Ben rapidly changed the subject as they reached their office. 'Still going strong?'

'Paul's amazing,' Belinda sighed happily. 'We're going away this weekend.'

'I know.' Ben grinned. 'I'm covering for you.'

'His ex-wife's got the kids.'

'Have you met them yet?'

'God, no.' Belinda rolled her eyes as she sorted out some paperwork. 'The last thing I need is someone else's kids.'

It was the last thing Ben needed too.

Of all the stupid things to do… As they worked on in silence, Ben was silently brooding. Whether he liked it or not, he was involved with Celeste and her baby up to a point. He couldn't just stop going over to see her while she remained his neighbour…

'Here.' Belinda broke into his introspection. 'I've got something for you.'

Ben went over to the computer and had to laugh as

twenty or so female faces pouted back at him from an internet dating agency's website. 'I typed in your details and came up with all these possibilities for you.'

'I'm not interested in dating, and certainly not this way,' he said.

'Oh, get into the twenty-first century.' Belinda laughed. 'At least you know what you're getting this way—I haven't got time to go out to the clubs. And I know Paul's not looking for a stay-at-home surrogate mother for his children—he knows from the start that my career comes first and I absolutely don't want a baby. Look, she's nice.' She brought up a woman's details and Ben read on.

'She says she wants someone with no baggage,' Ben pointed out. 'I've got a truckload.'

'We all have.' Belinda shrugged. 'You just have to lie a little. I mean, if you get to our age and have had any semblance of a life, baggage is the norm. Go on, Ben,' she urged. 'Give it a go.'

'Leave it, Belinda,' he warned. Colleagues he could deal with, friendly colleagues even, but Belinda was pushing the line. She was in love and hanging off lamp-posts and wanted to spread her happiness—but she was talking to the wrong guy. 'I couldn't be less interested in starting a relationship now.'

He meant it.

Four years ago tomorrow… He lay on the bed when he got home and closed his eyes.

Four years…

Had it been that long? It seemed like only yester-day—yet it had also stretched on for ever.

Four years… He snapped his eyes open suddenly, knowing that he just had to deal with the present problem that was Celeste before he could get on with remembering and mourning the past.

'I was wondering…' His voice trailed off. It had taken him ages to decide how best to deal with this and finally he had decided to drop by her place, to pretend nothing had happened, and then offer his solution. Except she had taken for ever to answer the door and when she did, it was clear that he had woken her up. There was a huge pillow crease down the side of her face and the usually sunny Celeste was decidedly grumpy and certainly not about to make this easy. 'Were you asleep?'

'Actually, yes, I was.'

'Sorry.' Ben cleared his throat. He didn't want to just drop helping her, but he did want to pull back and this might just be the way! 'I've got a day off tomorrow. I'm going to do a big shop because I'm having too many take-aways, and I wondered if you wanted to make a list. I could grab some stuff for you.'

'I'm fine, thanks.'

'It really is no problem. You said you were struggling to get to the shops—'

'I did my shopping this afternoon online,' Celeste interrupted. 'So I'm all right. I've got a friend coming over tomorrow and we're going to make a load of meals and stock up the freezer.'

'That's…great.'

'And the doctor said that I needed to rest a lot,' Celeste continued, 'so, I don't mean to sound rude, but...' she gave an uncomfortable swallow '...I'm having a lot of trouble getting to sleep, and I'd just nodded off when you knocked.'

'Sorry about that,' he apologised.

'You weren't to know.' She gave a slight smile, only it didn't reach her eyes, and neither did her eyes meet his. 'But it might be better if you don't...' she gave a tight shrug '...just drop over in future.'

'Sure,' Ben said. He should have been relieved. After all, he'd been hoping for the same thing. He was absolved from duty now, so why didn't it feel great? 'What did the doctor say?' he asked, not able to leave it there.

'I told you.' Celeste's usually sunny face was a closed mask. 'I'm to rest... Look, Ben, it's really not your concern.'

Then she closed the door.

He went back to his unit.

And as he had done for the last few years on this night, Ben tried and failed not to watch the clock.

The horrible thing about anniversaries, Ben had found, was the build-up to them—as if you were stuck in a portal, as if by somehow going over and over every detail, you could change the outcome, bargain with God.

Only not this night.

Oh, he did all that, but there was another layer there too.

Guilt.

Guilt, because when he surely should have been drowning his sorrows in whisky and thinking only of Jen, when he should surely be lacerating himself with thoughts of what could have been, this year he couldn't sustain it.

Instead, he found himself standing at the window and wondering about Celeste.

Found himself thinking not about what could have been, but what already was.

And what could be?

Time did heal.

He'd been told it, had said it himself, but only now was he actually starting to believe it.

It didn't consume him now, it didn't walk with him constantly, there was room in his mind for other thoughts, so on a day that was usually spent locked in mourning, he awoke, showered and dressed, went to the cemetery and told them he loved them—always had, always would—but instead of heading to her parents' home, instead of stopping, he started. He kept his appointment with the bank, saw the real-estate agent, looked around the house again, put a deposit on a boat, went home, saw that his sunflowers were dying, watered them, showered again, and got changed into shorts.

He did really well, actually!

Until Jen's parents rang.

And then so too did his.

Followed by Jen's sister.

And then it all finally caught up with him.

He tried not to look at the clock, tried not to remember ringing her from work, then tried to remember the *exact* tone of her voice when Jen had said she had a headache.

It had done nothing to alert him.

Well, actually it had, but he was a doctor and his wife was pregnant and also a doctor and between them they could dream up a million and one scenarios if they so wished. So she had told him it was just a headache...and he had told himself the same.

'*It's just a headache, Ben.*'

Except when he suggested that she take something for it, instead of her usual rebuff, he'd been concerned to find out that she already had. Jen, who never took anything, had taken a couple of painkillers.

'I'll come home,' he'd suggested.

'For God's sake, Ben.' She'd sounded irritated. 'It's a headache, I'm just going to go and lie down.'

Yes, by early evening it had all caught up with him again.

He didn't walk along the beach today, and he didn't jog. He ran. Only the beach seemed too small—he could see Melbourne miles away in the sunset, but he felt as if he could make it in a few leaps, that he would never run out of energy, that he could run all his life and still never leave it behind.

He wasn't wearing a watch, but he knew the time, knew it to the very second.

Ringing Jen and getting no answer, and telling himself she was just lying down.

He pounded the beach. His lungs were bursting but still, *still* he remembered walking up the garden path and trying not to run, because he was surely being stupid, because there was surely nothing wrong, then letting himself in and calling her name. It was five past seven, as he ran, Ben knew that, because suddenly he felt like swearing at the sky for cheating them, five past seven because he'd seen it on the clock as he had walked into the lounge, seen her kneeling on the floor, her hands on her head on the sofa.

So still.

So pale.

So gone.

Pounding on her chest, ringing the ambulance.

He wanted her and if not he wanted a Caesarean—he wanted life to be salvaged from the wreckage he had come home to, except he knew, knew, knew even as he laid her flat on her back that it was too late.

He ran along that beach, not as if the devil was chasing him, because nothing could catch him now. He was the chaser, pounding on anger, and regret and hate and the unfairness of it all.

Temper split his mind.

He didn't want Celeste and her baby.

He wanted *his*!

It was a relief to be off work, but it was also the longest, loneliest time.

Her request to stay at her parents' was met with a curt letter of refusal and a cheque, which Celeste would love to have not cashed on principle, but she couldn't afford principles right now. Although she'd have loved to splurge and get her hair cut and buy something fantastic and non-essential for the baby, instead she trimmed her hair with the kitchen scissors, bought another two boxes of nappies and paid two months' rent in advance, then crawled back into bed and carried on missing Ben.

And she did miss him.

Missed him more than she had Dean. Which made no sense, but it was how it was. Over and over she took out the memory of his kiss and explored it, remembered the moment that had ended them—and she wished she'd never tasted him, never been held by him, had never kissed him, because in that moment she'd glimpsed a different world. With just one kiss he'd shown her how good life could be—and then he'd ripped it away.

She thought about ignoring the knock at the door—but not for long. Maybe it was her parents to say they'd changed their minds, or the postman, or maybe, just maybe…

It was Ben.

'I hope I didn't wake you,' he said.

'You didn't.'

'And I'm sorry to drop round…' His four-wheel drive was purring behind him, the engine still going, no doubt ready to make a quick escape.

'It's fine.'

Ben wasn't finding this easy. The whole day hadn't been easy, in fact—but it was something he had promised, something he had to do. 'I went over to my sister's to get the car seat for you.'

'Oh!'

'Look.' He ran a hand through his hair. 'I don't want to offend you, so say if you don't want them, really, you just have to say. But she gave me a few things…a crib, a stroller, one of those jogging ones…'

'Do I have to promise to take up jogging?' she asked.

'No…' Despite the strained circumstances, she still made him smile.

'Only I might get challenged under the Trade Descriptions Act if I'm seen with it,' she teased.

'It's good for walking on the beach too,' Ben said. 'Well, according to my sister.'

She couldn't joke any more, really she didn't know what to say. It wasn't a question of being too proud to accept help, it was more that she'd had none, well, apart from her parents' cheque. But this was real help and real thought and that it came from him made it as bitter as it was sweet.

'Thank you,' she said sincerely.

'Do you want me to bring it in?' He gestured to the vehicle behind him and she said thank you again, her nose a bit red from trying not to cry.

She offered to help, but he shooed her away and she sat on the sofa as a lot of wishes were granted—just not the one she wished for the most, because he couldn't even look at her, Celeste noticed. Oh, he was kind and helpful and set up the crib and accepted a glass of iced tea while Celeste opened bag after bag, smiling at teeny tiny baby socks.

For Ben it was a nightmare.

All these things had been promised for him and Jen—the crib he was setting up now he hadn't got to do four years ago. The little socks and vest Celeste was holding up made him sweat, and even driving here had been hard, with an empty baby seat in the back...

Still, she needed it and he never would—it was stupid to let it go to waste and he had promised her the car seat that night.

That night.

'I'll leave you to it, then,' he said gruffly. It was almost more than he could stand to be in the room, surrounded by baby things, her home set up and almost ready now…almost more than he could stand to look at her, because she looked *terrible*!

So terrible, in fact, that he wanted to scoop her up and run—wanted someone to notice just how unwell this woman was. Where the hell were her parents?

'Did you hear from your mum and dad?'

'Yes.' She tried for upbeat but didn't manage to come close. 'They sent some money…' He could see her red nose, see the swirl of tears in her eyes despite the smile.

'And when…' Ben cleared his throat '…do you see your obstetrician again?'

'Next Wednesday!'

It was only Friday.

'When did you see him last?'

'On Tuesday.' Still the smile remained, but it was wavering now. 'If my blood pressure is still up they're going to admit me.'

'No protein in your urine?'

'No protein…' He was trying to be a doctor, trying to assess her practically, only it wasn't working. He knew they would be carefully monitoring her for preeclampsia, knew she was being watched, only he wanted her watched more closely, and as coolly as he tried to assess the facts, detachment wasn't working.

'You've got a lot of fluid, Celeste,' he pointed out.

'I know. I'm allowed one gentle walk a day, and I've cut out salt as well as sugar… They're watching me, Ben.'

And with that he had to make do.

Only he couldn't.

'Why don't you ring and get your appointment brought forward? I could take you there now,' he offered.

'Ben,' Celeste interrupted, 'thank you for all the lovely things—and thank you to your sister too. When I'm able, I'll get her a card.'

And with *that* he had to make do.

CHAPTER SIX

'HI CELESTE!' He gave a tight smile as she came over. The whole street had come out to watch the auction and Celeste had bypassed her gentle walk on the beach today and wandered down for a look—it was what people in Melbourne did on a sunny Saturday afternoon when a house was up for auction.

'Hi.' She was polite and said hello and then bypassed him, but Ben halted her.

'You're supposed to be resting.'

'I'm walking around a house instead of a beach!' Celeste pointed out. 'Anyway, I've got cabin fever. I'm going crazy being stuck inside the unit and at least they'll have the air-conditioning on in the house.' And then she gave him a smile. 'Thanks for yesterday, by the way.'

'No problem. I'm glad it's all going to good use.'

'I meant the doctor pep talk. I rang my obstetrician and they're seeing me on Monday now.'

'That's wonderful.'

'I'm going home to pack my case after this—I have a feeling they won't be letting me out.'

Then she moved on, wandered inside with the rest of

the crowd, and when Ben's eyes should have been on the competition, instead they were on her.

He wanted her.

As he walked around the house, stared into rooms, walked through the garden. It was Celeste's comments he wanted, not the real-estate agent's, and she gave plenty.

It *was* stunning. Her entire unit could fit neatly in the lounge, and Celeste was quite sure that if she could just lie on that lovely white sofa and gaze out at the water till Monday, with someone peeling grapes for her and massaging her feet, her blood pressure would be down by her doctor's appointment!

She loved viewing houses, wandering around them, pretending they were hers, and wishing it could be so. The kitchen was a hell-hole, though, but the agent steered them past it quickly and on to view the upstairs. The whole place was to die for—every room in the house, even the master bathroom, was angled for water views!

'There are no blinds,' Celeste pointed out, and Ben smothered a smile, because when he'd first looked around the home, he'd said exactly the same thing, only the agent hadn't ignored him! 'How can you have floor-to-ceiling windows in a bathroom and no blinds?' Celeste demanded.

'The glass is treated,' the agent hissed. 'You can see out, but no one can see in.

'Now, moving along, this is the master bedroom!'

'Divine!' Celeste breathed as she stepped in. A vast bed was in the centre, and there was a balcony set up with a little table and chairs…

'Are the windows treated in here too?' Celeste asked pointedly as the agent sucked in his breath.

She *did* make him smile.

And he *did* miss her.

She was writing on her little list again—just as if she was a serious bidder—and he could see the real-estate agent's lips purse as she stepped out boldly onto the balcony instead of following the pack back along the hall. 'Can you keep up, please?' the agent snapped, and Ben felt his teeth grind together.

'This room would make an ideal nursery…' Despite her obvious condition the agent addressed a loving young couple and ignored Celeste when she asked a question. How she wished she'd won the lottery, and could pull out the winning bid just to wipe that superior smile off his smug face and make him squirm. Ben saw her face redden as the agent ignored her and then caught her eye and gave her a wink.

'My partner asked a question,' Ben said coolly, watching Celeste's beam of delight as the agent practically gave himself whiplash, turning to face her. No, she hadn't won loads of money, but watching that smug smile leave his face was almost as good.

'I'm so sorry,' he simpered. 'What did you want to know?'

'Thanks for that.' Celeste grinned at Ben as they wandered outside.

'Ooh, it was my pleasure,' Ben replied. 'He's obnoxious.'

Celeste loved auctions—the crowd gathered outside the house, the real-estate agent pumping up the action—

yet she was always scared she'd put up her hand and outbid someone, like standing on the edge of a cliff and wanting to jump, just to try it.

There was some serious bidding going on, and Celeste watched on in glee. This was the most exciting thing to have happened to her all week.

Ben was trying to concentrate, but his eyes kept wandering to her.

He hadn't put in a bid yet—he would wait and see... God, even her eyelids were swollen. When he should be concentrating, when he should be focusing, instead he was thinking about her, worrying about her—and Ben didn't like the feeling a bit.

The bidding was slowing down now, the auctioneer having trouble eking out even a small raise in bids—and it was then that Ben put in his first offer.

He saw the flare of surprise in her eyes—she'd had no idea that he would be bidding. It wasn't something he had to discuss with anyone, Ben told himself, that was the life he had built for himself. Yet still there was a little pang of discomfort, remembering all the nights when she had spoken about her hopes and fears and dreams for the future, and he realised that he hadn't let her in at all.

The flagging crowd was suddenly interested, and Ben saw her smile. Just a little smile that winged its way over to him, telling him she was pleased.

Excited for him, even.

He was outbid, so he upped his offer.

And again she smiled.

He was outbid again, so he upped it again.

He looked over for her smile, for that bit of encouragement that he shouldn't need but somehow liked, and then he saw she wasn't smiling.

He had been outbid again, the auctioneer passing the bid to him, only Ben wasn't listening.

There was an aghast expression on Celeste's face, as if she had just received some shocking news—only there was no one talking to her and she wasn't on the phone. Her hands were both on her stomach.

He could hear the auctioneer's warning. Confused, but also needing to get over to her, Ben put in a ridiculously high bid, heard the gasp of shock from the crowd. Ignoring the rest of the proceedings, he waded through the crowd towards her.

'I think my waters just broke!'

'It's okay,' he said soothingly.

'No, it's not.' She was shivering, shock setting in as realisation hit. 'I'm only thirty-four weeks.'

'Thirty-four-weekers do very well...' He could hear his calm voice, only the blood was pounding in his temples as he pulled out his phone. 'Come on, let's get you sitting down. I'll call an ambulance.'

'There's nowhere to sit!' she shrilled. The sun was suddenly hot on her head, her mouth filling with saliva. 'Ben, I think it's coming...'

The real-estate agent had come over to congratulate him, the house apparently his now, but Ben wasn't listening.

'We need to get her inside,' he stated.

'Excuse me?' the agent said.

'Ben...' She was moaning now, whimpering in terror. 'I've got pain...'

'She needs to be inside.' Ben was walking her to the entrance at the side of the house, taking her weight. 'She needs some privacy…'

'You can't just go in!'

'I just bought the house!' Ben snapped. 'She's about to give birth. Where do you want her to do it—on the street?' He gave up walking her then and picked her up—and such was his authority that the real-estate agent actually opened the side gate for him. 'Now, call an ambulance,' Ben ordered, 'and tell them it's a premature baby…' He had her beneath the willow tree now and she was wriggling out of his arms, already starting to strain. Ben realised with alarm that there was no chance of getting her inside. 'And say there's a doctor in attendance.'

'Is there anything I can do?' The man he had waved to each morning, the man he had just bought a house from, was now there, being practical and helpful. 'Some towels,' Ben said as his wife rushed off and he struggled to be calm, to be professional. It was a delivery, he told himself, he was more than capable of dealing with that. Only he could see her terrified eyes…

'I need you to listen to me, Celeste.' He had pulled down her panties and examined her. The baby wasn't waiting for the ambulance, it wasn't waiting for anything… 'This *is* a small baby, so we're going to try and slow it down.' It was important that they did so, as a rapid delivery could cause damage to the fragile brain. 'You're not to push,' he warned Celeste. 'We want this to happen as slowly and as gently as we can…'

She had never been more petrified—the thought of her baby coming so soon and here, no hospital, no shiny equipment… Yet she was suddenly desperate to bear down, to push, only Ben was telling her to just breathe through it, to resist this desperate urge—and she knew why. 'It's too fast…'

'Your body will have been preparing for this for hours, you just didn't know.' He smiled. 'We just need to slow down this last bit.'

He was right. All morning she had felt restless— trying to lie in bed, to read, to rest. She'd had a shower and then gone back to bed, then decided to go and look at the auction…

'It's coming,' she moaned.

It was. Nothing was going to slow down her baby's entrance to the world, and she was so glad Ben was here and terrified that he might not have been.

'What if I'd been at home, what if…?'

'You'd have coped!' Ben cut short her what-ifs. 'And you're coping well now.'

'I'm sorry we're not talking.' She panted with the effort of not pushing. 'I'm sorry to do this to you…'

'I'm glad to be here,' Ben said, 'I've done this pl—' He didn't continue, as he'd just seen that the cord was around the neck, but not tightly, and he slipped it over. Only it wasn't just that which had halted his words. Yes, he had delivered babies over the years, yes, he had done this plenty of times before.

Just not like this.

Not like this, with his heart in his mouth, as he held a tiny head in his hand and guided a pale life into the world.

Not like this, as he delivered the babe onto Celeste's stomach, rubbed at its back, flicked at its feet. He knew it would breathe, the doctor in him knew that it had only been a minute, but for Ben it was one very long minute, the babe floppy and cyanosed, its heart rate tipping almost low enough that if it went down further he would have to commence CPR. He could hear Celeste's pleas and they matched his thoughts, willing the ambulance faster with oxygen for this little one. He turned the baby over, its back now on Celeste's stomach, and felt his head lighten in relief as the tiny baby startled and took its first breath.

'It's not crying,' Celeste sobbed.

'She will,' he promised.

'She?' Ben was no midwife—maybe it should have been for mum to find out herself, except the baby was too fragile and sick for anything other than practicality.

'You've got a daughter,' Ben said, 'and she needs to be kept warm.' He kept the little one on her mother's stomach, and wrapped them both in towels, relieved to finally hear the sirens.

'I got some string....' The woman who had got the towels had been busy and had the ambulance not been pulling up Ben would have cut the cord then. He was seriously worried at the babe's lack of response. She was breathing, but with effort, little bubbles coming out of her mouth with each breath. The paramedics were straight onto it—suctioning her little airway, even the tiniest oxygen mask swamping her tiny features as Ben clamped and cut the cord.

'We might radio through...' The paramedic looked at Ben, a quick decision being made between them without words—to attempt IV access and work to stabilise her here, or to scoop and run and get her to the hospital which was just a short drive away, depending on the traffic?

'Let's get her to hospital,' Ben said, and the paramedic nodded, wrapping her up in towels.

'We'll send another vehicle for Mum,' the paramedic said.

'No, I want to go with her…' Celeste was sobbing, shivering and shaking, stunned at the speed of it all.

'She needs to get to hospital quickly.' Ben's voice was kind but non-negotiable. 'Can you stay with Celeste for a moment?' He spoke with the woman who had been so helpful. She had brought pillows and blankets from the house now and was doing her best to make Celeste comfortable. 'I'm going to help them get the baby settled in the ambulance and then I'll be back.'

'No,' Celeste sobbed. 'Go with her. Please.'

There was a flash of confusion at his own thought process then, only he didn't pursue it—there wasn't time. He nodded his acquiescence and held the infant as the ambulance sped them the short distance to the hospital. Her little lungs were filling up with fluid and Ben held the oxygen mask close to her face, but allowing room for the paramedic to suction. There was a little probe attached to her ear and her oxygen saturation was low but not dire…

The ambulance swept through the streets, slowing down at High Street, which was filled with Saturday shoppers and weekend drivers, and Ben felt his tension rising as it braked and accelerated, the siren blasting out.

Then he looked beyond the mask and the flaring nostrils and he saw the creamy vernix-flattening dark curls, and navy eyes that were nowhere near able to focus, except he felt as if she was looking straight at him.

It was a bizarre moment of connection, and it was Ben who tore his eyes away first.

He was only the doctor.

This baby's mother was just a friend...

Then the hospital was in view, and he could see Belinda waiting outside. As the ambulance opened he didn't hand the little one over, but ran inside to Resus with the precious bundle—the resuscitation cot warmed and waiting, paediatricians and Raji there, and only then did he hand her over...

And only then did he realise how terrified he had been. A cold sweat was drenching him as he saw the urgency in the assembled staff, and he knew that this was no overreaction. He saw how very sick this little baby was and he was unable to speak for a moment as he struggled to get his breath.

He headed over to the sink as the paramedics gave the handover, and Ben took a long drink directly from the tap, before walking back to where they were working.

Raji had placed a tube down her nose and was suctioning her airway more deeply, the paediatrician had just inserted an umbilical line and fluids were now being delivered. She looked a touch more feisty than she had, her face scrunching in displeasure, little fists bunching and legs kicking a small protest...

'She was very flat...' Ben gave the Apgar scores. 'It was a very rapid delivery.'

'Thirty-four weeks, the paramedics said.' The paediatrician was looking her over. 'But she's quite big for thirty-four weeks—do you know where mum was having her antenatal?'

'I'm sure he didn't have time to ask,' Belinda said. 'You were at a house auction, weren't you, Ben?'

'Actually…' he cleared his throat a touch '…this is Celeste's baby.'

'*Our* Celeste!' Belinda blinked and then looked at the admission card that the receptionist had just filled in. 'Baby Mitchell…'

'She lives in the same street as the auction,' Ben half explained, 'and she must have wandered down to watch it.'

'Well, lucky woman…' Belinda breathed out '…that you were there.'

'She had gestational diabetes,' Ben said, which explained the baby's relatively big size for gestation, 'and she had her antenatal care here,' he added to the receptionist, and she rushed off to get the notes.

'Does anyone know if there were any other problems?'

'Hypertension,' Meg said as still Ben struggled just to breathe. 'She was signed off a couple of days ago.'

'Her blood pressure has been up,' Ben said, watching Belinda blink at the depth of his knowledge. 'She looked very bloated today, and I thought she was tipping into pre-eclampsia,' Ben added. 'I think she was going to be admitted on Monday.'

He felt sick.

The resuscitation area was impossibly hot, and Ben felt stifled, hearing the blip, blip, blip of the monitor. Even watching the team at work was incredibly hard. Oh, he knew they knew what they were doing, knew that babies were tough, even tiny ones, only they seemed so rough with their handling of something so very, very small.

'I'm going to go outside for a bit,' Ben said in a strangled voice.

'You might want to change first.' Belinda glanced up and smiled and only then did Ben register the state he was in.

He had a quick shower and selected some theatre blues, only instead of drying and dressing he sat on the wooden bench, dripping wet, with his head in his hands, her words playing over and over. *'What if I'd been at home, what if…?'* Scenario after possible scenario was playing out in his racing brain.

And not just for this morning.

Over and over the years he had beaten himself up with those very words—wishing he'd come home earlier, wondering about the outcome if he had. He'd been told that nothing could have been done for Jen, that even with the best of care she'd have died, or worse, that the brain haemorrhage she'd suffered would have left her a vegetable. But what about their baby? Could it have been saved if he'd been at home?

There was a myriad of conflicting emotions pelting him.

Relief, regret, resentment even, that he had been there for this child and not his own—and yet, even as resentment flickered it faded just as quickly. That tiny life he had held in his hands, he had willed and willed to live, had felt more for than a doctor should—and not just for the baby, but for her mother too.

Then he remembered his own stupidity, that he had contemplated staying with her after the traumatic birth of her baby.

Of course he should have gone with the baby!

Celeste was stable, another ambulance on the way… and yet instinct had overridden logic for a second, and all he had wanted to do was stay and comfort her.

No!

He stood up then and dried quickly, pulling on his theatre blues and making a firm decision. He wasn't going to get involved with Celeste—whatever it took.

He just couldn't go there again.

Wouldn't.

Couldn't.

CHAPTER SEVEN

'WHEN can I see her?' It was *all* she could think about.

The ambulance had arrived a couple of moments after they had taken her daughter, and she had been taken directly to Maternity. The midwives had been wonderful, keeping her up to date on her baby's progress as Celeste was examined and an IV inserted and bloods taken.

'Why do I need that?'

'Your blood pressure's still high,' the obstetrician explained, 'and you've got a lot of fluid retention. We just want to check your bloods and keep an eye on you, make sure everything's settling down…'

The midwives helped her to wash and freshen up and get into bed and then Gloria, who Celeste had guessed was the one in charge, finally came in with some real news.

'They've just transferred her from Emergency to Special Care. Once they've got her settled and as soon as *your* doctor gives you the okay, we'll take you over to see her. Here.' She handed her a photo. 'One of the nurses took this…'

Oh, she was tiny, with a little pink hat and tubes and things everywhere, but she *was* hers… The few moments she'd had with her daughter were imprinted on her mind and Celeste already recognised her, could walk into the special care unit now and pick out her daughter, of that she was positive…

'Now,' Gloria said, 'she's doing well, and she's on CPAP. That just means she's needing a little help with her breathing, to fill her lungs with air, and she's been given surfactant and medicines to help with lung immaturity…' She went through all the treatment her daughter was receiving till Celeste understood and then she *again* asked a necessary question, one that Celeste had so far refused to respond to. 'Is there anyone we can call for you?' Celeste shook her head.

'I'll ring my parents soon.'

'You shouldn't be on your own,' Gloria said gently. 'Is there a friend…?'

'Later.' Again, Celeste shook her head.

She wanted some privacy, didn't want to share this moment now with parents who hadn't helped, who apart from a terse phone call and a single cheque had done nothing. And neither did she want friends who hadn't really been there around her, or a father who didn't want to know—all of that she would face and deal with, but right now she just wanted to process all that had taken place by herself…

'Hey!' The door opened and Ben's face appeared. He was perhaps the one person she didn't mind seeing right now—after all, he had been there!

'Thank you.' How paltry it sounded, but she meant it from her heart.

'You're very welcome.'

'How is she?'

'I'm not sure,' Ben said. 'They moved her from Emergency half an hour or so ago…'

'Oh!' Of course he wouldn't know, Celeste told herself. As if he followed his patients up to the ward! Once he had handed the baby over, that would have been it for him.

'How are you doing?' Ben asked.

'Not bad…' She didn't elaborate, didn't want to bore him with the tests she was having. He was asking politely, that was all.

'Well…' he gave a tight smile '…I can't stay. I've got the real-estate ringing every five minutes—I need to sign the contract on the house.'

'You'd better go, then.'

'Do you need anything?'

'No.'

'If you need me to drop by the unit I can fetch some stuff. Do you have a bag packed?'

'No.' Celeste gave a weak smile. 'I'm not that organised. Could I ask you just to check the plugs and things?' she asked reluctantly, when he clearly just wanted out of there. 'I think everything is off, but I only went out for a walk.'

'Sure.' He handed over her handbag, which was on her locker, and waited while she gave him her keys. 'Anything else?'

'Nothing I can think of.'

'Well, I'm on a night shift tonight, so I'll drop these back to you.' And even though he was taking her keys, even though he would be going back to her flat and checking her things, his voice, his stance was as formal as if he were just another doctor doing rounds. 'Congratulations, Celeste.'

'Thank you.'

It was an exhausting evening.

There was no rosy glow of motherhood for Celeste to bathe in. She told her parents the news and as expected they arrived a couple of hours later, bringing with them their endless questions and practically blaming her for the stress they were under.

'What were you doing, walking?' her mother Rita scolded her. 'You were supposed to be resting.'

'The doctor said that I was allowed a gentle walk each day.'

'Have you rung him?' Rita asked. 'Whoever *he* is. Have you let him know he's a father?'

'No.'

'Well, don't you think you should? It is *his* responsibility...'

The time or place didn't matter. The same arguments that had ensued since the day she had told them she was pregnant carried on at the hospital bedside. So much for a baby bringing peace, Celeste thought, waving goodbye to the fantasy that the arrival of their grandchild would cast the arguments aside.

'When will we get to see her?' Rita demanded as Gloria came in.

'It's just Mum allowed in for now,' Gloria said, seeing Celeste's strained face. 'They're ready for you, Celeste.'

It was a relief to be wheeled out of the room and away from them.

'You can actually have one of them come in with you,' Gloria said once they were out of earshot. 'If you want—'

'No,' Celeste interrupted. 'I'd rather see her on my own first.'

They had to sit in a little annexe for a few moments until they were ready for them.

'You poor thing.' Gloria gave her a kind smile, as they sat there. 'I bet this is so not how you planned it.'

'None of it's how I planned it,' Celeste admitted.

'You are allowed to cry, you know.' Gloria put her arm around Celeste's shoulders and felt her stiffen. 'It's been such a difficult day…' Celeste wriggled away because if she started crying she wouldn't stop.

And then it was time… She was wheeled in to wash her hands, and then she was wheeled past the incubators and finally she got to see her daughter.

Lying like a little washed-up frog with all drips and tubes and that little pink hat on… Even then she couldn't cry, couldn't give in, because she felt she had to be responsible, so she listened instead as the special care nurse explained all the drips and tubes and that her daughter was comfortable…

'Can I hold her?' Celeste asked, when they didn't offer.

'Not today. We're keeping her very quiet for now, but probably tomorrow…'

So she got to hold her fingers instead and stared at her teeny pink nails and waited for this whoosh of love to come. It was there a little bit, only it wasn't exactly whooshing as she'd expected—because there was this huge plug of guilt lodged in its way.

'Have you got a name for her?'

'Not yet,' Celeste said. 'I wanted to see what she looked like.' She gazed at her daughter and tried to think of a name that might suit her, but her brain was too fuddled for such a big decision. 'I don't know.'

'There's plenty of time,' Gloria said. 'We should get you back—you're not well either, remember.'

She wasn't.

The obstetrician came in and explained that her blood tests had come back and the results weren't great. 'They should all settle over the next few days now that you've delivered, but we will need to keep an eye on you. You've got pre-eclampsia, Celeste.'

'Had.' Celeste frowned. 'Doesn't it go away once the baby is here?'

'Not straight away,' he explained. 'You're still quite sick. You were being observed for it as your blood pressure was raised at your last antenatal, but…well, you had a lot of other stresses that could have accounted for that. It's good that you've delivered. It could have been dangerous for you both had the pregnancy continued.'

It was a long, lonely evening—friends came and visited, but it was as if they were speaking a foreign language. Oh, they cooed and oohed at the photos, but when eight o'clock came and they headed out for Saturday night, Celeste just lay there with her eyes closed, not because she was tired but because she was scared she'd cry. She ignored the footsteps coming into the room, they could take her blood pressure without talking, and then she heard her keys being placed on the locker and screwed them closed more tightly.

Ben could see a tear slipping out of the side of one eye, and could only hazard a guess as to how hard this day had been for her.

He knew he should just put down the bag and walk out quietly. After all, he had resolved not to get involved—a young single mum was the last thing he needed. She was so young and fragile and he was so jaded and bitter, and his heart was closed so tightly. Only sometimes she managed to wedge it open a little…

'I know you're awake!' Reluctantly he broke the silence, smiling a little at her defiant answer.

'I'm not.'

'I packed a few things for you—your toothbrush and hairbrush…'

'Thanks.'

'Is there anything else you need—a nightdress or anything?'

'No, thanks,' she answered, her eyes still closed. 'Mum said she'd go shopping tomorrow.'

'How were they?' Ben asked, even as he told himself he shouldn't, looking up at the diuretic infusion and the magnesium infusion and then back to her poor, swollen face.

'Cross.' More tears were spilling out the sides of her eyes now, and he picked off a few tissues and put them in her hand. 'They're still cross with me.'

'They're worried,' Ben said.

'And cross,' Celeste said. 'And so are you.'

'Cross?' Ben frowned. 'Celeste, why would I be

cross…?' His voice faded as her eyes opened to him, because she was right. Cross was how he felt—or was he just worried?

He truly didn't know.

'Because we kissed…because you think I just go around flinging myself at men—'

'No,' Ben interrupted, 'I'm not cross at you for that, I'm cross with myself.'

'Why?'

'Because…' He blew out a breath, and he couldn't help but admire her for being so open, for just bringing it out. He sat on the bed, because he definitely wasn't a doctor dropping in now. 'Because I'm the last thing you need right now.'

'You don't know what I need.'

'You don't need *me*,' Ben said very firmly, very surely. 'Since Jen, I've had a few relationships and they don't work. You've been messed around enough without getting involved with someone like me, someone who doesn't want children…'

'You think I'm after a father for her?' Celeste asked incredulously. 'Some long-term commitment from you? Hell, Ben, it was only one kiss!'

'That shouldn't have happened,' Ben said.

'I know,' Celeste admitted. He was right, absolutely he was right. 'You're wrong about one thing, though,' she challenged. 'I'm not after a relationship. I'm having enough trouble getting used to being a mum without someone else in the picture. It's bad enough that her own father…' She started to cry then because she couldn't believe how wrong she'd got it, that the man she had thought she was in love with had thought so very little of her.

'Have you told him?' And he said it in such a different way from the way her mum had—not accusing. He just asked the question and watched her face crumple.

'I rang just before you came…'

'And?'

'He doesn't want to know.'

'I'm so sorry,' he said gently.

'I'm not,' Celeste sniffed. 'Well, I am for her, but not for me. At least I know where I stand. I will be okay on my own, you know!'

'I know that,' he said with a small smile at her vehemence.

'And I'm not after a partner or a surrogate father for the baby—it was just one stupid kiss and I regret it, because I really did like having you as a friend and I hate that it's been spoilt.'

'You were the one who told me not to drop round,' he pointed out.

'You were glad that I did,' she accused.

She was so honest, all he could do was smile at her again. 'We should have spoken about it,' Ben admitted. 'Tried to work it out.'

'That's what friends do,' Celeste said.

'That's what we are doing,' Ben replied. 'So I guess that's what we are.'

'Honestly?'

'Honestly,' Ben said, and to prove it he squeezed her fat sausage-like fingers. 'Have you got a name for her yet?'

'Nope,' she sighed.

'Any ideas?'

'About a thousand…'

'I'd better get down to work.' He stood up. He wasn't making excuses, he was already five minutes late. 'I'll drop by soon, but call if you need anything.'

'I will.' She gave him a watery smile, glad they were friends again, and so grateful to him for his skill today and for his honesty tonight.

Yet she had been honest too. She didn't want a father for the baby, neither was there a need for a relationship to survive….

And that thought was confirmed when at midnight she finally got to hold her.

She held this little scrap of a thing to her heart and thought it might burst as finally love whooshed in.

She stared at her daughter.

Just a few hours old and so, so , so raw and vulnerable and so reliant on her. No, she didn't need a surrogate father or a partner to make things work for her baby. She would take care of that all by herself.

She just wanted Ben for himself.

'We've been waiting for them.' The midwife cuddled her a little while later when she was wheeled back to bed and the tears finally flooded in. 'You have a good cry…' So she did, soothed that apparently it was completely normal to weep, to sob, that it was obviously hormones on top of an early delivery, estranged parents and a very new, sick little lady who was lying in a cot in Special Care, with a father who didn't care a jot…

Trying to convince herself that her tears had nothing to do with Ben.

* * *

'How is she?'

Ben had washed his hands and put on a gown over his clothes, even though he would only be looking.

'Good.' The special care nurse looked up. 'I'm Bron.'

'Ben.'

'You're the doctor who delivered her?'

'Yep.' Ben peered into the crib. 'I'm a friend of her mum's as well.'

'Well, she had a good first night—she's a restless little thing, aren't you, Willow?'

'Willow?' Ben smiled, because it was the perfect name for her.

She looked so much better than yesterday. Tubes and machines didn't scare Ben. If anything, they reassured him. She was a lovely pinky-red now, and pushing up against the side of the incubator as if she was trying to dig a little hole to climb into.

'I'm just going to change her sheet—do you want to hold her up?'

It would have been appropriate for Ben to help, rather than just stand and watch—and the most natural thing would surely be to just hold her up as the nurse changed the bedding, except, feeling awkward, he declined. 'No, thanks…' He knew he looked arrogant, but it was a price he was willing to pay, so instead he just stood there and watched as the special care nurse changed the bedding, then wrapped bunny rugs into an oval and wrapped them like a little cocoon to help Willow settle. She was a scrap of a thing really, all spindly arms and legs and with a little pink hat covering her dark hair.

She was cute, but no cuter than any of the others he'd

seen as he'd made his way over to her. They could have taken him to any baby and told him that it was Willow and he wouldn't have known any different.

And then she opened her eyes.

Even though she couldn't possibly be doing it, he felt as if she was staring right at him, just as she had in the ambulance. He stared back at her for a moment, and then once again it was he who looked away first.

'Thanks...' He gave a brief smile to the nurse. 'Thanks for letting me see her. It's good to know she's doing well.'

CHAPTER EIGHT

BEN dropped in on Celeste while she was still a patient and occasionally he saw her in the canteen and stopped for a chat and got an update as to how well Willow was doing.

She was doing *so* well.

Every day Celeste saw progress.

And not just with Willow. The ice was thawing with her mother too. She made the journey every other day, initially to see her granddaughter, but bringing in vital supplies for Celeste, then not so vital supplies and sometimes the occasional treat.

It was also Rita who provided an unlikely source of comfort as her milk supply steadily dwindled.

'The more you stress about it, the worse it will be,' Rita said firmly as Celeste sat in tears on the breast pump she hated so much, but at three weeks of age, Willow was only taking the tiniest of feeds from her mother before she became exhausted, and had to be gavage fed through a little tube that ran from her mouth to her stomach. Celeste was struggling to produce enough milk and hated the bland room where she would sit for ages, only to produce a paltry couple of millilitres.

'It's important that she gets my milk.' Celeste gritted her teeth. The lactation consultant had said so.

'It's more important that she gets fed.' Rita refused to back down—she was tired of the pressures that were being placed on her daughter and frustrated on her behalf. 'I couldn't feed you either, Celeste. I had to put you on the bottle when you were four days old.'

'And look how I turned out.'

The weight had fallen off her, sitting there, often teary, jangling with nerves, huge black rings under her eyes thanks to endless two-hourly feeds, broke and a single mum to boot. It was actually her first vague attempt at a joke with her mother in ages and for a moment Rita didn't get it. Then, as she opened her mouth to carry on with her lecture, she did, catching her daughter's eyes and starting to giggle, as did Celeste.

'You turned out just fine,' Rita said when the giggles had faded and the tears that were never very far away these days filled Celeste's eyes. It was the nicest thing her mother had said to her in a very long time. 'Go and get some lunch.' Her mum took the feeble offerings of milk, stuck one of Willow's ID labels on the bottle and popped it in the fridge. 'I'll finish up in here. You go and have a little break.'

Except it didn't feel like a break.

Celeste far preferred the safe routine she had established. Living in the small mothers' area, she was happy with her spartan room and evenings spent chatting with other anxious mothers. Her days were filled with feeding Willow or expressing her milk, gaining confidence with Willow under the nurse's watchful eye and taking for ever to choose what to order from the parents' menu cards that came round once a day. Only every now and then her mother insisted that she 'take a break'. And Celeste loathed it.

There really wasn't much to do.

The hospital *gardens* were a misnomer, the gift shop had long since sold out of her favourite toffees and she'd read each and every magazine at least twice. She'd popped into Emergency a couple of times, but it had always been at the wrong time, the department full and busy, and she'd sat awkward and alone in the staffroom. But mostly she loathed the canteen, where the best way she could describe herself was an 'almost but not quite'.

Almost a member of staff.

Almost a patient.

Almost a mother.

Except she had no uniform.

No ID tag on her wrist.

And no baby beside her.

Worse, her colleagues, if they were there, waved her over and after a couple of moments updating them on Willow's progress, Celeste sat toying with her yoghurt, listening as Deb raved about the wild weekend she'd had and Meg moaned at length about her stint on nights that was coming up.

And then she saw him.

Pushing his tray along as he chose his lunch, Belinda was by his side, dressed in a tight black skirt and red stilettos, her raven curls tumbling down her back as she laughed at something he was saying, and Celeste felt something twist inside her.

Belinda was so ravishing, so sexy and confident and clever and just...so much better suited to Ben.

She was quite sure that if they weren't already together, it was only a matter of time.

'Celeste!' So deep in thought was she that Celeste hadn't even noticed that her colleagues were clearing up the table. 'Did you hear us?' Meg laughed at her absent-mindedness. 'We've got to get back—you drop in any time.'

'I will.'

'And I'm sure you're not thinking of it yet, but when you feel ready, you come and talk to me. Try not to let too much time pass without coming back...'

'I won't.' She said her goodbyes and sat alone, glad of the break. Belinda and Ben wouldn't come over. Registrars didn't generally sit with the nurses, well, in the staffroom they did, of course, but not in the canteen. Meg had unsettled her—of course it was way too soon to be contemplating returning to work, but in a couple of months' time, that was exactly what she would be doing—it was just impossible to comprehend from this vantage point.

'How are you?' Celeste was slightly taken aback by the warmth in Belinda's voice, and even more surprised when she put down her tray and joined her. 'How's Willow?'

'Marvellous.' Celeste blushed slightly as both Belinda and Ben joined her.

'Do you have any idea when you'll get her home?' Belinda pushed.

'A week or two,' Celeste said, 'if she keeps on doing well.' But she'd lost her audience, Belinda excusing herself to answer her pager and suddenly it was just Celeste and Ben.

'You'll be starting to pack up.' Celeste dragged her mind to something that wasn't about Willow. 'It's just a few weeks till you move into your new house now.'

'Actually, it's this weekend,' Ben said. 'The vendor was more than keen for a quick settlement and I'm all ready to move in.'

'Oh.' She was stirring an empty pot of yoghurt. 'I was going to come home for a few hours on Sunday—the nurses are insisting I take a night off. I was going to pop over and say thank you properly...'

'I won't be there,' Ben said, and then there was a pause. 'Of course, I'm only down the road.' Except it wasn't the same.

They were friends, but mainly by proximity, and though she didn't want to rely on Ben, on anyone really, there had been a certain comfort to be had knowing he was just a few doors down.

'Have you got my phone number?' Ben asked. Celeste shook her head and he scribbled it down. 'Here it is.' Ben handed her a card. 'You call if you need anything.'

'Thanks.' She pocketed it as Belinda returned, but they both knew she wouldn't use it. Oh, they'd stop and chat perhaps if she was walking on the beach, but there would be no dropping round, no dinners in front of the television. Just as he was moving so too had she—she was a mother now, which, by his own admission, rendered her off limits to Ben.

Belinda said something that made him laugh and then they tried to include her in the conversation, but it didn't work. She hadn't read a newspaper in weeks, so she wasn't exactly up on current events, hadn't been anywhere except the special care unit, which meant she hadn't a clue about the new seafood restaurant Belinda was raving about. She was just so out of the loop that it was like watching a foreign film. Celeste was so busy reading the subtitles, she missed out on the humour and laughed too late, and by the time she'd worked out what was being said, they had already moved on.

'I'd better get back…' She was about to add 'to feed Willow,' but it was a detail they didn't need. The entire focus of her life was just a conversation filler to them. 'Good luck with the move.'

'Thanks.'

It was a relief to move.

To be away from her—even if it was just down the road—made him safe. There could be no dropping over, no hearing the baby cry as he walked past the unit.

Celeste got under his skin.

From the very first moment he had seen her on the beach she had entranced him—and every now and then, when she was around, somehow he forgot his rules.

But closing the door on the unit for the last time, there was a pang of something—a wave of homesickness almost for the weeks he had spent there, despite the argumentative neighbours and the lack of air-conditioning. It hadn't all been bad, Ben thought as he picked up his sunflowers, which now were up to his shoulders in height, and loaded them in the back of the hire truck, along with the rest of his belongings.

It had almost passed as home.

'I'm sorry to trouble you...' Ben was instantly awake, but as it was only his first night in his new home he struggled to find the light. He could hear the panic in her voice and it had him searching for his jeans the second it was on. 'My car won't start, and I can't get a taxi for an hour...'

'Wait outside,' Ben instructed, not asking what the problem was, because clearly there was one—Celeste would never ring at two a.m. otherwise. 'I'm on my way.'

Used to dressing for an emergency dash to the hospital, he was in jeans, T-shirt and running shoes in less than a minute. Another two had his car out of the garage and down the street, and she was there outside the units, waiting for him.

She'd got so thin. Even in these last few days the weight had fallen off her and she was as white as a sheet in the glare of his headlights. He pulled open the car door and she jumped straight in.

'Thank you. You'll be sorry you gave me your phone number,' she gasped.

'I'm not sorry at all—I'm glad you rang.' He could hear that she was trying not to cry, trying to stay calm, and he didn't push her with questions, just drove and let her speak and tell him the bits she wanted to.

'The car wouldn't start,' Celeste explained. 'I think it's the battery.'

'Don't worry about that now.'

'They said that she's had a couple of apnoea attacks...they haven't happened in a while.'

'Okay...' He forgot to indicate at the roundabout and cursed himself for his error as a car angrily tooted—hell, he did this drive most nights when the hospital called him in. He *had* to concentrate.

'Her temperature's high as well, so they're doing bloods...' He didn't answer, just stared at the road as she talked nervously. 'I told them to ring...' She gulped and then managed to continue. 'I mean, I told them that they were to ring me for anything. So maybe it's not that serious...'

He doubted it.

Despite trying not to worry about Celeste, Ben was. He'd seen her toying with her yoghurt, seen her dramatic weight loss, her nervousness—and she'd practically told him that the nursing staff had insisted she have a night off, so they wouldn't be calling her in the middle of the night for nothing.

'She was doing so well!' Celeste insisted, even though he wasn't arguing. 'I wouldn't have left her otherwise.' God, when did the fear stop? Celeste asked herself. When did you stop living in constant worry?

Get past the first trimester.

Get past thirty weeks.

Get her blood pressure down.

Get past a hellish labour.

Get past those first terrible few nights in Special Care.

Her leg was bouncing up and down, jiggling away.

When did it stop? When did she get to live without fear?

They were at the hospital and he could have just

dropped her off, only of course he didn't, so they parked in the emergency doctor spot and he used his swipe card to get them in the back way, without having to go through Emergency.

'How is she?' Celeste was shaking so much as she went through the hand-washing ritual. The unit was brightly lit even at night, but some of cots were covered in blankets to simulate night.

Not Willow's.

She seemed to have more tubes and people around her than she had on the night after her birth and Celeste was glad when the charge nurse came straight over and brought her up to date.

'She's stable, Celeste.' Her voice was kind and firm and Ben's arm around Celeste helped, just this quiet strength beside her as she took in the news. 'Willow gave us some cause for concern a couple of hours ago—she had an apnoeic episode, which isn't unusual here, but she hasn't had one for a while, then she had another, and she started to struggle a bit with her breathing. Now she'd had some blood gases and we've put her back on CPAP, and the neonatologist has taken blood cultures…'

'Has she got an infection?'

'There are some patchy areas on her X-ray,' the charge nurse replied, 'so we've started her on antibiotics.' They were walking over to her cot and Celeste felt her heart tighten when she saw Willow, seemingly back where she'd started, all wired and hooked up and struggling so hard to breathe.

All Ben wanted to do was turn and run, but instead he stood with his arm around Celeste and stared at the machines instead of the baby. At every turn he was pulled in closer, dragged further into a world where he didn't want to belong.

'She's been fine...' Celeste sobbed when she saw her, the only relief being that Bron, her favourite nurse, was the one looking after her. 'She was going to be moved to the nursery next week...'

'It's just a setback,' the charge nurse said firmly. 'Remember when you first came to the unit and we explained that these little one have ups and downs. Well, Willow has done exceptionally well...' On she went about roller-coaster rides and all the rest of the spiel that Celeste was sick of hearing and had dared to think might be over now. All she felt was that she was back at the start again, especially when she was told she couldn't pick Willow up.

'Just hold her hand for now,' Bron said. 'We're trying to keep her quiet.'

And with that she had to make do.

'Here's Heath coming now. You've met him,' Bron said.

'He's not her doctor,' Celeste pointed out.

'No, he's the consultant on call tonight. Have a seat in the parents room and I'll get him to come and speak with you.'

'Are you the father?' Heath asked Ben as he came up to them.

'No, just a friend,' Ben explained. Then they could see Heath wasn't listening to him as the charge nurse was urgently summoning him back to the cots again.

Celeste could only feel guilty relief that it wasn't for

Willow but for the little one in the next cot. 'Not *just* a friend.' Celeste looked at him. 'There's no such thing as *just* with you.'

Ben tried not to over-analyse that comment too much. It was just one of those things—she was grateful probably that he'd been there tonight, for his help these past weeks, and no doubt glad she didn't have to sit alone on this hellish night, because it wasn't actually Celeste who'd drawn the short straw.

The wait to speak with Heath was endless, and she couldn't go to Willow because, as well as working on her, they were working intensely on the tiny infant in the next cot. Ben thought his job was agony at times, but when the other baby's parents arrived, pale and shocked and visibly terrified, he wouldn't have been Heath or the charge nurse for a million dollars. Unlike Celeste, they got to hold their baby straight away.

Because it was already too late.

'We're concerned about Celeste,' Heath said.

Ben had sat with Celeste until Heath had taken them through Willow's X-rays and blood results and asked all the questions that Celeste was just too overwhelmed to ask, but would surely regret not asking later. Until finally she was taken in to sit with Willow.

'I'm not Willow's father,' Ben interrupted.

'Her partner?'

'No.' Ben shook his head.

'I'm sorry.' Heath frowned. 'Only Bron said that you'd been in a few times at night to see Willow.'

For the first time in his adult life Ben was coming

close to blushing—he felt as if he'd been caught out doing something wrong. Oh, he'd only been up a handful of times—and never when Celeste was around. He'd just wanted to see for himself how the baby was doing.

Clearly, it had been noted!

'I'm a doctor here.' Ben cleared his throat uncomfortably. 'And as I said, Celeste's a friend. I pop in occasionally to check on the baby. I delivered her...'

'I see.' But obviously he didn't.

'You said you were concerned about her?' Ben pursued.

'Look, I thought you were her partner. I'm sorry, my mistake—it's been a long night,' Heath said.

Ben realised that if he wanted to, he could just walk away now—ignore the slight indiscretion, say goodnight to Celeste and just fall into bed for what remained of the night. But he didn't want to.

'We're very good friends,' Ben said. 'If I can help in any way...'

'She just needs a break. It's exceptionally unfortunate that Willow got sick on the one night we'd persuaded her to go home. And with the baby dying in the next cot she's hyper-vigilant now,' Heath explained. 'It's common with mothers in her situation, but sadly tonight has done nothing to help with that.'

'What can I do?' Ben asked.

'It's not simply an overnight thing,' Heath said, standing up and shaking Ben's hand before heading back out to the unit. 'She needs regular support, needs to be encouraged to take a break every now and then— once Willow's better, of course.'

Which meant getting further involved with mother and

child—which Ben definitely didn't want to do. So instead he offered her more practicality as he said goodnight to Celeste. 'Give me your keys. I'll sort out the car for you.'

'I'll sort it out myself tomorrow,' she said.

'Celeste.' He wasn't arguing or debating the point. 'You *need* your car to work, for Willow's sake. So give me your keys, and if it's the battery I'll charge it or get a new one, and if it's something else…' He saw her eyes close in utter despair, as the water rose ever higher. He wanted to pull her out, to wrench her from the rising tide, except he was so very scared to.

Scared to love her.

Except somehow he already did.

Only the problem wasn't Celeste.

It was Willow.

CHAPTER NINE

He was up at six, on a rare day off. He had boxes to unpack and a kitchen to paint, but instead he wandered down the road, Celeste's car keys in hand. He'd have a look at the car, have a run on the beach and then he'd sort out the boxes. Ben opened the garage and after turning the key in the ignition the car grumbled into noisy life—so it wasn't the battery.

At eight he called the mobile mechanic.

'Do you want my advice?' The mechanic stared at what could loosely be called an engine and frowned heavily.

'No.' Ben gave a grimace. 'Just fix it, get it roadworthy, please.'

'The tyres are bald…'

'Get decent second-hand ones,' Ben said, because against that pile of scrap, four gleaming new ones would stand out far too much.

It took the whole day, but by six he was dropping her keys back at the hospital for her.

'How's Willow doing?' he asked her.

'A bit better, thanks.' Celeste looked completely wiped out. Her hair needed washing and there were huge charcoal smudges beneath her eyes, as if she'd been wearing black eyeliner and rubbed them, except she hadn't worn make-up for weeks. 'The first of her blood cultures should be back soon, but she hasn't had a temperature since lunchtime.'

'What about her blood gases?' he queried.

'They're better.' She shook her head in confusion. She wasn't thinking as a nurse but as a mum, listening to the doctors and the special care staff. 'She's to stay on oxygen…'

He wanted more information, wanted to speak with the neonatologist, to see the baby's X-rays and blood results for himself.

'I got to hold her,' she told him tremulously.

His demands had no place here, so instead he smiled. 'That's good news.'

'Mum's in with her now.'

All he could do was take her to the canteen and buy her a hot chocolate and some cereal from the machine, and only when he handed her the car keys did Celeste remember what he was doing here. He wasn't actually here to find out about Willow at all.

'What was wrong with it?' she wanted to know.

'It needed a new battery.' And a starter motor and brake discs and pads and muffler and… But he chose not to elaborate any further.

'How much was it? There's a cash machine here,' she said.

'It wasn't much. We'll sort it out when Willow's better,' Ben said easily. With a baby that sick, Celeste needed a car that started first time every time, Ben told himself. And he was saving his sanity too, he decided. At least he wouldn't be getting woken up at two a.m. any more…

Except he actually hadn't minded.

If the truth be known, he would have hated to have found out from someone else the next day what had happened.

He'd hardly slept in twenty-four hours but, despite that fact, his mind suddenly seemed clear.

Celeste needed a friend—a real one—and maybe he could be that for while, maybe he could be there for her, at least till Willow came home.

'I've been thinking,' Ben said. 'Once Willow's better, how about a day out?'

'Where?' she asked.

'On the water,' Ben suggested, but she immediately shook her head.

'What if something happened? It would take too long to get here,' she protested anxiously.

'We're not crossing the equator, just taking a ride out on the bay! We could have lunch.'

'I don't think so, but thanks anyway.' She shook her head.

'Don't say no,' Ben said. 'Just think about it.'

She didn't think about it.

There was way too much else to think about.

As Willow got over what had turned out to be a nasty bout of pneumonia and started to regularly put on weight, discharge day started looming. Celeste's milk supply had finally completely dried up and, regretfully for Celeste, Willow was now taking a bottle, but at least it did give her a little bit more freedom and meant she could get back to the flat every now and then—or even visit the doctor for herself!

'Celeste?'

Ben passed her as he was walking through the main entrance corridor. Amidst a hub of people and cafés and a gift shop, there was Celeste, as white as a sheet, and in her own vague world.

'Celeste…' He tapped her on the shoulder to get her attention. 'Is everything okay?'

She visibly made an effort to concentrate. 'Fine,' she finally answered.

'Willow?'

'She's good,' Celeste said without the usual elaboration of the past few weeks. Normally she gushed over every milestone, and Ben saw her lick dry lips.

'You?'

'I'm bit queasy,' she admitted. 'I was going to get a drink but there's a huge queue.'

'Go and sit down, I'll get you one.' That she didn't argue told Ben she really wasn't feeling well.

Of course there was a queue at the café, but he could be arrogant enough at times and he ignored it, going straight to the front and getting two bottles of water and a bottle of juice—oh, and a muffin.

'Here.' He put his wares on the table and Celeste took a long drink of water.

'How did you get served so quickly? I'd given up.'

'Perk of the job.' Ben winked. 'I got you something to eat…in case you're hungry.'

Celeste screwed up her nose. 'How much do I owe

you?' She scrabbled in her purse for some money, but Ben just shook his head.

'Don't be daft.'

'Add it to my slate!' Celeste said, and then leant forward, rested her head on her arm for a moment and let everything pass by, the noise, the traffic of a busy hospital, the glare of the windows, everything except Ben's concerned voice.

'Should I be taking your pulse or something?' he teased gently to hide his real worry.

'No.'

'You're not very good company today.' He lifted her forehead a little, then saw her grey face and put it back down to rest on her forearm.

'They told me to wait half an hour...' came her muffled voice. 'I should have listened.'

'Should I be sending for a gurney from Emergency?' he asked lightly.

'Please don't!' Slowly she sat up and gave him a weak smile.

'Better now?'

'Better.' She blew out a breath. 'That's twice you've saved me from embarrassing myself.'

'Childbirth is hardly embarrassing,' he pointed out.

'In the middle of the road, with a crowd gathered?'

'Okay.' He grinned. 'So it could have been embar-rassing—if I hadn't managed to get you into the relative privacy of what is now my garden! As would fainting outside the hospital gift shop. So what happened to make you feel like this?'

'I just had my postnatal check.'

'Oh.' He was a doctor, so why were his ears going a bit pink? He could walk into the staffroom in Emergency this very minute into a gaggle of nurses who wouldn't halt their discussion with him in the room.

'He suggested that I have a coil inserted, in the unlikely event that I want to resume sexual relations over the next five years!'

She *did* make him laugh—even at awkward things.

'You will want to, eventually,' he said.

'I doubt it!' She took another long drink and then picked at the muffin. 'It seems like a lot of fuss for nothing, to tell you the truth—well, not nothing,' she mused. 'Having had a family fallout, a baby in Special Care…' She broke off the list of her woes—he wouldn't be interested in all that, especially when she came to the part about how Willow's father didn't want to know her. 'Anyway, he also suggested that I lie down for half an hour afterwards.'

'You clearly didn't listen,' he said a little sternly.

'I felt fine.' Celeste shrugged.

'Well, listen next time,' he ordered.

Colour was coming back to her lips now, and to her cheeks. It had been nice to sit and chat but she'd been gone for a while now and wanted to be back to give Willow her bottle.

'I'd better get up to Special Care…'

She was still a touch pale. 'Maybe you should wait another ten minutes,' he suggested.

Which she probably would have, except the pager she wore went off, telling her that Willow was awake and ready to be fed.

'I should go.'

'I'll walk up with you,' Ben offered, still concerned with her colour.

They walked through the corridors and up to the lift, Ben seeing her right up to the entrance to Special Care, and as they arrived, Celeste was suddenly nervous.

'Do you want to come in?' It was, oh, so casually offered. 'You'll see a huge difference in her…'

'I'd love to,' Ben said, and she could hear the 'but' even before it was said, knew it was coming before it was uttered. 'But I really ought to get back to Emergency. Another time, maybe?'

'Sure.' She didn't get him—just didn't. He seemed to enjoy her company, was always there when she needed him, and yet sometimes all he wanted to do was get away from her!

'Hey…' He turned around. 'Have you thought about coming out on the boat with me?'

'I don't think so,' Celeste declined. 'They're saying that Willow might be ready for discharge next Monday, and I've got loads to get ready.'

'Well, I'm off next weekend,' Ben said. 'So the offer's there…just let me know.'

She was ready.

Well, as ready as she would ever be!

All the new baby clothes had been washed in soap flakes, there were nappies and baby wipes and bottles and formula, the crib that Ben had set up and which Celeste had lined with bunny rugs. All it needed now was Willow—and that was happening tomorrow.

The nurses had practically frogmarched her out of the department, insisting she spend a day at home and strongly suggesting she didn't come back till morning—that she should grab one last night of uninterrupted sleep while she still could.

Her parents, having helped her set up, had gone home, and with nothing to do, Celeste had decided to walk down the road to get a magazine, with the intention of sitting on the beach to read it. Or rather that was her excuse for walking past Ben's new house!

It felt strange, being out in the fresh air—strange to be out in the afternoon sunlight instead of in the nursery—but the nurses had given her very little choice in the matter, so she decided to enjoy it.

She was wearing denim shorts and a white halter-neck T-shirt, pre-pregnancy clothes that were actually a bit big for her now. Her feet were wrapped in thin red leather sandals, and it felt nice to have the sun on her legs, nice to walk along the street, though she felt as if she'd forgotten something, kept pulling out her phone to check it in case the hospital had rung and she'd missed it, or kept scrambling in her bag to check she had her keys. It already felt completely weird to be anywhere without Willow.

Still, the world had carried on very nicely without her. Flowers hung heavy on the trees, the bay was blue and still glistening in the background—and there was Ben, with his new boat all hooked up to his four-wheel drive.

'Very nice.' Celeste commented, walking around and inspecting *his* new baby. 'Very nice indeed.'

'I think I'm in love.' Ben grinned, running a loving

hand over his new toy, and all Celeste could do was laugh. 'How's Willow?'

'Very well. She looks like a complete fraud—she's way too healthy to be in hospital.'

'All ready for tomorrow?' he asked.

'As ready as I'll ever be.'

'You'll be great,' he said reassuringly.

'So, are you taking her out?' She wouldn't ask to go with him, Celeste decided, but if he happened to offer again…

'I've just got back,' Ben said. 'I went out with a friend—I'm still not sure about launching her on my own yet.'

'Ooh, no!' Celeste agreed, smiling, but her heart sank a little, realising that she had very literally missed the boat with him. 'The boat ramp is not the place to practise.'

'Yeah, I'm still a novice—but it is nice to be out there again. I'd forgotten how good it feels.'

'There's another launching ramp by the creek,' Celeste said, 'for when you do want to take her out on your own. It's probably the quietest one and you won't be holding everyone up.'

'You've done this before, then?' he asked curiously.

'All the time,' Celeste said with a cheeky grin. 'Well, when Dad and I were talking, I used to go fishing with him.'

'You?' Ben raised his eyebrows. 'Fishing?'

'No, daydreaming,' Celeste said. 'But I'm fishing now…'

It took a second for him to get her meaning and when he did he smiled.

'Let's go, then.'

It was the perfect evening to try out a new boat—the bay was calm, with barely a breeze. For a novice, he did a pretty decent job of reversing the boat and trailer down the ramp, then jumped out and dealt with the boat as Celeste took the driver's seat, just as she had when she had been out with her dad. Having parked his four-wheel drive, she then walked down to the water, Ben holding her hand as she stepped in. His new engine purred into life and she was so glad she had said yes, so glad, as Ben weaved the boat, to feel the wind in her hair and to just breathe again after these last few weeks.

Ben watched as slowly, slowly she unwound.

The weight had fallen off her since Willow's birth, and seeing her slender frame emerging he'd realised just how ill she'd been, probably since the day he'd met her. Too much time in the hospital, both as a patient and visiting Willow, had given her that pale, unhealthy colour. Still, the sea air was bringing back some much-needed warmth to her cheeks and when she didn't check her phone for a full ten minutes, Ben knew that finally, even if it was just for a little while, the Celeste of old was back.

They stopped and idled and Ben set out the food they had grabbed on a quick stop at the deli. In the distance, Melbourne glittered gold in the setting sun. Willow was coming home tomorrow and all was surely right in the world—even if it felt otherwise at times.

'Scared about tomorrow?' Ben asked.

'Scared but ready,' Celeste admitted.

'You're going to be a great mum,' Ben said.

'I'd better be…' Celeste smiled. 'She'll be home in a matter of hours.'

He unpacked tarragon chicken in mayonnaise, which tasted as good as they first time they'd shared it, washed down with sparkling mineral water. For Celeste it was bliss to just pause, to escape before life changed yet again tomorrow.

'You've got transport and everything sorted?' Ben checked.

'Dad and Mum are coming,' Celeste informed him. 'Come over in the afternoon if you like—I've got some friends coming round and we're going to have a little barbeque…'

'Shouldn't you take it easy the first few days?' Ben asked dubiously.

'That's the plan,' Celeste said with a flash of her old cheek. 'I'll get them all in and out in one hit!'

They could have headed home then, except they didn't. Ben was playing sailor while Celeste lay in the bottom of the little boat, her feet up on the edge, and listened to the dreamy lap, lap of the water. She couldn't remember being this relaxed since Willow's birth, since before Willow was born, since for ever, really…

When she opened her eyes to tell him so, she suddenly wasn't relaxed any more.

Because he was watching her, just sitting quietly watching her. When Celeste's eyes opened, he didn't look away, he just stared, and she stared right back at those contrary green eyes that both reached for her and resisted her. They stared in silence, reliving their one and only kiss in their minds, and all it did was confuse her, because in that second she was sure that without Willow there would be love between them.

Without Willow.

It was an impossible place and one she never wanted to visit. She could see a flash in his eyes and it could have been the breeze or the sun glare, or it might have been tears, because there was regret etched on his features, and regret laced with anger in hers.

Because without Willow, they'd be mere colleagues now.

Without Willow she'd never have been living opposite him.

There could be no without Willow and there could be no them.

'Rotten timing, huh?' She wasn't making a joke, and she wasn't making a stab in the dark as to how he was feeling—because out on the water, when it was just the two of them, with no past, no future, just this moment in time, there was no question of either of them denying it.

'It is,' Ben said, and he didn't have to elaborate—he'd stated his case from the very beginning.

'So I'm not going mad and imagining things, then?'

'You're not going mad…' He touched her hair, just holding one heavy curl in his fingers, and *how* he wanted to tell her, to explain, but how? Heath's warning was ringing in his ears. This was her day off from worrying and he didn't want to darken it with his grief, couldn't burden this very new mum with his fears for her, for her child.

'I just can't do it.' Ben settled for that.

'I know.'

'I said so from the beginning.'

'You did.'

'Can we still be friends?' Ben asked, and her answer was the same as the one ringing inside his own head.

'I don't know.'

Maybe this was their last kiss but it was the sweetest she had ever tasted.

He bent her head and brushed her lips and if real men didn't cry, that excluded Ben, because she felt the brush of damp eyelashes on her cheeks as his mouth met hers. It was the most fleeting of kisses but it was so mingled with regret and love that it would stay with her for ever.

She didn't have to tell him to take her home afterwards, he just started up the engine, Ben driving, Celeste pulling on massive sunglasses and trying not to cry.

The whole journey home was neither pleasant nor wretched, yet contained no more kisses.

'Do you want to come in?' she offered when he pulled up at her gates. She knew exactly what she was offering, knew because the air was so thick with want, there could be no doubt in either of their minds.

'Celeste...' His knuckles were white where he gripped the steering-wheel. 'Go inside.'

'Just for tonight,' she pleaded. She wanted a proper kiss goodbye, was greedy for more, and was trying to convince herself she could handle the morning after. Rejection was surely her forte—except she loathed it now.

''Night, Celeste,' he replied.

CHAPTER TEN

HE PROBABLY should have popped over.

Set the tone.

Resumed being nothing but friends.

Only it was too late for that now.

Autumn was coming. Every night the wind stripped a few more petals from the sunflowers. Heading for home from work nearly a week later and sick of the constant reminders, Ben pulled out the gangly stalks and went to shove them on the compost. About a hundred seeds scattered in the garden while he did it and Ben gritted his teeth. So much for forgetting! If he didn't get the seeds up he'd need a scythe next year just to get to the front door!

She was everywhere.

In his head, in his dreams, and as he walked into the house, he headed upstairs to change and his eyes moved straight to the beach, to where he'd first seen Celeste, instead of to the picture of Jen on his bedside table.

'What do I do?' He picked up the silver frame and stared into his wife's clear eyes and wished for just two minutes of her time.

Two minutes of her logical, practical advice, which

was a stupid thing to wish for—as if he should even be asking Jen about Celeste!

He wanted her to tell him, just a sign, one little sign, only he didn't even know what he was asking for.

And then he looked at the whole picture, not just at Jen.

He ran a finger over the swell of her stomach to where their baby lay, touched *her* only through glass, touched what he'd never, not even once got to hold.

But there wasn't time to wallow. He had visitors that evening, which proved difficult, and then he was called into hospital to deal with an emergency at around 10 p.m. He could hear the pounding music from Celeste's neighbours as he drove past her unit and despite his best intentions, it was difficult to ignore. However, he determinedly drove on, hoping the party would wind down early, or that she'd taken Willow and gone to her parents'. Surely a wild party next door was the last thing a new mum needed only a few days after bring her babe home.

Still, it wasn't his problem now.

'Sorry!' Belinda looked up from a packed Resus as Ben made his way over. 'You're about to get a page saying we don't need you after all.'

'Sure about that?' Ben checked, because the place was steaming.

'We were alerted for two multi-traumas,' Belinda explained, 'and on top of this amount of patients, I thought we should call in some extras, even though you're not rostered on.'

'Where are the trauma victims?'

'One died en route and one's not too seriously injured.

I'm just about to ring the parents—who'd have teenagers, huh? Perhaps I should have waited to call you.'

'Better not to wait and see.' Ben really didn't mind being called in, it was part of his job. 'I'll give you a hand now that I'm here.'

'No, you won't,' Belinda contradicted as she looked at some X-rays on the computer. 'Go and get some sleep—this is just a usual Friday night.'

'I really don't mind,' he persisted.

'Well, I do,' Belinda said. 'You're covering for me tomorrow, remember.'

'Ah, yes!'

'And I'm rather hoping that you *won't* be calling me in.' She winked at him.

'Going somewhere nice?' he asked.

'To a fabulous hotel in the City.' Belinda smiled. 'A million miles away from here.'

'You and Paul still going strong, then?'

'Absolutely. You know you really shouldn't knock the internet.'

Ben just groaned—she never let up! 'Okay, then, I'll head home. Just buzz if you do need help, though.'

He would actually have preferred to be working— wished that Belinda had handed him a pile of patient cards and asked him to wade his way through them, because as he turned into his street, instead of slowing down he speeded up a touch and turned up the car radio. Really, whatever was going on at the flats wasn't his problem. There were parties there every other night, and he couldn't forever be checking that Celeste was okay…

A group of teenagers was spilling onto the street, and

despite the car radio on loud he could hear the doof-doof of the music. Though he had driven past, regretting it, resenting it even, he executed a hasty U-turn, flashed his lights at the drunken idiots and pulled over. Opening the gates and heading up to her unit, he saw the lights were on. Hearing Willow's screams from inside, he knocked at the door.

When there was no answer he realised how scared she must be.

'Celeste,' he called during a tiny lull in the music. 'It's me, Ben.'

'What do you want?' He could see she'd been crying when she opened the door.

'I heard the noise on my way back from work. You can't settle her in this. You should have rung me...'

'You wouldn't have been home,' Celeste pointed out, but despite her flip retort he could tell she was still close to tears. 'It's only a party...'

Which it was—a very loud party, but next door to a very new baby and a very new mum, who just hadn't needed it tonight.

'I can't get her to feed, and the nurses said it had to be every three hours at the most,' she said forlornly.

'Come on,' he announced. 'Let's grab her things and you can both crash at my place.'

She was about to say no, about to close the door, but a small fight was erupting in the next unit, and, however much she didn't want to need help, tonight she did.

'Please, Celeste...' Even inside her flat the music was just as loud! 'Pack a bag and come and stay at my house tonight,' he begged again.

She would have argued, but she was too relieved. She wasn't sure if it was her own tension or the noise that was upsetting Willow, but after six weeks of tender care in the special care unit, Celeste was scared enough being on her own with her, without the invasive noise and chaos of next door.

She was trying to clip Willow in her little seat to carry out to the car, but Ben had other ideas. 'Just put her in her pram. It will be just as easy to walk…and she can sleep in it.'

She would never have walked outside with the party mob there, but with Ben she felt safe. He pushed the pram and bumped it down the steps as Celeste locked up. The gates to the units were already open and with his arm around her they walked in swift silence away from the noise along the street and only when it faded in the distance did he talk.

'You should have called the police.'

'What, and have my neighbours hate me?' Celeste said ruefully as they walked along the street. There was a nearly full moon, which provided plenty of light, the music was just a thud in the distance and she could hear the welcome sound of the water now. 'It was only a party…' she said again.

'It's no place…' He didn't finish the sentence, but Celeste knew what he'd been about to say.

'It's all I can afford, Ben,' she told him quietly.

'I know that.'

'There was a small house in town for about the same price—I should have rented that, but I wanted to be closer to the beach. The flat seemed fine when I inspected it. I didn't think to ask to see it at eleven o'clock on a Friday night…' She took over the pram, and was walking more quickly now. Willow, over-tired, was still crying, and Celeste was both annoyed at him and at herself. She was trying so hard to cope, so hard to do right by her baby, yet at every turn she seemed thwarted, at every turn life tossed her another curve ball… 'I'm doing my best,' she said as they arrived at his house. 'Though, I'm sure you don't think it's good enough—'

'I never said that!' Ben interrupted.

'No, but you think it!' she retorted. She was angry at him and she knew she shouldn't be. It wasn't his fault, he was being perfectly nice, but his home, his order, his everything only seemed to highlight her own inadequacies.

'Why don't you feed her?' Ben suggested soothingly. He carried the pram and the baby up the stairs and past his stunning bedroom to a rather nice guest room, where he parked the pram. 'Rest on the bed, the view's lovely. You can both relax and get Willow calm and settled…'

'And her mum too…' She was just a bit embarrassed at her outburst. After all, it wasn't his fault how he made her feel.

'I'll leave you to it,' Ben said. 'I'll find some sheets to make up the bed.'

'Thanks,' she said awkwardly.

'Come out when you're ready.'

'I need…' He was turning to go and she stopped him, rummaging through Willow's bag. 'Is there anywhere I can warm up her bottle?'

'Sure,' he said.

'Actually…' she picked up the hot little bundle that was her sobbing baby '…could you hold Willow for me?'

'I'll do the bottle,' Ben said, in an annoyingly calm voice that only made her appear more frazzled. 'I know where everything is.'

He took the bottle and she changed Willow while her screams quadrupled. She felt like howling herself. She knew he'd been expecting her to just lie on the bed and flop out a boob, to feed her baby herself…

She felt such a failure, felt so close to crying that she barely managed to thank him as he returned a couple of moments later with a warm bottle. He sort of hovered for an uncomfortable moment as she sat awkwardly on the edge of the bed and took it from him. Then Willow's mouth clamped onto the teat as if she'd been starved for a week and the only sound was of gulps and tears as an overtired baby finally took its bottle from an over-wrought mum.

Although Willow was gulping her bottle, she kept jumping and startling while she was doing it. Celeste kicked off her sandals and lay back on the bed, pulling Willow in tighter, but every time she almost relaxed, the baby would suddenly startle as if the noise, the angst, the panic from her mother was all about to start again.

It was nothing unfamiliar to Celeste.

The party had just been the clincher. In the few days since she'd been home from the hospital, practically every time she'd sat down to quietly feed her babe, her mother had 'dropped in', offering all kinds of sugges-tions—'Change her first,' or 'Change her after she's fed,' or 'Hold the bottle higher,' or 'She needs winding,'

each well-meaning suggestion from Rita only exacer-
bating the tension further.

Celeste desperately wanted to be back in the hospital,
wanted to be feeding Willow with knowledgeable staff
offering quiet encouragement, or even to put her to bed
in the hospital at night and go home, as she had last
Sunday, missing her but knowing she was being well
looked after—no, that Willow was being *better* looked
after than she could manage by herself.

'It's okay, Willow, it's all okay, Willow,' she said
softly, over and over again until finally Willow believed
it, until finally her little jerks and startles stopped, and
the gulps of tears faded. Celeste felt this unfamiliar
surge of triumph as her baby relaxed into her, scared to
move almost as Willow moved from resisting her to
this passive, trance-like state almost—seemingly asleep,
but still feeding.

She really was asleep, Celeste realised as she took the
empty bottle from Willow's mouth and watched her
little eyelids flicker.

So asleep that if the party down the street relocated
to outside the bedroom window, Celeste was quite sure
that Willow wouldn't wake up.

And she had done it all by herself.

She'd never been so alone with her baby and felt so
much a mum at the same time.

Celeste stared down at the perfect features of her
daughter, dark little eyebrows that looked as if they'd
been pencilled on, her fine pointy nose and little rosebud
mouth, and she thought her heart would swell and burst
there was so much love inside it for her baby.

A scary love that knew no bounds—yet still she felt so inadequate.

This little scrap of a thing was just so utterly and completely dependent on her, there should be no room to feel anything else.

Except she did.

She didn't want to move, didn't want to put her down. She just wanted to stay safe on this bed, holding her baby, watching the bay with Ben just a call away. To simply hold onto this first ray of peace.

'Don't fall asleep holding the baby.'

She could hear her mother as if she were in the room with them.

And she was right, Celeste sighed, heading over to the pram and gently lowering Willow in.

As she headed out to the lounge, Ben, sprawled on one of the sofas, looked up from the show on the television he was watching and poured her a glass of wine. It was the second little ray of peace she felt. For the first time since Willow's discharge from hospital, she felt as if she were home.

'She's asleep,' she told him.

'Good. How are you?' he asked.

'Better.' She took a seat on the edge of the sofa opposite him. 'You always seem to bailing me out. It won't be for much longer.'

'I know,' Ben said, then suggested that she choose a movie, so she did, kneeling down as she worked through his collection, and as she did she told him her most recent news.

'I mean, you won't have to keep bailing me out because I'm moving back home.'

His wine paused midway to his mouth. 'When?' he asked and then took a long sip, holding it in his mouth until she replied.

'Next weekend.' Huge amber eyes flashed towards him then looked away. 'Mum and Dad are painting the spare room for her and we're moving the stuff throughout next week. It's just not working, living here. You know what it's like, and Mum and I are getting on a lot better now…' She trailed off.

'How do you feel about it?' he asked shrewdly.

Celeste stared unseeingly at the DVD she was holding. 'To be honest, I haven't really stopped to think about it that much.'

So she did. She sank back on her heels and thought. Out loud.

'It's not what I really want,' she admitted. 'I asked them a few weeks ago, but that was when I was pregnant. I never wanted to live there with a baby—but it's best for Willow. We could manage on our own, but this way…' Celeste took a deep breath. 'She's nearly two months old—it seems unbelievable. I could put her in the crèche next month and start back at work.'

'Is your mum going to watch her for you?'

Celeste nodded. 'Only for work—she's warned me that she's not a built-in babysitter so we've agreed it's just for a year.' And then she told him her other news. 'I've spoken to Meg and she's going to help me with my application to transfer hospitals.'

'Back to your old one?'

'No.' Instantly she shook her head. 'To Melbourne Central…'

'That's my old stomping ground,' Ben said.

'It's much closer to home than here. Anyway, I'm going to be head down finishing the emergency grad year and then I'm going to do as many shifts as I can and save…'

She looked so young sometimes—she *was* so young, Ben reminded himself. Only that wasn't what he meant. She seemed so fey and carefree at times yet there was a deep streak to her that enthralled him—an inherent resilience that belied her apparent fragility at times.

And she'd clearly given this a lot of thought.

'You say you're getting on with your parents now?'

'It's a lot better than it was.' She'd chosen the movie and popped it in. 'I can't imagine living at home again, though. I couldn't wait to leave the first time!' She rolled her eyes and added, 'They're really strict.' She gave him a smile and this time sat on the same sofa as him. 'There'll be none of this…'

'What?'

'Sitting in the dark with a man, drinking wine!'

'You're twenty-four.' Ben grinned. 'And we're watching a movie.'

'I don't care how old you are, young lady.' She wagged a finger at him. 'When you're under our roof, you live by our rules.'

'You're serious?' he exclaimed, half horrified, half amused.

'Absolutely. It will be even worse this time around, given…' She nodded in the direction of upstairs.

'She can't hear you!' Ben laughed.

'I don't care whether she can hear or not. I've told Mum and Dad that there's to be no talk of "the mess I've got myself into" or "accidents" around her—that's *my* only rule if I move home. I'll put up with anything for a year if it gives her a better start, but I'll tell her her story in my own way, in my own time.'

'That's fair enough.'

'It's not her fault I didn't know her dad was married…' She stopped talking then, thankful for the dark room, because her face was red suddenly, not from embarrassment but near tears. They sat in silence for a while—the words that had never been voiced by Ben hanging there between them…

'How, Celeste?' he finally asked. 'How did you not know?'

'I just didn't.'

'What about nights like this?'

'Like what?'

'Like this.' Ben gestured at the simplicity of it all. 'Did you never wonder why it was always at yours?'

'He didn't come to mine.' Her voice was shrill. 'We went out, we were dating…'

He didn't get it, but it wasn't his place to push it, he'd already crossed that line, so Ben chose to leave it, surprised when it was Celeste who broke the strained silence between them.

'I shared with two other students. I knew what we were doing was wrong…' She stopped again and was staring unseeingly at the television screen.

'Wrong?' Ben frowned. 'I thought you didn't know he was married?'

'It's more than that. I can't tell anyone about Willow's father…it would cause so much trouble.'

'You can tell me,' Ben said, because though he could sense her indecision, he also sensed her burden.

'You won't say anything to anyone?'

'Never.'

'Because gossip…'

'I don't gossip.'

She looked over to him, at those guarded, remote features that occasionally softened into tenderness—and right now she was the lucky recipient of that emotion. She saw the honesty and integrity there too and it made her shame burn harder, so much so that she couldn't look him in the eyes as she shared her truth.

'His name's Dean. He was my lecturer at university.' When Ben didn't say anything, she wasn't sure if he understood the problem. 'It's forbidden for a lecturer to have a relationship with a student…'

'I know.'

'It happens, though,' she attempted to rationalise. 'All the time. I mean, it's between two consenting adults, and it's a stupid rule really…' He could see tears squeezing out of her eyes, and, as she always did, she closed them, trying to keep it all in.

'Not that stupid a rule, perhaps,' Celeste admitted. 'He must choose his targets—I mean, he had his story all set up. He said he shared a house with another lecturer—that was why we couldn't go back there—and as I was sharing with students, we always went out miles away. Of course, I assumed it was so that no one from uni found out about us. He told me that once I'd qualified, that we could go more public…'

'You never suspected?' He still didn't get it. Even if he and Celeste were only a little bit in each other's lives, that much of each other they already knew.

'I'd never really had a serious boyfriend,' she revealed, giving a tight shrug. 'Like I said, Mum and Dad were really strict, and when I left home, I didn't go wild or anything. Really, I didn't even know if we were going out at first, it was just a drink, or dinner…' She was squirming with embarrassment now. 'And we went to a hotel a couple of times…it should have been obvious to me,' Celeste admitted. 'I mean, he never answered his phone—it always went to voicemail.'

'Oh?' Ben frowned. 'Is that supposed to mean something?'

'He never answered his phone when he was with me either.'

'Okay…' Ben said, not that he really understood it.

'You're too honest.' Celeste managed a watery smile. 'So am I, I guess, because I never assumed he was lying. He never answered his phone in case it was another of his women—or even his wife.'

'How *did* you find out he was married?'

'He was away one day, another lecturer came in— explaining that he was taking over because apparently Dean's wife was ill…'

'Oh, Celeste,' Ben groaned softly.

The commercials for the film were over so she put her feet up on the table because that was what Ben was doing and took a sip of her wine and sat there, trying to watch the film while remembering the hurt—the very real hurt—and the fear a few weeks later when she'd found out that she was having Dean's baby.

It was a funny movie that she'd chosen, or it had been the first time she'd watched it—only it didn't seem so funny now. Instead, it was a romantic comedy of errors that just made her feel like crying.

Ben was on the sofa next to her, big and solid and so reassuring.

And there was a picture of Jen by the television.

She couldn't see the image, just the outline of the frame—but that made her feel like crying too.

As if the universe had got something terribly wrong, had tossed them all up in the air and they'd landed in the wrong places, the wrong rooms, with the wrong people.

Except she liked being here with him.

She needed a tissue, Celeste realised, had sniffed four times in the past fifteen seconds and it was getting embarrassing now, except she had to reach over him to get them, so she didn't bother. 'Here.' He pulled a wad out of a box on the coffee table and Celeste managed a wry laugh.

'Do you sit here crying at films often?'

'Nope…' Ben smiled at the image she conjured up. 'Jen's sister was over earlier.'

Oh, God!

She didn't say it, but she flinched at her insensitivity. Wallowing in her own problems, he just seemed so together, it was so easy to forget all he'd been through. 'Just for a quick hi, but she hadn't seen the house.'

'It must have been hard for you,' she said.

'Yes, it was,' Ben admitted. 'Thankfully I was called into work.'

'Thank you.' She stared over to him. 'I mean, really, thank you for everything.'

'I was glad to help.'

'And I'm sorry.'

'For what?' Ben asked, but was just a touch uncomfortable as to how she might answer.

'Because of how difficult things are between us...'

'They're not difficult,' he lied.

'Yes, they are,' Celeste contradicted, 'because I *want* to be friends with you, Ben, but I don't know how to *be* one...' He could see the tears rolling down her cheeks now. 'And please don't feel guilty when I tell you this, but it's part of the reason I'm moving home too—maybe things will be easier, maybe we might even manage to be *friends*.'

'I don't think so.' His fingers wanted to touch her hair again, he wanted to hold her, to kiss her, but it would be too cruel to them both.

But then she looked at him, looked right at him, and said the words that sometimes he'd wished too, stuck her toe in that closing door and kept it wedged that little bit open.

'I wish it could have been you. I wish Willow was yours.'

She meant it, she really meant it, and her nose was running because she meant it so much.

She wished it had been Ben, that he had been the one who'd made love to her.

Wished, wished, wished for so much more than the little they'd had.

'It would never have been me,' Ben said then. 'Because I'd have taken so, so much more care of you than he did.'

He couldn't stand that she was moving away, couldn't stand the thought of not seeing her again, couldn't stand not to touch her some more. 'Come here.' He pulled her at her wrist so she was right up against him and it was like climbing into his boat.

Sort of away from everything.

It was nice to have a cuddle with him while she cried—he was so big she *had* to lean against him, or she'd topple overboard! Nice when he hooked his arm around her and secured her there.

Just really, really nice.

It was for Ben too.

So rarely was he indulgent—but next week she was going somewhere she didn't really want to go.

Leaving him somewhere he didn't really want to be.

Tonight they were here.

And it was nice.

Nice to lie on the sofa with *her*.

Nice to hear her sobs recede and to feel her chest move as she laughed at the film.

It had been a hell of a day. Showing Abby and her husband Mick around the house, with Abby tearing up every five minutes, he'd even offered to take them out on the boat.

Except Abby looked too much like Jen and there would be three in the boat instead of four—so he'd been glad when he'd been called in to work.

It had just been one of those days, and it could have been one of those nights too.

Except Celeste was here and all it felt was right.

He was hovering on the edge of indecision, scared but almost ready to really make a new start.

A very new start.

Certain films shouldn't be watched with a supposed friend who was actually a whole lot more.

They were watching a passionate on-screen kiss—and it seemed to go on a lot longer than Celeste remembered from the last time she had seen the film.

It was like the time when at fourteen she'd been watching a serious documentary with her parents and suddenly they had been watching full-on sex.

Just exquisitely uncomfortable—but for all sorts of different reasons tonight.

His hand was hovering over her stomach, but she was too near the edge of the sofa, needed a little shift, a little hoist from him to bring her closer, which he didn't do, so Celeste wriggled back a bit.

Just a bit.

Ever the gentleman, he moved back a fraction and secured her, his hand on her stomach, and she felt like pulling up her knees, because she'd felt him touch her.

She couldn't remember how to breathe, because there was this feather-light stroking from his fingers on her stomach, just these almost indistinguishable caresses and a slight irregularity to his breathing as they continued to watch the kissing on the screen.

'When you move home....' His voice was hesitant, slightly gruff. 'Suppose we take things slowly...' She could hardly breathe, hardly dared to hope, scared to move in case he stopped talking. 'Suppose we go out...?'

'I won't have a babysitter—Mum only said she'd do it while I worked,' she whispered back.

'You could come here, we could have dinner, just start at the very beginning, get to know each other properly…'

'And Willow?' Her heart was in her mouth.

'If we take it slowly enough, maybe…' He could hear the blood pounding in his ears as he offered so much more than he had sworn he ever would. 'Maybe in time…'

He was offering her hope—offering *them* hope—that the impossible might just happen.

CHAPTER ELEVEN

CELESTE suddenly didn't care about the film, she wanted to see him, so she wriggled around and his legs had to trap hers to stop her falling off the sofa. He could see her lovely eyes shining in the darkness and he wanted to protect her, even from herself, but, God, he also wanted to kiss her, to just dive straight into that pleasure, but he had to make it very clear too.

'We'll just take things slowly.'

'I know.'

And then he could kiss her—properly this time—and she could kiss him too, a lovely slow kiss that wasn't awkward, just took a little adjusting to, because she was lower than him and rather precariously balanced, so he pulled her in a bit so that her bare thigh had to be clamped by his denimed ones, and as his tongue slid into her mouth, as their lips pressed harder, if she wanted to stay on the sofa, her other leg had to wrap around his.

He smelt like Ben…like the kiss from the first time, except she felt sexy now rather than tired, she felt alive rather than weary, and she felt wanted rather than looked after.

It made her feel dizzy.

She was sucking on his bottom lip, her little hand on his broad back and with the roughness of his jeans in her groin.

'Celeste…' He pulled back a bit as she pressed hard into him. 'I thought we were taking it slowly!'

'Not with this part,' she murmured.

Like teenagers, with no real intent, they kissed, except, unlike the rest of his body, his arm was going to sleep, so he pulled her onto her back and lay on top of her, his elbows sinking into the sofa as he kissed her deeply.

It *was* a kiss that was safe, because they weren't going anywhere more serious at the moment. At some level they both knew that, but it had to be verbally confirmed.

'We can't,' Ben said as her thigh slid between his legs and her hand slid up the back of his T-shirt, feeling the silk of his skin, the firmness of muscle, and she arched towards him. 'I haven't got anything.'

'I know,' she breathed. 'But I had a coil inserted…'

'No.' He stopped then, because she was just too precious to risk it. 'You're not to rely on just that.'

'So just kissing, then…' Her mouth was on his, her body this writhing mass of want beneath his. It was already more than a kiss but, God, it felt nice.

'I think we can manage a little more than that,' he promised. His hand was creeping up her top now, her breast soft and warm beneath his fingers. This was *so* much more than a kiss as his fingers skilfully caressed her nipples.

She'd considered her breasts useless, shrunken little failures, having not been able to breastfeed Willow, but now they swelled beneath his fingers, and the feel of his mouth and his tongue on them was sublime.

She was pressing into him, could feel his erection, and she wanted it closer...

'Ben...' she murmured softly. She could feel these little licks of pleasure in her stomach and it startled her, for he was turning her on her side, with nowhere to go except the back of the sofa and the gorgeous weight of Ben pinning her. Her hand crept to the front of his jeans; she felt the lovely solid length of him and heard him moan. 'Ben...' She didn't know why she kept saying his name, but she couldn't help it. Her fingers started working the heavy buckle of his belt, but his hand stopped her.

'No, this is just for you,' he said. He didn't mean it in a martyred way, he was lost too, but somewhere inside he wanted her to know that it could be about her, that it could just be about this...

He was kissing her hard, this lovely wet kiss that was so deep she didn't want to move or breathe again.

Was there any place nicer to be than on a sofa with her?

He was eighteen again—only it hadn't been that good then.

He was peeling open the zipper of her shorts, wriggling them down over her bottom. As he pressed her body against his, his mouth was on her neck, kissing her, trying to remember not to leave any marks, because it was the last thing she needed with her mother. He was glad he didn't have a condom in the house because he so badly wanted to dive into her. He was holding her hips now, guiding her along his hard length still safely under his jeans. He thought he might explode from the delicious pressure building, but was determined that he wouldn't—because even now it was still about her.

For Celeste was lost within herself, savouring and catching up on everything she'd ever missed—those little licks of pleasure inside her were building to a crescendo. She could hear humming, and realised it was her; she was humming as she coiled her legs around him, coming just to his kiss, coming just for Ben.

'Willow…' she gasped, feeling as if she'd been drinking as the piercing tone of her baby's cries brought her back down to a rather nice place. His kiss welcomed her back slowly as she worked out that she could, in fact, breathe, and then on wobbly legs and dishevelled she stood there in front of him, hauling her shorts back up her legs, more than a little embarrassed but at the same time not.

Then she gave him that wonderful smile and he smiled back and she decided that even if that embrace was all it could be for now—it was more than enough.

Quite simply it was the nicest thing that had happened to her.

Ben had never expected to feel again.

Over the years he had tried and over the past few weeks he had resisted, but feelings didn't listen to logic.

Finally, he was starting to believe.

There were two glasses on the draining board, her footsteps were on the stairs as she came back down from soothing Willow and there was this delicious presence that filled each room. For the first time in years he was glimpsing a future—not in bricks or gardens, or hours filled with work, but hours and—later on—nights with her.

Maybe he *could* get used to this.

'Hey!' She was standing at the kitchen, hands behind her back, her dark brown hair black in the low living-room light. Her eyes were glittering and she was wearing a provocative smile that demanded caution.

'How's Willow?' he asked.

'Asleep again,' Celeste said. 'How are you?'

'Good,' Ben said, because he was. Having Celeste here was making him feel wonderful.

God, she was gorgeous, standing there just smiling, her cheeks all flushed, eyes glittering, the top button of her shorts undone.

He was hard again so he turned away, made a big show of washing the two glasses, just to give himself time to recover.

She walked over and kissed him on the lips and he kissed her back, his arms wrapping around her, wet, soapy hands holding her, but she didn't hold him back, she just kissed him.

'Which hand?' She pulled her lips away and smiled up at him wickedly.

He frowned. 'What are you up to?'

'Which hand?' she repeated.

He was smiling and frowning simultaneously. He was beginning to get a hint of an idea as to where this might be leading, but he dismissed it, because he'd determinedly discounted it.

'Left or right?' Celeste prompted.

'Left.'

She pulled her hand from behind her back, and offered it to him but didn't reveal what was in it. 'Open it.'

Ben prised open her fingers and saw the little silver package, the key to heaven, and he was *so* tempted to reach out and take it.

'Celeste…'

'Before you say anything…' she laughed '…I didn't even know that I had them—I got a free bag of samples from the hospital, and I was looking for some nappy cream for Willow…' She didn't have to explain any more, so he smiled and interrupted her, reaching for her other hand and opening it to reveal the same contents.

'That's cheating,' Ben said.

'Why?'

'Because I can't lose.'

'Maybe you deserve to win.'

God, since Jen had died, sex had been just that—sex. Good, bad or indifferent, that was all it had ever been.

But with Celeste?

He stared into those amber eyes, his body charged with the memory of before and the possibility of after, her kiss still wet on his lips.

'I don't want to rush you,' he said gruffly.

'I *want* you to rush me,' she murmured back. How could she explain how different he made her feel? Sex had been a mystery for Celeste before Dean, yet how it had been for them was completely different from what she'd so far experienced with Ben. For her and Dean it had been a logical, preconceived act. Booking into a hotel on a Friday night, she had prepared for the occasion all week, nervousness mounting like the waxing moon and disappointment waning after the event.

But tonight, pressed into him, kissing him, ignoring

the film like two teenagers necking in a cinema, it had been the closest she had ever come to her body—to the bliss of a kiss and the intimacy of two people blocking out the world and letting someone else in.

It was neither logical nor preconceived.

And she certainly wasn't smooth and spraytanned!

But all it felt was right.

'You know I'm moving back home, Ben, so we won't be able to see each other that much, but just for tonight…'

'Are you sure?'

She was about to say something flip, but she stopped, looked into those lovely green eyes and there was no question—this was how it should have been, this was what it was all about, because this was Ben, and always, always, she'd wanted him. Now, finally, she could have him. That he wanted to forge some kind of a future with her—however that might turn out—just blew her mind.

'Absolutely,' Celeste said. 'Except…' She screwed her eyes closed.

'Say it,' he urged.

'I don't want to disappoint you.'

"You could *never* disappoint me,' he said emphatically.

'Oh.' She gave a very wry laugh. 'I might just surprise you.'

A mother she may be but she had little more sexual experience than an amoeba—and most of that had been gained tonight in Ben's living room.

He kissed her to the bedroom and beyond—only that didn't quell her nerves.

As Celeste dashed to the bathroom, Ben took a moment too…quickly turning over Jen's photo.

Celeste stood in front of the mirror, talking to herself and berating her lack of preparation for what was about to happen. Her bikini line stopped at all stations and as thin as she might be, thanks to Willow, bits of her wobbled in a way they never had before. Even if Ben assured her that he wasn't comparing her to his wife, Celeste was—imagining Jen's perfect white sports bras versus her rather faded maternity one.

She sighed heavily, girded her loins and went back into the bedroom, to where Ben was waiting for her. She jangled with nerves and cellulite for every second of the disrobing, torn between shame and want, but then Ben started kissing her again, hands stroking her, seemingly not fazed at all by her post-pregnancy body.

Rather liking it, in fact, Celeste soon realised. So why waste two hands covering yourself when there was six feet three of male pressed against you?

'We'll take it really slow…' he said, laying her down on the bed carefully. He lay down too, facing her, and then he kissed her. His legs without jeans were right up against hers—scratchy, big, muscly legs—and she was suddenly quivering with a mixture of excitement and fear, feeling as if she were about to turn over the page of an exam and hoping to hell she'd studied enough…

'What are you scared of?' he asked, quirking an eyebrow at her.

'I don't know,' she whispered back, closing her eyes once again.

Ben hated the man who had taken her confidence even before it had had the chance to bloom. Hated her self-doubts, but he had assurance enough for them both. But that she was scared of something so very, very wonderful saddened him too.

She was shaking with nerves as he took her in his arms. It felt so very different from before, because this time she knew where it was leading. He was so lovely to lie with, so big and male...and all hers. While they kissed she explored his body slowly, her hands running down his arms, feeling them solid and strong. Then she progressed to his chest—hard and flat and smooth. Her mouth moved there and she kissed the skin as his hands stroked and soothed her. Wrapped in this warm cocoon of skin and muscle and Ben, her hands slid over his hips and met solid thighs. She could feel him caressing her waist and over her hips, and it was Ben's mouth exploring her now, kissing her pale breasts, one hand moving to the front and making tiny circles on her soft stomach. Had there been a muscle working there, maybe she'd have thought about it and held it in, but there wasn't and anyway Celeste wasn't really thinking, her throat too tight with nerves as his hand crept downwards. Then he was stroking her and she made little noises, pretending to like it, but was too embarrassed to really. He kissed her again, so she stopped making all the right noises and kissed him back, concentrating on that, and tried not to resist his fingers slipping deep inside her, as his thumb stroked her softly and rhythmically.

She suddenly couldn't breathe, so she pulled in air and pulled it in again, and made the same sort of noise she'd been making before except now it came from a different place, this involuntary place that also made her sigh and moan and forget everything except Ben and how he was making her feel.

She held a man in her hand for the first time, exploring him, feeling him slide beneath her fingers, just touching and exploring, delighted with what she found. Ben was patient till he couldn't be patient any more. Her inexperience worried him, not for himself but for her—she was far too trusting and naïve—so he handed her the condom, which was something she should know how to do. But he ended up guiding her clumsy fingers as she rolled it down his length but, too eager, too nervous, she ripped it.

'We've only got one more!' she cried, embarrassed with her clumsiness. She wished he'd just do it for her, but Ben was insistent.

'I'll go to the petrol station if I have to and get some more if you rip this one,' he growled. God, he hoped he didn't have to! Practice may not make perfect, but a patient teacher helped and Celeste heard his moan of pleasure as she slipped it on slowly. Terrified of her nails, she unfurled it with her palms and then she was holding him lovingly for a moment, proud of her handiwork, as his fingers slipped deeper into her slippery warmth.

'I don't want to hurt you…' he gasped. He was suddenly right there at her entrance and she was tight with expectancy and fear. But then he was in just a little bit, two hands holding her hips and just gently stretching her till fear abated and she relaxed, willing him in further. But he was so supremely gentle, so strong and sure that there was pure bliss in there being no rush.

Always, in her vast repertoire of twice, there had

been an 'is that it?' moment. Is that what the world raves about? Is that all there is to it?

No, *this* was all there was to it.

All she wanted and all she wanted to be...

He was pushing her onto her back now, his huge frame moving over her, and it felt sublime...till she lost her rhythm and Ben dealt easily with that.

'Stay still.' His words were a low whisper in her ear.

'Still?' Wasn't she supposed to be writhing around? Surely lying still...

'Stay still,' he said again, so she did. She just lay and felt the blissful feel of him within her, the scent of him, of them, and she *really* did try to stay still, except her hips kept lifting, her body kept arching to his.

'Stay still...' he repeated, and she tried harder, except she couldn't, and suddenly she was lifting to him, moving with him, just locked in their own rhythm and Ben wasn't telling her any more because with that pause, she'd got it. Without trying hard, suddenly it was easy.

The skin of his chest was against her lips and she licked it, sucking his salty flesh, her legs around his, ankles trying to grip except he was so broad she could barely manage it. Then she felt the shift in him, something she'd never anticipated in the guarded, reticent Ben, because he was locked into this magical place too. There was no way she could define it, nothing specific with which to gauge it, except suddenly he was moaning her name and forgetting, deliciously forgetting to be gentle. Celeste was urging him on, not with words but with deep kisses on his chest and hands that slid over his buttocks and pushed him in harder. He was all over her, and so into her it made her dizzy, this full focus of him on her, until she was coming, a deep, deep orgasm that pleaded for him join her. And he did, giving in and just diving forward, shuddering his release and tipping Celeste to a place where there was no sound or silence or thought or want—just them and the beat of their bodies matching and minds colliding. She'd glimpsed pure magic and she never wanted to come down or go back or move from this place again.

He kissed her out of it, back to the world and then Ben rolled away from her and Celeste was suddenly scared, scared of losing whatever it was they had just found, scared of this place receding. Then it was her kissing him. On top of him, she kissed him hard, her hand threading into his hair, a silent plea for him not to leave her, for him not to retreat again inside himself because she had seen him now, seen *them* perhaps, glimpsed a marvellous possibility of them together, and she didn't want it to disappear.

CHAPTER TWELVE

'BEN RICHARDSON.'

She hadn't heard the phone ringing, just Ben's voice as he answered it. 'Belinda Hamilton is on call this weekend. No, I've seen her, she was there earlier tonight.' She felt the sheets move, Ben climb out, the shower taps on before the conversation was even over, and then two minutes later Ben, still dripping wet, was beside her, pulling on jeans. 'I've got to go into hospital for a bit.'

'Problem?'

'A bit—Belinda's not answering her pager.' He kissed her and it soothed her, but almost on cue, the moment he had gone, her three hours of sleep were up anyway, because Willow woke up. Celeste padded downstairs and prepared her a bottle, then brought her into bed to feed her. It was the easiest night feed Willow had ever taken, so blissfully easy. The bottle was gone in a few minutes and Willow was back asleep. She deserved a cuddle for being such a good girl, Celeste thought, and moved the pillows, cuddled her daughter in and determinedly ignored her mother's voice in her head that told her she shouldn't have the baby in bed with her.

And that was the scene Ben came home to.

Having dealt with the issue at work, he'd stopped at the petrol station, had bought *lots* of supplies and was ready to fall into bed. On the drive home it had all seemed straightforward, and Ben had felt so sure.

Then he'd called at Belinda's. Sure she was home, he had hammered on her door and felt this flicker of fear, the same fear he had when he'd come home to find Jen.

This silent house and the appalling feeling that something was wrong.

'Belinda!' he shouted. 'I'll call the police if you don't open up.'

'I'm sorry!' The door pulled open and he saw her eyes were swollen from crying. 'I just can't go in.'

'What's happened?' he asked, appalled.

'Can you just cover for me?' she whispered.

'Sure.'

'Can you ring the switchboard and tell them to page you if there's a problem?'

'I'll do it now,' Ben said, stopping the door as she went to close it. 'Belinda, what's going on?'

'Gastric flu…'

'Don't give me that!' he exclaimed.

'Please, Ben.'

It was none of his business. So long as she was okay, that was all that mattered, but his heart was still racing as he let himself into his home, the metallic taste of fear on his tongue and he downed a glass of water and then another before heading upstairs.

And then he'd seen them both on the bed, curled up like two kittens, sleeping, so sweet and perfect and innocent. But he'd glimpsed the past tonight, tasted fear again as he'd knocked at Belinda's door—and maybe that, Ben decided, was the sign he'd craved from Jen.

Maybe that was his warning.

Celeste stirred and half awoke, could see Ben sitting on the edge of the bed. 'How was it?'

'Busy enough, I just had to sort out some backlog, as they couldn't get hold of Belinda.'

'That's not like her,' Celeste frowned. 'Do you think she's okay?'

'She's fine,' Ben said. 'Well, not fine, as I stopped by her flat on the way back. She says she'd got gastric flu but my guess is...' He didn't finish. Belinda's personal life was her own and shouldn't really be gossiped about. 'It doesn't matter.'

Celeste knew she'd just been relegated, knew, though it was almost indefinable, that what she had feared— losing what she'd just found—had already taken place.

'I'll put Willow back in her pram.' She thought Ben might take the baby from her, but he didn't, so Celeste slipped out of bed and down to the guest room where she tucked her daughter into the pram. Then, as Willow woke up and started grumbling, she wheeled the stroller back to Ben's room and parked the baby in the corner as he undressed and climbed into bed.

It took a few moments to settle Willow and by the time she returned to his bed, Ben was asleep.

Or pretending to be.

She stared at his keys and the phone and the little paper bag from the garage, knowing what it contained and realising they wouldn't be needed.

Wondering what, in that short space of time, had changed things so much. She told herself she was imagining it—overreacting.

Maybe he *was* asleep after all and not just pretending.

The view from the bed was magical and it should have soothed her as she got into bed and lay next to him—only it didn't.

They'd agreed to take things slowly, dinners and dating—and the sex certainly hadn't been a problem. Even as inexperienced as she was, Celeste knew that for certain—what she had shared with Ben was so much more than she had ever expected or anticipated. So what had gone wrong between them?

Though cool and sophisticated wasn't really her forte, though she wanted to curl into him, to wake him with the kiss her body was demanding that she give, to roll over in the soft warm bed and feel his arms wrap around her, she resisted the temptation.

This was way too important to misjudge. So instead she slipped a reluctant body out of bed and checked on a still sleeping Willow, deciding to take advantage of the peace and have a shower, because if she'd stayed in bed she'd surely break the strained silence.

He lay still, hovering on the edge of the decision.

Ben knew that she was awake, knew she was waiting for him, knew that last night had confused her.

It had confused him too.

With Willow in the room, he hadn't slept a wink. It wasn't the little snuffles that kept him awake, it was the silences that killed him.

He walked across the room, checked that she was still breathing, which, of course, she was. In fact, as he looked down at her, she promptly opened her eyes and smiled at him.

Only Ben struggled to return it. Instead, he tried to go back to bed, but she'd seen him now and was starting to cry.

God, he hoped Celeste wouldn't be long in the shower.

Ben headed down stairs and made coffee for them both and a bottle for Willow, gritting his teeth as the cries grew louder, wondering if Celeste would be out of the shower by the time he got back up stairs.

Hoping so.

He walked back into the bedroom and put down the bottle and mugs, listened at the bathroom door and could still hear the shower—surely she could hear Willow crying?

Surely!

Ben stared into the stroller, picked up the baby's little soother and popped it in her mouth, but Willow spat it out in disgust, her eyes fixed on him, real tears at the edges, pleading with him to pick her up. So he tried, telling himself to pretend that he was at work where he operated on automatic, except this wasn't work.

He wanted to pick her up, even put his hands into the pram to do so...then he pulled back and tried rocking the pram instead, willing Celeste to come out of the shower and tend to her babe.

What the hell was he so scared of?

Cross with himself, Ben paced the room. He would just go right over and pick her up and be done with it.

Then he heard the bleep of Celeste's phone.

Dean

He didn't read the text—just felt the chill of a shadow, a big black bird in the sky that could swoop down and take them at any given moment…

'Willow!' Shivering wet, wrapped in a towel, Celeste headed straight for the pram, scooping her daughter up in her arms, feeling her hot, red face and turning questioning eyes to him. 'She's been sobbing!'

'I was about to knock and tell you,' he said lamely.

'To knock?' Celeste stared at him open-mouthed. 'Did you not think to pick her up?'

'I was making coffee,' Ben said defensively. 'And her bottle.'

Which sounded logical and reasonable, Celeste realised—except babies were neither logical nor reasonable, and Willow had needed to be held.

'Can you hold her for me?' Celeste's voice held just a hint of challenge. 'I just need to get dressed…'

'I have to shower and get dressed too,' Ben lied. 'Switch just called, I have to go into work.'

'Ben…' For someone usually so emotional, Celeste's voice was ominously calm. 'I'm not asking you to feed her or change her, I'm asking if you could hold Willow for two minutes.'

'Sorry.' He shook his head. 'I've got to get ready.'

'Ben?' She couldn't believe it, couldn't believe the way he was acting. 'I'm not asking for—'

'Look,' Ben interrupted, 'she's not my…' He didn't finish, his mouth snapping closed before this morning turned into the mother of all mornings, but Celeste finished for him.

'Not your *problem*?' That wasn't what he'd been about to say, but it was easier to nod than to explain. 'God.' Celeste gave a mirthless laugh. 'I really know how to pick jerks, don't I?'

Ben didn't answer so she spoke instead.

'Just how *slowly* did you want to take it, Ben? What, by the time she went to school, maybe we could move in with you?' she said scathingly.

'Willow's father just texted....'

'Don't blame this on him!' Celeste retorted. 'You've been off with me since last night.' When he didn't answer that, she asked again, 'Just how slowly did you mean, Ben?'

'I don't know.'

She stared down at her daughter, *the* most important person in the world to her, and she knew what she had to do.

'I'm not putting her through this.' Willow was starting to whimper. Her mother's arms were a nice place, but it would be even better with a bottle. 'I should have listened from the start—you don't want kids and I've got one.'

Her phone bleeped again and Celeste gritted her teeth. What the hell did Dean want?

'You'd better see what her father wants!' Ben was done. She was right, Willow deserved better than him, and the only way out was to end it—really end it. 'After all, she's his responsibility.'

'Correction!' Celeste spat, hating him too much at this moment for tears. 'She's *mine*.'

He didn't respond, just headed for the shower.

'You might be glad to get rid of me and Willow, Ben,' she called to his departing back. 'But you've no idea what you just lost.' He closed the door behind him and knew, because he knew Celeste, that she'd be gone when he came out, that she wouldn't hang around to debate the point. He turned on the shower full blast, and prayed she'd go soon, because while the water might drown the sound of Willow's tears, it wouldn't drown his.

It wasn't Willow that was his problem.

He sat on the floor of the shower and held his head in his hands.

It was his own daughter.

It was a hurt like she'd never known.

A rejection not just of her—that she could deal with, had dealt with in the past and could deal with again now. It was the rejection of Willow that was as acute as a sting but didn't abate like one.

Was this the price of motherhood—that the man of her dreams could walk away from her so easily?

Well, let him.

'How long will you be?' Her mother hovered at the door, holding Willow.

'I don't know,' Celeste snapped. After weeks of nagging for Celeste to speak with Willow's father, now that the moment was here, her mother was demanding timelines! Did she not realise how hard this was? 'There are bottles made up.'

'You will be coming back to get Willow, won't you?'

That didn't even deserve an answer, so Celeste just gritted her teeth.

'Maybe you should take her with you…'

'Mum!' It wasn't a snap this time, just a plea for her to stop fretting, worrying, fixing… And then Celeste got it, answered the question that she had wrestled with for weeks, no, for months now. Seven weeks into motherhood and Celeste was starting to get the swing of it—this aching, endless worry lasted longer than the pregnancy, longer than the first days or months. She was stuck with this fear for her child for life—as was her own mum—and now when her voice came, it was gentler, more reasonable, friendly even. 'I'm not going to parade Willow in front of him—he hasn't even asked to see her. I'm just going to see what he wants.'

'What do *you* want?'

'I don't know,' Celeste admitted. 'For some sort of father for Willow, I suppose…'

'What if he wants you back?' It was the first real conversation they'd had in years and Celeste was finally able to answer honestly.

'He lost me a long time ago, Mum. I'm only meeting with him now for the sake of Willow.'

'Be careful,' Rita said, and Celeste nodded.

'Don't wor—' The words died on her lips and then Celeste smiled. 'Okay, worry away if you must, but you really don't have to. Whatever he has to say, Willow and I are going to be fine.'

Seeing him again, all Celeste felt was older and maybe, possibly, just a little bit wiser.

There was none of that giddy rush she'd had as a student when he'd walked into the lecture room—no blushing when he spoke or hanging on to his every word.

Whether she'd wanted to or not, she'd well and truly grown up and could see Dean for what he was now—a rather sad attempt of a man who'd played on her naïvety, who had taken full advantage of a perfectly normal crush when he *really* should have known better.

The rules were there for a reason.

It was a very short meeting, and not at all sweet. He wanted assurances that his perfect life wasn't about to end soon, that Celeste wasn't suddenly going to change her mind and come knocking—an assurance she was only too happy to provide!

'What will you tell Willow?' he asked diffidently.

'The truth.' Celeste looked at him coolly. 'Probably a nicer version of it. I'll miss out the bit where you offered to pay for an abortion—but she'll grow up with the truth. And when she's old enough, what she does with that truth will be her decision, Dean.'

Then there was nothing else to say, nothing at all, so she didn't bother. Just stood up and walked out of the café and took a big breath and then another one.

Until finally she blew the last one out and let him go.

Then Celeste put one foot in front of the other and did it again, just kept on putting one foot in front of the other, which meant she was walking.

Walking away and getting on with the rest of her life.

CHAPTER THIRTEEN

'WHAT'S going on, Belinda?' It took till five on Monday to talk to Belinda. All day she'd been avoiding him and, clearly thinking he'd already gone home, she walked into the office and did an about-turn, but Ben halted her.

'Nothing.'

'I need to know why you didn't answer your pager on Friday night.'

'I'm sorry about that. I honestly felt so unwell, I just…'

'Belinda, I covered for you, but I'm not going to be fobbed off,' he warned.

'He's still married.' Belinda crumpled as she admitted it. 'I found out on Saturday night…that multi-trauma…'

Ben frowned.

'It was his son.'

'Oh, Belinda.'

'I rang his number but ended up speaking to his wife…I recognised the surname, then she called him to the phone…' She could barely get the words out for crying. 'I just couldn't stay in the department and see him, face her. You think I'd be used to it by now…'

'Used to what?'

'Being let down.' He could scarcely believe the change in her from the confident, outgoing woman he'd first met. 'I'm so embarrassed.'

'Embarrassed?' he asked, bewildered.

'I just feel like a fool,' Belinda admitted. 'I knew he was busy, I made so many excuses for him—he was at work, or with the kids… I guess I just gave him a million and one reasons to justify why he could only give me such a little bit of his time.'

'It's not your fault,' Ben said, and it wasn't Celeste's fault either—if the stunning, streetwise Belinda could be taken in, what chance had Celeste had? 'You were just…' he gave an uncomfortable shrug as analysing emotions was not his strongest point '…trying to be happy…'

'Like we all are,' Belinda said. 'Only we just end up hurting a whole lot of people along the way.' She took a gulp of her coffee. 'I feel such a fool,' she said again despairingly.

'*He's* the fool,' Ben insisted.

'That's not how it feels from here.' She gave a watery smile. 'I'll be okay… I just need to lie low for a bit, lick my wounds…'

'I can imagine.'

'But I'll get there.' Belinda blew out a breath. 'Get back out there soon…'

Ben realised he would never understand some people—never get how someone who had been so hurt could, in such a short time, be talking about getting back out there, laying their hearts on the line, only to have them broken again.

Why?

Except he suspected he was starting to know the answer. It was he who was the fool—he worked that one out as he drove home that evening.

There were all these people out there, searching for happiness, trying not to be lonely, and he'd had it right there, not once, but twice, *right there* for the taking.

He'd just been too scared of getting hurt again to move on and take what was on offer.

He had wanted a world that came with iron-clad guarantees—and because that was impossible, well, he'd stepped right off the planet. Made some half-hearted attempt to move on with his life—only by *his* safe rules. He'd rather have sex than a relationship, and the more meaningless the better, because then you didn't get hurt. And no children or feelings involved either, please, because that could hurt too. As could biological fathers that might pop up…

Only being lonely hurt more than the risk of loving.

And now he'd lost her too.

He got stuck in his street as a small rental truck pulled out of the units—his big black bird swooping down and taking her away. He could see her car in her drive and knew she was inside her flat, organising the moving of her stuff over to her parents' house in preparation for the coming weekend. If she went to live with her parents, he knew he had lost her for ever.

He finally realised that this was his moment.

That *this* moment was all anyone had.

And he had to start living in it. He took a deep breath and headed for her door.

* * *

'It's not a good time, Ben.'

He could hear Willow's cries as she went to close the door on him.

'I need to talk to you.'

'And *I* need to feed my baby!' She opened the door, her face angry. 'So I hope you can stomach being in the same room as her as you say whatever it is that you have to.'

Willow's screams were louder and louder as they walked through her tiny unit. Everything that was them was gone—the crib, the flowers, the throw rugs, the ironing board by the wall. Just the drab furniture remained and as he followed her through the place, the kitchen was empty, except for a kettle and a jug and a bottle warming.

'It's coming, Willow…' He could hear the strain in her voice as she tried to keep it light for her baby. 'The microwave's gone with the removal…' He watched as she tested the bottle on her wrist then placed it back in the water, and then she snapped, 'I'm just going to feed her and then I'll be gone. I've decided to go before the weekend. There's no point hanging around now.'

'Don't go.'

'Just what the hell do you want, Ben?' she asked wearily.

'You.'

'Well, sorry, but I'm already taken…' Even though she was in the lounge, Celeste had to shout over Willow's screams. 'And I wouldn't have it any other way.'

'I don't *want* it any other way,' he said desperately.

'She isn't going to go away, Ben. I'm not going to

pretend she doesn't exist so we can sleep together a couple of times a week!'

'I want Willow too…' She had no idea how hard that was for him to say, no idea of the terror of that admission, so she scorned him instead.

'Oh, so you'll *tolerate* her so you can have her mother.'

'No, I'll try harder. I want her too,' he said again.

'Just leave it, Ben!'

'Jen was pregnant when she died.' Real pain demanded respect. Real pain could be felt and heard and acknowledged, even if we don't know how, because even Willow fell silent. 'About the same stage as you when you had Willow.'

'You should have told me,' Celeste said, shocked.

'How?' Ben shook his head. 'It's not something you just slip into the conversation—and especially being pregnant yourself…' he gave a thin smile '…you didn't need to hear it.'

'No.' She admitted the truth of that. She'd been struggling enough as it was.

'I wanted to tell you after you had Willow…but…I lost my baby, Celeste, and I couldn't do it to you. Give you that fear that you might lose yours too.'

'How?'

'A subarachnoid haemorrhage. Just like that.' He clapped his hands and it made her jump, but it seemed appropriate. She'd learnt about them at uni—a sudden, severe, thunderclap headache—and she felt like crying except it wasn't her place to right now. 'I came home and found her…' And then he corrected himself, because it wasn't really Jen that was the problem, he had loved and lost her and would miss her for ever, but in that he had moved on—had almost reached that place of acceptance, just not quite. 'No, I came home and found *them*.

'She was buried inside Jen and I never got to hold her and I never really got to mourn her—and I don't know how to start.'

'You just did.'

He nodded, screwed his eyes closed and pressed his fingers against them as, dizzy with images, like a roundabout, he willed it to stop.

'Tell me,' she implored.

'I can't go there,' he said, because he truly couldn't. 'I didn't want to love you, but I do, Celeste, and I don't want to love Willow, but I know I will. I'm so scared of losing you…'

'You did, though, Ben.' She was still angry, so angry with him. 'You don't want to fall in love in case something happens, so you'd rather just let us go…'

'I'm here now.'

'Half of you!' Celeste exclaimed. 'And the other half is stuck in a place where no one can visit. Well, Willow and I deserve more than that.'

'I'll give you more than that,' he vowed.

'When?' Celeste demanded, and Ben couldn't believe his ears.

'What are you asking for, Celeste?'

'Your love,' Celeste said, and her heart was breaking, but she was determined to be very, very strong.

'I just did. I told you I love you…'

'No, Ben.'

'And I *will* love Willow.'

'No.' She absolutely meant it.

'I don't know what you want here, Celeste!' It was Ben that was angry now—he'd never been more open, more honest, had never revealed his heart like this since Jen died, and now he knew why. 'What? Do you want me to say that I love Willow?'

'Anyone can *say* it,' she pointed out.

'Okay?' He picked up the bottle. 'Am I to hold her, to feed her?'

'I'm quite capable of that.'

'What, then?' Ben demanded, because he didn't know what she wanted from him, didn't know what test she had in her mind that he had to pass.

'I want you to *let* yourself love her.' All she did was confuse him, because he *was* going to love her, in time, he knew that it would grow. 'And when you do, we'll both be here waiting for you...'

'I don't understand you, Celeste.'

'Well, *I* don't understand *you*.' She picked up the bottle and walked into the lounge and picked up Willow, feeding her in silence as he stood at the door and watched.

'You can't just demand instant love,' he protested.

'I can,' Celeste came back immediately. 'She's already got one poor excuse for a father—she doesn't need another, hanging around, waiting for love to grow.'

'You're impossible!' he growled.

'I'm very straightforward, actually,' she replied calmly.

'Say goodbye to Ben.' She stood up, held up a little hand and waved it at him. 'We'll see him when he's ready.'

She put Willow in her crib and tucked her in. 'Now, if you'll excuse me, I need to get on with my packing.'

'That's it?' he asked incredulously.

'That's it,' she confirmed.

'I've come over here, I've told you why, I've told you I love you and that I'll do everything I can for Willow, and it's not enough?' He walked over and looked her in the eyes. 'It's not enough for you?'

'No.'

She meant it, he knew that she meant it, he just didn't get it. 'I don't understand you, Celeste,' he said again helplessly, and kissed her on her taut cheek. 'I'll go.'

'Please.'

'I'll *never* understand your mother,' he said, looking at Willow. He stroked her little cheek and again it was Willow who looked into his eyes—the same way she had the day she'd been born and the next morning too.

Once more, Ben closed his eyes, only this time he opened them again, and she was still there, smiling— patiently waiting for him to love her.

He didn't want to do this—he felt as if he were dying— in fact, he was sure it would have been easier *to* have died.

'She was made for you, Ben,' Celeste said softly beside him, staring down at her daughter and under- standing the world now. 'Because you'd never have done this yourself—you'd never have done it again.'

She was right—and somewhere deep inside him something aligned. Because even with Celeste, without a certain little lady being born into his hands, under his tree, he would never have taken that chance again, would never, ever have risked having another baby.

Yet he risked it now.

He looked at this little new life and remembered all that hope, all that love, all that promise he'd once had...

'She was never born.' It probably didn't make sense to Celeste, yet it was so vital to him. He could feel the petal of Willow's cheek as soft and white as a daisy and it felt as if he was being hollowed out inside. He still wanted to run, only there was no beach long enough, no universe that could contain the grief that split him. 'There's no birth certificate, and we hadn't chosen a name...' It hadn't felt right to name her without Jen.

He could never separate the two, had grieved for Jen and their baby, but had never actually separated them, had never let himself grieve just for the baby. 'She was never born.'

'She still *was*, though,' Celeste said, her voice there beside him, her arm around him—and if he'd been there for her before, she was there for him now. 'She still *is*.'

'Daisy.'

He stroked Willow's cheek and finally named the daughter he should have had. And just as he had cut Willow's cord, Willow let him cut his daughter's—her little star hands holding his as grief pitted him. In holding Willow he got to hold his own baby, pressed his lips to her soft cheeks, got to hold Daisy just for a moment, and then sent her back to rest with her mum.

'I love you.' He said it to Willow who was there now, only he didn't just say it, he felt it too. He held her close, but he didn't just hold her—he finally let himself love her, finally let himself hope, and he promised her silently that he would always be there for her. 'And I love your mum too.'

'She knows that,' Celeste said.

'Don't go to your parents'.' Holding her baby, he turned to Celeste. 'Come home.'

And it was home—even if she'd never lived there, his house was already her home.

'Well, I'm all packed.' She was smiling and crying, so very, very proud—and safe too—and for the first time in the longest time absolutely sure. 'I'd better ring Mum and tell her. She'll be on her way soon.'

'What will she say?'

'She'll probably be relieved.' Celeste laughed. 'I'm not the easiest person to live with.'

'I can't wait to find out,' he murmured.

He didn't want her, didn't want them in this shabby, bare unit a moment longer. He wanted them home where they all belonged. The boxes and crib and bags and baby baths and car could all wait till later, so Celeste rang Rita and Ben packed a quick bag for Willow, and they walked down the street pushing a pram, only as a family this time. She was *such* a good baby, because she slept for a couple of very necessary hours while Ben and Celeste kissed and made up and cried a bit too, and when Celeste finally fell asleep in his arms, Ben stayed awake, just so he could feel her warm skin. Then he heard Willow, who was starting to stir in her pram, and he finally felt what had been missing for all those years.

Peace.

A peace that wasn't shattered by Willow's lusty cries, a peace that remained as Celeste chatted incessantly on as she brought in the baby's bottle and then handed him an angry bundle as she decided that instead of feeding her daughter, *he* could do it while she explored the spa in her new bathroom!

Peace as, fed, changed and content, he put Willow back in the pram and wound up her mobile for her.

Peace perfect peace, Celeste thought as she lay in the spa, her toes wrinkling, knowing how much he loved the two of them, mother and daughter. She stared out at the glorious view and at a wonderful future too.

'Marry me!' Celeste shouted to the silence.

'I was about to suggest the same thing,' Ben said, standing in the doorway grinning. 'We should get married out there on the beach, where we met...'

'I take it that's a yes?'

'It's a yes...' He looked out to the beach and he could almost see them—see their wedding, Celeste holding Willow, the celebrant, with family and friends gathered around, and he could almost see Jen, holding Daisy and smiling. And it was a blessing, a long-awaited blessing, to be able to think of them both and smile.

'Oh, well, if you insist.' She laughed.

Lost in thought, he had no idea what she was talking about. 'Pardon?'

'I suppose there's no talking you out of it...' She gave a martyred sigh. 'I guess you'd better climb in and ravish me.'

He didn't ever compare, because there was no comparison—two more different women he could never imagine, and yet he loved them both. But it was then, when he least expected it, that he got his sign, the one he had been longing for from Jen, because just for a second he could have sworn he heard Jen laugh, could have sworn he heard her letting him go with grace, urging him on, to live this wonderful life.

And Ben laughed too.

Laughed as he climbed right in to join Celeste to do as the grad nurse ordered.

Ravish her.

EPILOGUE

Never, not once, did she wonder or doubt.

Not even a little bit.

Despite her mother's gloomy predictions, despite what she'd read in the 'blended family' section of a baby book, which Celeste had finally thrown against the wall—not once did she think that their baby would change how he felt about Willow.

Because without Willow, there would be no them.

'It won't be long now.' Ben squeezed her shoulder as she lay on the operating table—with all the passion of a doctor to a patient, but that was what he did sometimes.

They'd experienced three pregnancies between them and all of them had been different.

This had been a textbook pregnancy (if you excluded her massive weight gain), and had gone brilliantly till the very last minute—but eight hours of huffing and puffing and still their baby wouldn't come out!

She'd worked part time till seven months, because that was what she did.

She had told him about her backache and sore ankles

but had spoken to the obstetrician, rather than him, when she'd had a ripper of a headache.

And he'd massaged her tummy and kissed her bump and done all the right things throughout.

They both had.

Jollied each other along and assured the other it would be fine.

'I'm scared…' She wasn't even sedated—they had been so mean with drugs that she was thinking of writing a letter of complaint. So much for being a doctor's wife! An epidural might numb your stomach, but it didn't numb your brain.

'What if it changes things?'

No matter how neatly folded, no matter where it was stored, your baggage came on the journey with you— and every now and then you had to cough up and pay the excess or watch as Customs ripped open the zipper and demanded to know what a chocolate bar was doing hidden in your bra.

As if you could explain how it got there.

As if you had meant to pack it and haul it to the other side of the world.

Except you had.

'I don't want it to change anything,' she wailed.

'Change can be good,' he said reassuringly.

It was only the three of them, her and him and Willow. And she was scared for them, scared for the coming baby—scared of change. Only it was happening, whether she wanted it to or not.

'I'm scared, Ben,' she said again.

'I know.'

She could see tears swimming in his green eyes.

'Remember Willow—she was so floppy and ill…'

'And look at her now.'

She knew they were making the incision because the OB had told her, but she only had eyes for Ben.

Could hear the gurgle as they suctioned her waters and she was petrified.

'How can I love it as much as Willow?'

'Wait and see,' he suggested gently.

It was a him.

This beefy whopper of a boy that they held up over the drapes, with a flat nose and bunched-up forehead, who screamed and cried and kicked all the way to the little cot set up for him.

'No wonder I needed a Caesarean.' She just had to smile, had to cry, had to gaze in wonder.

And, of course, so did Ben.

He walked over and stared at his son, got the footprints on his T-shirt and then came back to Celeste.

'You should see the *size* of him!' he said in awe.

'Now do you see why I moaned when he kicked?' she gasped.

She got a quick kiss when they brought him over all wrapped up—but so was she, so she couldn't really touch him. But there were too many people around for real tears.

'Go with him…' Celeste said to her husband.

It was all a blur from there. They were a bit more generous with drugs, and she was stitched and sent to Recovery and then to her room. And Celeste sort of remembered her mum coming and Ben's mum too and a lot of noise…

And later, much later, she woke up.

And remembered.

She wasn't scared of Ben's feelings, not even a tiny bit, okay maybe, just maybe a smudge…

But he had his back to her and his son and a fretful one-year-old on his hip who he was showing the moon to, and that left her alone to stare at her new baby.

She was scared of her *own* feelings.

He was so little.

A huge baby, but really so little and new and wrinkly and perfect, and she was so scared she wouldn't get this right. Then he opened his eyes…

Just stared right at her and demanded she love him.

She would very soon, except she was really tired. 'Ashley…'

She was too sore to pick him up, so Ben did it for her, balancing Willow on one side as he scooped up his son and handed him to her.

'It means "from the ashes",' Celeste said. 'I looked it up.'

'I bet you did.'

'Baby!' Willow forgot for a moment how tired she was. Delighted with both her *finally* awake brother and her vocal skills, she'd recently discovered chanting. 'Baby, baby, baby!' And she clambered over the bed and a catheter, coming dangerously close to a Caesarean incision, and then smothered her brother with kisses and germs followed by lots more gooey kisses.

Then Ashley got a kiss from Dad.

And then Celeste got a kiss from a suddenly very needy, tearful Willow.

There was almost too much love to go around, Celeste thought, very near tears herself.

'I'm going to get her home,' Ben told her.

He'd seen her watery eyes and he understood.

Knew when she needed him, even when she didn't admit it.

And knew when she needed to be on her own too.

The midwives walked in on his kiss to Celeste, but that was okay, because there would be lots of kisses later—she needed wise women with her now.

Tonight was for Celeste to meet Ash.

Ben understood that.

Tonight was the time for Celeste to discover that there was plenty of her to go around.

'Push the button…' He stepped in the lift and guided Willow's hand to the 'G' button—but she managed to miss and they headed for the roof instead!

'You're as unpredictable as your mother!' he huffed.

'Daddy!' She'd said it so many times, but she said it again—started up her chant and continued it all the way to the car park where he strapped her in and drove her home. 'Daddy, Daddy, Daddy!'

He was hers and she was his and never let anyone say otherwise.

He made her milk, put Willow in her cot, kissed her goodnight and turned on her mobile.

Then rang uncles and cousins and friends and deleted the text he wanted to send to Celeste in case it disturbed her sleep—he'd tell her himself in the morning.

Then he checked in on Willow and changed his mind and sent the text anyway.

Willow sound asleep—give ash a kiss—i love you.

And amid a frustrating attempt at a feed with an angry, hungry baby, and with nipples that hurt, a midwife smiled and handed her the phone. Celeste read her text, but didn't reply. He already knew she loved him too, so she just did as instructed. She leant forward and placed her lips on an angry forehead, erased crinkles with soft lips, felt the melting in her heart as Ash snuffled towards her and, after just a beat of a pause, Celeste resumed trusting again.

Felt the sweet weight of a new baby in her arms—and wanted it, could do it, was doing it right now…

It really *was* that simple.

Love grew if you let it.

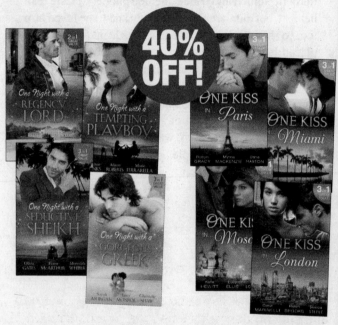

MILLS & BOON®

The Chatsfield Collection!

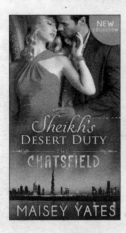

Style, spectacle, scandal…!

With the eight Chatsfield siblings happily married and settling down, it's time for a new generation of Chatsfields to shine, in this brand-new 8-book collection! The prospect of a merger with the Harrington family's boutique hotels will shape the future forever. But who will come out on top?

Find out at
www.millsandboon.co.uk/TheChatsfield2